CA
A
HOROSCOPE

*

DOORS TO MANUAL

SUZI STEMBRIDGE

Published by Komboloi Press:
This edition published in 2018
© Copyright: Suzi Stembridge B.A. Hons (OPEN)
M.C.I.J. March 2011

Digital edition first published in 2011
Paperback first published by New Generation Publishing
in 2015

Cover photographs courtesy of Oliver Stembridge
www.picture-life.co.uk Copyright © 2018

Frontispiece - Acropolis at Athens & a Vickers Viking aircraft

THIS BOOK IS VOLUME ONE IN THE COMING OF AGE SERIES

Other books in THE COMING OF AGE SERIES:
THE SCORPION'S LAST TALE
BRIGHT DAFFODIL YELLOW
THE GLASS CLASS

Also by the same author

THE GREEK LETTERS QUARTET:
GREEK LETTERS Volume 1 BEFORE
GREEK LETTERS Volume 2 AND AFTER
GREEK LETTERS Volume 3 THE EYES HAVE IT
GREEK LETTERS Volume 4 MUCH MORE THAN HURT

THE WHOLE SERIES ENTITLED JIGSAW

3

For Heidi & Oliver

With thanks to Simon and to Sarah

In August 2018 CAST A HOROSCOPE was the winner of a 'CHILL WITH A BOOK AWARD'.

Cast a Horoscope is the first volume in the series *Coming of Age* and one of eight novels, set against a historical and topographical background spanning six generations charting the fortunes and adventures of Rosalind, her partners and offspring or their ancestors, their families and friends and entitled "Jigsaw".

A book, written about a generation which lived at a slower pace, where it really did seem to matter how you dressed, what you did when, and where young people grew towards adulthood only slowly; the days before Facebook, texts and even fax machines. In the nineteen-sixties, words such as stewardess and flight deck had yet to be coined and health and safety were never even mentioned.

About the author: Suzi Stembridge lives in Yorkshire with her husband and has worked in travel for most of her life, after bringing up two children. She has travelled extensively, particularly in Greece and the rest of Europe and has a keen interest in history and culture. She founded and managed the tour operation Filoxenia Ltd and the travel agency Greco-file Ltd.

www.greco-file.com

IN THE BEGINNING

It was extraordinary how the dream would reoccur

Because in the beginning, the girl was innocent
Her mind was free; her heart untied.
Her love affair was with herself, with youth.

There was a pear hanging from every branch and the
sun which shone through the trees created a close
imitation of the shapes of dried bones, by casting a
shadow of a delicate network over the fertile earth.

In time, the images in this dream would haunt her as
real live images of things that happened in a faraway
place named Cambodia, or as it was called in modern
times, Kampuchea. For the moment that was history in
the making and too close to her immediate perception of
the news to be believed as realistic or even to be
frightening. It was happening to others.

She had coped with the Nazi concentration camps which
occurred during her childhood, but which she had only
learned about in her late teens. She had coped with
Waterloo and the War of the Roses in the schoolroom; in
time, she would cope with Pol Pot: but in maturity
Kuwait, Yugoslavia, Somalia, Iraq and ISIL, along with
the event the world learned to call 9/11 would crowd in
on her and on others with fears of nuclear disaster,
famine, environmental issues, Aids, Ebola, global
warning, forest fires and floods loading a fierce
depression upon thinking mankind.

The girl had to grow and mature before she could believe in and accept death.

So, for the time being, the sun was with Adam and the breeze was with Eve. The massive forces of God were bringing together their reluctant bodies, albeit bodies of skeletons, into the orchard where the living stronger trees which existed outside her dream grew up toward His Heaven, but remained rooted in the powerful evil earth.

Now it was a naked, winter pear tree, and barren. Its branches rattled against the panes and to their disturbing sound she woke.

ONE: NEW JOY WAIT ON YOU

August 1960

(i)

With a buoyant step Roz Peters entered an aircraft for only the second time in her life. Uppermost in her mind was the knowledge that she, as the sole air-hostess, would be entirely responsible for all the thirty-six passengers of a Vickers Viking aircraft. She had been told the night flight would be full. Once through the door in the tail she walked up towards the cockpit which was on stand-by lighting. She stopped where two small steps took her up over the wheel axle. Although there were passenger seats in the forward section before the cockpit door she felt inhibited to go further.

As the Ferryair Captain climbed on board, using the same and only entrance to the dark aircraft Roz was facing him. She welcomed him and introduced herself, lighting the entrance from the galley at the back with a standard issue torch. She had thought that if she switched on the cabin lights at night she would harm the aircraft, much as using the headlights in a stationary car flattens the battery. Roz was confident that her Captain would have been told that his regular hostess had gone sick and she was taking her 'stand-by' place, after completing only one training flight instead of the prescribed six.

However, without attempting to reply to the young hostess' welcome or to reassure her, the stocky short Captain merely put down a switch marked 'cabin lights' and strode up to the cockpit. 'We are on ground power now,' he snapped as he marched up the aisle, with the tall first officer silently following him. They shut the forward door to the cockpit leaving Roz in the empty cabin nervously replacing the torch and awaiting the arrival of her passengers from the departure hall. A ground hostess led out the passengers, all men.

To her amazement, Roz found her nervousness quickly evaporating and she was able to remember the procedure she had been taught the previous day, particularly when it came to demonstrating the emergency procedures. She was glad she had spent all that afternoon swotting up from her manual, although the expression 'if the aircraft has to ditch it *may* float' was reverberating through her head, she was not going to alarm the passengers by telling them that. It was midnight and she didn't feel ready for bed, just for work.

'How long have you been in this job?' one passenger asked her as she helped him fasten his seat belt.

She replied 'half an hour!

He laughed, 'that makes two of us.... I've never flown in a chartered plane before.'

Rosalind remembered sitting in the London flat, fed up after a hard day's shorthand and typing, and that was little more than a month ago. On her application form as she applied for this new job, she had given her full name, Pandora Rosalind Peters, and made a split-second decision to be known henceforth as Rosalind or if pushed simply Roz. 'This will be truly a new beginning,' she said aloud.

She gave her new passenger friend the gin and orange he asked for, but she did not know how much gin to put in the plastic tumbler. In return, he fiddled with his lapel and detaching a small gold pin he gave it to Roz. It represented a WW2 Spitfire and it was solid gold. 'We're all businessmen, seasoned travellers on scheduled airlines, but this time,' he said, 'we're going to Hamburg to play hockey, would you know, travelling by a small unknown charter airline!' She didn't know how to thank him.

When they landed Roz was still stacking dirty dishes into the sink.

She stood in the galley entrance and smiled, 'Goodbye!' she said cheerily to the businessmen, hoping that they would not notice how very unship-shape things were in the galley behind. At least the bar box was locked. During her brief training Julie Rhodes had stressed 'this is most important; otherwise customs officials might impound the aircraft. In Germany coffee is still expensive after the shortages caused by the Second World War, so it's also wise to take the precaution of locking that in the box too.'

When the passengers had disembarked a customs officer climbed aboard and sealed the bar box and asked Roz first in German, and then scornfully when she did not reply, in English, 'are you staying overnight?'

She told him no, and followed her crew, ten paces behind, in the direction of the restaurant. She felt anxious and lost, and wondered if she should be following them, wherever they were going.

She remembered the fun she had had at the meal break on her one and only training flight with Julie to Paris. Fun was the right word! Fun described everything about this job, at first. Even the sit-down in the crew room when they went through the manual had been conducted with an air of humour. Again, she recalled how when describing the safety procedure during the ditching process she had read out that ominous phrase that stuck with her: 'The aircraft may float'.

'Do you mean that when an aircraft has to ditch in the sea, they don't know if it will float?' Her tone was incredulous.

'Oh, I am sure they have a good idea, it probably won't! It's just that isn't the sort of trial practice run anyone is prepared to do!' And they had all laughed and trooped out to the aircraft for Roz's first training flight.

On that first flight, on the turn round, the Captain, Bill Turner who had appeared so easy-going had amused the two girls over lunch with nicely blue stories and his First Officer had asked for 'French Coca-Cola' which had turned out to be local red wine served in Coca-Cola bottles so that no-one would notice that they were drinking. But now it was two o'clock in the morning and the restaurant was shut. The Captain was annoyed, but Roz was not hungry. He appeared annoyed about the flight in general. Like Roz he had not been rostered for it, but had been called off standby early that evening.

By way of general conversation Roz explained to the Captain, 'I've been asked to do the flight although I'm not yet fully trained, because there was nobody else available.'

'It's the same throughout this blasted company, everything done on a shoestring.' The Captain growled and spoke with a thinly disguised Yorkshire accent. 'Young lass, you might as well know now, as find out later, but in this Company, you work twice as hard as

10

any other. It's the aircraft and the passengers that are nearest and dearest to Lionel's heart. And Lionel - if you didn't know is our chairman, - normally spotted in mucky overalls, and spanner in hand, in Hanger number one. Crew, well then, they're just an incidental cog in the wheel. By the way the name's Duncan, Gerry Duncan.'

He didn't wait or seemingly even expect Roz to respond or to introduce herself. He swung round rudely turning his broad back towards her and called the Agent over to organise some food.

He turned round again and smiled. Middle-aged, broad shouldered, fair crinkly hair, rude, he might be, but Captain Duncan had an incredibly appealing smile. It seemed to appear from the corners of his mouth and it would grow, lighting his grey blue eyes as it grew, until suddenly where there had been a stern frightening face, there was a gleeful generous expression which it was impossible to resist.

'Frankfurters mit sauerkraut - or something,' said Captain Duncan using the smile to cover for his lack of German language. 'Big airport this, restaurant should be open you know. Really this is disgraceful.'

'I am sorry sir, we usually do have a twenty-four-hour service,' replied the agent in perfect English. 'Just at present we are engaged in a little redecoration.' The agent nodded to give weight to his excuse and added. 'If you would like to use my office I'll soon organise a plate of cold meat for you. I am sorry that you have been inconvenienced.'

The flight on the way back to Yorkshire was going to be empty and there was no hurry. After the meal which had been described to crew by the agent in a humorous tone as 'an Assiette Anglaise', but which was in fact anything but English and quite delicious, the Captain and the first officer talked about local affairs between themselves.

They were discussing some new bungalows, which were to be built at Guiseley near the airport. The conversation did not include Roz.

With her meal now finished Roz excused herself to the Captain and crossed the dark tarmac to climb aboard the empty aircraft. The crew cabin light was illuminated in the galley and she wondered idly how she could turn it off, and why it was on.

Shortly Captain Duncan arrived back at the aeroplane, followed closely and almost respectfully by the younger first officer. The Captain fixed his eyes on the shivering girl and his wry look frightened her.

'Well Miss, you certainly have not been trained!' He curled his lips sarcastically before adding, 'I did wonder when you would notice the crew light. We rang for coffee when we had just crossed the English coast over Bridlington.' He continued to stare at Roz, and pressed the 'crew call' light on the panel in the galley and it went out.

'God knows what would have happened in an emergency. I certainly don't. No doubt you expected Mr. Smith here to scream for you through the cockpit door? Whatever you forget, whatever else you forget young lady, never forget to check this call sign, frequently, on this damn antiquated flying machine. Do you understand? When the crew needs *you*, they can only attract your attention by illuminating this sign. And this means my dear child, when you are in the passenger cabin you have no indication that this light might come on, unless you keep going back down to the galley to check that it has not. So of course, hard on your little legs it may be, but you must keep on going down to the galley to check. Do you understand? This isn't one of your new-fangled Viscounts or Comet 4B's with bells that ring in the cabin; this is your original pig-in-the-sky aeroplane. And if the light has come on in the galley, then of course you must answer it immediately. Do you understand?' The thickset well-built Captain Duncan spoke the last phrase with emphasis.

'You are young!' He stated as an afterthought.

'She'll learn, Gerry, give her time, for Christ's sake.' The taller, dark and handsome first officer spoke sympathetically, but it was the Captain that was looking at Roz straight in the eyes. He had grey forbidding eyes, steel grey eyes which when he wasn't smiling were quite cold and Roz wanted to avoid his glare, but did not dare look away and so she mumbled her reply.

'I'm sorry, Sir. I'm sure I'll remember now.'

The Captain recognised the contriteness in Roz's voice and his look softened. No longer was it a look of anger, nor could it be described as lecherous, but it was certainly somewhere in between, and Roz controlled a shudder. He was such a portly middle-aged man, for all his uniform, self-confidence and winning smile, and Roz decided that she was not going to like him, but as quickly again his mood changed.

He turned to walk from the rear of the small twin engine aircraft up to the tiny cramped cockpit, but as he did so, suddenly he said, 'Come on, if you've never been in a cockpit before, now's your chance. The flight's an empty leg home, and a night take off is one of the most thrilling things you can experience.' Again, there was the haunting smile. It was easy to see why his face in repose was a mass of smile lines, for when he smiled for the second time, the whole face was lit with warmth and humour and Roz Peters began to understand that on this evening he had been experiencing a bad mood because he had been called out on standby. When crossed the Chief Pilot of Ferryair was not easy to be with.

They helped her sort out the tangle of safety harness and to erect the minute jump seat behind the Captain's seat on the left-hand side. The first officer strapped the girl tightly into the seat and climbed into his own seat on the right. Her heart was thumping, whether with fear or excitement it was hard to know.

There was an ear-shattering noise as the Rolls-Royce engines were started, especially from the port engine which made Roz's seat vibrate. She thought of the emphatic words of one of the Australians who was dating a flatmate, when he had heard of Roz's new job, 'You should consider that there is only a thin sheet of aluminium between you and providence...'

She shuddered with anticipation and the old troop carrier began to bump down the runway.

She could see very little from her position behind the Captain, but leaning forward she could distinguish the coloured lights of the airstrip and the edge of the runway illuminated by the taxiing lights on the wings. The Captain positioned the Viking aircraft in a small circle marked out by white lines on the tarmac.

He ran up the engines to a point where Roz thought they would surely explode. By comparison it was silence which followed.

The Captain turned around and signalled for Roz to put down a switch on her right-hand side. Terrified for fear she should touch the wrong one, she paused, waiting for his confirmation. He smiled and reassured her and she flicked the switch down.

The Captain said something to the First Officer, who nodded and undid his seat belt.

Quickly he handed her a set of earphones and a mike and she was live to the control tower.

The Viking turned, positioned, took a huge breath of power and accelerated down the brightly lit airfield, travelling as fast as a racing car, travelling faster, until there was suddenly no ground beneath them.

The Captain reached for the stick, the green lights went out, the wheels were up and the Yorkshire coast was the destination.

It was a short flight and fascinated by the confident movements of the two pilots Roz stayed where she was in the cockpit.

She had never known such a thrill as this.

It was no exaggeration to say she would never have as greater thrill unless she was to fly an aircraft for herself.

She thought she would be committed to this method of travelling for the rest of her life and as the plane circled the German plain below to get its bearing on its westerly direction, glimpses of the early morning sunrise flirted with the horizon.

22 June 1971

(ii)

Rosalind was prepared for chaos that afternoon. It was a date of unhappy memories, for the last ten years it was a date in the diary which she had to keep full and keep herself occupied so that unwelcome reminiscences did not well up and overwhelm her.

Today she could sense trouble as Alice stood in front of the heavy closed entrance door waiting for her mother to pull it towards them and allow them in but before she could do so, four large louts barged through the turnstile into the door pushing it into Alice's face and nearly knocking her smaller sister Sara backwards down the steps into the street.

'I'm very much afraid we won't be able to make next week's lesson. May we cancel it?' Rosalind asked the cashier as she bought the twin's tickets 'If this is normal in the Easter holidays we'll wait until the school children go back and the baths are less crowded.' She spoke pleasantly, for the sake of making conversation. Rosalind was an assured young woman, not yet middle-aged, but full of confidence, more mature in the social sense. Some people resented this attitude in middleclass women.

'You can't cancel it.'

'But the children can't come.'

'Yer'll have to pay. Yer're on regular. Yer can't cancel.'

Rosalind muttered 'in that case we might take our patronage elsewhere and use the more modern swimming baths in Slaithwaite', wondering vaguely as they were only nearby, why they didn't anyway. She supposed it was the excellent reputation for teaching children to swim at these old-fashioned baths. That they were dirty was only half of the problem. She felt less confident now. Her husband would be amazed at the discomfort which his wife suffered in the name of the twins' leisure.

Alice loved swimming; Sara was not too keen.

Having changed the children Rosalind led them to the edge of the pool.

The atmosphere was steamy and hot.

There was no sign of Mrs. Jones, their instructor.

Presently she found an authoritative-looking person from whom she enquired the whereabouts of Mrs. Jones. She was told 'Mrs. Jones is on 'er holidays. You'll just have to wait while Mrs. Ramsden gets into her costume. She'll take 'em.'

The twins' mother realised that things were not quite equal in fast-changing Britain. 'I see, I can't cancel our lesson, but there is apparently no compulsion for the baths to honour your commitment.' As she hadn't spoken loudly there was no telling whether she had been heard or not.

They waited uncomfortably, the twins picking up their mother's mood. Periodically five heavy adolescent girls, who were busy asserting their independence by jumping into the pool precisely where the girls and their mother were standing, bombarded them, thoroughly wetting them with huge splashes. They moved away from the girls' frolics but to no avail, the girls' movements seemed to drench the whole baths.

Roz became soaked. Despite the heat, dark-haired Sara in her little blue bikini was shivering, probably with fright.

At last Roz stood in the comparative safety of the spectator's gallery and watched the two small bodies moving through the water beneath her. The smell of chlorine and wet bodies rose. What a penance, Roz thought. This was the children's third lesson. The atmosphere was oppressive, hot and damp. It was a ghastly experience.

Alice was thrown suddenly from Mrs. Ramsden's grasp as a youth adorned with flippers and snorkel chose that precise moment to surface under teacher and pupil. Roz saw Alice was ruffled.

One of the large and budding adolescents passed on her way from the changing cubicles around the gallery to the ancient mangle where she could wring the stale chemical water from her swimsuit. Now changed from her swimsuit the girl was dressed in a Marks and Sparks dress which Rosalind recognised as being on sale at least ten years ago, long before Rosalind married. A hand-me-down and the girl's dreary affected walk emphasised it. A hand-me-down of some consequence. Rosalind had worn one exactly like it on her first trip to Greece. Possibly it was her actual dress. Most of her old clothes had been given to charity when she married.

Rosalind remembered how horrified her mother had been when, just before her mother died, she once wore a garment in her wardrobe bought cheaply with pocket money whilst still at school.

'Oh darling, you don't *need* to shop at Marks and Spencers you know,' Daddy wouldn't like it if he knew you bought your clothes from a chain store. You can always use my account at Marshall and Snelgrove if you need something new. Daddy has worked awfully hard to afford for you to have these little privileges, dear.'

18

'M & S,' Rosalind had replied, hating her mother's pre-war values. 'Same thing, Marks and Sparks, Marshall and Snelgrove. Both chain stores, what's the difference?'

She had continued to wear the frock from Marks and kept it for years. It had been a happy dress.

She had worn it on the first night she had spent in Greece.

'You should enjoy life,' Rosalind wanted to tell this moody teenager.

'You don't know what cares may befall you later. Youth passes, be warned.'

But her voice was echoed in thought only and the girl would never hear it.

TWO: PUTTING THE JOYSTICK ON AUTO-PILOT

June 1960

(i)

London at the beginning of the swinging sixties was, for Pandora Rosalind Peters, simply the centre of the world. Here she had come like so many other twenty-year-old secretaries to seek her destiny.

London on that June evening was so hot that there was heat from the reading light, which made the red-haired girl want to switch it off, although it was ten to ten and growing dark at last. Roz stretched up an arm, extinguished the offending light and caused the furniture to take on a dim outline, which would have suited her pensive mood seconds previously. Unfortunately, the movement broke the spell and she reflected crossly that London was no different, unless less exciting, from any other place she knew. Obviously, at twenty her repertoire of places was not exactly vast, but at twenty, or even twenty-one, one *feels* to have knowledge.

She sat wearing the old rust coloured cotton sweater of a previous boy-friend. Only that. Daring in the sixties. Her towel, lay within reach, carelessly thrown over the settee; bright orange it fought with her red hair and the peculiar colour of the sweater. The girl hugged her knees and sat on the floor.

A week ago, June twenty-fourth had been her birthday. She had reached twenty years old.

She had deliberately not drawn the curtains. Kangaroo land they called this part of Earls Court in the early sixties. One house was white, one grey, while further down the street, by day, the painters were painting the sills of another overlooking a small exclusive park, blue.

Here only fifty years before, horses and coaches, footmen and butlers carried on their precise lives, kept a tranquil peace and life below stairs was yet to become a basement flat. Now to this quiet residential square had come the Australians in their swarms, bringing sunshine and noise, loud laughter and voices, but a sense of humour and even she would admit to a quality of life which was pleasant.

Soon her three flatmates would return with Australian boyfriends from a first date. The previous night they had also introduced new boyfriends and also the night previously.

It was the way of things; the girls were literally gaining experience and chalking up a score. At breakfast, they would gleefully recall their conquests.

But Pandora Rosalind Peters was preserving her virginity. The effort required to do so made London tiring but she refused to give in to a nation such as the Australians whose few known representatives had always demanded the same prize. How was she to know in 1960 that her own son would in the late eighties reverse the action by jetting out to Australia with two of his pals. And when he did could she count on the pommies behaving better than the Aussies in a foreign land? But by then, of course, there was the pill, and there was Aids - another world, another set of values.

The swish of the traffic flowed in through the open window and the balmy air warmed her exposed body parts. She had a slim body. She could not deny that the semi-naked pose made her feel sensual.

'Dear Gal,' the Aussies of the sixties had said to her, 'now why should a lonely Australian boy be paying for a bint's dinner if he didn't expect just a little kindness in return. Aw, come on it won't hurt.'

She had found in London that it was not just the Australians who went in for this sort of reward; it might just as easily be one's boss, when one needed a rise or even to keep one's job.

London was a miserable city. She would study peoples' faces on the Underground. A man had sat opposite her earlier in the day. He had possessed a suitcase. The carriage was nearly empty, but the man had disposed of the case by setting it on end, on his knees, thus protecting himself from the stares of the other travellers almost completely. Yet it must have been uncomfortable for his baggage was less than an inch from his nose.

Alternatively, he might have set it on the floor or left it on the seat next to him. She had wondered where he was going, was he happy? Had she been able to study his face she knew she would have been unable to recognise any feeling in it. He was as much of a zombie as someone who had managed to repress his traumas sufficiently so as to become a successful case of psychoanalysis.

She recognised that to live with oneself one should like oneself and she doubted herself more than most. It was possibly the reason for her possessive attitude to her virginity.

There was no good reason for her shyness or insecurity, although to lose one's mother as a teenager did not help; but she was good looking, her pale complexion and auburn curls almost classed her as a beauty. She was small about five-foot-three and she had an excellent slim figure. She also had the ability to be outgoing, given the chance to come to terms with strangers. She was sure maturity would improve things.

She had worked through her lunch hour and when her boss had sent her out on an errand to Unilever House, she had decided to try the restaurant opposite her offices for a late snack. The white net curtains over the windows presented a reasonable front and under the neon sign there was a notice which proclaimed 'FRESH-CUT SANDWICHES' and another: 'LUNCHEON VOUCHERS ACCEPTED.' Strange habit, she thought for bosses to pay for employees' food rather than increasing their pay packet.

Stepping inside the restaurant she realised that the half dozen eyes of the proprietor and his family in the otherwise empty cafe were in some inexplicable way preventing her from walking out again without bothering to seek a table. She sat down near to the door, at a table with fewer crumbs on the sticky plastic cloth and instantly regretted her decision to stay.

The owner had come over to her at once and flicked the grunge to the floor. Some landed on her lap. He was dressed in a once-white laboratory overall, unfastened and obviously unwashed in branded detergent. His long greasy hair dirtied his collar. She wondered how the English got away with it. In France, the man at least would have worn a cheerful apron and the furniture if cheap would have been cheerful.

When she looked at the menu the man smiled. She gathered some courage and ordered a coffee only and the man stopped smiling.

There was a notice on an old-fashioned hat-stand; a tall Victorian tree of slender mahogany, with branches like a pruned apple tree at the top only, and with symmetrical knobs where the apples should be. Elegant really but in 1960 it was awfully unfashionable. The notice on this work of craftsmanship said: 'IN THE INTERESTS OF HYGIENE DOGS ARE NOT ALLOWED IN THIS RESTAURANT.' 'The place might be cleaner if dogs were allowed in to eat the crumbs off the linoleum.' She spoke aloud but no one heard.

The coffee came, and as it cooled she read The Daily Telegraph; an advertisement caught her eye.

She stood up to leave as two smartly dressed city gentlemen, without bowlers, came in and ordered afternoon tea. From the enthusiastic greeting they received it would seem that they at least regularly attended the establishment and the girl had difficulty attracting attention to get her bill. The coffee had been scarcely drinkable, and it had cost seven pence, nine pence with cream, nearly a shilling for one cup! She felt it was exorbitant, and in that moment a decision was reached to leave London.

Not only that, but she decided she would revert to her second name and be known as Rosalind; Pandora, or even Pan, the names of her childhood, no longer suited.

Now, sitting alone in her overcrowded mice infested flat, it seemed the answer was in the threepenny stamp on the letter that she had just sealed one hour ago. In London, she was no more liberated than the cooks and under-house-parlour-maids who had worked from the basement some fifty years ago. It was Rosalind's opinion that as nations go, the British were placid people, uncomplaining, but it was time for a change. Change as radical as producing modern Americans from Pilgrim Fathers.

Perhaps London needed to lose its reserve, to brighten its image. The city was just a great false congregation of unhappy and lonely citizens. At least the American and the Australian nations portray an image of joy, however much the prim British frowned. Yet post-war London stood on the threshold of a new experience, for this was the beginning of the swinging sixties and Roz was yet to realise it.

Just a half mile from the cafe where Roz had sat that afternoon, Carnaby Street would spring to life, and all within easy distance would feel the sweet smell of success and Roz was about to detach herself.

The Arabs believe that your death day is predestined. If you don't die in a tunnel at Mecca you will surely walk under a bus. But Roz understood nothing of fate and all she could do was write and address a letter to the Airport at Leeds/Bradford, kiss the envelope for luck, and hope it would take her back to her roots and to security in Yorkshire.

She hated the South. Twice she told herself she hated the South but she was not at all sure that the North appealed so much more. Already she was a lost and lonely soul searching for roots, for happiness, for an elusive security and the stability that man's increasing mobility had made so difficult to achieve. Trees and men both sow seeds, trees take roots, men wander seeking fulfilment that is rarely attained until the wanderlust settles or dissipates.

Had her mother not died when she was just sixteen she would never have left home. Or was it because of Derek and Lucinda that she had come to London? Did it matter when your cousin, your best friend in all the world, so close as to be like an elder sibling, the person you trusted most and to whom you looked up, married the man you had set your heart upon.

Did it matter? Was that preordained by some great god?

Roz knew there were other men...she had yet to meet them, and yet....

A noise in the keyhole reminded Roz that her flatmates and the Aussies were due home. Hurriedly sitting on the folded copy of the Daily Telegraph, she hid the Situations Vacant on the second page. She covered herself with a towel and tried to present the impression of one freshly out of the bath.

August 1960

(ii)

'Do you think we dare ask her for a cup of coffee?

'Doubt it! Not after your remarks in Hamburg, you might discover it was sweetened with salt!'

So, the novice air hostess, sitting in the tiny cockpit of the Viking aircraft for the first time on that August evening in 1960, on the empty leg back from her first trip to Germany, wearing headphones like the rest of the crew, observed that the Captain's remarks to his First Officer were made by pressing down the lower switch on a panel on the dashboard, which corresponded to the one on her right, just behind the jump seat.

She experimented, bravely she felt, and not without results. Her remark, 'or she may be tempted to turn you both into frogs!' was met with a cheeky grin from both pilots.

Wisely young Roz Peters limited her conversation to that one reply, remembering to turn off the radio when she had finished speaking. This was fortunate since later she deduced from the absence of pressure on her ears and from the brief indications to ground control that they were descending.

'Any other traffic in the area?' asked Ben Smith, the tall First Officer, at the end of his request for clearance into Yeadon, increasingly becoming known as Leeds-Bradford International airport.

'No! Not tonight, only fools and Ferryair fly at night, the wise birds are sheltering in their roosts,' was the quick retort of the English control.

'His wit is too much for me at this time of night,' and the fair-haired Captain did not laugh, or even smile. It was well known that Yeadon did not normally accept night flights. On this flight from Germany the sombre Captain attended to the undercarriage and the green lights came on. Turing to the small port window he looked out. 'I've got a wheel.'

The First Officer likewise looked out of the starboard window.

'I've got a wheel,' he mimicked without any hint of sarcasm, but Roz saw he wagged his bushy eyebrows as he turned in her direction.

She had not understood that such things were checked visually and she thought that the procedure was amusing and also unnecessary since she assumed that the purpose of the green lights, now illuminating the dashboard was to indicate that the undercarriage had come down.

Now she realised that such things were never left to chance. 'I never thought that where things can be visually checked they are, I suppose that's because the lights might operate while the undercarriage itself might still be malfunctioning.'

'She's no fool,' quipped the first office turning to give Roz a smile.

After they landed in the early hours of the morning Mr. Smith, the First Officer, continued his friendly patter. 'I insist that Miss Peters join me, and Captain Duncan, for a wee dram.'

The Scotch was drunk directly from the bottle in the draughty crew room. 'It never fails to amaze me that the operations officer forgets, not just occasionally but most times, to leave out the key for the traffic office where some glasses are kept.'

'You'd think someone would remember we're working these abominable hours.' Gerry Duncan's remarks were still scathing. 'We were better treated on our return from those grim Berlin airlifts.' Tales of ex-RAF and the relief of the Berlin blockade were favourite topics of conversation with all crew. For these men, it was as though peacetime was too dull, but to Rosalind, although fascinated by their bravado tales of a war and its aftermath all of which happened whilst she was still a child seemed out of her sphere of interest, indeed by now Roz was too tired to enter into any conversation.

Her father and his friends would converse endlessly about the Cold War although they tended to clamp up when she came into the room. She was still at an age when older adults would protect her from the cruel realities of life and now she was actually entering into that harsh, unkind world. She perched nervously on an upright chair, picking at the skin around her forefinger. She had understood that if the crew bus was not available at night, she should call a taxi to run her to her flat.

However, she felt she could scarcely argue with the Captain when he offered her a lift and she left the empty building with him and stepped hesitantly into his German Mercedes. It had a left-hand drive.

'I see, one of these 'Chinese' motor-cars,' she said. She spoke gaily, in the curious Goon humour of the sixties.

'The only good thing to ever come out of that damn country,' said the Captain with feeling. He scowled to close the conversation; clearly, he did not like to be reminded of his war efforts. In particular, Hamburg, which had been totally decimated by eight square miles of firestorm in 1943, weighed heavily on his conscience. In fifteen years the pain of the war years was scarcely erased. Roz pushed back her auburn hair, taking off her airforce blue forage cap, she loosened her tight jacket and still felt uncomfortable.

How this gloriously petite young girl had come to be acting as a stewardess in the very early days of cheap package holidays, without previous training and no experience was due to one of those acts of fate, of chance, which favoured the young in those days; before qualifications mattered and before the Baby Boom heralded unemployment.

Three miles and ten minutes brought Roz to her lodgings. She thanked the Captain for the lift, before leaving the car.

'Good night young lady. It was a tough initiation but I think I can report that you'll learn fast,' and the man smiled, a tender almost protective smile, as he leant across her to open the car door.

The huge tree outside the lodgings, which Roz shared with another stewardess, was lit by the headlights of the German car, casting a delicate shadow across the street. Dawn was breaking and an unseasonable August wind took the heavy branches of the green tree in its wake and tossed them lightly against the windows of Roz's flat. She unlocked the door and went inside.

THREE: PUPPY LOVE

Mid-August 1960

(i)

Three days after returning from Germany, Rosalind Peters received her week's briefing from the crewing officer. She was rostered out on tour. It arrived by morning post and Roz discovered it on her way out to the hairdressers. It scheduled her departure as August 16, gave her destination as Athens, listed the crew as DUNCAN, SMITH & PETERS, and included a list of catering requirements essential for three weeks absence in Greece. It was company policy to take as much with the outgoing aircraft as possible, saving the expense of uplifting items such as coffee and minerals en route, which were costly on the continent. She was very apprehensive, but Greece was Greece and she was excited.

The day of departure was warm and it increased Roz's anticipation with thoughts of hotter Greek sunshine and bluer skies. She had been briefed by Julie, her flatmate, on all the pretty clothes her suitcase should contain and she commissioned, with some trouble, since they objected on principle, one of the loaders to carry her case across the wide expanse of tarmac to the aircraft. Everyone was smiling; it was a beautiful August morning with a clear blue sky with an occasional puff of white cloud and young Roz Peters was going to Greece. She could not believe it.

The passengers were as excited as Roz; most of them having never flown before, let alone to Greece.

Now she knew him better, Ben Smith seemed pleasant enough and she received a shy smile of recognition at Yeadon and thereafter each time she offered him a cup of coffee.

He also accepted the daintily prepared lunch which Roz had uplifted, thoughtfully and only for the crew in Rome. Ben was tall, rather gauche personality, the type that seems too big for a tiny cockpit.

Captain Duncan was not so co-operative and had apparently thrown his lunch box out of the window for he proudly displayed the remains littered around the wing, in its shiny new livery. This particular plane had recently been in use as one of her Majesty's 'personal aircraft used for the Queen's flight'.

Roz thought the contents had landed dangerously near the propeller and wondered what would happen to the disintegrating pieces as they fell on the Italian peasants below; hard boiled eggs, salami and pieces of tomato from heaven. However, she didn't trip into the trap of questioning the pilot's wisdom in opening his cockpit window in flight as no doubt the whole exercise had been conducted for this purpose. Roz knew full well that the little Viking aircraft - ancient even in 1960 - were not pressurised like modern aircraft.

One half-hour refuelling stop in Rome had provided the stewardess with a much-needed cigarette, which she accepted from the Captain, although she generally avoided Rothmans. The Rome Agent was a busy Italian who was simultaneously delighted to see them and sad that the crew would not stay to be entertained in the Airport Restaurant. Aircrew in the early sixties expected a royal welcome as a right. It was company policy to feed the crew on a long flight, during a transit stop, and Roz had not eaten since breakfast and it was three in the afternoon. Clearly, it was a bad day for hungry stewardesses because Captain Duncan had no appetite.

The office of the agent in Rome was in a cellar underneath the main building, and Roz drew a comparison with an air raid shelter. She thought the similarity was so great, that fifteen years before this was probably exactly what it once was.

It was a poor substitute for a gay Italian cafe and a bowl of Spaghetti. The Captain had offered the agent a cigarette also, who took the packet to put into his pocket. The Captain did not look surprised. English cigarettes were a luxury in Italy. He busied himself preparing the papers. The construction of the load sheet and the passenger manifest were still new to Roz and she crossed over to watch the Captain draw them up.

'At this rate, we will be in possession of a proper little Miss Efficiency at the end of our trip' and a casual observer would have said that Captain Duncan winked, but Roz retreated a small step backward and wondered if she would ever feel an empathy with this man.

Roz was warned to complete her cabin duties in good time to experience her first landing in Greece. A ten-hour day had made her tired and the crew had not been especially communicative, but that was as she expected.

However, in contrast to the previous Hamburg flight, as the Viking approached Athens the galley was immaculate. The bar box was counted and accounted for, and provided the crew light was not flashing, and Roz was prepared to take that risk, she was perfectly safe secured tightly by her seat belt, gratefully and illegally

33

having accepted a kindly lady's invitation to sit next to her for landing. The galley had no window and the jump seat provided for a stewardess was no place from which to observe one's first landing at Athens!

Indeed, to appreciate Athens to the full, in those days when it was not much bigger than a small town, it was best to fly in at night, to see from the air the brilliance of the floodlit Acropolis.

The kindly passenger had actually flown into Athens before but she was as excited as the young stewardess when the magnificent sight of the illuminated Acropolis came into view. The Viking circled slowly in its approach round the hills of Athens, turning deliberately in a graceful and rhythmical ritual, grateful for its safe arrival. The electric atmosphere from the blue street lights and the yellow floodlights and the red neon signs seemed to penetrate the regal little aircraft's skin, slowly 'Oscar Romeo' landed on the ancient soil and taxied to the terminal; parking cheekily next to a monstrous Comet 4B of Olympic Airways.

Outside the air just smelt hot. It was exiting.

(ii)

Intoxicated by excitement Roz carelessly handed her personal case to a catering official who offered to take it across on his trolley and with a half skip and half walk she shot off in the direction of an entrance marked prominently in Greek and English 'BAGGAGE ONLY'. One foot over the threshold, the restraining hand on her shoulder proved only to be her Captain's but as he remarked she was lucky it was him.

'Greek customs officers, like many Eastern gentlemen, prefer foreigners to abide by the rules,' he told her, leading her into immigration. 'They also don't like crew or passengers to import spirits; at least they certainly give that impression! You should take care!'

'Any brandy?' they questioned Roz. She shook her head and showed them the five packets of Stuyvesant in her blue shoulder bag.

'Ehete alla?' She looked blankly at the man. 'Is it all?'

'Yes,' she said. Was it all foreign countries which had the penalty of loss of the hand or other useful limb or were they not far enough east? The customs officer believed her, so she never found out. When her Captain also denied the possession of any brandy in his pilot's bag, they actually inspected it and found nothing, fortunately.

Directly outside the long airport building the First Officer rescued her small hand baggage from the boot of the large American taxi and carried it somewhat triumphantly into the back of the taxi whilst the Captain instructed Roz to sit beside him, allowing his first officer to sit in the front seat.

She had been relieved to discover her main baggage safely stored with passengers in the Customs Hall. The catering official who had helpfully whisked it away from her at the aircraft had separated it from the rest of the crew luggage and there was one awful moment when Roz had wondered if she would ever see her case again. Of course, these episodes had not endeared her fair-haired Captain towards her and it was with some trepidation that the young girl now sat down next to the small slightly overweight pilot.

However, as the taxi began to move the Captain smiled his wonderful smile. 'This is the craziest ride into town you will ever witness. It's why I insist my co-pilot sits in the front! They tell you Italians drive fast. Not by Greek standards, they don't!'

As the car was passing through the gates, Ben Smith opened his briefcase and removed a bottle of duty-free brandy. 'Voilà'.

'But, see,' said Roz. 'Snap' and she flourished her own bottle of illicit booze.

'Incidentally, my name's Gerry, and you're Rosalind. There's no need to keep referring to me as 'Captain' off duty.' It seemed a belated introduction when Roz remembered the Hamburg flight, more an indication that she was accepted as one of the crew. Captain Duncan clearly did not bother to get to know his crew unless forced to spend three weeks with them.

'Have a drink?' said Ben, and he cheerfully passed around the now opened bottle of brandy. 'And pass it on to Gerry, I don't think he'll mind if you wipe the neck!'

Roz had never drunk neat brandy before, after a day of fasting, out of a bottle, but by now she was beginning to understand her crew. After the Hamburg flight, she had thought that Ben might have been tired or thirsty, now she suspected that this was his normal routine.

The hooting of the taxi, the swerving and sudden stopping for apparently ever-changing traffic lights captured much of her excited heartbeat and eventually brought them off the dual carriageway which ran parallel to the sea and onto a street which seemed to have a never-ending succession of car salesrooms, chandelier or furniture shops. They turned left towards the city centre. The great silhouetted columns of the Temple of Olympian Zeus on their immediate right reminded them where they were and by craning her neck upwards to the left Roz could distinguish the dim outline of the floodlit Acropolis. They passed into the brightly lit streets of the modern town and the three English persons took a final gulp from the brandy bottle and the Captain replaced the top on the bottle.

Roz felt it was rather difficult to climb out of the taxi, at the same time ensuring that her air-force blue forage cap with its gold trim and wings was straight. Unused as she was to sampling neat spirits she realised that she must compose herself at all costs, and her deportment in such matters was important. After all, she was in uniform.

In the hotel Captain Duncan perhaps realised her predicament for whilst he appeared to pay no extra attention to her, he assisted in filling the registration card, carefully explaining that she must put name, father's name, address passport number, although the Greek form was excellently translated into English underneath.

The dark-haired Greek receptionist put three keys on the desk and the Captain picked up the middle one and handed it to Roz.

'We always put our hostie into the middle room, don't we Ben?' They both laughed when the remark brought the desired expression of horror on her fair-skinned blushing face and she quickly changed her response to a watery smile. The bonny Greek girl went on filling in the registration cards without even looking up; she was obviously very used to the idiosyncrasies of aircrew.

'Five minutes everyone and then sandwiches and six beers in my room, alright?'

For Roz, the remark did not seem to give any alternative and although five minutes did not give her much time for a shower she was hungry. She washed in the luxurious hand basin, gazed longingly at the bath and at the white covered bed in her room for it was a quarter to midnight and remembering tales she had heard in the crew room, she picked up her glass tumbler from the washbasin, collected her six-transistor radio from her case and arrived having changed her shirt and armed with another half bottle of Hennessey, at the Captain's door.

A radio was already playing as she entered the room, so she tried to place hers unnoticed on the bed and as the Captain was sitting on the only chair, and since he did not rise, she sat rather hesitantly on the one divan whilst the large dark-haired first officer sprawled over the other.

Captain Duncan noticed the radio and since it was probably the smallest he had seen, picked it up and examined it.

'I think she really is one of us!' There was a note of approval and the man smiled kindly.

Ben had also seen the tooth-brush-glass touch and nodding his head, said with unmistakable admiration, 'yes, this one has passed the test!'

They ate the Salami sandwiches which were unbuttered and left a repeating lump in the throat. 'More than a hint of Garlic in these,' said the first officer, and he wrinkled his nose in disgust. They drank the beer, or rather the men drank most of it, and then Ben drank some brandy with ice, because at night in Greece in August it was hot.

The Captain opened the long French window and Roz carefully left the bed where she had been lying and unsteadily crossed over to the balcony. Already she was both tired and exhilarated.

Captain Duncan joined her outside on the balcony. 'Good hotel, eh?'

'Is it new?'

'Very, the plaster is hardly dry on the walls. You can smell it. It is the pattern of things to come. You mark my words in a few years' time Athens will be over-run with good tourist class hotels.

'We still should have been booked in at the Astir Beach Hotel,' interrupted Ben from the bedroom. 'Wonderful place. A complete chalet for each guest, right on Glyfada beach and much nearer the airport.'

'Listen to him!' mocked the Captain, 'What gives you the impression that the directors of Ferryair would bear that sort of expense?'

'It's not expensive...not that expensive,' retaliated Ben, his dark bushy eyebrows waggling in protest. 'The only drawback is that it's ten miles from town and cabs into town are exorbitant.'

'As I've just found out to my cost.' But Gerry Duncan exercised a remarkable control on the sarcasm in his tone. Deliberately changing the conversation, he said, 'there is a very good night-club down there.' He pointed informatively over the balcony opening his steel blue-grey eyes just a little more, to better observe the scene for himself.

'The drinks will be expensive though,' teased Ben and laughed as he saw Gerry unconsciously jingling his change in his pocket. The Captain was considered tight with his money.

'Do you see where I mean?' asked the Captain, ignoring Ben. 'There under the blue sign! A great pity the music is westernised though. I feel that in Greece you should do as the Greek do. Trouble is, a lot of smart Greeks frequent that particular night-club and to them the Western music is chic.' He said chick. 'In twenty-years-time, there will be little in Athens that retains that special Greek atmosphere. See,' he went on, lazily pointing his short thick arm over the rail to pin point Constitution Square, 'down there, by day the soldiers in the royal uniform guard the Royal Palace in their outrageous uniforms, with a swirl of their white kilts which they call foustanellas.' In a few years' time, there would not be a Royal Palace, as such, but they did not know that.

There was a full moon outlining the shapes and shadows of the great city.

'Do you see the pointed hill with the church on top, Roz?' It was the first time he had used her Christian name; a name so new to her, since she had only recently foregone Pan, that it made her jump. 'It is twice the height of the Acropolis. One tourist in two hundred knows its name, and one in a thousand can pronounce it correctly, Lykabettos.' Lickavittos was how he said it. 'I think it is nearly 1,000 feet high. I suspect it follows the Christian idea that you build your churches nearest to God. Imagine how excited you would have been if you were an ardent church builder and you found a virgin conical rock like that one and imagine the problems that would face you when you were determined to actually build on such a precipitous foundation. All over Greece there are hundreds of such churches and monasteries built on inspiring pinnacles, the most famous being those of the Meteora, the Monasteries of the Air. It's a quite a climb up Lycabettos but very good for the figure, young lady, and you do have a wonderful view for your labour!'

'It looks very high.' Roz whispered, gazing at the dark shape of the mountain, uncertain of her power of speech after her alcoholic experience, she rarely drank more than the odd sherry. Also, she was tired; too tired to talk, too tired to look at her watch. Here she was in Athens, in modern history the capital of a Greece united, in ancient times a city of most people's dreams but far from united. A place to which she had been transported free; a place that cost other Britons a great deal of money to visit and Roz was ashamed to admit that she felt tired. So, she turned away from the window and sat upright on the bed. If she had allowed herself to lie down she would have fallen asleep. It was a little cooler inside.

The Captain stayed on the balcony. He didn't seem to notice that Roz was no longer beside him. 'Lykabettos is a classical name, you know. It was supposed to be the rock Athena was carrying to form the bulwark of her citadel, but she dropped it!' Ben laughed from the other bed but the Captain ignored the interruption. Rising there in all its majesty in the

41

moonlight the mountain did look accidental. 'They say it is best to climb it in the evening, just before the sun sets or to get up early for the sunrise. When the sun is high in this country the views are very hazy.'

'They should put a cable car up there,' said Ben. The huge swarthy man was lazy.

'I hear that they might just do that thing, a funicular railway.' Answered his superior, exercising the tone of advantage in his reply. We, and I mean us, as aircrew, are destroying our own environment you know. Bring them all to see the beauty of the world and what do they all want – facilities and funiculars. Pah!'

'I know what they've done to Spain, but I mean they wouldn't do anything to Greece,' Roz's voice sounded small, hesitant. 'Greece is so much older and after all tourists have been coming here since Byron.'

'Oh! that we were all so young and innocent sweet Rosalind! Tourists have been going to Spain since the Ottomans trailed to Cordoba, and tourists have been coming to Greece for two and a half thousand years, ever since Pericles laid the foundation stones for his imperial temples on the Acropolis, ever since Aeschylus and Euripides competed in the drama festival and Aristophanes had them rolling in the aisles, ever since the Athenian has remained legendary for his hospitality. But now the twentieth century will abuse that hospitality. The word in Greek – philoxenia - literally means friends of strangers.'

'Never mind Gerry,' Ben said, excusing his senior officer. 'Like everyone else in the company you will soon realise that his cap is a regular little hive; bees in the bonnet aren't anything when it comes to Gerry's repertoire of facts and figures. This gentleman collects facts like everyone else collects stamps.'

'Which you plagiarise by entering them in that diary of yours,' said Gerry undeterred. 'Ben fancies himself as a writer, a recorder of facts, and I suspect would rather be a writer than a pilot. But like most writers he's inordinately lazy, relying on others to do this research. Now remember young Benjamin in case you don't know it already, there is at the present time only about four thousand miles of tarred highway in all Greece. In a country of this size, which is an infinitesimal amount by European standards! And I would lay you a bet of four thousand pounds that in five years that this will have doubled; and in ten, maybe, doubled again. We aircrew are bringing a few people to Greece, thirty-six on this particular trip, a few more come each month and they'll all go home and just as they did with Spain they will urge their neighbours and fellow countrymen to follow suit. 'Where did you go for your hols, Mrs. Jones? Oh Really? How nice, was it? Yes, we'd love to see your photos.'' The Captain's mimicking, mincing voice was excellent; he had the gift of being able to take off any accent, almost any tone, and Roz looked at Ben and started laughing.

'However,' continued the Captain, 'when we go out into the hot dusty streets of Athens, tomorrow, ninety degrees in the shade, we shall count all those home-movie-makers from Sweden, Germany, America and possibly discover a few British. You will both be able to do a little mental sum and perhaps you will see what I mean. Meanwhile make the best of the capital city of capital cities here with just as many amenities as you need, without too many hotels and still with a very ancient and very Greek life to revolve around.'

'Tomorrow, then, we'll see the sights. I'll believe that when I see it,' remarked Ben. He stirred slightly, he sounded extremely lethargic. 'For your information Roz, Captain Duncan is a bar-room sightseer. He can give an excellent history lesson, but I've yet to see him go sightseeing. That's why I've to keep a diary – to swot up on all the places I'm supposed to have seen, otherwise people would not believe I've ever been abroad.'

'That's not entirely true, and you know it. I've an absolute passion for the Valley of Kings at Luxor and particularly for Karnak; also for Knossos in Crete, which many don't share. But for the others, they are often so small after you've read about them in such enlarged terms; and that goes for the Acropolis and Egyptian pyramids for that matter.' The grey eyes twinkled. 'You mark my words, young Roz; I know the Acropolis is an inspiration to many; in the setting sun or the moonlight its marble ruins are breath-taking, but they are ruins, destroyed by an over-ebullient soldier, a Count, who ordered his army to fire on the Turks, who imprudently stored gunpowder in the Parthenon in the seventeenth century. You believe me, if your history is good and you've read a lot about them you'll be disappointed.'

'But I haven't read a lot. I'm just an ignorant girl, almost still a teenager. Dying to go home and tell them all about it!'

'Alright, you make a point. We shall visit the Acropolis and see the Parthenon, the temple of Athena Parthenos. We shall all inspect this monument that has no equal, this Doric architecture that is beyond criticism, presumably because it disobeyed all previous rules about Doric architecture, and even employed four Ionic columns in the central area. And you know I'd much prefer an English Lake District walk to touring the old sites!'

Roz had to laugh, tired though she was. Forewarned is forearmed, so they say.

Roz woke that first day in Athens and looked at her watch. It was one o'clock, perhaps understandable because it was only eleven o'clock British time. The previous evening, they had talked beyond history. Ben was a Catholic but this did not prevent the conversation turning to religion after they had exhausted politics. Roz had resisted the tiredness, which knotted her stomach and made her limbs itch and she remembered conducting some quite heated arguments in the early light of dawn. The evening had successfully broken the ice and served as an introduction to her companions for the next three weeks.

As always, when in a strange place, Roz lay in bed on her back for several minutes wondering whether she was supposed to get up and order breakfast – or indeed lunch. Finally, she decided to get up and shower. Since she was very hungry having eaten hardly anything the previous day, she lifted the telephone receiver and cautiously asked for room service. The excellent English reply gave her confidence and she ordered 'Café complete, with fruit juice and a boiled egg.' She had already been warned that nobody ate lunch much before two or three in the afternoon, nor dinner before nine so she supposed breakfast after midday was quite reasonable.

She debated whether to call the captain's room, decided not and turned on the shower. The 'phone rang. She had to answer it although her body and hair were wet through. She felt too alone to let it ring.

Wrapping an enormous white towel around herself she dripped into the bedroom, the dry heat of the afternoon almost drying her without the towel. A very false Greek accent gave her ten minutes to be in the bar downstairs. Not to be fooled, Roz pretended not to recognise the voice as Ben's and said she did not accept invitations from strange men. Nevertheless, when she arrived at the bar some twenty minutes later, with her light breakfast thankfully consumed, there were three orange coloured drinks lined up on the bar. They glistened with ice in long inviting tumblers.

'These three are for you, we're two ahead, so you will have to do some rapid swallowing if we're going to have lunch in ten minutes.' She arched her eyebrows, attempting to appear oblivious to their teasing, but only succeeded in emphasising her lovely hazel eyes, which were quite green that day.

She questioned the alcoholic composition of the drinks.

'Screwdrivers; vodka and orange, fresh orange, so very good for you!' Ben qualified this by waggling his great dark eyebrows. Roz was relieved when they drank the second and third drink for her without being asked.

'Well, are we going to drag young Roz up the Acropolis then?' asked Ben, possibly trying to conceal the fact that he would like to visit the ruins himself. To Roz, Ben was the antidote to the rather sarcastic Captain, who, despite his touching way of appearing to father the young stewardess, in fact frightened her. She was thankful the more handsome dark-haired first officer seemed less complicated.

He wasn't a bad looking man; his black hair and slight Mongolian features, together with huge eyebrows and swarthy skin made his a very interesting face. But he was so untidy. Roz even expected him to put on his mackintosh as they explored the sights of Athens in the heat. His smile was his most disarming feature. He had a dimple in his chin. He also possessed a quality rare among aircrew; he was a widower and therefore technically unmarried. He had been a widower for thirteen years; thirteen was his son's age. Ben was twenty-one when his eighteen-year-old wife died.

'Lunch,' said the Captain. The single word used so abruptly recalled the Captain's usual sharp manner, which he had apparently forgotten now he was off duty. His slight Yorkshire tongue seemed to have mellowed to the transcontinental brogue, which was common among aircrew, and sitting at the high bar at that moment in his Hong Kong made twelve-ounce lightweight suit it would have been difficult to distinguish him from any regular globe-trotting salesman. It occurred to Roz that no one had yet mentioned whether the Captain was married or not; last night she had assumed that he was.

Gerald Duncan twisted his heavy frame off the bar stool as if to leave and stood facing the exit into the dull modern reception hall, his grey-blue eyes focused on the unmistakable smart grey uniform of another pilot, now crossing the foyer.

The two Captains met; inevitably one slapped the other on the back, whilst their respective crews stood discreetly in the background. There were general introductions all round.

'My crew: Ben Smith, Roz Peters, meet Captain Williams. Harold is with JTL.' He pronounced it Jaytell. Gerry mentioned the world's most exclusive charter company founded by John T. Lines. 'Flying rather grander kites now, Harold, eh?' Ferryair's short almost tubby chief pilot spoke not without a note of envy.

'Well, how about a drink?' Ben echoed the universal aircrew greeting. Roz was thankful now she had ordered the light breakfast to line her stomach.

'Must get out of these togs, first, Old Boy. Wouldn't do you know, to be actively seen drinking it off ... we've had one hell of a trip. Couldn't get pressurised and spent three hours circling Belgrade. Of course, those local loaders ... had we been in Albania and not Tito-land I would have said Chinese ... ha, ha, of course the damn loaders had not locked the rear hold. Saw your charmer at Ellinikó! Made me rather nostalgic these little twin-engine jobs. Always look minute on the apron beside these modern jets. Hear they're starting on the new terminal next year, time this town had an airport worthy of it, rather than what others would call a simple cattle shed.' And as though Harold Williams could not help rubbing salt into Gerry's wounded pride, he persevered. 'Still good that old Queen's Flight Viking then, Duncan? Must make up for a lot really, having one of Royalty's cast-offs to bum around in. Rather like having an aging Rolls Royce, I expect.'

It was said kindly enough but Gerry obviously winced. Roz wondered if Captain Williams gabbled like an old woman out of nerves or authority.

She felt a genuine pang of sympathy for Captain Duncan but he answered lightly without ill feeling. 'Well, at least we don't get pressurisation problems with her, if that's what you mean, Hal?'

Captain Williams, no doubt, was now aware that he had touched upon a sore point. 'Tell you what,' he said. 'We're all rather hungry and there's a magnificent little restaurant in Monastiraki just around the corner. Take the street down away from the Grande Bretagne. I'll meet you there, with my mob, in half an hour.'

48

Williams smiled paternally at his silent crew of four, a first officer, engineer, a hostess and a steward.

Not a great believer in exercise, in the heat of the midday sun, Gerald Duncan's crew took a taxi to the restaurant, but Captain Williams had not been overestimating when he said it was just around the corner. It was.

The wooden tables and the woven wicker seated chairs contrasted with the smooth browny-purple leather furnishings of the bar they had just left. Gerry immediately ordered a bottle of Retsina, stating categorically that it was the only wine to drink in Greece. The proprietor tried to persuade them to sample a carafe drawn from the enormous barrels which provided part of the furnishings of the room, but Gerry ever on the side of caution insisted on a bottle variety. Without any question, Dolmathes, stuffed vine leaves, and artichokes were on the table when the others finally arrived.

It was for Roz and the other stewardess to draw the line at the local fare which was provided for the main course. While the men sampled larks roasted and split in half, head, eyes and no bigger than a sparrow, Sally announced she was a vegetarian, which in 1960 caused something of a stir and the girls quickly changed their order to a Greek salad, Roz who was ravenous was tucking into Ben's side dish of moussaka as greedily as she dared, but she should not have worried, the dishes just kept coming.

Even Roz, new as she was to the ways of aircrew could have foreseen the rest of the afternoon's events. No sooner had they come out of the restaurant into the bright hot sunlight, after a long and huge lunch, leaving a happy waiter with a most generous tip, then the

49

girls began shop-window gazing and the male party and the female element drifted apart down the narrow-cobbled street towards the fashionable shops of Odhos Ermou, progressively moving away from the old town and the shadow of the Acropolis.

The first group of shops showed their windows full of fascinating gold jewellery, beautiful inexpensive shoes and leather bags. The rift between the sexes was strengthened and it was suddenly apparent to the girls that they had seen the last of their escorts for some time. They continued up towards Constitution Square, known in Greek as Syntagma, and down a small street Roz could see the bright lights of the hotel entrance, but no men folk.

Sally, the Jaytell girl, was predictably bitter. Even her limited conversation over lunch had convinced Roz that Sally was no lover of male aircrew. 'Their manners are always disgusting; my kid brother would know better than to leave women alone in a strange town. Still, sometimes if you're with a decent crew they like to take you to a nightclub in the evening. Air-hostesses come cheaper than club hostesses. It might be a good idea to have our hair set in anticipation?' Sally sported a large beehive creation, which clearly needed the practised skill of a professional hairdresser.

However, this seemed a sensible suggestion to Roz. For one thing, it would be cooler than wandering the Athens streets. She did not feel fully acclimatised yet. The shops were only just opening again after their afternoon siesta and the heat still was hitting them full frontal, although it was well past four o'clock. They really had no alternative because the crew had absconded with the funds and at least if they used the hairdresser in the basement of the hotel they could charge the expenses incurred to the hotel account.

'Are there good nightclubs?' Roz asked Sally.

'Good nightclubs and good restaurants and very Greek. I do hope they will take us to Vakhos, that means Bacchus, God of Wine.' Sally tossed her flaxen hair knowledgeably. 'Or even the Palea Athena, where there's dancing.'

Two hours later, beautifully coiffured and manicured they emerged.

They had not really expected that the men would be waiting for them and, sure enough, the crews' keys were still hanging in the receptionist's office and the girl's retired to Roz's room feeling sure they would return if only to get some female company. Mixed, as Roz's feelings were for the Captain she thought basically he was an honest person and would not wittingly leave a naïve twenty years old alone in a strange city.

As nine o'clock approached however, the excitement of coffee and cakes served in luxurious style in their room and the effect of a slow indulgent bath waned and Roz became rather tired of Sally's almost constant brittle string of complaint and unfavourable opinion of air crew which she appeared to have gained in her two years flying experience.

Roz consoled herself that this was her first day in Athens, and there were another seven to come. Now that she understood the way of this crew, who seemingly moved from bar to bar, she had no doubt that she could occupy her own time in the ancient city. It had been enough to walk through the sun-blistered streets under the vivid blue sky and smell the heat, the cypress trees which intermingled with the hills and the bleached white houses, everywhere throughout the city. Even the dust so characteristic of Greece was not objectionable. A fine dust covering the city, a dust of time, but it was more of a soft talc than a desert sand.

The girls' rooms were opposite and Roz was called into Sally's room. In every sense, in old-fashioned terms, it could be called a boudoir. Under the auspices of 'sensible luggage' for crew, (which was never weighed as passenger's limited amounts were), Sally had managed to transport several perfumes, talcums and other feminine toiletries. Restlessly Sally began sifting through her wardrobe where she had hung close on fifteen dresses.

'I'll ring for a valet, some of these could do with a wash, at least a press.'

'Wouldn't that be very expensive?'

'Very. I've got to have something to occupy my mind.' Sally smiled. 'They'll be ready first thing tomorrow.'

'But Sally what a waste of your night stop allowances.'

'Not mine, duckie! Expenses on the company. I never do any laundry at base, keep it all till I'm in a reputable hotel.' She pressed a bell marked 'VALET' and sat down on her bed.

Roz sat down and drew her knees under her chin. It was all very different to expectations. She was wearing only very brief black pants and bra, bikini style, partly because she did not know whether to dress for dinner or not yet and partly because it was still so hot.

'I wonder where that valet has got to?' said Sally petulantly.

There was a knock on the door and she called 'come in.'

Four crew men, all but the Captains, Gerald Duncan and Harold Williams, closely followed each other, despite the girlish screams, into the room.

'Come on, lazy women! We're going on a freight run to Cairo ... pack your bags, excess banana cargo!'

Roz tried to grab her wrap but the first officer prevented her and she leapt into Sally's bed. Sally who was dressed anyway, protested loudly and hysterically.

At that moment, the 'phone rang. Sally answered it and peace ensued.

'Yes ... no, it's Sally, yes ... no, I'm perfectly happy here! What tonight? No ... why ... because you what? Because you like the chandelier better?' By this time the boys were laughing. 'No! I don't want to move from here. You must be joking ...' And Sally put the 'phone down.

'That was your Captain,' she accused Roz. 'He says we're to pack our things and move to the Astir Beach Hotel at Glyfada. He says they've booked rooms there because they like the chandelier better in the hall there!' The words almost exploded in rage from Sally's mouth. She had three suitcases to pack.

'Told you zo,' slurred the engineer.

'You're mad!' and Sally swept from the room, adding 'and drunk of course.' This way she confronted the valet answering her call in the door.

'Did you need the valet service Madam?' asked the man who was American.

'No.' Then as Ben started just quietly pushing the dresses from Sally's wardrobe into her suitcase... 'Yes. Please pack my case. We've to leave urgently.'

Twenty minutes later they were all downstairs awaiting a car to take them the ten miles to the coast, whilst Gerry politely explained to an irate Management that aircrew were always unpredictable because you never could tell when they would be called upon to do an unscheduled flight.

'Bet you're glad though, that you hadn't just let the valet take all your clothes to the laundry!' Roz giggled as she whispered to the still seething Sally.

'Bet you're glad you don't have to ferry excess bananas,' returned Ben, who had overheard Roz's remark.

(iii)

Bushes of rhododendrons and azaleas separated the chalets, each with lawns of green and a sandy path to the door. A million stars patterned the sky and the light from the patio threw subtle shadows across the grass. The memory of an excellent meal remained and the mood from the savage local wine lingered with the small group of people seated on the patio.

In 1960 Glyfada might have been a million miles from the city centre of Athens of which it is now part.

An almost heavenly perfume surrounded the garden villas; hibiscus, honeysuckle, even geranium. Any pangs of conscience that they had suffered when they left the irate Athenian hotel manager with seven empty bedrooms, earlier that evening, had been forgotten in the excitement of occupying the little chalets along the shore of Glyfada. There were moths of all colours and sizes, darting busily between orange and olive trees and Ben was gently rubbing his knee against Roz's under the tablecloth.

Sally had never appeared at dinner leaving the rest of her crew blatantly in search of female company.

A waiter had been called to clear the table and Captain Duncan had turned back a round of local brandy, warning Roz she would surely go blind if she drank it too often, since it contained wood alcohol.

Roz was grateful for his advice but did not know whether to take him seriously.

The conversation led to general reminiscences of previous stopovers. Aircrew, it seemed, all too often behaved with eccentricity, frequently vacating perfectly adequate hotels with rooftop restaurants and views over Athens to the Acropolis, just on a whim! And the effects and results of excess ouzo, arak and other potions were described to Roz in detail, presumably as a warning.

Gerry could not be dissuaded from describing how they had once convinced their pleasantly non-aggressive first officer that the best cure for a hangover was a trip along the canals of Rotterdam after Ben had spent a particularly heavy night on the Bols Gin.

'Destined for disaster ... I was,' Ben was experiencing some difficulty with the repetition of d's and s's at this late stage of the evening but laughing at himself.

Gerry continued, 'we got Ben on board...made his usual dash for the ship's bar, claiming it was medicinal but of course, and I suspect in this case it was. The real laugh was his gear. The girls were all ready for sunbathing on the deck and there was Ben with his city suit and bow tie!'

'No need to say more. I'd also have had my mackintosh, don't tell me!

Ben laughed at himself.'

'Halfway through the canal trip the dozy bugger goes and demands an introduction to the Captain of the barge. Naturally intending to provide a passport to the best harbour bar for the evening. It's extraordinary the way the fellow has with everyone, for the next thing we know is that the skipper of the barge is loading us into his own private launch, (wealthy chaps some of these barge owners) to take us across to the quay to physically show us the best nightspot in port. Benjamin then vaguely remarks that he wasn't aware that he was at sea and I actually think the launch was the first indication he'd had that day of being afloat at all. In fact, the barge's bar was just another quayside joint for all Ben knew. However as soon as the quay was really in sight, that red-bearded engineer, the one who came to us from the Corporation, has to go and say, 'last one onboard's a sissy.' Gerry paused. In 1960 those from the Corporation, BOAC, the precursor to British Airways were much looked up to by other aircrew. 'Then blow me! Ben has to literally go and step into the water and down he goes like a cat loaded with bricks and when he came up for the second time I actually managed to grab him and him still holding the gin! Ben! Do you remember? You claimed that in one minute you swallowed enough polluted Rhine water to prevent the Dutch dykes bursting again. Your city clothes were unrecognisable. One of the girls lent you an outsize sweater she must have stolen from her father or some such unlikely person, while the least the red-bearded engineer could do was to lend a pair of swim trunks.' Everyone was laughing. 'The trouble was you're an obstinate fellow, and you would insist on keeping on your red-spotted bow tie, complete with red socks and outrageous walking boots. In this fancy dress, you insisted on walking into the Rjin Hotel and demanding your room key.' Ben grinned and the dimple in his chin was prominent. Gerry, on the other hand, maintained his cool, amused and captivating smile.

Roz wondered if all aircrew were irresponsible. It was as though it was an enormous hangover from the tensions of the RAF and Berlin Airlift and Roz thought possibly the younger generations were missing something by not having to fight so hard for their lives. Perhaps life now was valued too highly.

The conversation became more serious and was gradually creeping round to the subject which aircrew

57

seem unable to leave alone, that of escapes and near misses. As the Captains became more technical, Ben suggested that he and Roz might walk down to the water's edge. Away from the light of the chalet, he held back the creaking branches of the ancient olive trees to allow Roz to pass down the sandy paths. Huge fuchsias hung gracefully from the bushes, quivering like dancers but mere shadows in the starlit night, and all the time the cicadas kept up their incessant chatter.

Ben put a long arm round Roz's shoulders catching a thread or two of her auburn hair 'Would you like to go to a club?'

'Perhaps tomorrow?' She was tired, a little nervous and overwhelmed with a desire to do the right thing and make a good impression on her companions.

'Good idea,' Ben sensed her unease. 'The bills aren't heavy if the Captain comes too. Always allowed to get away with more expenses. Doesn't seem fair, mind you. It makes life a hell of a lot easier for a Captain than a first officer when he has more allowance for entertaining the fair sex!'

The gentle sound of the sea washing and lapping the beach gave them both the same thought and they paused to listen. 'Shall we?' they both began simultaneously and laughed.

'Yes let's! It'll be beautifully warm,' finished Roz,

Minutes later, both in bathing costumes, Roz won the race over the sandy beach into the sea.

'Careful!' cried Ben, 'The water's deep, just there.'

Ben's warning was too late and Roz's carefully cherished hairstyle suffered. Laughing she allowed herself to be ducked and in the warm water they played and lingered for over an hour.

There really is a sound of silence in Greece near the calm barely rippling sea, the flisvos.

Although such limited nightlife as there was in Glyfada in those days, whined and moaned with Greek popular music in the background, on the seashore Roz was only aware of the peaceful lapping of the ink-blue sea and the relaxing sense of calm it produced. Even the ever-honking traffic and squealing tyres went unheard and far out in the Aegean the carbide lights of the fishermen flickered. Finally, they reluctantly waded out of the warm water and raced up the beach for towels. As they slowed to draw breath, Roz said, 'you must have been everywhere, to me this is all exciting, for you it's common place.'

'One day you'll almost certainly go to Jerusalem,' Ben put his arm round Roz's shoulders as they walked back to the hotel. 'Equally certain is the fact you'll find it a big disappointment; even bona fide pilgrims are generally unimpressed.'

'Is it true that you can only stay in the Jordan quarter because the airport is in Jordan?'

'That's true, well done you for knowing that', Ben realised that he was sounding somewhat patronising so he added, 'and that part is a very depressing town. No electric lights, well mostly, excluding, of course, the modern hotels and that means the maximum employment of daylight hours. Consequently, the sunrise at about five in the morning brings a hive of activity which lasts until sunset, also at five o'clock, which ensures a virtual shut down. I can assure you being woken at dawn after a hard day's flying is no joke, especially when all hoteliers in the Middle East seem to be experiencing a boom in trade which they celebrate by adding more and more extensions to their buildings, naturally employing wailing Arabs for the work. At our hotel, last month, the carpenters and the masons began their hullabaloo at dawn. Complete pandemonium! Can you visualise the demons in the word pandemonium! Hands in the air - tumultuous uproar, I always think it is such an expressive word! No wonder Milton made it the capital of his hell in Paradise Lost. And that's Jerusalem, paradise - lost.'

'You make it sound better than that! I'd love to go there!'

'We took a car out to the Dead Sea, eventually, just to get away from the noise. It was a small hotel, still part of Jordan, but none the worse for that. In fact, it was extremely good and great fun. I'm reminded of it because you can't sink in the sea there and with tonight's exception is the most romantic place I know for a midnight swim!'

'Does that explain how Peter walked on the Sea of Galilee? Isn't that very salty also?'

The older man looked at the pretty young girl. He felt like a father, her father, yet he was only just over thirty. It was not that she was much younger than he was, ten years maybe twelve, but it was that she was only just older than his son, by a few years. Of course, he had been talking to Roz as he would talk to Geoff, his son! 'Yes, it's salty; so I believe.' He squeezed her slim shoulders again. She was lovely. 'I can assure you that I'd no trouble falling asleep on the Dead Sea, after one particularly heavy session at the bar. But then, that night, I hadn't a hostie like you, had I?'

Roz appreciated the warm sensation created by the words. She recognised the mutual attraction. She was comforted by the support and she walked closer to him, snuggling a little more under his arm. She didn't feel so frightened now and he recognised her empathy, but he went on talking.

'The others said I slept on the Dead Sea for two hours - probably an exaggeration, but unfortunately I was in no fit state to argue with them.'

Roz felt protective. What she had been told about his loss of his wife in childbirth and his subsequent predilection for alcohol brought about a strange tenderness in her feelings for Ben. Probably if he had a wife still living he would be a model of sobriety. As it was he was always dining out on the tale of some first-rate party, or telling exaggerated fiction and rushing for his diary to record it. He was a sensitive man, clearly better at expressing himself on paper than orally; a fact which has been true of many writers who came after Homer.

He was very talkative this evening however. 'I love the Near East; it is so romantic. Black, black sea and menacing black mountains, sea or desert, mountains or forest full of bandits and a great round golden moon. You do realise if they actually get a man to the moon, nobody will be able to believe in the old Man-In-The-Moon again? Do you think the moon might be to be our symbol of romance then?'

'No not really, I don't think you need a moon, sometimes the stars are quite sufficient.'

61

Ben wondered if she was teasing him, and sensing him stiffen, she went on, 'Why could you only stay in the Jordanian sector of Jerusalem?''

'Well,' he sighed audibly. Since his wife's death, he found he did not know how to create intimacy. Once past the initial communication, he found himself stumbling and unsure of himself. He simply longed to stop talking and cuddle Roz instead.

He repeated 'Well, you land in the Jordan half and then there is all this trouble between Israel and Jordan, so although the Israeli's will let you into their side, the Jordan authorities won't allow you back. Extremely tricky sometimes. They won't even allow you to fly over the country. We have passengers sometimes who want to see both sections of the city. They have to drive to Tel Aviv and have an EL AL plane take them to Cyprus where we eventually rejoin them. The biggest trouble is the Israeli customs who stamp their passports either as they arrive or leave and so they won't be able to visit another Arab state until they get a new passport.'

'I've a special Israeli passport.'

'Yes, we all have. Ever since one Captain with a Tel Aviv entry stamped on his normal passport had to be taken off the Middle Eastern and Southern Med runs altogether, including Greece, just in case he was diverted to Arab countries. It was surprising how it limited his flying. In fact, he was even jumpy about Malta and Gib. But you be aware young Roz, never ever, hand your Israeli passport to an Arab in Cairo or anywhere, by mistake. The Arabs have a nasty reputation when it comes to the treatment of criminals.

Roz squirmed and he plucked up courage and took her hand.

He was nice, she thought. More mature than the boys she had known in London. She began to relax as though she was on holiday, not working. She knew it was going to be a happy trip. A job which became a holiday, what more could she ask for?

They parted at the path which led to her chalet.

Thank you for the swim,' he said. She appreciated his manners. Then he left her.

The Captain's accommodation was next to Roz's. He was at the door lighting a cigarette as she appeared. Without speaking he took hold of her arm and kissed her neck. Then Gerry let her go and went inside his chalet closing the door.

Roz went inside her own room and locked her door behind her. She shivered a little. The man's kiss had given rise to an uncertain effect on her whole psyche. It had been quite different to anything she had experienced. It was Ben whom she had expected to kiss her that night.

It was too hot to close the window. She arranged the window so that the Venetian blinds were open but secure.

The next morning, when she woke, the window was still open, but the blinds were no longer secure. Gerry was standing next to her bed, dressed in dark red swim trunks, His paunch hung a little over the waistband. She could count the hairs on his chest. There were three.

'Come on lazy, it's nine o'clock. Let's have a swim. I've ordered breakfast for two outside my room in half an hour.'

'Clearly,' Roz retorted, 'with such an athletic crew I'm going to be much in demand.'

That evening, it was Gerry who set the pace by ordering Lobster Thermidor and this led to promises for lunch the next day to take Roz down to Tourkolimano, referring to the pretty fishing harbour by its Ottoman name although it was increasingly called Mikrolimano and is still, to this day, a yachting basin and caique fishing port in the heart of Piraeus.

Here she was told, she would be able to rub shoulders with the famous, watch the tall yachts come and go, and choose her own fresh lobster alive. This thought made Roz wriggle and the others laughed.

The band in the nightclub played cha-chas and the singers swung into hit tunes. The clientele wore little black dresses and evening dress or low backed white dresses to reveal very brown backs and their menfolk wore more casual suits. The waiters wore dinner jackets and even bottles of Demistica and Retsina had to be served on ice, as was the vintage French wine. It was all very smart. The Head Waiter brought Nescafe; Roz failed to see why this was considered a luxury in Greece, she much preferred the sweet Turkish type coffee.

Twenty years previously, Greece was entering perhaps the first stable period in her history. Yet the beginning of the nineteen sixties was to see the end of the first of Constantine Karamanlis' governments.

It was hard for this aircrew, cocooned in the luxury of the Astir Hotel, to appreciate just what metamorphosis had taken place within Greece in that last decade, and even that what understanding they had was conditioned by their immediate needs. Greece was still a very poor country, a land whose independence was in places less than a century old.

It was Hal Williams (from the JTL crew they had joined up with,) who suggested that they took a taxi into the town and slummed it, (his words), round the back streets of the Plaka, at this hour of eleven at night.

But accelerated by the effects of the wine, Gerry Duncan stood up, turned down the nightclub idea and announced his immediate intention of retiring.

Roz was glad he went. She knew he thought he had terrified her the night before.

He left the table with the ship's funds' saying he would pay all expenses the next day and warning his crew to keep prices cool. He effectively quashed their hopes of going up to Athens for the nightlife, but Roz was tired after the day of fresh air and sun and she didn't mind.

Gerry was forced to pass the table on his way back from his visit to the Gents and he must have recognised the distinctive shape of the champagne bottle which had been ordered immediately he had left, nor could he have avoided overhearing 'When that one's cut he doesn't bother to make a noise, he just expires! Come on, get that bubbly opened.' It was said with exaggerated weariness and even Roz laughed in response to the JTL engineer's remark. Captain Duncan was not universally held as a popular commander, but even she recognised that Gerry kept his drinking fairly well under control.

When Ben finally escorted Roz back to the chalet he was the worse for drink. But this was obviously nothing new for Ben. Roz noticed that Gerry's light was still on and his shutters down. She lay on her bed and pulled the single sheet up, but although she turned twice in rapid succession between the sheets it did not assist her falling asleep. She got up and moved over to the window, drawing the blinds behind her so she could see the knurled old olive trees framed by the light from the path lights; the fuchsias looked sad in their sleep but perfume softened the air and mingled with the profusion of red flowers that is Greece in the late summer. The shadows of the huge mountains behind the chalets seemed to throw an aura of protection over the whole Attic coast. She was sad Gerry thought her a child.

FOUR: YOU'RE ONLY YOUNG TWICE

(i)

It was not until the Viscount with Captain Williams in command left Ellinikó, two days after Roz's midnight bathe with Ben and her kiss from Gerry, that she could clarify her thoughts. The Viscount took off in a northerly direction for Istanbul, acknowledging the waves of Ben and Roz who were lying on the beach, exaggerating its authority by flying unnecessarily low over the hotel. Their rendezvous would be in Rhodes a few days later.

Gerry lying some way from Ben and Roz was nearly asleep in the sand, he rolled slowly over to fry his stomach, picking up the sand much the same way as a piece of wet fish would collect the brown crumbs previous to cooking.

'Hal Williams should get himself an aeroplane to fly instead of a Whistler', he murmured, but his crew heard him. 'Always a good pilot, can't understand why he doesn't organise himself a Comet.' But there was a note of envy, which nobody missed and it was known that many of the air-force boys of the old school were missing out in these days of larger and more sophisticated aircraft. To make matters worse, Gerry told everyone that he had once piloted much more impressive machines himself and it was only the climate, or his wife's health or some such reason which had brought him back from the Middle East. This was a myth. He had been stationed in Cyprus and the Middle East, but his machinery was no more impressive then than it was currently. But so far no one had questioned this fact and on this basis, he was now Chief Pilot of Ferryair.

However, he seemed to bear some sort of grudge to which even his crew were sensitive and they chose to ignore his remarks and left him vigorously building small fortresses round his feet with his toes.

Ben and Roz wandered along to the beach and allowed themselves to be charged seventy drachmas for a pedalo. It was not until Ben was propelling Roz in the direction of the diving raft that their extravagance registered.

'When you think of all the beers you could buy for eighteen shillings *and drink*, in half an hour!' Ben remarked. He sounded rueful.

'But what a much pleasanter half hour spent in the sea than in a bar!' Roz laughed and tossed her red curls away from her face. The sun reddened her cheeks and she despaired of going brown gracefully.

'Don't you like drinking?' Ben looked alarmed.

'Not until it comes out of my ears,' and Roz jumped off the machine with such energy that she nearly upset it and Ben too. She guessed that three days ago she could not have made such a retort to a man, particularly a senior crewmember.

Gerry had ceased attempting to protect himself with sand castles and was watching them play. Since that first physical contact with Roz he seemed to have had the greatest difficulty in performing even the simplest of tasks. Even their pre-breakfast swim, two days previously and the meal later, was obviously a source of embarrassment for him. He had said very little, but when Ben had joined them he looked almost relieved.

This inability to communicate with Roz obviously annoyed him and accusing himself of an old man's fancy did nothing to improve his temper. He had ignored her almost completely for the last thirty-six hours, addressing her only occasionally and only as a Captain might be expected to address a hostess during a stopover.

For Roz's part, his display of infatuation amused her. It would be foolish to say that she had not noticed it but on the other hand she hoped she did not much care. Her first flight with Captain Duncan to Hamburg had taught her that this man had an independent personality and she was still not sure she wished it to be otherwise. She was aware though that she was giving it considerable thought. It was difficult to forget that kiss.

Now she considered the figure on the beach watching her green swimsuit tumbling in and out of the vivid blue sea. Green was definitely her colour; it highlighted her complexion and contrasted with the autumnal coloured curls, which were forever her glory. It brought out the green of her eyes. She climbed onto the diving raft and sat dangling her feet in the water. 'Gerry, oh Gerry,' she breathed, 'kiss me, kiss...kiss,' she repeated it the last time so quickly that it was almost audible. The emotion surprised her. 'Kiss me, come and play with me in the water, Gerry, where no-one will see if you hold my hand,' she willed. She watched the imposing sun-soaked figure rise and prepare to bathe. She watched him walk into the sea.

Now she knew that the very thing she had sworn would never happen was in embryo. This man was married. He had a wife at home, in Yorkshire, in England. But in the exceptionally hot sun in Greece, which warmed her blood, it was extremely hard to remember exactly where Yorkshire was or to care. Just once, whilst he swam Gerry looked Roz's way and as he reached her, his eyes twinkled, as he looked first into her eyes and then down at her thighs. After that it was impossible.

'Oh hell,' said Gerry silently to himself as he swam over to touch the girl. 'Why do you sit there, daring me? *Why* do you sit there, why do you do it, damn you? You're driving me insane. Do you know that Roz?'

The mountains of Hymettos rose up behind the beach at Glyfada, the sky was dazzlingly bright, the sand was too hot to walk across without shoes. At sunset, there would be an afterglow on the mountain famous for its honey and its marble since ancient times. These were all facts and had nothing to do with human emotion. That a statue of Zeus had in classical times crowned the summit, might be attributed to human intervention, as was the proposal that the cairn was now to be a radar station.

'Can we climb Hymettos, Gerry?' It was as though Roz was answering the unheard questions of Gerry's with another question, but she did not stop him fondling her toes in the water. Ben was swimming some considerable distance out in the blue sea; the pedalo tied safely to the raft.

'Yes, if you like,' he answered. The short tubby man was very gentle with this girl for all his apparently forthright mannerisms. No one would have called his thick features handsome, but suddenly to Roz he was very appealing.

Again, he went silent. The words he thought were not spoken aloud and however much he wished otherwise… 'And you won't believe this Roz, but I've never reacted to an air stewardess in this way. You're the first girl I've ever spoken to like this since I courted my

70

wife. I've been very faithful.' He lied; in fact, there had been another, but he had forgotten so it didn't count.

As if she had heard him she casually touched his hand, as though by mistake.

'I do believe you.' She might have said, or indeed might have thought, for she could almost hear him thinking. But she could not understand her own calm feelings for a few days ago this man's temperament had aroused an intense dislike. Now she lived to make him happy, to see him smile, to catch the crow's feet lines which framed his merry eyes when they did smile.

'There's no shade on the mountains at this time of the year,' he said aloud. Gerry too was shy. 'It really is hot, too hot. The violet glow may look inviting from here and I can imagine the herbs that will scent the air. There will be thyme and sage and wild mint. In the spring the sage has beautiful, almost global yellow flowers; they call it Jerusalem Sage. It's a beautiful mountain, even more beautiful than the mountains of Cyprus and the English Lake District, my other passions. Spring is definitely the time to climb the hills in Greece, only the spring. Great plumes of white heather and wild lavender; anemones, poppies and field marigolds; indescribable scents and colours. Whereas at this time of the year we can only take home memories of pinks and reds, tamarisks and bougainvillea and, I'm afraid, sunstroke'. He sighed. 'In the spring, Greece has a more delicate air.' This was a very safe conversation.

'Gerry,' she spoke his name aloud although she really only meant to think it. It was charged with feeling.

'My lovely innocent Rosalind,' he answered and his face was soft and a little sad, entirely different from his public image. But silently he continued, 'I think I could almost fall in love.'

71

'Do you love me?' She wanted to ask, but stayed silent. 'But it could only be platonically,' still she was thinking, not speaking outright and she looked earnestly at the sun-reddened man and wondered if that would be the right word. 'Otherwise, there would be too much heartache.'

'Yes?' he questioned, for it was she that had said his name aloud and his grey-blue eyes earnestly returned her look. He thought, 'even if we could love platonically. The designation of love as Plato described it, love free from carnal desire, love growing from mere human passion and ascending into a state of ecstasy, but all free from physical contact. An ideal and impossible state, yet I promise you that I'll try, at least I'll try for a platonic relationship.'

The young girl did not reply to his single questioning 'yes' but looked towards Jerusalem. A strange habit that she had had since school days when she had had an Arab school friend at boarding school and when it had been romantic to mimic the rituals her friend practised without understanding anything about them. But now she promised also. She promised a platonic relationship with this man.

Mecca is in the same direction as Jerusalem, even when faced from Greece.

She looked out over the blue Saronic Gulf and promised as the young do.

She was very young.

He wasn't, but years later she would remember the poignancy of this rendezvous in the sea and wonder that they could even think that it would be a platonic affair.

February 1972

(ii)

At three forty-five she picked up her twins from school and drove them to her friend's house for tea. She opened the door and the twins tipped out of her car.

Sara's wool beret fell off and she tripped over the unfastened seat belt and gashed her knee open, which meant that the family's entrance into Penny Sky's front garden was undignified, to say the least. Rosalind cursing, Sara wailing and Alice plaintively repeating her urgent question, 'who was the old lady who had the sweet shop, Mummy. Tell us about her.'

'Later', snapped the adoptive parent. 'One thing at a time, Alice. Now look, Sara's dropped her glove. Oh God, there's some oil. Don't tread - I said don't tread in it!'

The girls were five years old. Sara was slightly smaller than Alice and her hair was dark. They were adopted, but Alice had red hair, like Rosalind, but more like Andrew.

But Roz did not think about Andrew often. Well, she did, she thought about him almost every day, but it did her no good to admit to doing so.

But suddenly there it was, a naked, winter pear tree, and barren. An alarm sounded in her thoughts, always symbolic, nothing to do with Andrew, and yet ever present when she thought about him. The pear tree lounged over her friend's front porch, the same tree which during her childhood had been hung with soft ripe fruit. Rosalind immediately said so but the friend, tiny

Penelope Sky, replied the tree was sterile and that her husband planned to chop it down in the spring. Rosalind was sad to hear this, but it was not difficult to understand for the crisp Yorkshire winter winds seemed to bite into the clean branches of the tree, which spookily tapped against the panes of the upper windows.

She brought the tree to the attention of the two small shy children who clung to her anorak jacket as she passed through Penny's Yorkshire porch. Rosalind seemed happy to give some details of her own childhood to the twins. But had Rosalind's really been the golden childhood she described to the children?

As a child, Rosalind had loved Penny's recently converted house. It had been a small working cottage, improbably called Hangman's Cottage. It lodged at the end of a long lane, near to the big house where Rosalind lived as a child. Make believe stories had revolved around its solid Yorkshire friendliness and its grim name. The old lady who lived there had sold sweets and in exchange wartime children had given her ration book coupons. Coupons they had coveted and begged from parents and aunts. Coupons clenched in tight grubby little fists, lest they were dropped in the puddles on the rough lane leading to the little cottage, high on the Pennine hills.

There was a rule that coupons should not be removed from their respective rationing books, until the time of sale, to prevent such generosity as kindly adults often practised, but here the old lady would accept the loose black-market coupons from the children of the neighbourhood.

Now there were no scissors kept by glass stoppered jars of handmade jelly babies and humbugs, in turn, kept in a large old oak sideboard, which took up the full length of the wall in the dark low wooden beamed room. Now there were no glass jars and there was no dark black Yorkist range in the chimney recess, and no rag-tag rugs on stone slab floors. No Yorkshire ham hung from the rafters - mould on the edges. This was 1972 and the cottage now had a light bright-modernised kitchen, the windows were admittedly releaded with diamond panes, but in the best of taste and where the Yorkshire porch with the pear tree stood, there also was now a huge modern double glazed single paned glass door.

Nor were there any ration books, these children had pocket money and Alice, red, curly-haired and like her mother to look at, although adopted, asked 'Mummy! Did you have no doll's house because there was a war?'

But Rosalind's early childhood had not been deprived. Wartime children knew no other way of life and enjoyed it. War had provided an education in appreciation; life could be rapacious for those who survived at this time but it also could be sobering. How could a modern world now appreciate the wonderful conveniences it currently enjoyed? It had since forgotten the deprivation of war. Now, Penny Sky's refreshing house conversion, (or so it had been called in the Yorkshire Life magazine), was traditionally but inexpensively executed in the very best of taste, and the application of selected pieces of Victoriana had been combined successfully with the style of the early seventies.

One decade of affluence had shifted the world's axis and a new generation was altering its values. The age was changing. The little old woman had sold sweets for coupons to a child and in return had earned lasting love. Love that Rosalind could remember bestowing even now, but she wondered if she was alive, and if she was, where she was.

No longer was it a necessity to be well educated, in the sense that meant paying for education, in order to become middle class, but in the seventies, as opposed to the nineties it was still an advantage to be middle class. People, or a good two per cent of the population of Britain, still considered it important to talk 'well' which might mean trying at it in the seventies, and Rosalind was proud that her voice was moderate, no accent but 'transatlantic' enough not to be considered refined. Her years as an air-stewardess had helped here. Penny had to try that bit harder, Southerners or at least those that prided themselves on speaking properly and to whom such nonsense was an important passport to success, sensed with Penny that her dulcet tones had to be considered before they were aired, but unlike Roz she had not had the advantage of actually 'living' in London.

The first flakes of snow had fallen as Rosalind left Penny Sky' home. Little more than a flurry that would soon pass and they caused no alarm, but the road from Norland to Sowood was quickly spread with fine white sleet. Rosalind hated driving with the twins in the car at any time. In adverse weather conditions, it was a loathsome experience.

For one thing, churlish four-wheel drive machines bossed and threatened the other general road users. Huge fearsome resprayed ex Post office vehicles; Gipsys, Land Rovers and virile Range-Rovers that never ventured forth in the ordinary run of things now took over the narrow roads like military tanks.

They swept past Rosalind, wife of the well-known local newspaper editor, with such a nonchalant swish that on arrival at her own established property of character overlooking the Thwaiteburn Valley she was exhausted and never more had wished to change her country life-style back to the town.

So that February evening with the twins safely in bed at last, and a babysitter arranged, Rosalind asked her husband to take her to see Ken Russell's new film, 'The Boyfriend' in Leeds. They drove fast, particularly on the way home. This was not unusual and his wife did not usually try to stop him.

Recently she had begun to wish he would drive a little slower. The roads were unlit and still slippery from the snow, and the miner's strike of that year had sunk the country and her husband, a newspaperman throughout, into the depths of depression. Rosalind cautioned him and he replied defensively, still hyped up on the two double whiskies of the interval. 'A man must be allowed some excitement in his life you know', and as usual she wished she had kept quiet. The editor with his now almost completely bald head, even as a young man he had suffered from alopecia which with a serious lack of eyebrows and eyelashes meant a relatively inexpressive face, always seemed so straightforward, but there were times when she found him taciturn and cold.

From mid-November to late March in the mid to late twentieth century, nine out of ten days winter is a most foul season in Yorkshire. Even outside Leeds, the wide crisp views of moorland and dale relieved the industrial scene but did absolutely nothing to improve the climate, lift the spirit or break the damp, grey charge of the monotonous northern light; day or night everything hangs heavy with a glove of perpetual twilight in the sodium glare. Indeed, it matters not that these hours are night or daylight, nothing can defeat the dense atmosphere that fits a northerner's soul like a glove. Rosalind was aware that true northerners like her husband revelled in the sense of proud solidarity and belonging, that such an inheritance gave them. She knew also that twenty percent of these northern natives were forced to fight the lighter ambitions which urged them to break their shackles and run for a land where the sun would rise, and the weapon was alcohol, but for herself, with a mother descended from the plains of Cheshire, she merely announced she hated winter Yorkshire and knew she was forever branded a traitor.

On this dark night, the road from Leeds city swept through the gloomy grimy snow-covered industrial towns anything but industrious as the bewitching hour approached, and Rosalind decided that they were all beholden to the same clamp of respectability and the same decencies which engulfed the suburban stockbroker belts of the South of England, it was as tedious. It mattered not that they had broken free of the arterial roads and ribbon development of 'des. res.' even their own home, on the moors, and the homes of friends, Penny Sky's cottage, their own fine farmhouse, all desirable oases by the standards in the industrial valleys, all were marked by a disease.

It was called 'middleclass' and it fitted over the wide hilltops of the new commuter belt like a woollen Yorkshire cap. As always, she would be fighting to overcome it.

They approached Halifax in her husband's company car at two minutes before midnight and drove over the North Bridge and through and straight along the Huddersfield Road. In the '72 power crisis there wasn't a light showing along the whole length of the road. What were they all doing in the candlelit miners' stricken gloom, behind the dark walls? How could they do it, in the full knowledge that everyone could speculate upon their actions? How can people live in semis, flats, apartments, tenements, and caves and know that people know when they're doing it?

One thing was certain if this dark state of affairs went on much longer the birth rate would rise. Marriage was merely a licence for lust, thought Rosalind.

Half asleep and somewhat sad and defeated she mulled over her day. Mostly the thoughts happened when she was about to fall asleep. The driver braked hard as a car suddenly shot from the deserted Salterhebble petrol station. Rosalind shifted forward alarmed but held safe by the seat belt and not thoroughly woken she sunk into even deeper sleep.

He woke Rosalind as they drove into the drive-in garage of their fine converted farmhouse. He did so gently and she smiled at him, filled with the love he so rarely accepted from her. Her dream fleetingly washed through her whole body, from mind to crutch, a soft pear accepted from the little old lady, her childhood confidante who had sold her sweets, bitten with lily-white teeth, as suddenly she shot like Alice in Wonderland, from childhood to maturity and fulfilment of a woman's life to give birth to a soft pale pink pear. Her husband had wanted to father her child. So far it had not happened.

The next day, the last day in February in a leap year, dawned like spring. Rosalind woke early. It was dark still and her husband was snoring and their adopted twins still asleep. She got up, which was unusual for her so early and she drew herself a bath. It was deep and hot and she filled it with powerful foam essence. Even in the dark, the morning was concerned with spring. The wind had dropped and Rosalind was restless. It was as though in the few days before spring everyone relaxes, waiting for the first birds to consummate their winter vigil, watching to see if the buds will grow.

She felt cocooned in her bath, aloof and distant from the world, its man-made rules and conventions; a world where almost all are influenced by society. A mere image perhaps, but like the gods of ancient times necessary to provide a framework for man to live his life by. It was as though those who tried to reject Society, to opt out, must crawl, infused with hate into an obscure shell, a self-constructed shelter of the mind; and she drew a parallel with the atomic shelters constructed by energetic civil defence workers.

Protection there was an illusion. Just as the protection of her bubble bath was an illusion. Those that emerged later, after the bomb, when the fallout had dispersed, would find an earth that clearly did not need them, a world ravaged by war, or perhaps just by pollution and the passing of time. And she watched fascinated as she pulled the plug from the tub and the water and bubbles deserted her recently comforted body and left it naked.

Ten or twelve years ago she never questioned life, its origin or its purpose, now Rosalind was frightened. Past events, which she thought she would be able to forget, were being remembered and recalled when not wanted.

Once Rosalind had made a mistake. It was a particularly big mistake. As she climbed out of her bath she remembered that tomorrow her husband, the journalist would fly to Belfast. No doubt he would return with dinner party conversation about his day down the

Shankhill Road, or in the Falls area, and her friends, and his, would be agog and would congratulate him, and her, for being so brave. So very brave to go, and to let him go and secretly they would envy their excitement.

21 August 1960

(iii)

Considerably more suntanned, Gerry, Ben and Roz left Athens for the island of Rhodes two days after the swim at Glyfada. They had actually made one brief visit to the Acropolis.

They had climbed from the west to the Propylaea, up the steep ascent with the sun blazing down on their uncovered heads. Contrary to Gerry's warning Roz was not at all dismayed by its size but more impressed by the lightness and stability the marble ruins imposed.

Through the magnificent entrance, she had caught her first close glimpse of the Parthenon. It was the background of Greece, the mountains surrounding the Attic plain, the sky that was so clearly only Greek that had fired Roz's imagination. Without her escorts, she made her way slowly towards and right into the awesome temple, unaware that in a few years it would not be possible for the public to walk inside the sanctuary. The construction of the whole magnificent and mathematical project seemed a secondary task to the positioning of the ruins.

Her peace and appreciation did not last long.

Gerry was quickly beside her recounting some tale about the Erechtheum. He maintained that it was a temple where they sacrificed seven virgins every year. He didn't need to describe the rites in detail to make Roz's skin tingle. It was as though with Gerry that it was more what he said than what he did that held the inexplicable fascination for Roz. She had playfully taken hold of Ben's arm and tried to seek some protection from the magnetic aura of the stocky but powerful Captain. And as Ben, sensing none of Roz's panic, had responded to her touch, Roz revelled in the jealous glint that had passed through the Captain's grey and steady eyes.

Ben, in fact, welcomed Roz's display of public affection. If he was aware of Gerry's feelings for Roz he had not shown it, although, since the swim when Gerry had joined Roz on the diving raft, Ben had not shown much interest in her. And yet of the two men, Ben would be considered by most to be the more handsome; he was also the younger man - and unmarried. He would be right to expect some of Roz's attention.

It was the Erechtheum that had impressed the travellers most. It felt to be a living building. It was proof of the quarrel of the god, Poseidon, with the goddess, Athena, over the possession of Attic. It had amazed Rosalind that the old olive tree which still grew in front of the temple, could be considered to be so ancient as to be the fruit of Athena's lance; a symbol of her prowess and apparent reconciliation with Poseidon. The god had been no match for the goddess. He had merely produced a spring with the thrust of his trident. Athena had been judged the winner and henceforth the pair forgot their quarrel and worshipped in harmony. Gerry had said the tree was the same one, but it was so small she did not believe him.

But if Roz was becoming mesmerised by the magic of Greece, so she was also becoming hypnotised by Gerry. Yet when she rationalised this, to her he appeared a rather fat, near middle-aged man, with little to commend him save his gently teasing eyes relieving his rather Socratic looks, a body which had seen better days, and which when hurried almost waltzed rather than walked, with a slightly effeminate gait. This walk was unique to Gerry; those that knew him would see him coming down the street, far beyond the point where they usually recognised their friends. Those that had not seen him for some time also rarely forgot him.

This was not the type of man for whom Rosalind would normally have fallen.

Also, she had known her crew for little more than a week.

Before they left the Acropolis, they had crossed over to the side of the citadel to gaze down into the huge Theatre of Dionysus. Roz was left in no doubt of the legacy of history as she looked down on this graceful auditorium. She relived the Greek tragedies that nearly seventeen thousand Greeks would have witnessed in one performance. She felt she would never cease to be grateful to Pericles for his foresight and inspiration and the enduring elegance with which he had endowed his city. The Acropolis had become a reality for Roz; the core of ancient civilisation and she told Gerry to forget his books. She had been enthralled.

So much so she had been quiet throughout the sedate lunch at the expensive Floca Restaurant. Gerry Duncan had persisted in voicing his theory that Roz should be disappointed with the sightseeing excursion, but she was in no mood for being drawn into an argument and she concentrated on appreciating the excellent food.

That night, after her first visit to the Acropolis Roz and Gerry had talked into the small hours of the mysteries of ancient Greece. They sat on the patio, smoking to discourage the insects and listening to the sounds of the night between their soft conversations.

84

Ben had gone to bed drunk.

As Roz went to bed Gerry had kissed her for the second time.

There was an idyllic unreality to being.

Tomorrow she would 'work' for one hour while the Captain and his First Officer flew the Viking to Rhodos.

It was a rare thundery day with some menacing heavy cloud as they drove to the airport in a taxi from Glyfada. 'Ho-hum. We're going to have fun with that lot!' Ben winked, his eyes looking somewhat the worse for the last night's exercise of fluid intake. 'Be ready for a game of netball with the lunch boxes, Roz!'

Once airborne the Captain did not switch off the FASTEN SEAT BELTS sign when he extinguished the NO SMOKING sign. Disregarding the regulation that a hostess should also remain strapped into her seat whilst this sign was illuminated Roz distributed the lunch boxes. The flight was scheduled for little more than an hour, how else could she get through? But Ben was right and the contents of these boxes consequently became scattered over the cabin after one particularly large air pocket and the nasty pieces of egg and mayonnaise had to be picked from the old ladies' hair. A large proportion of the passengers were sick and Roz cleaned up and administered unto them. The crew, like Roz, had hangovers. But still, Roz hesitated to call the hour's experience 'work'. It was merely a method of transport to the exquisite island of Rhodes.

They arrived over the diamond-shaped landmass on schedule. There was a crosswind right across the runway. Making his approach for the second time Roz answered her Captain's cabin call. The skipper was asking his co-pilot for the alternative.

'Beirut, unless we go back to Athens,' was Ben's reply. 'We're sweating on fuel though.'

'I'm not going back through that filthy muck again,' Gerry was emphatic. 'Let's have a final attempt here. Roz, make quite, quite sure that both YOU and the passengers are well strapped in. Don't sit in the galley. Use that empty passenger seat.'

They landed.

The wind got under the machine and they found themselves airborne again without any power.

The wheels came down hard, very hard for the second time.

Roz knew the runway would be getting shorter.

She could feel the brakes forcing her body back into the seat and everything from the galley, well secured though it was, slid forward, fell onto the floor and rolled into the cabin. The bar box moved forward and hit the rear bulkhead behind the passenger seat with a heavy thud. Inexperienced as Roz was she realised that it was a miracle that a tyre had not burst. She smiled calmly at her passengers as she said goodbye to them. She did not mention the landing and neither did they, although some of them looked rather shaken. It was the sort of experience that nobody mentions until two or three days later, in the bar. In flying one does not speak of chance, luck is not a word in air-pilots jargon; flying is entirely a matter of skill.

Two days later in the bar of the Hotel des Roses, Hal Williams made a scheduled appearance. That he had been expected was confirmed by the speed with which the 'screwdriver'' cocktails were produced, at the bar.

Roz had just come out from the sea after bathing with Ben and they were all using the veranda as an extension to the bar. The sky was clear but on this day, it

86

was a soft blue, the sea was a little more vivid. From where they were sitting they could see over the Strait of Marmaris to the darker forbidding hills of Turkey.

As the island of Corfu lies majestically under the eye of Albania, Rhodes is torn from the womb of Anatolia, protected geographically by the fatherly frowning hills of Turkey, but menaced historically. Greece has never enjoyed calm frontiers. Yet the island of Roses is as aloof and unrelated to the barren land of Asia Minor as a stepchild is to his guardian. White ships pass through the straits by day and by night; they are symbolic of peace. Hands off Rhodes, they cry.

Moored away from the harbour Roz could see the defiant shapes of four warships reminding her that Rhodes was still foremost a port, a free port perhaps, but enjoying its uneasy peace only because of the presence of these warships.

Rhodes in 1960 had been reunited with Greece for a mere thirteen years, after a history of invasion and foreign influence. It began four and a half thousand years ago with the invasion of pirates from the Middle East, and more recently with successive invasions by the Turks, in the sixteenth, seventeenth, eighteenth and nineteenth centuries and the Italians and Germans in the twentieth century.

In 1960 a few palm trees formally governed the garden of the hotel, surrounded by a hedge of hibiscus and a pistachio tree which hindered the view of the unfortunate bathing huts erected on the public beach adjacent to the hotel's whiter sands. None of the crew suspected that in twenty years' time people would go topless on these same beaches in their hoards.

In Rhodes, as elsewhere on the islands with their own airport, the town in twenty, thirty years would also be choked with high-rise hotels, with buildings and sun beds alike concertina-ed into the tiny promontory between Kassou and Koundouriotou Square.

By the millennium years, it was wall-to-wall tourism bringing reports of rape and other crime, which would have been unheard of in the first half of the century.

Yet still, as then, the poetry of Rhodes is within her vegetation. In the two days spent on the little island, the warmth and perfume of the massive red hibiscus and oleanders aroused a sense of peace and a strange sense of returning home to a well-loved place, a sentiment for which the 'Isle of Roses' is renowned. This feeling can persist, even for first-time visitors.

After the episode at the airport, when the entire staff of the control tower and the small airport had turned out to congratulate the Captain on his skilful landing, they had been displaying more sober habits. If these were demonstrated not so much in liquid consumption they were apparent in other ways and they explored the delights of the ancient city leisurely. Everywhere they were influenced by the soft days spent under the dazzling sun and the pink reflection of the buildings and sandstone against the gay blue sky. Purple bougainvillaea covered the Italianate sidewalks and the legacy of arcaded golden stone facades; everywhere they went were flowers and perfumes. It was good to be alive.

But now Hal had reappeared with his crew and Roz surmised that the peace would be short-lived. The subject of the landing was broached within minutes of his arrival and the technicalities of the particular airstrip were discussed in detail. Roz gathered from the conversation that the runway ran between a series of minor hillocks that was further complicated by the presence of one such protrusion in the centre of the actual runway. She listened to Hal's rebuke fascinated and open-mouthed, 'even the local pilots boycott this airport unless the conditions are favourable. It is a curious fact, but all pilots naturally assume an airstrip to be flat unless they *know* to the contrary, and a sloping runway is therefore always dangerous, especially one which rises and then descends.'

It seemed that Gerry's skill apart they had been lucky and Gerry took Hal's admonishment in good part. Both might be senior pilots but in the pecking order of things clearly, Hal's airline was the most prestigious and therefore his opinion counted for more.

Now Roz found herself sharing a room with Sally.

She was sorry. Gerry tried to come onto her side.

'I'm sorry,' said Gerry to the receptionist at the hotel. 'My company is not prepared to pay bills for their stewardesses to share rooms with another company's personnel,' but when it turned out that Sally alone would be billeted in another hotel he relented. The town boasted few luxury hotels at this time and increasing tourism made those that existed well booked. So, Roz said she did not mind sharing. It was a consolation that she might be discouraged from accepting any advances that Gerry might make.

'Weren't you terrified?' asked Sally as she changed from the smart grey and yellow uniform worn by J.T.L. 'What a silly thing for Gerry Duncan to do. Nobody tries to land in a crosswind. Didn't Control tell you about the wind?'

'Should I have been frightened?' Roz was removing her swimsuit prior to lunch.

Sally shrugged; the yellow cotton blouse looked good with the blonde girl's colouring. 'I would've been very frightened. I think I'll keep this shirt on till after lunch.' She pulled a mustard shaded dirndl skirt from her case. 'You forget I'm still green when it comes to flying, by the time I had realised that it was happening it was all over.'

'Well, I've been thinking that I'll resign when I get home. You can only push your luck so far. And the psychologists are saying there is more to flying than mere skill. It's temperament that counts. I read it in a magazine. And the trouble with this crew is that they drink too much.'

'Don't they all?' Roz's remark was a statement, not a question and as such, it represented the attitude of the ex-forces personnel all over the world; all continuing their little acts of heroism by flying or sailing careers in the more realistic world of civilian life, but forces of the second world war school, nonetheless. Roz considered her lipsticks and chose a slightly orangey shade. With her colouring, particularly now so freckled and reddened by the sun, make-up was a problem.

'You never quite know how much control these cowboys have. It is all very well, this eight-hour abstinence limit. They absorb so much alcohol into their blood-stream and saturate it so that they stay intoxicated. Do you know I could swear Captain Williams was sick in his hat as we got out of the car here, you should have seen the porter's expression!'

Unfortunately, Roz laughed. 'That's yucky!' she said with disgust. 'Why don't you get yourself a ground job, chief hostess or something and see if you can reform the ways of our erring crews?'

'The international airlines are getting very hot on this issue now; no booze will be the norm soon so I might just switch to the Corporation.' Roz knew Sally was referring to BOAC, and it was every girl's dream, not easily achievable, to work for the Corporation.

(iv)

Beyond the medieval walls bearing the escutcheons of over one hundred and fifty Grand Masters lies the old town of Rhodes. Here behind the forty-foot thick walls there lies a masterpiece of medieval architecture, protected by a walled perimeter of two and a half miles. The fifteenth century Street of Knights has been carefully and lovingly restored after the First World War to all its medieval glory. The Palace of the Grand Masters and the Mosque of Suleiman give a strange mixture of Eastern and Western architecture and their philosophies. An old city is a cool place, even in the height of summer, the sunburnt cobbled streets merely whisper during the day to the sound of tourists, but at night the atmosphere of the town changes, and becomes charged with secrecy, piracy and murmurings from its dealings with the sailors.

Naturally as a port, Rhodes supported, as it had done for centuries, some nightclubs of certain notoriety and repute on the waterfront. Some were inglorious, more so than others.

It was to one of these nightspots, a floating room moored in the harbour, that Gerry and Roz were to escape that evening. After coffee in the hotel lounge, sitting in chairs covered with Sanderson prints Gerry looked at Roz in such a way that she said, 'Excuse me, I will have early night and write some postcards.'

She did not use the lift but took the palatial staircase two at a time until she reached the second floor. She knew she just could not afford to become involved with what she considered to be a middle-aged man. She guessed he was about thirty-five years old. She was twenty years old. Naively, she didn't consider his marital status. Age seemed the only barrier.

Her bedroom had shuttered windows, overlooking the sea, ink black in the Rhodian night. The bed was covered with more chintzes and the furniture was dark English oak. There was an ornately carved alcove which contained a large old-fashioned wash stand with double mirrors; this amenity was in excess of the private bathroom whose doors were concealed in the oak furnishings and much to Roz's annoyance had been a feature of the room which she had overlooked until Sally arrived and had attempted to hang her clothes behind these carved doors.

A curious noise peculiar to the East emitted from the radio, which the girls had left on as they went down for dinner. Roz collapsed on the bed without turning it off. She really was tired. The half-expected knock on the door happened before she had time to regain her breath.

She had not locked the door and she did not move.

'Come on. It's as bad as getting a dinosaur to gallop. We're going dancing.' There was a sense of the imperative in her Captain's voice.

They used the lift down to the basement and walked along the beach to the town. On the waterfront Gerry took Roz's hand. After all the initial overtures, it was a strangely insecure grasp, as though he was nervous also. Although they had kissed in Athens it was as though this was the first experience of physical contact. The warmth of his large hand rose into her body. She smiled softly and looked into his deep sad grey eyes, still twinkling in their seriousness.

Gerry took a taxi. Not because he hailed one but because the taxi stopped and solicited their custom.

'Poo pame? Le nightclub, taverna?' asked the driver.

'Nightclub with atmosphere,' gesticulated Gerry, trying to be expressive by waving his arms about as the English do when abroad.

They drove slowly down the wide promenade. The hibiscus bushes were dark shadows, stage props for the playing fountains overlooking Mandraki Harbour. Here once the huge Colossus strode the harbour entrance, tradition has it with less historical fact that he was a giant shepherd overlooking the fold, for Mandraki literally means sheepfold. An enormous bronze Helios, created from the spoils of Demetrios' siege machine, a huge contraption in itself which when it had been pitched against the town in the siege of 305BC would have seemed an unlikely object to bring good fortune upon the Rhodians. However, when Demetrios tired of besieging these brave citizens he retreated leaving them the artillery, the sale of the proceeds raised the cash for their colossal statue.

All this Roz was to learn later, now from the taxi she could see and sense the elegant Italianate buildings, of which their hotel was one, which came much later in modern times, mere shapes in the night, with arcaded facades, bombastic almost in style; a presence on the other side of the boulevard.

Captain Duncan leaned over the driver's shoulder, uncertain where they were being taken, but certain because the driver looked Turkish and he a tourist that it would be somewhere he did not really want to go. Gerry said as much to Roz, quietly, just in case the chap did understand English.

At the marketplace, the large polygonal white building built in the Turkish style loomed from the dark. The driver stopped and enlisted the help of a Greek friend who was lounging against one of the numerous cafe tables on the pavement, as an interpreter. It was established that the couple were looking for a place to dance and to drink and a smile crossed the local man's face. He also got into the large American taxi, just for the ride. They passed through the ancient gateway into the old city of the Knights of St. John.

'City of Knights. St. John. Jerusalem.' said the new friend, the Greek, beaming happily. 'New Gate,' he roared with laughter for the New Gate was obviously as old as the City walls. They had discovered the added bonus of a guide for their evening trip. 'Very Turkish,' he went on equally jovially, suddenly slapping his colleague who was driving the taxi, smartly on the right arm. The Turk dropped his hand from the steering wheel and the taxi wavered a little. The car seemed outsized in the narrow streets.

'Obviously a member of the Goon Show,' whispered Gerry.

'Very goods. Yous like tour tomorrow with guide. Very excellent. 'Thavma!' Gerry shook his head in negative response to the Greek, but the man went on beaming. 'Tomorrows,' he persisted, 'I takes yous both to Old City. Street of Knights. Castle of Knights. Hospital of Knights. Alls the Knights yous like!' More hearty laughter. 'Yous sees, Mister! I gives yous best tourist in all the Greece.'

They laughed politely and the taxi stopped. The Turkish taxi man pointed to a little taverna built on a raft in the water. It was the year of Thor Heyerdahl and his Kontiki adventure.

'Bests taverna in all the Greece,' said their friend.

Gerry weakened and tipped them both.

Both Greek and Turk smiled happily. A rare instance of two traditional enemies living in harmony, but this was Rhodes and like all the Dodecanese well used to the Turkish influence.

'Kalispera.' They said in unison.

'Kalispera,' said Gerry. 'Efharisto.' He smiled. As they walked over the shaky gangplank he said to Roz. 'Always liked the Greeks. They may have caught onto the tourist bandwagon, but they're always cheerful. They never take offence the way the Arabs can, if you don't accept their offers.'

'What did you say to them in Greek?'

'Just Kali-spera, good evening; Ef-hari-sto, thank you. Gerry took Roz's arm to steady her stiletto heels along the wooden boards of the gangplank. 'Probably this place is sorely needing the attention of tourists, which is why we've been deposited here instead of somewhere else. It may not be very good.'

Roz laughed in reply. She did not have any doubts as she walked into the little restaurant on the water that this was going to be an enjoyable evening. It was lit with bright lights and the tables were painted in a bright sea-faring blue. Later this would come to be known as Greek blue. She stumbled a little as she crossed the wooden plank floor and her stiletto heel caught in a crack. She smiled apologetically, but Gerry just placed a tighter grip on her arm and steadied her. He too was concentrating on his step; Hal's return had quickened his drinking pace.

They chose a table away from the music of the Greek trio and the singer all too obvious in her tight black dress, and they faced their seats out towards the dark black sea. There was no moon. The other guests were mainly Greek couples. They were likely to be the only British people in the room, although there seemed to be a couple of Germans and Americans.

Alone with Gerry again, Roz found there was a need for conversation. Yet Gerry was clearly a man who was only inspired by sudden bursts of discussion. He could sit silently for a long time and Roz was still shy. Whereas in Athens when they had been alone they had talked easily, here in the public eye of the band and the lone singer, small talk seemed difficult.

'How about a glass of Ouzo?'

She had yet to try this drink. 'If it's like Pernod, which I understand isn't dissimilar, I think not! How about some Turkish coffee?'

After the Turkish invasion of Cyprus in the mid-seventies, it became an insult to ask for a Turkish coffee, and this faux pas of the later tourists was not so easily excused as it was in the sixties. A request for Greek coffee would procure the same beverage.

She did not hear what Gerry actually ordered from the waiter because he spoke in Greek, but when a bottle of local wine arrived she was not really surprised.

Obediently she drank the health of her Captain and made no protest.

The need for conversation became greater. Finally, Gerry broke the ice.

'Why did you fall for this job then, Miss Peters?'

Roz's short answer 'Boredom' didn't stimulate him further.

Roz's turn to think of a conversational subject.

The singer sang 'The White Rose of Athens,' in Greek.

'Memories of Edith Piaf.'

'Yes.'

'I like her. They say she's not well, don't they?'

'Probably lives life a little too much.' Gerry refilled her glass.

Roz noticed she was drinking fast. Because he rose, Roz also stood up and crossed over to the balcony with him.

'Do you really know what might have happened on this trip, young Roz?' If she answered Gerry did not hear. He expected her to reply in the negative anyway. He continued, 'I'm going to vary the standard version and say that I LIKE you, a lot in fact. But as you know I'm married and you can accept that as being the reason why I don't take you girls to bed, ever. Seventeen years of marriage and I've always been faithful to my wife. Seventeen years of flying. I don't expect you to believe it, nobody does!' He took Roz's hand and she surmised that he had paused to allow her to reply.

'Did you start flying as a commercial pilot as soon as you came out of the RAF?' She used the word, Raf.

'Yes, my young friend. Change the conversation! YOU have been warned. Always, if in doubt, if you think he might be seducing you, change the conversation.

'Roz, I'm trying to do the opposite to seduction! But to answer your question, no. I went into the family business after the war. Father had a prosperous milk-round as a side-line to his West Riding farms. I was the youngest of three sons and my brothers were given a farm apiece. If you think that was unfair you should consider that the milk-round I received was extremely profitable. Together with some land in Wharfedale, which I acquired, I probably got the best bargain. Anyway, I'm not much of a country farmer. Too fat, too short, not athletic enough. I think father realised that much. The milk-round was merely a question of directing other people to do the work.'

The strange thing was she had heard he'd been in the Middle East.

There was something that didn't quite tie up about Gerry Duncan. And the worst of it was that she didn't believe him. He seemed to vary his past according to his mood.

'Why did you give the milk-round up? Did you have to get up at six in the morning?'

'No fear – and who said I had given it up. With a wife with expensive tastes, no kids mind, just an expensive wife, I couldn't afford to give it up. Flying, however, is my life, my hobby if you like, so I just put a manager into the business. It's a system, which works. Pennies for holidays. I don't fly in the winter. I disappear to Cyprus, for a month or so every winter. Very pleasant and quite peaceful.'

To Roz, he didn't look like a member of the new jet set. In ten days spent together he had mentioned little about his married life.

'Richest pilot in the company and the meanest, that's me!' Gerry led Roz back to the table to sit down. A fly that had been worrying the wine bottle made its way over to Roz's red hair. It flew loudly around her head.

'It buzzes like a young aeroplane!' she announced stupidly and smiled.

Gerry smiled in return and looked at his watch.

'Have you ever been lonely Roz?'

'Well yes. When I was living in a London flat, in a way I was lonely.'

'That's only half of what I mean. You can be in a room full of people at a party and panic because no one will talk to you, you can be married and have lots of friends and still feel the feeling of loneliness. It is a stronger emotion, I can't explain it. I feel lonely tonight. It's not a permanent state, it's like malaria, it reoccurs when one is most vulnerable and needing sympathy when one is with a pretty girl and can't dance holding her close.'

'Because you're married and old enough to be accused of being my father?'

He looked directly at the girl. 'Yes. And there are no more questions like that, please. I've put my cards on the table. We're approaching a very dangerous situation, and the outcome is up to us. At the risk of being rebuked will you dance?'

'I should be delighted, Captain. That is if the floor is large enough to accommodate the clumsy manoeuvres I shall make at this time of the night!'

'Then the pleasure is mine, M'mselle, although on closer examination I do doubt that the floor be larger than the original round table.'

Then, with good reason, for it was midnight, the English grandmother clock in the corner struck twelve. It had been unnoticed until that moment. 'I expect if you examined it you would find 'MADE IN ROTHERHAM' on the face'. Roz's auburn hair had fallen into a fine fringe, but it was too late in the evening to push it back. She looked her best in the russet coloured dress. The wide belt she wore and the full skirt, a little shorter now and just below the knee accentuated her tiny waist.

100

When they danced the skirt moved to show her knees.

'At least you didn't run away to catch your pumpkin and lose a shoe.' He looked at her dainty feet and she smiled apologetically for they were bare.

'How old are you Roz? You seem much younger than twenty-five.'

'I am. Why is everyone so interested in my age?'

'Merely a company rule that all stewardesses must be over twenty-four, that is twenty-five.'

'I'm twenty, but nobody told me that. They asked me how old I was too, at the interview.'

'Hmm, I'm surprised.' He danced a little closer. 'Are you a virgin?'

She looked at the worn pragmatic face, slightly smiling. He wasn't being meddlesome. He really wanted to know. 'They didn't ask me that at the interview!'

'What lovely hazel eyes,' he told the tiny girl. 'You're altogether too beautiful for this job; you're too pure. Lionel Rhodes was a wicked man to employ you. You must take great care of this virginity. It is a gift too great to be abused. I shall appoint myself as your keeper!' He laughed and with great seriousness and very suddenly he said. 'My wife doesn't allow marital relations, I don't sleep with my wife.'

The grey eyes were sad. Did he mean what she thought he meant? Her limited experience had not told her how to react to a middle-aged man's confession. Suddenly she was aware how hurt he would be if he knew she thought of him as middle-aged. A wave of tenderness engulfed her; he was purely a man in his prime, a young man in his prime, whose wife would not allow him to sleep with her. That is what he had meant when he had spoken of loneliness. Roz was an immature woman, only recently a teenager who thought she knew it all and the thought made her blush.

The music quickened and they danced faster. Slowly other couples on the floor retired to the edge and watched them dance. Gerry's small figure became primitive, graceful, exciting and in an equally sensual way his feet moved at the double to Roz's less energetic movement. The Greek rhythm took charge, Gerry danced exceptionally well, it was a natural talent, and because of his lead Roz also found that she danced as she had never danced before. It was simply because no one had ever danced so naturally with her before. There was absolutely nothing formal about it. It simply wasn't related to the dances she had learnt in the ballroom dancing classes she had taken when she left school.

Finally, slightly awed and exhausted Roz was led from the floor, Greeks applauded and the few other European tourists smiled; the Manager produced a bottle of Demestica with his compliments. Gerry declined but assured him that he would return the next night. They left.

Roz stepped deftly towards the same patient taxi, waiting for them at the end of the gangplank with the driver holding his door ready open. But Gerry was holding her arm and he steered her away.

'Wait for us,' he called to the Turk. It must have been one of the phrases he understood for he nodded. They walked under the Pole Star and Roz was conscious of how small Gerry was. His shoulder was scarcely above hers.

'Dear heart,' he spoke awkwardly not in the fashion of the early sixties. 'Let's walk along the quay for I know I won't be allowed to say goodnight to you back at the hotel.'

There was no reply to that. Her thoughts, in any case, were contradictory; the attentions of married men seemed ludicrous and unnecessary, at Roz's age there were so many unmarried men. She was flattered for she was desired. She was needed and she hadn't the slightest intention of giving.

She was young and faultless and she was an air hostess, one of the most coveted jobs by her contemporaries. But as suddenly as her ego arrived it left and in its place emotion put a little pity mixed with kindness. Suddenly the pressure of Gerry's hand on her arm meant something more. She had danced with him and now it was as though she read his touch. She recognised the feeling as something more than liking her company. She walked closer to him. Without warning, he unexpectedly led her across the road and quickly through a vivid red door with a bright light hung above, jangling from its support.

'Hal and Ben Smith,' whispered Gerry and tightened his grip on her arm as they crossed the threshold that perhaps gave a somewhat duller impression than its bright exterior might have intended. Roz squeaked. 'Sorry did I hurt you? Couldn't risk him seeing us. Might get back...might tell the wife,'

A coward to boot thought Roz crossly, she was a little ashamed of him. She could sense his quickened heartbeat, it irritated her, they had nothing to hide. He directed her to vacant table arranged between partitions, like an eastern railway carriage. She was not the only female in the room. Gerry pushed a girl away, who considering her direct approach might not have seen Roz. Roz thought nothing of it.

There were only two other tables occupied. At one table, four excited sailors were playing a game with beer bottle tops.

On the other hand, their playing cards, from the crumpled role they had assumed in the ashtray or on top of the beer bottles might as well have served as bottle tops. Roz said so and started to giggle.

'Shut up, Roz, for heaven's sake. They might turn nasty.'

It was the first time in Gerry's new role that he had spoken sharply to her. It served to remind her how much she had disliked him a few days ago. She looked peeved.

At the other table, a lone local boy slept together with six girls each in a tight flowered print dress at a table, which was meant for four persons at the most. It was all rather squalid and still Roz remained unperturbed.

The relief and almost positive assurance that Hal had not seen them obviously gave Gerry no regrets about entering this dubious bar and he did not apologise, but when Roz said, 'Isn't it over there?' and looked directly at the Greek word Τουλεττα – tooleta, he winced.

'Really necessary?' he asked.

Purposefully she walked with a forced dignity, the kind she thought the occasion demanded, and four pairs of male eyes accosted her as she tapped her heels defiantly over the stone floor. Once her goal was achieved the success of crossing the room and the undeniable knowledge that she was feeling rather ill caused her to sit in the only possible place. In the next moment, the floor raced up towards her and her head exploded as it hit the hard floor.

It seemed only seconds later that she picked herself up to shake the russet coloured skirt, but it was, in reality, a great deal longer. Still, she had no feeling of time, no knowledge of Gerry's anxiety. She leant against the wall. The one thought in her mind was she was extremely drunk. This did not appear to alter her reasoning. The wall did not move but stayed fortunately very firm and comforting. There were none of the other wild fantasies associated with drunkenness. The floor too now stayed still and the only thing she could reasonably call unsteady were her legs. This was her greatest problem. There were no adulterous desires; only now a very pressing desire to find the strength to move from this small room, which in relation to the rest of the brothel, (for it came to her in a flash that this indeed was a brothel), must be very dirty indeed and almost certain to smell.

She would be unable to recall there being an actual smell. Some instinct guided her and she made the decision to return to their table, but there was no guarantee that she would reach it.

In fact, she did, and Gerry worried though he had been, gave no indication of his anxiety. As she sat down he called for the bill and passed her a glass of soda. 'The water could be risky here,' he said.

They left without Roz saying anything. There is a time during some evenings when every action seems natural and no action is excused or criticised.

Vaguely in Roz's memory, there would be a drive in a taxi, with the faithful driver. There would be lights in Rhodes, still illuminated as they passed into the new town. Modern white lights on new standards of white concrete and the beam they cast was also white. There would be cultivated green bushes to line the

105

boulevards, black now and glistening in the night. The old wall would divide the old town from the new; it was a very ancient town; it was a very modern town.

Roz lay heavily on Gerry's round comfortable shoulder, her head carelessly resting on his collar-bone, missing the natural hollow of his shoulder above his breast. He didn't complain. White broad steps led up to the revolving door of the hotel. The brightly lit entrance hall could be seen clearly through the doors, the concierge on the left side, the reception desk on the other. The revolving doors spun. A porter must have pushed them. Another porter said 'Goodnight Madam.

Gerry said, 'Goodnight.' The corridor to the far staircase, the secondary staircase seemed half a mile in length. This was the staircase used by day as being most convenient for Roz's room. If she used the main staircase now the porter might suppose she was also using Gerry's room. She was very young and very drunk.

She did not care what the porters might think. It was not considered to be their business. But she walked the hundred-foot corridor to the second staircase with six eyes watching, her head held high and her stole dusting the marble floor as she went.

At five o'clock she was washing sheets in the bath. It would be dreadful if the chambermaid should discover them in the morning. She could not remember being sick, neither could she remember falling asleep. Now she changed from the very creased brown dress, into a pale cream nightdress and slept on top of the blanket. It was a hot night but she was not entirely confident that the sheets would be dry in four hours.

As she climbed back onto the bed for the second time, she was aware that she ought not to be alone in the

106

room. She had forgotten Sally was now sharing her room. She sat up on the bed and stepped onto the floor. She was quite still. There was no sound; no breath from sleep and Roz crossed the carpet to the canopied veranda. As she opened the shutters the sound of the tide moved in. The hills of Turkey faced her over the Sea of Mamaris and a dark navy-blue sky gradually surrendered to the soft rays of dawn, releasing enough light for shadows in the room. Sally was definitely not there.

At nine o'clock the tall girl stood over Roz's sleeping figure.

She was clad in a towel and presumably a swimsuit.

'Hallo there! What happened to you last night? Captain Duncan lace your drinks then? You woke me washing those sheets. You should have more sense than to mix your drinks.' Sally was clearly trying to cover her tracks and banking on the fact that Roz had been too drunk to notice she had stayed out herself, most of the night.

Roz hesitated.

'Oh! The sheets? Yes, I had a female accident. Don't suppose you've any S.T.s? Must be change of climate or something.' Now, she thought, she would probably have to cut out swimming for a couple of days to make that ring true. Never mind there were too many jellyfish. She didn't care if Sally didn't believe her.

However, it did seem sufficient excuse for Sally to say more kindly, 'Too much excitement if you ask me! Anyway, I'd watch it...Ben's mooning after you as though you were right out of a Doris Day movie, and if you try to play one against the other, one of your crew might cut up nasty, and you would deserve what you get.

My advice, but you don't need it...choose your boyfriends off the airfield. Don't play around with the home team. They're a waste of time. They're all married anyway.'

'But Ben's not married!' protested Roz, and fell silent. She wasn't interested in Ben Smith. But later she might have cause to think that her words had seemed important enough for Sally to remember them, at least.

24 August 1960

(v)

If Gerry had asked Roz, three hours later, how she laid in the sun with a hangover she would have replied she did not know. Waves of nausea swept through her head each time she opened her eyes but Gerry did not enquire after her health when he joined her on the beach and she had to roll onto her stomach to comfort the dimple in her tummy when she noticed the ghost of a smile in his cheeks. Last night she had told herself that she did not care for him.

Now she stared at his huge sandaled feet; the only part of his body she could see easily from her horizontal position on the sand. 'Hideous!' - she thought – 'how English a man must be to wear such footwear. Definitely not my type!

'Yet I love him! They clash with the sand and they chew the dust from the road...ugh! She thought of Derek the suave and handsome Englishman. He would never dream of wearing sandals or short sleeves with a jacket or of committing any of the other faux pas in dress that this crew did!'

Her thoughts turned to Sally, who she saw in the distance. Sally had been left on her own last night, where had she been and Roz recalled the attentions Sally had received from the Greek barman before dinner. Force Majeure!

It explained everything, particularly the empty bed whilst Roz engaged in her starlit laundry.

The morning passed slowly.

'Roz, I think you should take care, your skin is very red.' Gerry showed concern about her unshaded body. 'I will call the boy over for you,' and he raised two forefingers to emphasise his call of 'Boy.'

The Boy who was seventy at least and whose dusky skin, textured like seersucker, belied the fat tips, which had supplemented his income, on and off, for over forty years, came slowly nearer. Gerry said. 'A sunshade please,' and indicated to another large umbrella erected nearby. But the man's grey skin remained unmoved and the eyes only queried the words slightly. Gerry understood and reluctantly put his hand in his pocket. The drachmas had the desired response and the parasol came slowly.

Roz said, 'Thank you.' Gerry moved over and sat nearer. His form fell clumsily into a canvas seat, but deck chairs the world over have managed the weight of their expensive clients adequately.

The morning continued to pass slowly.

Gerry might not be thinking at all. He looked very relaxed.

Roz could not stop sensing the proximity of the man who was sitting so near her.

Then Ben arrived with Sally.

Quietly, so no one heard them approach and just as silently they placed a cigarette in Roz's slightly opened mouth as she was dozing. Roz screamed and everyone laughed, except for Roz who said coarsely, 'Keyriste.'

'Another version of that word, young lady is Kee-bab,' said Gerry sharply, 'and you might do better if you memorise it.

'Come off it Gerry, everyone swears a little nowadays you know.' Ben gravely blinked his blue eyes so that his shaggy black eyebrows seemed to hide the pupils.

'Not in my crew, they don't...'

'What do you say, Lofty, I'll buy you one those cool Cuba Libras the Greek barman does so well here.' Sally looked expectantly at Ben, obviously the invitation must be for her, the tallest of the assembled company, but she answered him coolly.

'His name is Dimitri and he is off duty this morning.' It was unfortunate.

'Really?' he said, quietly but giving the word it's full meaning of genuine surprise. Sally heard Ben though and to Roz she said,

'Come on ducky, we can't use the public rooms dressed like this, and perhaps if these scoundrels mean it I might be just a little thirsty after all.'

As Roz did not move she repeated earnestly, 'Come on Roz,' and set off up the wooden strip, barefoot towards the patio. Here the egg-sized pebbles inlaid into the path in the style used in the old village of Lindos, made Sally pause to put on her sandals and she waited for Roz.

Ben was watching Sally while Gerry thoughtfully pushed the sand into little heaps again, mainly driving the particles with his big toes. 'Must watch Mr. Dimitri, he might make other things besides cool drinks!'

'Yes, young Sally has a vicious reputation; a great pity they all turn out this way,' endorsed Ben. 'Two years flying and they become as hard as diamonds. Is it Air India that compulsorily retires its girls after two years? Perhaps they're right. I would hate to see our little hostie go the same way.' They were both aware that Roz was listening to their conversation, but she felt the time

111

had come to take her leave, and she joined Sally on the patio.

'They're nice,' she said casually indicating to the Egyptian styled sandals.

'Yes, I got them in Bond Street.' But Roz being a Yorkshire girl thought first of Bond Street, Leeds and the impression, if Sally had wished to create one, was lost.

After lunch, with the two crews, Gerry excused himself from the coffee table muttering that he was going to change some traveller's cheques. 'Sally!' He surprised the elder girl as he walked passed the chintz-covered chair where she was lounging. Her lips clearly dithered at the sound of her name; her heart might have fluttered. It was obvious that she loved to attract attention.

'Yes, Captain Duncan?' she spoke elaborately.

'Sal, you said at lunch you needed some stamps.' Gerry could not help the smile that flickered across his lips and his cheeks dimpled. What had she expected him to say anyway? He added, still mischievously, 'If you and Roz can waylay Ben, I'll fetch Hal and we'll go down to that market we were talking about at lunch.'

'You mean the Old Slave Market?' Sometimes there was a touch of humour in this girl, which appealed to Gerry, and his steel blue-grey eyes twinkled. Nobody had mentioned the words Slave Market before. The light in Sally's light brown eyes was attractive, he had misjudged her earlier, and she was wearing the same corn coloured skirt which had suited her so well in Athens.

Another job, a different career, somebody's private secretary perhaps, something dull like textiles or chemicals and routine good humour and Sally would be a different person. Nevertheless, he knew her to be a remarkably good stewardess; putting passengers before crew every time, as she should, but which few girls did. Most put crew first. The same bad habits, which if only he would admit it, he was training Roz to adopt.

'Always take your crew a cup of coffee before you start with the passengers,' he had told her, 'after all it is your pilots who are doing all the work.'

Now he studied the blonde girl. 'Yes, Sally. I mean just that, hurry or we'll miss the sale!'

'It would be a pity to do that. You would probably get a good price for us!' She added wickedly, 'especially for young Roz, she looks so innocent'

'Now then, cut it out. You're corrupting my already evil thoughts,' but although his eyes twinkled he spoke firmly, reminding Sally that there was a limit to such free conversation.

Minutes later five of eight crewmembers gathered in the huge hall. They walked down the wide drive passed the hibiscus and rhododendrons. Roz plucked nervously at the sticky green leaves that protruded from the railings as she passed, rolling them into a ball and letting them slide to the ground.

'You're in a destructive mood,' remarked Sally.

'Well young Rosalind, has that very loquacious young lady,' said Gerry, and Sally coloured thinking he was being uncomplimentary, 'warned you that you're about to do a favour for me. I see you've clad yourself to advantage.' Gerry observed the cream silk shirt and light brown full cotton skirt, complimented by a wide brown leather belt and as Roz pretended not to understand he went on, 'we're selling you to the White Slave Trade. The market of the world is here at the Nea Agora in

113

Rhodes. I am surprised your chief hostie did not warn you before you left Yorkshire.

Roz went pale, but she suddenly felt fabulous. Her bones felt as weak as her soft flesh, she wanted to collapse against Gerry's strong body and seek protection.

'I love you for your embarrassment,' whispered Gerry as Roz came closer to him, and she really was lost forever.

Ben, slightly late on the uptake, as usual, said, 'I'm surprised too. They generally call you into the Kremlin,' referring to the Flight Operations Office, 'and say, very confidentially of course, 'Miss Peters, we must ask you to exercise great care on this trip. Captain Duncan is under a fair amount of suspicion. We believe, we've no proof of course, that he may be a member of the White Slave Trading Company...of course,'' Ben's imitation of the female voice was almost perfect, ''as I've said before, we've no proof, but we do advise you not to go out with him unchaperoned.''

For one awkward moment, there was silence, and Roz blushed, had they indeed been seen last night?

Ben said quickly, his dimple in his chin unhidden, 'Sad thing is they don't realise that I'm in the racket with him. Poor Julie, must be overworked, it is unheard of for her not to warn the new girls!'

Gerry laughed; glad the moment of tension had passed. 'She's no such thing.' His laugh and tone of his voice sent a delighted shiver up Roz's spine. 'Julie is the most loyal chief hostess I know. She just realises that Roz is an excellent and saleable specimen I suppose I shall have to let Julie have a small percentage of the profit.' He sighed.

Roz thought it was silly to let Gerry excite her with this foolish game. Silly was a lovely word, it tickled. And then just suppose it was so?

The teasing just possibly could be true. She could not help feeling that she'd love to become Gerry's slave. Was she hoping? The thought that there was nothing she could do to prevent it made it more exciting. She was in Rhodes where she spoke no Greek and knew no other English person. It was a terrifying experience to resign yourself completely to fate. How terrifying was suddenly the reality, and she blushed. She was being a fool.

In truth, she was merely naïve and very young. In an age when mass travel was yet to come and package holidays were in their infancy and life had a slower pace with strict mores, Roz was no more an innocent abroad than any of her contemporaries.

Then Ben broke into a run and leapt over a flowerbed, and his action halted Roz's thoughts and prevented their analysis further. Such fantasies were only the product, she was sure, of the resinous wine at lunch and the hot blistering sun of Rhodes.

Or was Gerry really the first man she had truly fallen for? What about Derek, was he a mere boy? Was Derek, if she was brutally honest, the reason that her life had taken this turn and brought her to this eastern paradise? Her life with Derek seemed like something she had perhaps dreamt but bore no similarity with her life now.

The others were infected by Ben's high spirits and followed down the wide promenade with a half skip, even the staid and more sensible Gerald had a bounce to his walk which although characteristic was exaggerated.

Everyone felt young, looked happy and foolish. Hal who was almost fifty looked the most ridiculous, but it was he who said, 'Anyone for leap frog?' He bent down and to her surprise it was Roz who neatly jumped over his spine, and her face registered surprise that she achieved it.

Gerry found he had to laugh. 'I bet you've never had so much energy since you were in the sixth form.'

Hal straightened up and said something quietly to Ben.

Ben was beaming, his was the type of face associated with beaming and he did it well. It suited him and again it triggered off the dimple in his chin.

'A mere pixie!' Ben's words startled Roz as he suddenly appeared beside her. '*You* can't be twenty-five?'

'You're the third person in twenty-four hours to remind me of my tender years. No, I'm not twenty-five, just twenty.' The day Roz had applied for the post had been a week after her twentieth birthday.

Hal deliberately entered the conversation. 'A mere chicken'.

Roz sensed that they were both anxious to talk to her. Hal sounded like her father.

She was not experienced in small talk and the sudden necessity to put the men more at ease, made her tongue-tied. It was as though they were trying to say something to her.

She looked sharply at the Senior Captain.

Hal was trying to say something. 'You are very young for this game you know. I hate to see young girls hurt. Ben tells me you've only been flying a couple of weeks or so. It is very easy to be influenced by bright lights and hot sunshine, free wine and superb hotels...do

116

forgive me for mentioning it, but nobody likes to see a pretty girl get swept away with the general tide.'

'Please don't worry. I'm perfectly alright.' Immediately she uttered the words she blushed and wished she hadn't said anything.

Harold Williams gave her a strange look and a smile curled around his lips. Roz felt uncomfortable and Ben sniggered, and moved apart to walk on his own.

'Forgive me, my dear. Let's talk about other things, perhaps I can tell you a little about this town. Not at all like Athens, is it?'

'I already know all these light rose-coloured buildings along the promenade were built by the Italians between the two world wars.' It seemed pointless to ask him their origin or anything else when she already knew the answer, equally it seemed rude to tell a man so much her superior that she knew a lot about the town anyway. Gerry had already told her.

So, she asked, needlessly, 'Where was it that the Colossus stood?'

'Some say it strode the harbour here, a great bronze statue, commemorating some awful siege, which the Rhodians resisted and erected to the Sun God, Helios. I think it was about ninety feet high and built by a villager from Lindos, but you know it took this sculptor Chares twelve years to build and only stood for sixty years thereafter because along with all the other splendid statues in Rhodes it came toppling down in an enormous earthquake. It must have been pretty impressive though because it remained immortal for over twenty-two centuries afterward.'

'And now those deer with antlers mark the spot?' queried Roz pointing at the statues.

'No, it's a romantic notion, but modern thinking says it stood back away from the harbour and the port.' He sniffed, well pleased with his history lesson. 'People tend to minimise the classical influence of Rhodes, but it was first and foremost, second to none, not even Athens, in philosophy, rhetoric, and fine arts particularly during some later periods; and yet the Romans destroyed it all so thoroughly, in a mere fit of jealousy, that everyone now relates its history to the medieval period.'

Roz nodded and looked silently at the surrounding yellow and pink stones, which were almost white like a well-beaten cake mixture. This was the modern heritage, but to her in the bright light of the sun, this was Rhodes, and with this she was satisfied.

Rising apparently out of the blue velvet sea, the island had been so favoured by the kiss of the sun that Zeus had given it to his son Apollo, pleased that the young sun god had chosen to be born there. Fortunes may wane, but in Rhodes it seems they always wax again. White ships passed through the straits, graceful with the sinister Turkey on the north side and the pale yellow and white colouring of the Greek island on the other. To these colours, two equally clean sharp contrasts, the scarlet of hibiscus and the green of the leaves could be added. Roz closed her eyes to imprint the scene on her memory and saw no other colour except for the frame of blue, velvet blue sea and blue, silk blue sky.

Hal was right when he said the birthmarks of Rhodes could not be related to the sister city of Athens, and it was impossible to believe that they shared the same heritage and lineage. Athens was worn with yellow dust and badly needed spring-cleaning.

Some would say that this state of affairs just got worse through the century. Indeed, was to remain until Athens was awarded the Olympic Games of 2004, when mutterings were made and some progress ensued with the planting of trees, making of parks and the removal of the hoardings which had previously shown Athens to be so much part of the Middle East. Then with the global credit crisis a few years later and retaliation against the Greek Government's austerity programme, there was the worry in 2011 that the gloss would come off the country again. Greece ever destined to struggle.

Every trodden footstep seemed to move ancient atoms and disturb quantities of history, yet the paving stones of modern Athens were probably no older than those down the Kings Road, Chelsea.

Nothing in Athens of the nineteen sixties asked for attention, but everything impressed the visitor with its sheer physical bustle. One could imagine that the city bustled with the same atmosphere in the days when it pleased Pericles.

Everything in the Attic town vanished into a symmetry of sun and dust, everything from the shouting pictures outside the modern cinemas with unintelligible Greek ciphers captioning the descriptive illustrations to the more fashionable streets where men in national costume stood selling trays of Greek nougat, sticky and sweet, or enormous sponges. Since time immemorial Athens had obviously been a loud town.

In Rhodes on the other hand, all these things happened, but none were noticed. Even twenty, thirty years later, after the invasion of the tourists of the seventies, Rhodes was to keep her peace with certain dignity. Perhaps Greeks in national costume were not far removed from their villages as to stand out, or perhaps the pistachio nuts and America films with Greek sub-titles just fitted better into the background.

The exceptions were the Italian buildings which dominated the new town and the Turkish influence which soaked the old town. Rhodes did not suffer from its foreign influence, it embraced it and was actually enhanced by it, but beauty was the noun substituted for history, for despite the ghosts of the Knights firmly encamped behind the forty-foot wall of the Collachium visitors stared at Rhodes rather than studied it. Perhaps it was that the town was too obviously furnished with everything in perfect working order so that history failed to catch Roz's imagination.

Beauty overwhelmed the town, and even mass tourism of the eighties and nineties would be unable to dislodge the ever-pervading heavy grey stones of history and the medieval old town was made a World Heritage site in 1988.

Almost all the work in the new town had been done by the Italians, during their brief stay, but Roz gathered there was little praise for the Fascist architecture from the local people and Mussolini would be right to assume that there had been little appreciation for the several bombastic Italian-styled buildings which the Italians were obliged to leave when they were expelled from the island during the Second World War.

Near these fine Italian structures, two Greek guards stood to attention, as blue as Her Majesty's soldiers are red and equally as erect.

They should never have dared Roz to do it, but Ben's sense of humour often became distorted. So, of course, Roz had little option but to wade through the fountain as they were passing.

There was a shout and the blue Greek was already cocking his rifle.

Suddenly everyone felt that they knew the Greek words for 'to wade, the fountain, is forbidden.' but it was Gerry's look of complete incomprehension that made Roz's heart fall as well as her wet foot from the rim of the fountain, as her eyes met his she hung her head. She knew it hurt him to consider her a child and suddenly angrily she needed to be a child.

For the second time that week she was aware that nothing would ever steer her along an innocent path again. Nothing could be the same from now on.

She shook her foot and put it back into her shoe.

There actually does come a point in everyone's life when they do finally 'put away childish things.' Roz reached it at that precise moment. She felt as though she was in command of the mystery of life. She adored Gerry and nature intended that this love should be mutual. Only a moral code appeared to hinder them, a code that she believed was a wicked creation of man's convenience. The complete system of the modern code of ethics seemed precariously unbalanced.

Marriage was no longer the factor of love, sex was an abysmal reason; love was all, love was the criteria on which to base one's feelings for life. Pandora Rosalind Peters was in love with Gerald Shaw Duncan. If everyone followed her simple supposition of love, the inevitable danger of the world becoming overweight with prudish people intent on destroying the natural fibre of life and love could be prevented.

She had been told that the Greek word for life and God's love were logically the same: Zoë. A lovely word, she would call a daughter Zoë. Now there was every reason to suppose that the Goddess of Love,

Aphrodite still lived on this ancient island. Here was not just an excuse to sympathise with the early Greeks for their simple belief in the Gods of right and wrong, here was evidence to support their wisdom in this religion.

Yet Roz could not trust her newfound convictions. She was herself, neither strong enough nor courageous enough to defy her moral education.

Gerry moved over to walk near Roz.

'I'm sorry,' he said at first, very calmly. A small portly man, insignificant but for his smile, and she thought she loved him. She was ashamed. She blushed.

'You're a very silly little girl Rosalind.' He went on, 'Grow up...first leap frog and then paddling in the public fountains...you must always remember that you are a representative of your own country, visiting another; often less fortunate countries. That was not the sort of behaviour that I would have expected from you.'

Of course, the Nea Agora, which was to be the scene of the 'Slave Market' was the same Turkish polygonal building where their taxi-driver had met his Greek friend the previous evening. Here under the trees in the interior, the old men sat watching, conversing and smoking their pipes.

But the magical spell, which Roz had felt cast over her earlier, had been broken.

The new market was the focal point of the new town, overlooking Mandraki Harbour with the resplendent caiques, the large overgrown yachts, the wealth of princes and rich men, and the three windmills. Roz was almost disappointed to find the whole building was far too recent a construction being probably a mere forty years old in 1960 to ever have been employed as a slave market.

On the perimeter of the building, the little shops with their fascinating quality goods captivated Roz. No wonder she had been warned not to spend all her money in Athens. Everything was ridiculously cheap. Rhodes was a duty-free port. A status which it had mostly enjoyed since ancient times. The goods, which were marked handmade obviously were, many pottery pieces and jewellery being made locally. She bought a turquoise blue vase richly decorated by hand with seahorses and dolphins, heavy chunky pottery but very pleasing. Gerry muttered something about having a suit made and inferred that the tailors were as good as in Hong Kong and would make up your cloth for you within twenty-four hours.

Characteristically he never did anything about it.

They spent four more Elysian days on the island. Most of the time it was hard to move the crew from the beach or the bar. But on the final day, they had gone to the lovely bay of Lindos, hiring a car. Just Gerry, Roz and Ben.

They had motored slowly over the charming but atrocious road to the Valley of Butterflies, following the inland route over the mountains. They passed small white shrines with lights kept permanently lit, lesser villages and many white goats and they terrified themselves by urging Gerry on as he drove down the narrow single tracks: covered in shingle and sharp white pebbles.

Above the Valley of Butterflies, they stood higher than the vegetation and threw pebbles into the undergrowth to disturb the silvery pink butterflies.

Galaxies of shimmering insects rose adding to the colour of the wild flowers. Biologically these milling 'butterflies', pretty creatures that they were, they were told, were moths. Eventually with the burgeoning number of tourists to help conserve the dwindling numbers of these fragile creatures – panaxia (species Quadripunctaria Poda, sub species: C. q. rhodosensis) it became forbidden to clap or disturb them in any way.

They drove on to Lindos, observing pink oleanders around the peasant doorways of the settlements as they passed, tree-lined hillsides and everywhere the smell of thyme and myrtle. They passed orange groves and olive trees. They wanted to trespass and steal the fruit but when they did diverge it was off the road to visit a small wayside settlement, set a hundred yards from the actual road, as Greek hamlets often are. Here was a taverna with a rough wooden balcony overlooking a great gorge and valley below.

Immediately their car stopped it was surrounded by small laughing boys who encouraged them into the cafe. No one spoke English or understood their need for a drink, despite Gerry's laborious attempts in Greek. A gesticulation for a bottle of wine produced a jug of locally brewed Retsina, probably the only wine they sold.

Curiously the taste of the resin, which is reminiscent of cellulose, became more enjoyable as the level of the jug's contents was lowered. And anyway, who could go to Greece without sampling local wine? It was definitely a drink for the open air, for relaxing with, under a blue sky and catching that quick crisp air of the Dodecanese.

Presently their small sun-kissed hosts returned with an old man, they had obviously gone some distance to collect him from his house.

'I speaks the English because many years I live in Americas.' He said this to Gerry. He was a wizened little old man who immediately elected Gerry as the senior member of the small group. 'But I comes home to die. My name is Niko. Yous the first guest to our village.'

An old woman came out of the house and offered them a piece of cake. It was obviously a very special cake, made of fruit. Niko translated that her son had recently married, hence the special wedding cake.

'Yous special people, our guests, the first tourists. *Krima,* pity, but goods for the island. Many peoples now get rich, like American!' and Niko patted his stomach and smiled a toothless grin. 'Soons we alls very rich,' he went on grinning.

They said goodbye to their friends at the primitive taverna and on this perfect day, they continued over the crest of the island where the mountains rise incredibly higher than the English Lake District and dazzle the view. Sea, mountain and plain, all visible at once and magnificent beyond description.

This was their last day on this enchanted green isle with the silver-green olive trees, the green of much darker cypresses and blue-green hinterlands where little white villages are masked by olive fonds. Scarcely visible from the roads, were women riding side saddle on donkeys who always gave a queenly wave and older women garbed in black and grey and peasants in the fields, who would give the only indication and hint of a hamlet's presence.

Nearing the coast, they were suddenly overpowered by the panorama of Lindos with a zigzag road oscillating down before rising up to the little township. Here was their first view of the beach, and before she knew it, they were running down the path to the golden sand and Roz for the first time in her life was tempted to swim in deep water.

The Acropolis of Lindos majestically stood sentinel to the little cube-shaped whitewashed houses that formed the more recent village under the citadel, but even these houses were mainly seventeenth century. There was nothing very modern about Lindos in 1960.

The glass-green sea, clear and tempting encircled the little promontory with its sandy beaches. 'This is pure heaven,' said Roz and the rest concurred.

Back from the beach, they left the car, for indeed all transport in Lindos was by mule and donkey or by foot, and spurning the invitation of a donkey man they made their way on foot uphill to the narrow streets, cluttered with the small white village houses. Attractively arranged on the narrow streets, dazzlingly white, Roz could see through the open portals that many had pebble mosaics for courtyards, patios and staircases.

In the heat of the day, they only glimpsed a surface impression of the architecture and history that tourism was yet to spoil. There were no hotels, no cars and only a sprinkling of tourists in the village centre. It was an idyllic place. How long would it survive?

Gerry refused a ride by donkey putting the animal's welfare first, committing them to walk up the steep hillside, climbing the four hundred feet to the Acropolis, which hid its glory from the foot of the hill.

'Curious how the medieval aspect of the Castle of Knights is visible from the village and afar, but as we reach the outer gate, this relief of a large trireme is dominated by three banks of oars. It's hewn out of the rock giving it a new dimension. This site has not only

126

medieval ruins but takes history backward through time,' said Gerry.

Hot and exhausted, they explored the Byzantine Church, the remains of a classical temple dedicated to the Lindian Athene and a Doric Stoa; additional evidence that Lindos had been occupied since ancient times by the Minoan civilisation and by the Mycenaean settlers from the Peloponnesian city of Tiryns.

'Unlike many other ancient sites which echo one aspect of history, here it all is, in a nutshell, but also unlike some other sites, in glorious technicolour. The dark grey relief of the trireme, the glory of the pink sandstone temple and the dazzling white aspect of the village all set against the vivid blue sea and sky. Few places on earth evoke such a climax,' Gerry was still pontificating but no one looked bored.

Finally drunk with the experience they climbed down from the rock, walked past the huddle of houses, their shoes squeaking on the smooth ancient paths and found an empty taverna under the plane and mulberry trees. Here they were treated to a fresh, roasted chicken,

'I swear the owner killed it as he saw us coming up the street,' said Roz with some feigned horror.

To escape the heat of the day they sat in the tiny front room of the taverna, which also boasted a magnificent mosaic cobbled floor and a huge olive tree growing from the floor and up through the roof. They followed their meal with a chaser of large watermelons, red and juicy.

That afternoon alone on the beach, again they swam under and through the clear warm water and finally they found their little Fiat and drove back up the swinging road, along the coastal road, back into the town of Rhodes.

And all the time they had made small talk and Gerry had never once shown emotion or feeling. He was playing the part so perfectly that Roz was sure he must love her. Now she was sure that one day they would find again the sense of touch.

It was as if a fine invisible web covered them both, stretched when they moved apart. It gave them no need for words. Their time would come; and the world would explode. Yet Roz, not really quite sure what she would feel, now curled up, on the back seat of the car immediately experienced a sensation of lightweight emotion, as she watched the gentle scene of rocks and trees and little houses on the roadside and the car swept through the more barren landscape of the coast back into the city.

They left the Hotel des Roses and drove to the airport for the flight allowing just enough time to reach their destination to land in Crete before dark.

For their comfort, they had delayed the departure of the flight until the sun had lost its power but equally, no pilot lands on a Greek island at night if given a choice, or at least they didn't in the early sixties when Herakleion still sported a grass runway.

Roz cried with two small dewdrop tears as the taxi drew away from that imposing residence the Hotel des Roses, with its mock arches, in its huge entrance in the yellow stone walls. The legacy of the Italians and the little red roofs of the peasant houses and the Turkish settlement were left behind on the road to the airport. Windmills and fig trees followed the coast all the way, and there was a gentle breeze to the end of the day.

Here and there, there was an orange or lemon grove. The view of the sophisticated Miramare Beach Hotel, the one hotel on the coast outside the town, people taking their final swim of the day in the blue pool. More windmills, olive groves and coves. It was a memory for life. Roz said goodbye to the land where she had grown up.

If she were to go back in the future, if ever, it would never be quite the same. There were plans for Rhodes to grow up, also.

28 August 1960

(vi)

They landed at the little green grass airstrip running beside the sea on a Sunday evening. The flight was at an interesting low level, skimming the blue sea where occasionally a white wave broke and small green islands disturbed the symmetry patterned by intermittent white rocks, islands with evocative names such as Chalki, Karpathos, Kassos, virtually unknown to tourists except for the few yachtsmen who brave these seas, inhospitable as this corner of the Aegean is thought to be.

Gerry had called Roz up with the crew call to the cockpit. 'Take time from your passengers to look at this sunset.' And while the sun-set, the whole Western sky was coloured in varying soft and brilliant shades of pink and gold.

Below them, the rough ridge of jagged mountains which formed Karpathos reached up to the little aircraft, but it looked a forlorn, barren island, almost unwelcoming, although Roz doubted that any Greek island could be inhospitable.

Gerry turned the 'plane full circle so all the passengers could appreciate the magnificence of the Western sky and once again heading west he said, 'there you see Minoan Crete; we'll just make it without the undercarriage lights. Landing in ten minutes, Miss Peters!' His grey-blue eyes twinkled, mischievously.

'That's mean!' the girl protested. 'I've all the supper boxes and glasses to collect yet.'

'What's mean?' he asked. 'You'll remember a sunset over Crete all your life. Don't tell me you'll remember or even lose any sleep over an unship-shape galley!'

He was right of course. Roz laughed and left the cockpit and her passengers seeing her smiling face, laughed too. Gerry already had the 'FASTEN SEAT BELTS' sign illuminated but Roz ignored it and with the assistance of the cheerful passengers who stacked up the boxes and passed them back as best they could she had the aircraft reasonably tidy as they landed heavily on the undersized grass airstrip.

As they left the airport it would seem the whole population of Herakleion had turned out to greet them. True as the aircraft landed and taxied to the small customs hall, the crew noticed they had congregated against the perimeter fence, clapping as the chocks were put on the wheels. Women in black, shawled and toothless, men in black and grey with hats and pipes; girls and young brides in tight black skirts with gay blouses and, of course, beautiful high heeled shoes.

For this, of course, was Sunday, and Sunday at its best. Very orthodox.

The taxi that was to bring them to the heart of the little metropolis arrived with darkness. Once in the town, there was more of the same, huge crowds of people and to Roz, it seemed that there were millions of people living in this tiny city, and Sunday was the night of the Volta.

In reality, Herakleion was built on a waterfront with gossiping Venetian buildings jostling for a sea view. Behind the quay, the town was compact and approaching modernity with several smart Greek whitewashed buildings, the smell of new plaster pervasive, with modern shops and restaurants.

The Ferryair crew could not move across the pavement to approach their smart small second-class hotel for the ebbing and flowing of the meandering people. Dark people, some in gay clothes, but Roz's auburn hair stood out, and suddenly the mass was aware that strangers were in their midst and let them pass. Another instance where in Greece the same word means both stranger and guest. In ancient Greek barbarian was the word that meant stranger. It is clear that it was imperative to use the word xenos for the stranger, who was a guest rather than a barbarian: the gift of Greek hospitality and friend of strangers, philoxenia.

In their new hotel rooms with cool bare terrazzo floors beneath them they were able to look from the mock Venetian balconies into a world apparently full of sparrows. The chattering of the population continued. The Volta was in full swing. It is a courting ritual. In Greece, this exodus from houses into the squares and market-places happens every Saturday and Sunday night, but nowhere is it so pronounced as in Herakleion.

It was a sad night for the crew.

In Gerry's inside pocket was his wallet. In this wallet was the briefing he had received on arrival at the airport.

It stated simply:

DEPART HERAKLEION   08.15
UPLIFT 36 PAX ROME.
      E.T.A. YEADON   19.30

'That doesn't give much time for the unexpected, does it? Have they gone mad? We can't possibly keep to that schedule!' Ben was outraged as Gerry showed him the telex. Neither man mentioned any disappointment at being called home. Perhaps it was only Roz who felt it. In the airline business, one anticipated the unanticipated. And then it hit her. Gerry would be going home: to his wife.

'They've probably got it about right.' Gerry spoke calmly. 'Bit of a bore though. End of the trip and all that jazz. And it's a long day. They've got us empty from here to Rome so there're no counting duty hours on that leg if we're pushed. Better order lunch boxes for us all, Roz.'

'Does that mean we're going home?'

'Brilliant, absolutely brilliant deduction dear girl!' The irritation he felt was now pronounced in Ben's tone.

'Better have an early night.' Gerry said quietly.

That seemed to be the end of it. Nothing was said of Roz's thirty-six passengers who she had taken around the Aegean and now appeared to be abandoning so blithely in Crete. She supposed some other crew would have the pleasure of their company and she had failed to say even goodbye to these people she had come to know well. Somewhat soberly she retired early in the evening and still the town sang to its chorus.

A little later Gerry crept quietly into Roz's room.

'I thought you might like a nightcap and a quiet talk before you retired.' He smiled. 'We won't go out. I don't like to be seen with a stewardess when there is only one other crewmember. It always looks wrong unless there is a group of you like there was in Rhodes. Pity though there is a place on the quay, past the old harbour called 'The Glasshouse,' which has a charm all of its own. I'd like to have taken you there.'

'I don't want to go back, Gerry.'

'Me also. You know for a youngster you're a good little hostess. I shall put in a favourable report when we get back. Perhaps that will mean we shall be able to fly together on some other trip, but it doesn't always follow.'

'You mean that I might not be crewed with you again?' Roz was incredulous.

'Could happen, there is a good percentage of other pilots in the company and other lasses for that matter. Roll on the day I say, when, if new-fangled machines take off, they will make up the rosters...or perhaps not, there would be less chance of being rostered together then!'

'I've enjoyed this trip.' Roz was trembling; the thought that she might not fly with Gerry again seemed too much to take in. Had she been terribly immature to allow herself to be influenced by this rather ordinary man? But she knew the answer; Gerry was not ordinary, underneath the sarcasm, he was a gentle person, behind the plain features with the receding hairline was a kind heart and great intelligence, and there were always his eyes. So, different from Derek, there was no danger of this being a rebound romance.

'I've enjoyed it too. I've enjoyed it very much. I'm only sorry that I can't round it off by showing you Knossos. Old Arthur Evans, they used to call him 'little Evans' you know and he was in his forties, older even than me!' he paused, 'before he ever started digging in Crete. But he certainly discovered something and spent most of his fortune on what is possibly the most interesting ancient monument to be seen in the Western hemisphere. Everything is in proportion. The rooms have roofs and although some of the paintings are as unreal as the souvenirs you buy, all reconstructions, and although Evans has been heavily criticised and they say you can't tell the original from the restorations it is the very extensive restoration and rebuilding that has preserved it from the elements of weather. The gypsum stone of which parts are made would apparently have dissolved like sugar in the acid rain unless some form of preservative hadn't been used and had the results of the diggings remained untreated all Evans' work would have become a heap of ruins.'

'I thought it never rained in Greece.'

'In the winter, it rains a lot. It can rain in summer, although that is often some spectacular storm. It is a wonderful discovery; literally the ancient life penetrates the atmosphere as you walk around. Tell you what, borrow my book of C.W. Ceram's "Gods Graves and Scholars" and let me have it back in Yeadon. You can always leave it in my pigeonhole in the crew room. Don't lose it though...and read the chapter on Crete if you read nothing else.

'Weren't all the women of Knossos bare-breasted?' Roz giggled, childishly but Gerry was carried away with his own recollections.

'Fully clothed in tight gowns, hugging the buttocks like corsets and their little tits thrusting forward and up, completely naked from open fronted bodices whilst the neck and shoulders were firmly enclosed as the was the behind. Can you imagine anything more appealing?'

Then Gerry held Roz round the waist as he kissed her.

She was wearing a very pale green dress, almost the colour of apple leaves. Apparently accidentally he touched her cool skin. The touch electrified the surface of Roz's body. Gradually his caresses became urgent and the feelings, which his large and gentle fingers disturbed in her body, opened the sides of her mind as though her head and her brain had expanding walls. Rushing into the cavity left vacant, came space, space as wide and as calm as an ocean. Unexpectedly she shook and curled up against Gerry's body.

'Oh Gerry,' and he squeezed her tight as they listened to the chatter of the crowd, the clip of multiple heels upon the pavements, the song of their laughter. Just love play, the entire world over it was the same, the order of the day, between the sexes the coquetry of flirtation, the soft impeachment of love which becomes the most natural and almost unnoticed action in the world. Inside the hotel Gerry was actively demonstrating his affections but everywhere over the world the foreplay was being re-enacted in crowd scenes such as the one below the balcony.

The Volta was merely a courting ritual.

'I am sorry Roz. I was wrong.'

'It was wonderful.'

'Yes, it was and I am married. With Holly, I've every problem known to men, but I just can't divorce her because she is frigid. She is my wife and she loves me for all her cool passion. She took me in from a war, which wrecked me, physically and mentally, and Holly made a whole man of me, but she would never give me children.'

'Gerry, hold on. I haven't asked you to divorce your wife!'

'I know. I haven't asked you to marry me.' He flicked a red curl from her eyes.

'If you did, I would refuse.'

'Yes, it is only that I said I would always remain faithful to my wife. It is a point of honour with me.'

'And in my old-fashioned way, I've also sworn not to make love before my wedding night.'

'As it happens neither of us has betrayed ourselves, we need not feel guilty, not entirely that is, but if I ever see you again I can't be responsible for my actions then. After the trip, this trip, we must never see each other again. Do you understand? I cannot request not be rostered with you, that might affect your career, show you up in a bad light but you can ask not to fly with me. That way there won't be any awkward questions asked. Many girls make similar requests for obvious reasons and they won't ostracise me because you refuse to fly with me. If I made a similar request they would assume you were a lousy stewardess. So, will you do that thing? Will you promise me?'

Roz did not nod.

'Otherwise, I cannot be responsible for my emotions and my deeds, but I love you, my little girl. I do.' He kissed her gently. She was small and he a short man, being protective when he bent over to touch her lips.

Gerry left her. When the door had closed Roz lay back on the bed and considered as logically as she could the whole situation. A middle-aged man, a man whose own marriage had clearly failed was obsessed by her. When she was forty he would be nearly sixty. How could she love him? But she thought she did.

Then as quickly as a sudden rainstorm would come in from the sea, with every ounce of common-sense with which her mother had endowed her, she told herself she was not in love with Gerry.

Like a storm, it had been a fury, a torrent that had surged and broken and passed.

Infatuated possibly but not in love.

All Gerry had done was to awaken response and sensuality as a bud breaks into flower and with a feeling of warmth and softness still expanding in her body and the gentle rhythm of the chattering local gossipers, Roz fell asleep.

When she woke she felt less confused.

Roz had an 'adopted' sister. Her cousin, in fact.

She would discuss it with her.

Lucinda would know what to do. Lucinda always had an answer.

This was Roz's first thought when she woke the next morning.

A year ago, there had been Derek.

FIVE: BEYOND ADOLESENCE

March 1972

(i)

The pale March sun went behind a cloud. The pale English sky slowly darkened and slowly and softly huge flakes of snow fell from above. Some slowly, some faster, all racing now...huge flakes of snow; the type that a now more mature Rosalind remembered watching as a child, mesmerised. Twirling, fighting, dropping gracefully, caught in the wind, covering the earth that thought it was spring, with a white shawl, at first like lace, where here and there the daffodils and daphne showed their cheerful colours.

Then the sky cleared and the light brightened; the large fat snowflakes were going and fine drizzle slowly melted the beautiful magic which had covered the world.

In a desert Rosalind thought she would long for snow, it was so restful.

A week ago, a neighbour had set fire to his shrubbery, burning leaves. The snow had now settled deeper on his garden, where in the hot freak sunshine of early March that previous week, a spark had set fire to the dry earth.

The fire engine had come, inspected the then dying flames that had frightened all his neighbours and gone away without using a hose. Now the snow found the burnt ground more hospitable than the fresh green buds of spring and there it lingered, covering the scorched earth.

Suddenly the snow and drizzle stopped and once again there was a long view over the white Yorkshire valley. Trees, quietly budding, now had a delicate emphasis, smoke rose silently from a chimney and the birds were cheerfully singing again. A beautiful world, really it was.

On this day, when her husband was again in New York, Rosalind was supposed to go into his office to take some correspondence he had left at home by mistake.

He was the editor of a large regional paper.

There wasn't a cloud in the sky; it was hard to imagine the heavy snowstorm, which minutes earlier had whitened the Thwaiteburn Valley.

Rosalind was unhappy that his role as a writing journalist was drawing to a close; she had married him, happy with his professional image but recently this seemed to have developed with bigger responsibilities, bringing with it the more cynical and tough characteristics that make wealthy men. Indeed, it has been suggested that the successful businessman or entrepreneur is a character unto himself, a type, who risks all, even gambles with affection to achieve his aim, success.

It had its moments as a hypothesis, but Rosalind could not really believe that the hard work, which earned such men as her father, a MBE, which James Peters still insisted he had accepted only to please his wife, had been born entirely of a compulsion to gamble with chance. Such hard work had obviously given Rosalind a great deal of security in childhood, including an expensive education and if she was happy to expect the same for the twins, Alice and Sara, she realised, so it must be with her husband.

It was also probably true that the 'Nouveau Riche' made snobs of its second generation. She was this second generation, but what were to be the characteristics that they were bound to foster in the twins? Would they rebel and fall prey to the views of the left, or would it be merely the world, which naturally persuaded its each generation that the views of the left were the right views. But no one could tell what would happen in ten or fifteen years' time. Indeed, were it suspected by this generation that in their mid-sixties they would be struggling with their pensions; that the Western economy would be vacillating, endowment pensions faltering, they would have been aghast. At the moment life was good to a point. It was the speed of change, which had increased over the last century, not just the natural changes brought about by each growing generation, and that was frightening.

The only thing that was certain, was that whatever the outcome there would be change. Nothing could remain static. Her children would be the adults of the twenty-first century, whereas her own generation, the war children were brought up with entirely different standards in a world of much lesser and slower change.

Soon it would be summer. Rosalind was looking forward to summer. It would be fun this year; the children were old enough to enjoy it too. She pulled on her long fashionable winter snow boots, covered her red hair with a neat beret and set out with the letters for the office, first calling at the wine merchants as she had promised her husband she would do.

September 1960

(ii)

The mackintosh-clad figure of Ben Smith arrived in the crew room of Yeadon airport as Roz Peters was making a decision. She had just decided to go home to visit her father. It was exactly one month since her first flight to Hamburg but Roz felt that she had been responsible for thirty-six lives in the sky for many years. Three weeks with Gerry Duncan had made it impossible to remain a novice.

Indeed, had anyone prophesised a month ago that Roz would have had enough training and confidence to undertake the Maastricht schedules, particularly with Bill Turner, who although fun to fly with, kept up an alarming timetable, Roz would have been amused at the thought. Now she had just completed a day of three schedules, there and back three times in one working day.

Ben gave Roz a shock and she jumped as he walked into the room.

'Hallo!' He looked genuinely pleased to see her and took off his epaulets. He fastened the buttons on his untidy mackintosh and tightened the belt. He replaced his black tie with the blue and red striped tie of the air force and he was ready to drink in the public bar. 'Have you seen Gerry Duncan lately?'

'No, but he went out this morning.' Roz did not want to say that she knew he was due in from Zagreb at eleven o'clock.

'Still owes me thirty shillings from the Greek trip, such an old Shylock. Did he give you your night-stop allowance?'

'No, he told me we'd spent it all.'

'Typical, still I suppose we had a pretty fair time. Can't go robbing the company, really can we? Still you fly out on a trip with Bill Turner and you'll get your night-stop allowance practically intact when you return.'

Their night-stop allowance was thirty shillings a night. For a trip of twenty days this really increased the stewardesses' meagre salary of seven pounds a week, and of course whilst abroad there was no need to pay for meals.

'How about a spot of Chinese fodder?' Ben did not sound as nonchalant as possibly he had hoped.

'No thanks, I'm actually just off home for a couple of days.'

'Shame' said the tall pilot with the dark hair, and shaggy black brows, which wriggled as he talked. He looked hard at her with his dazzlingly blue eyes. 'Maybe see you around then, when you get back?'

'Yes, I expect so.' Roz spoke tenderly; poor Ben, he had such a sensitive face, round and gentle, like a puppy with such a mass of untidy hair. Roz knew he had a son, who was now thirteen years old; his eighteen-year-old wife had died giving birth to Geoff, only one year after Ben had married her.

If only he would stop wearing that gabardine, Roz thought, and make some attempt to tidy himself up.

Even so, when she set off in the taxi from her digs for the bus-station, she did not bother to change from her own uniform. She was proud to travel home wearing it. It gave her a kick. Immediately she forgot Ben.

The bus to Leeds, where she would change for Halifax, was waiting at the Yeadon bus stop as Roz arrived. She found an empty seat, the last one and she settled back. It was difficult to decide just how much to tell her father about this new way of life, but she must collect her thoughts before arriving home. However truthfully or simply she expressed herself she had no doubt that he would try to read something into her life.

Already it was going dark with the reluctant, heavy light of autumn in the dusk of a lovely September evening.

The presence of the trees with their now changing hues was very comforting. A state of Englishness; something one noticed after time abroad, the trees emphasising the protective role they play in the environment. For Roz who liked travelling it was part of the feeling of movement and change, and she was happy watching the fields and ditches pass by marrying themselves through the magnificent golden autumn colours as darkness grew; a ballet with the rhythmic sound of the wheels passing over the road.

Soon they would be in Leeds. Rural areas gave way to denser housing. Roz loved to watch people in their houses. Uncurtained windows as dusk turned to dark, some eating, an increasing number watching television, and children going to bed, but these subjects were only incidental chapters punctuating her thoughts.

She knew that in her personal world she had grown up.

The last three weeks had been a swan song to her childhood. A period in her life when the auburn-haired beauty with hazel coloured eyes had become conscious of self, had matured so quickly that she felt that life had only just begun.

Nevertheless, as the bus ran nearer to Leeds her confidence decreased. A pattern was beginning that would stay with her a lifetime were she to know this. Mercifully for Roz she did not.

How could she tell her father, and Lucinda, of her new life? There would be suspicion, non-belief in her innocence. Would her father, always acutely astute, know that her love affair was only a love affair with flying, strangely touching and almost platonic? Almost certainly after Derek they would be looking for signs of a rebound. Even if they were not deliberately questioning, they would be teasing.

She had left home sad, shy, unconfident, dwarfed by her vivacious, clever cousin, the orphan Lucinda and she was coming home now as a grown-up person.

In the dark, the contrast to the soft nights of Greece was accentuated by the grimy haze, which was now enveloping Leeds.

Roz began to wish that she had accepted Ben Smith's offer of a Chinese meal and suddenly she could not face the thought of arriving home unannounced. Far from surprising her father, Roz knew she would startle him, shatter his routine and so, once off the bus she rang from a nearby call box.

James Peters naturally assumed, at first, that his daughter was ringing from the Leeds/Bradford Airport. 'But darling! I would have met you in Leeds if you had let me know! And Rosalind love, your bed isn't made up and Jessie has gone home now.' Jessie was the housekeeper.

'Don't worry Daddy, I'll soon make it myself.'

145

'Do you want supper?' Her father's strong voice sounded plaintive. 'I've just had dinner.'

'No, I'm not very hungry. Actually, we had a huge meal in Maastricht, at teatime. Bye, must rush to catch the bus. Can you meet me in Halifax in about an hour?'

Roz was dispirited by the call. Her widowed father hated his evenings to be disturbed. She looked at her watch to find it was already ten o'clock. Working such irregular hours, she found time had little meaning. Why couldn't her father accept things without fuss? He had Jessie to keep things running smoothly.

She had been with Mr. Peters some years and was the first housekeeper not to live on the premises. When Helene Peters died, James Peters did not consider it 'proper' for Jessie to live in, especially when the girls grew up and went away; the elegant, but no one would call her pretty, Lucinda married and his dear daughter Rosalind, who was genuinely pretty, off on that flying job.

Nevertheless, he was so totally used to being waited upon that he could not accustom himself to not having servants working around the clock. People, even daughters just did not arrive at eleven o'clock at night, expecting to be put up for the night. Not in Roz's father's world, where nothing was ever anything but conventional. For a man who was a product of the first half of the century he was surprisingly straight-laced and would expect his only child to be the same.

Suddenly she remembered that she had not given Julie her standby number. She must telephone her first thing tomorrow; otherwise, she did not dare to think what would happen should she be called out for a flight.

As quickly as it was remembered it was forgotten.

Here was Halifax and the first thing she saw as she stepped off the bus was her father waiting in his pale silver green Bentley.

'Thanks Daddy, thanks a lot for meeting me,' and Roz wriggled a little to fit her back into the right place in the luxury car.

'How was the last trip then?'

'Do you mean our bus service to Maastricht and return, Maastricht and return and thereon ad infinitum? Or do you mean my last real trip, the marathon?'

'Obviously I mean Greece, little goose!' James Peters smiled kindly at his daughter. He was not tall and apart from his undoubtedly prosperous bearing the most noticeable characteristic was his rimless glasses.

'To be paid to visit such countries finally convinces me that you must be on to a good thing,' he said. 'Although don't forget I did once go to Greece myself and travelled as far as Mt. Athos.'

'It was wonderful, Daddy.' Roz had never heard of Mt. Athos and the significance of her father visiting the monastic peninsula in northern Greece before the Second World War was not going to spoil her excitement now.

'I just could not believe it all,' her tale was continuing unabated. 'Did I tell you we had a stowaway on the last flight back? It seems incredible; you know Herakleion Airport is tiny, sorry you probably don't, grass strip and all...and we had a real live stowaway. It's the last place one would think of something happening, isn't it?'

'I don't know, such things are becoming a serious hazard and shouldn't be taken too lightly, but carry on.'

'Well, I was just checking everything in the galley before take-off, when there was this knocking on the rear door. It's the only door on a Viking, but we always call it the rear door, just so the pilot remembers where it is, I suppose! The Captain was revving his engines up and he was just about to take off. I couldn't believe it! I rushed up front, we'd an empty aircraft and I told Captain Duncan not to take off! He looked so angry! He must have been poised there like a racehorse before the flag went down. I suppose I was lucky really, that he hadn't taken off and I got into the cockpit before he did so, for he wouldn't have realised I was not all strapped in. Anyway, I had an awful job getting him to believe what I was saying was true. I think he thought I was joking.' Roz remembered the fierce expression on Gerry's face as though she might be being too familiar and teasing him. Now she shuddered a little with the recollection.

'If you were not so excited, I think I would have thought you were joking!' said her father.

'Anyway, in the end,' she went on, her eyes green with the thrill of the recollection, and her reddened skin slightly flushed, 'he sent the first officer down and together we opened the door where this enormous Cretan peasant was standing. He really was enormous, most Cretans are, and he had this thick mass of hair over his head and face, black hair. He looked quite mad. Thing is had we not noticed him before the Captain swung the aircraft round, his head would probably have been sliced off by the props. This first officer gave him a hand and he jumped into the plane, whereby the joker tries to

148

make bird imitations with his hands, shouting, 'Rhodos, Rhodos, Athinai,' presumably wanting us to take him to Rhodes or Athens. We sat him down and the first officer said to me that we'd just taxi back to the terminal and find out what was going on. It was then that I saw his knife. It was awfully primitive, more like a toy knife, the kind kids play with, in Elland streets, only it had this fancy sheath, covered in blue velvet and ornately worked in silver. You know Daddy, I was quite scared!'

'Damn lucky...I'd say, more like damn lucky!'

'But the Greek police said he was quite harmless. Apparently, he had relatives in Athens and Rhodes. He was a little simple and he had once been taken on an aeroplane trip to visit them. So, every time he fancies going again, he tries to hitch a lift.'

'None of these facts you or the crew knew when you welcomed him on board,' said her father sternly. 'Do you know in America there is a new word. It is called hi-jacking. More and more gangsters are realising that they've only to board a plane and thereafter the crew is in their power, particularly with pressurised planes where one bullet through the skin will sink the thing. Just threaten the crew and they'll have to fly you to Cuba or Russia or where have you. Too damn dangerous for my liking. Never trust anyone Rosalind. You still a virgin, then?'

She thought - oh no, Daddy please don't ask me - but she said, 'Of course I am.' And it was true.

'Hm...' said her father, 'you don't look innocent anymore. Pity.'

Only her father could talk like that without giving offence. 'You've grown up young lady! Still it's a good thing to hang on to virginity, far too much promiscuity these days. Men don't respect it Roz, you know.'

The Bentley swung into the narrow entrance where the two great elms marked home. Great big trees emphasising the strength and stability of this family home. It was as if her father had planned his little talk to finish at the point where Roz was bound to experience the greatest emotion relating to her homecoming. The car continued up the long drive and at the top the headlights picked out Lucinda and Derek standing on the steps of Bankfield Hall, waiting for Rosalind: the newly-weds had been brought in to welcome her home.

The solidarity of the Calder Valley claimed her, once more.

Roz woke with the rays of early autumn sunshine reflected from the turning trees and the golden fields through the corn-coloured curtains of her room.

She realised that her father would already be away to Church.

He always worked exceptionally hard and relaxed with even more effort.

After Church, he would call at the Bridge Inn for a pint of beer before lunch, if they were beagling in the district he would have skipped Church. A self-made man perhaps, and a product of the Second World War forces, but his daughter found something nicely warm and kindly about him. Nevertheless, she understood when people told her he was very demanding in business.

Her mother had been different. Always slightly contemptuous of trades' people Helene Peters had come from Cheshire where, she told her daughter, people were well bred. Curiously Rosalind thought it was her father whose background was superior; her mother's family had only 'arrived' later in life and her mother's childhood had been one of being brought up in modest circumstances. By marrying James Peters she had done well for herself and although Rosalind's great-grandfather had himself been a well-respected Manchester financier, the rest of her mother's family had not done as well for themselves.

Roz reluctantly pushed back the warm honey-coloured blankets. A certain inbred modesty made her pull down her soft blue nightdress over her knees before she moved from the bed, although there was no one to see. Always she allowed it to ride up around her waist whilst in bed, to feel the crisp cool seduction of the sheets. Moving to the window she stood and surveyed the peaceful scene. A few cows, brown and white Ayrshires, some hedges that she knew would be thick with the brambles of the season and beyond the confines of the small estate, the endless walls, dry stone walls rolling over green dales and moors and here and there in the distance, some sheep, with greying fleeces suggesting that this county was industrialised. It was only the clever site, mixed with not a little luck that had ensured the view was not a forest of mill chimneys and pylons; a West Riding view which was in Roz's eyes was more typical than the one her parents' home, enjoyed.

The garden of the house was large and well kept, with neat lawns and growing trees. The Scots Pines and the Monkey Puzzles were nearly a hundred and fifty years old, but the house was Jacobean.

Stretching her body with her arms lifted above her head she took off her nightdress. The cool air from the window brushed over her skin.

She had a lucky figure. Gerry had called it perfect. She loved it. At twenty years old to know that you are not too thin, nor too fat, to know that the shape of your bottom and the shape of your breasts conformed; this was incredible luck! 'You neat little poppet,' Gerry had said the day they had swum at Lindos on Rhodes.

The sound of Jessie's voice disturbed Roz's daydreams.

Rapidly she dressed. A Marks and Spencer's bra and pants, her mother would have been horrified to know that she did not wear 'proper lingerie', obtained from a 'proper corsetiere,' a little X-girdle and a new pair of tights had to stand in for the rigid constructions her mother had been accustomed to wear, but even Roz did not know that within the decade even the lightweight girdle and stockings would be abandoned in favour of merely tights and pants! As it was the stockings were new, a pair bought by Julie in a marvellous new weave and shade from C & A's in Holland, and quite unobtainable in England.

Why couldn't the English manufacturers emulate these smooth silky fashions which the Dutch did so well, Roz wondered? They lasted much longer without laddering. To these preliminary garments Roz added a fine Italian sweater, which she had perversely bought in Athens, it was dark blue and went well with the lovely cream coloured skirt she had bought in Fenwick's before leaving London. Finally, with a brush through her red curls and with her shoes also from Athens, in smart navy calf, she made an appearance downstairs as the 'phone rang.

There was a strong smell of Yorkshire roast beef from Jessie's cooking, as Roz answered the 'phone.

It was Julie's voice on the other end of the line. 'Rosalind Peters, you're an idiot; you didn't give a standby number. They're going hairless in the Kremlin. I'm not well and they wanted you to night-stop in Manchester for me tonight and fly to Paris tomorrow, first thing, back to Manchester the same day. I think I've got a tummy bug from Valencia. One hell of a nuisance! Yes, I know it's daft to nightstop in Manchester when it's less than an hour's flying time from Yeadon, but it's something to do with regulations. If we were going from here, I might've felt better by tomorrow. But they want you on the spot tonight, there it is ducks, can you get yourself to Manchester tonight? You're all to kip at a hotel just outside Altrincham, I'll give you the address, I'm afraid it's all rather you than me. You're to pick up some French associates in Paris, fly onto some factory with a private strip and hang around while they all tour round.

'Oh' added Julie, 'apparently you'll have half a dozen John Bulls, V.I.Ps to ship out and back to Manchester as well. All very top drawer, so press your uniform. Sounds daft to me, but it seems they're friends of my Dad's and they want to use Ferryair particularly. That's why I was to be the hostie.' Julie Rhodes always found it difficult to be dissociated from her father, Lionel Rhodes, who was chairman of Ferryair.

'What time is E.T.D.?'

'My roster says take off 7.30 a.m. which means being at the airport by 6 a.m. for a flight like this. It will be a champagne affair you know. Anyway, now I've located you, you'd better ring Operations. Let them know you've got my message. And by the by, don't run off again love. It frightens me. Others have lost their jobs for less.'

'Well,' said her father who had come in from church as Roz was on the 'phone. 'What's all that about?' His face had a clean healthy look about it; a twinkle in his eye, not unlike Gerry's and a breath of September sunlight came in with him.

'I've got to be in Manchester,' and Roz told her father of her untimely departure. But her father merely smiled.

'How would it be if I were to take you over to Manchester, and we'll have a night out at the Midland Restaurant, the French Restaurant?'

Roz rang operations who told her that she could make her own way to the hotel, but that she was to report in good time, the eight hour no drinking rule had been doubled to sixteen on this occasion.

'Sorry Daddy, no French Restaurant, I've to be at the hotel near the airport, by seven-thirty this evening.'

During lunch, it occurred to Roz that nobody had mentioned, neither had she asked, who would be the Captain on the flight.

(iii)

Her father kept his word and drove Roz over to Cheshire, to a village hotel. He said he had business in the morning in Manchester and would stay overnight in the city.

Since her mother's family had come from the same village they parked on the green, near the church in which her father had married her mother, and after a quick look inside, walked down the steep hill to the small hotel, past the neat little cottages with thatched roofs. As they walked she thought of her parents' own lives, of her mother's ambitions and the rewards of her father's business, which she accepted as of right, and her father's worthier aims. She thought of her mother's early death. She thought of her own life.

She said, 'you've pinned too many hopes on me, haven't you Daddy? As an only child, I mean. Here I'm in a profession which is always referred to as a bloody flying waitress, working for a second-rate company come to that, no BOAC I'm afraid. That's no achievement for an only daughter, is it? Especially one who, if she had played her cards right could have been married by now to such an eligible gentleman as Derek Lean.' Her father merely grunted. 'In her way Lucinda would've suited you better, as a daughter, I mean. But you know I am happy now, much happier than I've been since Lucinda got married. You can put your mind at rest, I will be a good little girl. I promise. My only danger is that of ego, I might become very conceited. I feel so clever, being paid for visiting the world.'

'My only worry, my dear, is the one we briefly touched upon last night. Don't be persuaded by any of

155

these good-looking young men you're working with to take a risk. It isn't worth it. It just isn't worth it.'

Roz laughed. 'Really Daddy, if you were to see the crews, I doubt you would describe them as young or good-looking,' and suddenly she was a little bit ashamed of associating with these rather ordinary middle-aged men, glamourised only by the epaulets on their uniforms.

They walked onto the gravel in front of the hotel where a Volkswagen minibus, red and black in the colours of British European Airways was parked.

The acknowledgment that the crew must have arrived at the hotel disturbed Roz. She did not like stopovers with an unknown crew.

Her father pushed open the glass door of the hotel.

In the hall stood the Ferryair crew,

Ben Smith and a Captain whom Roz did not recognise.

She walked over to the two uniformed men, Ben eternally in his mackintosh and the other man also, although it was a fine night.

'Hello'' she said lightly, and Ben beamed through his glasses, his face lit with pleasure when he recognised Roz. The second man sniffed, and searched for his handkerchief; and Roz looked enquiringly towards Ben for an introduction. She was not immediately impressed with this stranger who must surely be her skipper. With no introduction forthcoming Roz moved forward to introduce her father to Ben hoping this would prompt Ben to make the other necessary introduction, but then a third uniformed figure came down the stairs.

This was a moment when Roz failed to function as human.

Ben's companion nodded. 'Be off then, Guv. Pick you up at six tomorrow morning then.' The peaked cap was of course no more than a BEA bus driver's perk. The raincoat hid the unbraided suit.

Roz faltered and introduced her father to the real Captain, who had just walked down the stairs. 'Daddy, this is Gerry...I mean Captain Duncan, and this is Mr. Smith.'

Clearly, her father was surprised. He too must have expected younger, more upstanding, tidy and good-looking men to be British pilots. Instead a rather plump little man stood before him, the ordinary build somewhat relieved by the distinctive fair hair, the sharp nose and the slightly protruding eyes. Four gold rings around his sleeves, an immaculate suit and clean shirt but although Gerry was international, the senior captain of the company, Roz realised that her captain did not look outstanding, whilst Ben was still embarrassingly wearing his shabby gabardine.

'Hallo there' Ben beamed yet again. 'The happy trio is together again.'

Roz wished her father had not come in. Gerry said. 'You leave her in good hands, Sir.' And for a moment the glance which Roz's father gave the man questioned whether he was being sarcastic. Gerry offered the older man a cigarette, pulling a packet out of his pocket, but the businessman refused. Lightly kissing his daughter on her cheek, he left.

Gerry rang the bell and an hotel assistant showed Roz to a pleasant little room overlooking the gardens and beyond the green fields that were still Cheshire. The outskirts of Manchester sprawled haphazardly west from the centre of the city, but here its black and white timbered houses interspersed with red brick cottages or yellow sandstone buildings stood out in the jumble of architecture, the village fighting for survival and miraculously conserved from the huge jaws of the suburban encompassment of circumjacent Manchester.

Thirty years ago, there could have been no threat to the green of Cheshire's heritage, there were fields where now there were neat little houses with their neater little gardens. Now it was over populated, thought Roz as she stared through the window. She was not to foresee that as the airport grew so too would the dormitory villages spread into one huge conurbation of desirable real estate: Bowdon, Hale Barns, Wilmslow, Timperley, Sale. More houses for more people, less food for more people. Spring here she suspected would be a jealous show of lilac and cherry blossom, forsythia, polyanthus, primula, bell hyacinths, daffodils and tulips. Now in the autumn, the competition was between beech and sycamore, a legacy of the fields, which the neat little gardens once were, with ageratum and antirrhinum, a legacy of endeavour.

The gong rang for dinner.

A leisurely and pleasant meal was served in the Swiss style dining room. Ben did most of the reminiscing and the two others listened.

Roz drained the dregs in her coffee cup, and Ben bemoaned the fact that their early flight forbade a nightcap.

Gerry pointed out that he had already turned a blind eye to the sixteen hours no alcohol ban, which had been imposed by the Operations department on this

158

occasion, and allowed Ben a beer or two with his meal. Both Gerry and Roz had abstained.

'Goodnight,' said Roz eventually.

'I'd like a breath of fresh air, are you coming?'

'Good idea'' said Ben immediately.

'I wasn't actually inviting you, old chap.'

'A fellow knows when he's not wanted,' and Ben left in a genuine huff.

'Oh dear,' said Gerry. I didn't mean to upset him. See what you do to us both! Come on stretch your legs, you'll be cooped up in that flying machine all tomorrow. I hope Ben hasn't been drinking at lunchtime as well, he is putting it back rather.'

They walked slowly along the road under the high walls and huge trees; in the distance, traffic lights marked the entrance to the main Chester Road.

Roz told Gerry that this was her mother's home village and pointed to the house where her mother's family had once lived, now masked by trees, the house was the one her great-great-grandfather had built in the Victorian era, a status symbol of the then upwardly mobile classes. It looked substantial, even vast and she wondered why her mother had always told tales of childhood deprivation.

'Gerry, that stowaway on the aircraft at Herakleion. I got into awful trouble from my father for having let him on board.'

'Better that we had chopped that peasant's head off with the blades?'

'He seemed to think so, yes.'

'Well for that matter, so did Lionel Rhodes.'

'But he was harmless.'

'As it turned out; but in these days of pressurized aircraft one bullet hole in the side and that's our downfall, literally. You see, young Rosalind, I nearly didn't believe you when you told me, and that too is dangerous. I thought you were playing a practical joke; it isn't every day that someone comes knocking on an aircraft outer door. And, if you're deadly earnest and I still think you are teasing, then it is time we stopped flying together.'

'Do you really think that 'hijacking' will become a serious threat? Can't the government clamp down on it?

'Dear Roz, if you thought about that and all the other dangers you'd probably get a new job tomorrow. In America, from where everything nasty comes, it is becoming big business. Governmental pressure is useless against a determined terrorist with a planeload of passengers held hostage. It is a sign of the times. In future, even if you don't do it consciously, vet your passengers. In a few years' time, hostesses will be out of date, we'll need bodyguards at our rear!'

Roz could not see Gerry's face in the dark, but she sensed its solid seriousness. Walking apart they were silent, small beings casting long shadows from the streetlights.

'You know the funny thing is,' said Gerry suddenly, 'I thought Julie Rhodes was on this flight.'

'She went sick, I was on stand-by.'

'She isn't sick...I met her going out on another flight when I left Yeadon this evening. I asked her why the swop and she said, 'Just some whim of my father's', and bustled away the way she does.'

'How very odd. Why should her father do that? He's a friend of yours, isn't he?'

'Yes, his wife is a friend of Holly's. They were at school together. One of the well-known girls' public

160

schools, but then I expect you were at one too!' It was not a question so Roz did not answer it, it seemed too silly to say, 'not that well known, like my cousin Lucinda's school,' it was just another area where she felt inferior to Lucinda, and Gerry knew nothing of Lucinda. Lucinda with the huge teeth and protruding upper lip but in all other aspects perfect. Miaow.

'In fact, it was my wife's friendship with Lionel's wife which brought us back from Cyprus and the Middle East to work for Ferryair. Lionel was expanding his company and he needed a chief pilot. It sounded attractive at the time and Holly hated being abroad and shed no tears when I accepted Lionel's offer. But it has now become obvious that Ferryair cannot expand without a bigger runway at Yeadon, and that the boundaries of the road make the perimeter too stringent for much runway expansion so luxury Viscounts and worn-out Vikings seconded from some Middle-Eastern sheik are really no real exchange for the Britannias and Comets which I'd be flying now, had I stayed abroad.'

'So Mr. Rhodes rather misled you?'

'You could say that, but it was my own fault. Holly wasn't happy abroad and I hoped it would please her. I hoped we might have children if we came back to England.'

'Would you like children?'

'Very much. A marriage is nothing without a child.'

'And there is Ben, with a son, envying you for having a wife!'

'Yes, but that's not quite the same thing, poor Ben.'

They arrived back at the hotel, to find the front door had been bolted.

'That was a longer walk than I intended,' said Gerry looking uneasy as the manager let them in. It was a quarter to eleven, and they said goodnight and went to their separate bedrooms.

In Roz's room, on her bed, lay Ben, fast asleep with a half bottle of Scotch standing half empty on the table. No glass, just the open bottle.

'Come on Ben! For Christ's sake get up. I want to go to sleep.'

''Lo there, Roz. Come to bed.'

'Do get up and go back to your own room, Ben. Hurry up, they will hear us.' It was not a big hotel and Roz was frightened any disturbance would be heard over the whole building.

'Ssh, love,' said Ben loudly, sitting on the bed, the dimple in his chin was prominent and he winked at Roz. His eyes were full of small boyish mischief. Roz felt terribly sorry for him.

'Come to bed with me, there's a girl,' and Ben began to sing the song, the 'Lily of Laguna.'

She put the top on his Scotch and handed it to him. 'Get out please, Ben. I like you, but I do hate you when you're drunk.'

At this point, there was a knock on the door.

'This is a quiet hotel Madam. Can you and your friend keep your voices down.' Hypocrites, Roz thought, she was sure they were the only guests in the hotel.

Ben started to giggle and he attempted to kiss Roz. She ducked and his face fell into the eiderdown where he promptly fell asleep, if he were as drunk as that Roz thought he might be sick; she decided to enlist Gerry's assistance.

When she arrived back in her room with Gerry, Ben had left.

'You great goon, Roz. I see love and wistfulness and then great happiness...Oh, Roz! I do love you so!' The man was wearing a burgundy wool dressing gown, with his hands resting on the girl's shoulders he stared straight into her pensive hazel eyes. He picked a rust coloured curling hair from the girl's shoulder and dropped it to the ground.

'Sshus, Gerry.

'Can we, I wonder Roz, if we can, in the full knowledge that we've both thought about it, about what we are doing, knowing that we love each other...'

Gerry was inviting her to do the very thing that previously they had sworn they would never do, which only hours before she had promised her father that she would not do. She had no words, but her eyes spoke with a sad acknowledgment of fate.

'Knowing that if we don't do it tonight, then we shall probably do so at some weaker moment and not appreciate it.

'Yes,' said Roz.

She was trembling.

'Say to yourself Roz, that you love me and that you trust me. I shan't harm you...nor will I allow any harm to come to you.'

Outside the world lived.

Within Roz, a revolution slowly travelled around and through her body; wound her up like a spring and reaching far down into her fingers and toes undulating, and oscillating back through every nerve in her body with fearful determination.

Gerry took every precaution not to harm her. He took every care to extend her whole being in an extended

163

moment in time, which she knew she would always remember.

And outside Cheshire put out the lights and went to sleep.

Suddenly Gerry hesitated.

'I love you too much - I can't go on. I mustn't. I love you too much to make you pregnant. Even with precautions the risk is too great. I only intended this to be for you.'

There was a footstep outside the door.

Roz tightened and froze. She felt the result of her involuntary movement. Quietly Gerry trembled and Roz hugged him. Every bit of her body experienced the gift Gerry had given her, they lay silent and still, together.

Eventually, Gerry spoke. 'I spoilt it for you.'

But in the stillness, the warmth and peace of his happiness she felt no sense of loss. She was terribly happy.

There was another single footstep.

Someone had been listening.

Gerry shook himself and rose from the bed, throwing on his dressing gown. He kissed Roz. The footstep passed.

'Love you, I do really…always remember that, dear Roz.'

Gerald Duncan left the stewardess's room.

As she lay the warmth continued to caress her body and a feeling of wellbeing surpassed her guilt. She felt marvellous.

The Ferryair crew arrived at the airport at six-thirty a.m.

By seven-thirty the 'plane was ready and fifteen smart city gentlemen looking particularly British were led out to the aircraft, complete with briefcases and bowler hats. Roz wanted to laugh at their image of correct attire for a jaunt to a factory in Provincial France; only one man at the head of the procession was dressed in a brown sports suit.

The man at the head of this procession, Roz realised, as they grew closer was her father.

'I thought I would surprise you, Miss Peters,' and he laughed. 'Laid on this little surprise for you with my old friend Lionel Rhodes.'

Roz blushed.

She went quite scarlet. That was her colouring, the red skin and auburn hair made her blush.

A scarlet woman in fact.

Miss Peters seemed a misnomer, now a Mistress; the father had met his deflowered daughter for the first time.

Roz remembered the look of the hotel staff, those that were around at six in the morning as they had eaten breakfast from a table laid the previous evening, and grudgingly had been given a pot of tea to go with the cereals, the rolls, butter and marmalade, and the milk which had stood out overnight, although covered with a small cloth doily weighed down with blue beads around the edge.

One's misdeeds were broadcasted remarkably easily or was it Roz, in her guilt, imagining things too freely,

A further shame rushed over Roz.

The job; it wasn't given to Roz on merit. Obviously.

Her father clearly had known Lionel Rhodes; and clearly, he had engineered her recruitment to Ferryair after she had told him of her application following the advertisement in the press, how shameful! He had made sure she would be on this flight.

Momentarily Roz hated him. But he, her father appeared not to notice her blushes or discomfort and passed into the cabin, laughing and congratulating himself on his amusing knavery. His little deception had been a success. How proud his daughter would be of him!

But Roz knew now why she had got the job so young.

SIX: MURPHY'S LAW

May 1972

(i)

In May, there had been a training course for the staff journalists and Rosalind and the kids had joined her husband for the four-day seminar at Coylumbridge, along with the families of the staff journalists, who like Rosalind were paying for the privilege. "Even a thriving paper such as ours has a limit on 'freebees'," had said the editor when she grumbled at the cost.

They all enjoyed that and they did a little spring skiing and the children charged around the Aviemore Centre, knocking down delegates and holidaymakers with the lethal battery-operated kiddie cars, a kind of skidoo for juniors.

There was something about the Spey Valley air, the size of the mountains, rising so abruptly from the plains and forests that completely overtook Rosalind, revitalising her as never before and they had booked a small house for a private visit in October when they could stay longer and appreciate the autumn colours. Rosalind then brought the children home, the families of the staff journalists left, leaving the editor to complete his business, a week's training course in Glasgow with the journalists.

But he returned home a week later, out of sorts. Rosalind did not pick up his mood immediately; she had

had a troubled week with the children, mostly caused by the unseasonable weather. There had never been a May as bad as this in England. Every day it poured and the wind blew. The children were waiting to put on their summer clothes and take off their Chilprufe vests.

In contrast to Rosalind, her husband was always a fairly placid person, although when things went wrong, he was prone to sudden bursts of anger, and when he poured himself an exceptionally large gin, before sitting in his favourite armchair Rosalind knew something was wrong. He usually drank very little.

His eyes were huge, his face, generally smiling, was stern and his acute lack of hair made him look more middle-aged than he should be.

'I know you expressed doubts Rosalind at the time I decided on the Scottish trip,' he confided stroking his baldhead. 'There was only one day in the whole week when we weren't working flat out. The new technology which the lads were studying had its practical side too, and every minute of the time in Glasgow was spent either in newspaper offices, case-rooms or the lecture halls. Everything on paper was going for it.'

He explained to his wife, 'Perhaps it was the hotel we were using for that final weekend was too remote, well away from any town let alone a city. Six thousand acres of moorland together with a golf course surrounded the house and perhaps predictably a kilted laird who in the guise of hotelkeeper lived up to his reputation for hospitality. It was a man's pub, a drinker's pub, and after the week's work on Saturday they all played a round of golf and some of the men spent much of the afternoon fishing. It was a beautiful May day with which Scotland can sometimes surprise her visitors. The

168

sky was as blue as the Mediterranean and there was not a cloud to be seen.

'It wasn't until later in the evening that I smelt trouble,' he told Roz. 'Four of the men, with the laird, were sitting in the smallest wooden bar room, carelessly arranged to remind one of a ski-holler with pictures of Glenshee, a pair of wooden skis with ancient bindings and a pair of equally ancient ski sticks. You know the thing! To belie the Alpine image there were also a few tartans thrown in. The Canadian born barman had put on an old tape, which was issuing forth the whine of bagpipes.'

'Sounds fairly standard stuff,' said Rosalind a bit bored by the long-winded tale, if she was truthful, always a fault of her slightly pedantic husband.

'Throughout I was becomingly ill at ease. Something was going on between the men and I couldn't place it, it was uncanny. I felt uncomfortable for a reason I couldn't explain. They'd excuse themselves at regular and rather too short intervals and would disappear upstairs one at a time. I retired to bed at about one o'clock. I felt they were being particularly anti-social and I was peeved that the company had paid out for this trip at my instigation.

'About half an hour later, and as I was dozing fitfully, I was startled by a commotion on the stairs just outside my room. There was a copper gong outside it and someone had knocked it over.'

He paused and got himself another drink before continuing. He told his wife that immediately he had opened the bedroom door he knew why he had been so disturbed in the bar. It was pot. The men were smoking pot. The smell in the corridor hit him.

The three journalists were on the floor. Two of them were attempting to lift the third pressman into his room. The third, Tom Morton, was rigid.

'I'm dying,' he said mournfully, scarcely audible. He was completely stiff; he could not even unclench his hands. The other two men looked as white as ghosts. Between them they carried the ossified, inflexible Morton into his room, which was opposite the editor's. Here they put him into the large rosewood bed and stood anxiously around.

'Well, it's obvious what you three have been up to!'

'He's just tight, Boss. You know Tom, always did get drunk a bit quicker than anyone else.'

'He might be high, but you needn't kid me. He isn't high on alcohol. I can smell the stuff. What do you think I am? Green, a schoolboy; of course, I know what you've all been up to. What the hell do I tell your wives?'

'It's like this, really it is perfectly harmless. I can't understand it. But nobody gets a bad trip like this, but no one, not on marijuana. He must've taken some drugs as well.'

'Of course, he has. I know that. He has been on tranquillisers for weeks, since the libel case with Lewisons.' It was the second man who spoke.

'Heavens above!' the bald man had exclaimed. 'And he's been drinking, don't you chaps know any elementary rules about pot. Never mix it, even better, never smoke it. Ye Gods!'

'Why didn't someone say so? I didn't know...why the hell didn't you tell me that, Jack?' asked the first man.

'You knew, if you thought hard enough. Anyway, the stupid fool should've realised himself. Probably thought you'd call him a sissy! You did have that look about you, when you first suggested we tried it out.'

'The whole thing is absurd,' the editor recriminated. 'You've behaved like teenagers and you might lose this pub its licence if anyone finds out. I know you think the place is in the wilds of Scotland but that doesn't put you above the law, you know.'

Tom Morton chose that moment to be sick. In the ensuing chaos, the senior man had lost his temper. He fired all three of them.

When Rosalind's husband arrived home he had to explain to his Chairman how he had taken his three best journalists on a seminar and fired them at the end of it.

December 1960

(ii)

It was the last week in December and three days after Christmas, Roz was in Tangier, sitting in a dark bar often frequented by aircrew and run by an Englishman called Roger who always wore an old Oundelian tie.

She was listening to Captain Smith, who was immensely proud of his shining new rings adorning his uniform sleeves, discussing the large Bull Mastiff, which lay at Roger's feet. Roger was three or four times the size of his dog in height and width respectively. The dog was the largest Roz had ever seen.

The wood panelled bar, in comparison, was small. There were six high stools along the bar and either you sat on these or stayed outside, where in summer trade was done as a pavement café, for when the six seats were occupied the house was full. The bar, in fact, had been tailored, perhaps a size too tight, for the sandy-haired proprietor and his dog. Both wore a fixed expression of content and the master never spoke about more important matters than his dog, or the weather, or to discuss the cordial situation in Tangier where lime-juice had become particularly difficult to obtain except on the black market.

Roger was noticeably not interested in England or her affairs. It was a bar peopled by a species common in Tangier in the sixties and if it was to be run by an ex-patriot Englishman then Roger was as expected.

Both the bar and Roger were a hangover from the days when Tangier was a freeport; when everyone had something to hide and discretion was paramount to social discourse. Roz suspected that Roger had nothing to hide, but liked to pretend that he had.

It was the fourth day of the trip, they had flown out on Christmas Eve and the cool bar was the only place to logically encamp during the warmth of midday. They had spent most of these off-duty days there, including Christmas Day. What else would an aircrew without friends and family do to occupy their time?

The other pilot in the crew was called George, which was unfortunate and although he was obviously nicknamed 'the Automatic Pilot', nothing could label him more accurately. Every movement he made was thorough and deliberated. His first decision was always his final one. In the four days Roz had known him she had never known him change his mind or make a mistake. Since he rarely spoke – no doubt for fear of being in error – both Roz and her new Captain found him tedious and boring and did their best to avoid his company.

It was significant that Ferryair had rostered an unmarried crew out at the festive season but Roz felt it was an unfortunate combination and Christmas had been a disappointing occasion.

Although Ben was supposedly drinking less since being made up to Captain, at this season his festivities seemed to consist purely of getting drunk and George's merely of going into deep thought. She formed the habit, when Ben failed to hold her attention of staring at the Automatic Pilot right through the long coarse eyelashes to the brown eyes caged behind. It was often minutes before she realised the rudeness of her gestures for the eyes never flickered.

Now sitting in Roger's bar, Roz was passing the time staring at the Automatic Pilot imagining the beautiful shape of the swimming pool at the Rif Hotel in the pilot's glassy eyes, trying to blot out the less than desirable situation she found herself in this Christmas. Ben's loud voice enunciated details about mastiffs between gulps of Cuba Libra. What a way to spend Christmas!

On four successive evenings in his paralytic state, Ben had proposed to Roz.

Last night she thought he had, at last, received and understood her negative response.

A hand moved from a slightly lower direction than the brown cadaverous eyes and rested heavily over Roz's hand, which was on the bar. She blushed and tried to move her fingers without success.

'Don't worry my dear,' said the voice quietly but thickly and stiff from a European accent. 'You're always looking at me; beautifully you stare so I know what it is you want. You want me and we can arrange it. You see these eyes of mine, I know they've not the expression; the one is of glass and the other is trained to stay with it. I trained it still. In this way, I don't betray the handicap I have.' George uttered in far from perfect English but too quietly to attract the other occupants of the bar. He was a Pole now nationalized as a British subject.

Roz shuddered. It was a pity he awoke such feelings of disgust in her. She was aware of the courageous work the Poles had achieved for the Allies in the war.

The Pole continued to speak, 'You see my dear, your eyes, now they are beautiful, very beautiful and green and they express everything and so I know you desire it, as I would like you to appreciate me. It will be arranged.'

Roz was tempted to retort aloud, but she controlled her indignation.

What did these pilots think she was? A call girl or something?

Nevertheless, she realised that this lean objectionable man with his dirty moustache was not entirely inhuman, he had natural human responses, but on this occasion, he had made a mistake, chosen unwisely.

She muttered the fact to herself – 'It might be your first mistake, but by Georgy Pole you've made one.' She wondered if the man had hair on the palms of his hand or perhaps it was just the beads of sweat from the hand which had covered hers, which made the back of her hand tickle. She did not dare to look.

The situation was becoming intolerable for the man smiled more and his moustache became moist with the continual licking of his lips. Why did men lick their lips when they were sexually hungry? It put most girls off.

Rather than being of assistance, Ben was also an increasing problem.

Roz could see George give Ben a sideways glance, not convinced that Ben was drunk enough yet to present an excuse for George to have to escort Roz back to the hotel. On the other hand, she was sure that Ben had drunk far too much to notice, even if George were to drag her screaming from the teak-panelled bar, far less to care.

She pushed a stray auburn strand of hair behind her ear and thought vaguely that it must be washed.

This was her answer to the problem. Before she had even formed the words of her excuse she slid from the red Moroccan leather stool and announced. 'I've an appointment with the hairdresser at three.'

'He is closed from one o'clock to six. The siesta hour in Tangier.' Roger said it pleasantly enough but Roz could have murdered him.

She glared at Roger. 'No, he has promised to stay open for me. Because of New Year, they rang from the Hotel you know.'

The hurried untruth did not convince anyone and George said nasally and nastily, 'Let Ben pay for this round, Roger. I'll have to walk this young lady to her destination; not a safe place, this Tangier, you know. It's not safe for the fair sex.

'Your English is terrible, George,' Roz said rudely. 'I'm going to spend a penny.'

'Upstairs,' said Roger, pointing to two steps, which led into a larger room. In the gloom and dark Roz could just make out a staircase. These led to a veranda which overlooked the bar below, but there was no sign of her own needed ladies room and anyway she did not really want to go. She counted to thirty slowly as an estimation of the time it would take and prayed to Gerry that something would save her from this evil plot. She desperately needed Gerry now. She had not seen him for months.

On the half landing on the way downstairs, she found the little room she had lost.

She came back into the bar as the native boy was coming from the street. He made very little movement as he parted the raffia which hung over the door and it immediately returned to its place without swinging.

Almost immediately the strands were parted again, this time with more definition and with a certain importance. A man came into the bar, hesitated whilst

176

his eyes adjusted to the dim light and allowed the Arab boy to move into the back room so that the intruder could pass to the only spare stool. He asked for a Cuba Libra in hesitant French.

Roger grinned. 'Why my old pal, if it isn't you, you ole son of a gun. It's six months since you've been in here!' There was a silence in the room, which had been silent anyway before the man had entered. Only this silence was noticeable.

The man acknowledged his fellow colleagues quietly.

He did not order drinks all round although George and Roz were clearly without. He might have been expected.

'Ben,' said the stranger, 'nice to see you and congratulations Skipper, haven't seen you since you got your stripes. They told me at Bordeaux that there was another Ferryair plane ahead of us. Didn't see her though. Funny, small field, thought you wouldn't be able to hide her.'

'No, you wouldn't.' Ben had woken from his stupor and the reminder of his rank seemed to allow him to talk without a drunken slur. 'We're doing this new schedule, where we slip crews. Mosey Marsden has the kite somewhere between here and Lagos.'

'Hmm, that's interesting, thought they wouldn't let you take a Viking around these parts any longer. Something to do with landing in hot weather, isn't it? New rule?'

'Yep, but we're freighting down to West Africa and then only pax up from Gib after the New Year. I suppose you're going to tell me that you are now only on the Viscounts?'

'Something like that, a New Year cruise; all luxury destinations, next stop Malta, then Cairo and then Jerusalem!'

'Well that is what they called our package, Lisbon and then Tangier; that is why we've been graced by young Roz's company. You remember Roz Peters, don't you? From the autumn trips?'

'Of course, hallo Roz!' and Gerry smiled in Roz's direction and the excitement which had been mounting inside her, exploded with a return smile. This is why she had not seen him for many weeks; he had been upgraded to the larger aircraft.

'Actually, very glad to see you all, we came through some filthy weather and at Bordeaux they were saying a kite had difficulty lifting over the Pyrenees near Tarbes and had to divert on one engine. Hate that area with all those gorges and moguls. And when we didn't see the plane on the apron thought it must have been Ferryair. Operations are reporting a spate of US and night-stops recently. Ops get very twitchy when kites go US.'

'We've been here four days,' slurred Ben proudly and Gerry looked at him critically.

The Polish pilot George scratched at the turn-up of his left trouser with the sole of his shoe. 'Captain Duncan, it is a long time since the meeting we had, you perhaps not now remember the exciting time we had together in Germany. Perhaps you prefer to forget?'

Gerry looked perplexed but noticing the glassy stare involuntarily his hands dropped to his knees and his feet to the ground, but he remained seated. 'I'd forgotten and I'm sorry I've forgotten your name also.' He sounded genuinely apologetic, still trying to place quite how he knew the man, where he had met him, and that being obvious it made George's curt reply sound sharp and rude.

'George. George Kenyon. Like you I've forgotten my name. My other name, I have forgotten it. Gone.' And immediately after this, he said. 'Come.' The Pole grabbed Roz's hand. 'You're going to the hairdresser, aren't you? Or have you forgotten that? I will walk with you because, as our friend says, he will be closed and then you will be at, at a loosen end, as the English say, for the rest of the afternoon.'

Gerry had never understood a situation more clearly or so quickly before. He obviously realised the Pole's intention, every bit of terror the invitation held for Roz was registered in her petrified green eyes.

But it was actually Roz who saved the situation.

Calmly and she by no means felt calm, she worked out her strategy.

Gerry had answered her prayer, miraculously and she must use it.

'No George, most kind of you, but I want to go back to the hotel first, to change. You see, this dress only comes off over my head and to have my hair done and then to take off the dress would spoil my new coiffeur.' She laughed to make the excuse sound feminine.

'We'll have another round,' said Gerry. 'I fear the lady is giving you the brush off, as we Anglo-Saxons say. Ladies prefer to have their hair done, knowing that the menfolk are enjoying themselves and not hanging around waiting for them. A man waiting for a girl makes her impatient you see and this impatience is relayed to the hairdresser who in turn does an inferior job.'

Only Ben laughed, because Ben was insensible to the drama.

179

Roger's last seven years work had taught him a most persuading tact, which rarely failed. He was already pouring out the drinks. 'Better still,' he said. 'Have this one of me. I haven't seen my old pal Gerry for many a moon.' George, Roger sensed, had never refused a free drink in his life.

He was right. Roger admired no one, he merely observed.

'I had no idea you were employed by Ferryair,' said Gerry when George toasted his host. A free drink was more important than a lay.

'I'm not, you know. Freelance work mainly you know.'

Roz left the bar.

She walked past the hairdresser and noticed that it was indeed very shut. She gave an expansive glance in the window of the shop next door. The shop sold Moroccan leather poufs, camel saddles and Moroccan rugs and precious little else. It advertised on the plate glass door that the assistants spoke French and American. There was no mention of English. Naturally, all the goods were expensive. Her memory was keen and she recognised the goods as being twice as expensive as the replicas they had seen yesterday in the Kashbar.

She walked from the seafront where the trains ran beside the Palm trees along the Avenue d'Espagne to the main shopping area. Here the smart shops kept good supplies of Western commodities and here the town looked prosperous and clean. But from here she could also look down on the dirt of the harbour and the vacant area of sinking soft sand, which the sea never appeared to wash. Turning slightly west she could see the muddle of white plastered mud walls and corrugated brown roofs set closely together in a lump, like mosaic made from broken pots and where the conglomeration was most intense it looked like the scattered contents of a rubbish bin.

This was the Kashbar and it annoyed Roz that this area of native poverty and a stinking and crude way of life had been deliberately fostered with the idea of attracting tourists. Nothing too nasty, just a perpetuation of nineteenth-century mores in the twentieth century.

Here every visitor exchanged gold for bargains bartered for over cups of unclean mint tea. Years later drinking herbal mint tea, fashionable in the nineties would remind Rosalind of this day. She never chose to drink it for preference.

No doubt the prosperity of the Kashbar was due to the tourist, the marriage of the travel operator with the cunning Arab. Certainly, it did not strike Roz as a genuine Arab market.

It was a ghetto, inasmuch as it made the outsider feel like a trespasser. How ungratefully she had reacted to the friendly Arabs who piled their goods and hospitality upon them yesterday, allowing them to remain all morning in their shops if they had wished. How strange that the colourful scene should not have impressed her more.

Her body still felt warm and happy with the satisfaction of seeing Gerry unexpectedly. How small this world really was! The airways of the world could bring the Ferryair community as close as living in the same neighbourhood.

Roz returned to the hotel and collected her key from the receptionist. She was rather tired but supposed that she must attempt to wash her own hair and set it in the style of a professional dresser. First, she thought she would sleep. Perhaps she would have dinner with Gerry.

She wondered who his crew might be.

Perhaps he would call her. She had only seen him once since Manchester. She wondered where the Pole had met Gerry before. Neither man had seemed overjoyed to see the other one. The room was warm; she took off her clothes and put on her dressing gown.

At four o'clock the 'phone rang.

Her heart jumped and she answered it with the sure knowledge that this would be Gerry.

It had been three months since she had seen him and so often she had wondered at the magnificence of the evening in Cheshire. She had wished to see him often. She needed him. But pride and respect for his own family life had prevented her from seeking him out.

Gerry did not know she would be in Tangier; she wondered if he was as excited as she was. Did he know how desperately she now needed him?

'Hallo.' She whispered trying not to sound too provocative as she picked up the ringing receiver.

'I thought it would be alright,' a voice spoke. 'The hairdresser was shut, eh?' A flood of disappointment surged through her veins. She would give this Polish pilot short change.

'Good job, you know,' George continued. 'Now we need you. Ben's had a bit of an accident. Have you your little first aid box that you must carry round with you?'

'What's the matter?'

'Nothing serious, can you bring the box to my room, we need it quickly.' Roz heard him sniff over the 'phone. 'Hurry, won't you?'

Still clad only in her dressing gown and slippers, Roz shut her door and carrying her little emergency kit she hurried towards the elevator and in minutes was knocking at George's door. He opened it, smiled weakly and let her in, closing the door behind her. He locked the door and put the key in his pocket.

'Where's Ben?' There was a note of panic in Roz's voice.

'Now then Miss Peters, don't tell me that invited to a Captain's room you haven't been before?'

Roz said more assuredly than she felt, 'Come on George. Let me go. I'm not your girl. I'm not the type. Please.'

'Oh no?' and as quick as a flash the Pole caught her ankles and the small of her back and threw her down in the wide armchair.

He forced his mouth over hers. The moustache scratched and smelt stale, tobacco and rum. The brown eyes stared. She could not scream. He put his arm heavily over her precious tummy. He pinned her legs with his body. His brown eyes went on staring.

Worse her body responded. The same warm feeling she had experienced loving Gerry flashed momentarily through her and she could not move.

She knew she could not resist his strength; why couldn't she scream? She tried and as the moustache caught her teeth she felt she would be sick as the man forced his tongue into her open mouth. His hand was surprisingly gentle. Her body was enormously excited but she hated the man. Her body seemed to be acting independently of her mind. Suddenly the force he was exerting on her body, pinning her down hurt and she tried to kick out. He was ready for it and with the full force of one arm and the rest of his body pinned her against the chair.

Now terrified, no longer excited, she closed her eyes, and waited for the inevitable.

But the strong man put his hand on her stomach and gently kneaded it and pressed it. Alarm and terror showed in her eyes. But suddenly he lifted his body off the girl but still pinning her down with one strong arm across her body, the other stroking her stomach.

The first aid box had arrived with her in the chair. The man shifted his position and sat down on her lap with her hands pinned underneath and although she tried to struggle she could not move.

He took a handkerchief, mercifully clean from his sleeve and forced it into her mouth. Surprisingly she found that she could not even spit the gag out.

Then from the box, he took the bandages and completed the gag and tied her hands and ankles. He tied them very tightly but they were not too uncomfortable.

The pale blue dressing gown had fallen apart at the centre fastening as the man evil in his intent, fondled her stomach and Roz was frantic to close it but quite unable to do so since her hands were tied. He began caressing her stomach again and the inside of her stomach moved.

'You're pregnant,' he said suddenly. 'Nod your head if you are pregnant.' He seemed ecstatic.

She tried to remain still. Her eyes gave no expression, save that of terror.

'If you don't tell me, if you do not admit it, I shall attempt to abort you. I am very good at this. Would you like that? Sometimes pain is exciting…pain for women is very exciting. Women are lucky. You are lucky.'

The man was crazy. Anything rather than this. She would rather he raped her.

Of course, she had been hoping for a miscarriage, a natural abortion, but in any way but this way. For Gerry's child to die in this way. Suddenly she knew she must save Gerry's child. Her child. She must bear Gerry's child. She loved Gerry.

She tried to say it aloud, but no words came, of course. She nodded her head. Yes, she was pregnant.

The man stood up. She found from the position he had tied her and laid her back on the chair that she could not move. He stood in front of her and looked at her and still the brown eyes did not move. He knelt and began to kiss her naked stomach. Gently and lovingly.

'I adore pregnant women. In me it turns on the animal. You wonderful, beautiful bitch,' he said quietly. 'Whose child is it? Which foul lecherous husband by you has been corrupted? You whore... you girls have your own lover never, from another woman you must steal, the husband...or perhaps you've not. Perhaps it is the poor simple Captain Smith who follows you with dog-like devotion, around. He told me about that last summer on a long summer trip you were together. Greece. A romantic land eh? Clever, silly, little, bitch. You! An animal, female, little, about to experience pain, one of the most excruciating, satisfying pains of nature. A suffering and a pleasure which to the male, is denied, you know! Never can women be equal, you know, not to men. The women, they are smaller. A simple fact, but the truth it is. Because frail they are, they can suffer. Men a lifetime, spend, trying to equal the suffering of women. Fighting, warring, living dangerously, always hoping for the suffering that will make them equal to the woman. You know? Suffering a pleasure that only through torture that men can know; readily available to woman in child, either by the birth or by the abortion. Which way shall we give you the pleasure, my little sow?'

His gentle mood vanished and the one eye flashed. An emotion had got the better of him. Now Roz was terribly afraid. The situation was unreal. The man was mad, crazy, disturbed.

Suddenly the neat black briefcase, which she had often noticed throughout this trip, first in the cockpit and now on the table, seemed sinister. Always locked, always polished. He got up and crossed to this case. It was like a doctor's case. He unlocked it. Perhaps he had the instruments with him...what were the correct instruments? She thought a knitting needle would do. Girls in the post Second World War period, spoke in hushed tones of the perils of abortion, their mothers cautioned against sex before marriage, virginity was stressed. The growing liberal attitude was rarely openly discussed and some mothers still found it difficult or impossible to discuss sex, either before or after marriage with their daughters.

Would it hurt? Of course, it would. She remembered how she had heard or read of girls dying in the pain of amateur abortions. She remembered the period pains she sometimes had, it was difficult to imagine one ten times worse.

If she fainted now, she thought she was about to do so, perhaps it would serve as an anaesthetic.

'You're pregnant,' said the Pole again and opened the case with a key. 'You unlucky woman.'

Roz tried to move and realised that the bandages securing her wrists behind her back had been cleverly attached to the feet of the chair.

'You're completely in my power,' he said sensing her urge to move and free herself. 'You cannot help but comply with the wishes I have.'

186

He moved towards her carrying the unlocked and opened the black case. He put the case down and grabbed one knee in each hand. He parted her legs, stretching them far apart, but the bandages around her ankles, tying them together, made the position wholly unnatural and uncomfortable.

He put his hand in his case and brought from it a small leather-bound volume. 'You read my manuscript. Now. Aloud. If you tell anyone about this manuscript, ever, I, the world, shall tell that you are pregnant. I, the world, shall tell it is my child. I, it, the child, shall claim. This will be my child,' his voice always squeaky rose in a triumphant crescendo as he struggled with the English language and finally achieved a short sentence with the correct grammar.

Roz defiantly closed her legs. He seemed not to realise that no one would possibly believe it was his child, since she had only met him four days ago. A sudden hysteria made her want to laugh and she could not for the gag, but the glint showed in her eyes.

He saw her eyes and he grabbed her breasts and squeezed them hard. His hands returned to the closed knees.

'You want the abortion, then? You sit how I say.'

Again, he opened the legs, this time hurting her as he forced them apart. Her terror returned. She was petrified. She couldn't shake her head and in her absolute fright she began to cry.

Tears welled up in her hazel eyes, brown now not green, for the pain of it and for the indignity. She thought of her deceased mother Helene, the formidable, upstanding wife of James Peters, correct in every social etiquette. How she wouldn't have believed her daughter could be in this position.

A product and child herself of the First World War era, Roz's mother's own upbringing had taken her into the roaring twenties when relaxed morals still abided by strict rules. When these partying young people became parents themselves during and soon after the Second World War it was as though they brought back the values and morals like those of their grandparents, products of the Victorian and Edwardian eras. Upper middle class was a social position which these upright British citizens took seriously. Many started married lives with maids or nannies to look after household duties, children enjoyed private educations, the cars on the roads were mainly the property of these families; and fifteen years after the end of the second world war not much had changed in their expectations.

Roz had found herself in a despicable and unspeakable position, and in this the Pole's own confidence that she would not speak of this outside this room, had some foundation. This kind of thing did not happen to nice girls.

Strangely he produced another handkerchief from his pocket and wiped the tears from her eyes. He undid the bandage around her right-hand wrist and he removed the gag. He handed her the book and she began to read the volume aloud as commanded. She felt cold and naked sitting in her strange position and very vulnerable.

The book was about the size of a diary but the pages did not have dates.

They were numbered in Roman numerals. It was old. Only a few pages seemed to have been written on, in beautifully formed script. She realised it would not take her long.

It began:

'MEMORIES OF A WARSAW GHETTO' she read aloud. (How strange she thought, that she should have linked the Kashbar with a ghetto, only that afternoon.)
It went on:
'People breeding. I hate it and wherever I am reminded that one of each sex brought together makes another of either sex, I want to exterminate the whole of one sex. It is immaterial which sex. Illogically now, since from the camp, I am liberated, where the whole process disgusted me, I have the pleasure to take thirty girls. It is, I mean, that I have had the thirty girls to enjoy. I am happy to give them a little masterfulness. It is this that pleases me. Perhaps I have served the girls well?'

Roz turned the page, it was blank, but the page following was written in the same ink …
'I am not a jew…;' (written with a small j) 'like my Wife;' (written with a capital W) 'and it is not that I am the Nazi. I believe in the manufacture of people in the way other people they keep the stud farms or breed the pedigree stock. This theory is the same as the one of my Jailer at the Castle. His mind I had the pleasure of Analysing. So, with Hitler I sympathise on the morning of the Big Plan. My Big Plan. This is the day that the essential ingredients I mixed together into the Big Plan of Escape; three englishmen for who I will also make escape possible have promised me refuge in England. For us the War will finish. Now I am liberated. I am

seeking the solicitor of the englishmen in London, on my arrival there. It is a solution to my Home Problem.'

Roz turned another page. *'I need not return to Poland. The englishmen will not know that murdered the jew, my Wife, I have. That I supply the Gestapo with a chronicle of my relatives, all jewish, to save the pure Polish blood of myself. For two years the Germans they suck my blood and then one night they burst open the door of my Warsaw flat. Fine and prosperous was my flat. In this fight they have the success of sticking a bayonet through my left brown eye. My Arian eye.'*

Another blank page. Roz realised it was a confession.

'The english prisoners,' she read, her clear voice still trembling with fear and emotion. *'They know and the free englishmen so they will know when I arrive in England that the Gestapo have brought me to the prison. There they interrogated and tortured me through the healing of my left eye.'*

Roz hesitated, looking for further entries to read in the journal.

The Polish officer put his hands on her knees. *'Read on,'* he said roughly spreading her knees apart again and lifting her dressing gown up around her thighs. She dared not move and found another page of the neat copper plate writing of a generation that had not the use of typewriters.

'Read clearly' the man commanded.

'I am free. I am naturalised. I now speak the english language well and I write it clearly.' A date, or what appeared to be a date had been crossed out in ballpoint biro, as opposed to the blue ink of the rest of the entry. Roz could not read the date. She thought of her father, the forceful businessman of conviction,

190

intelligent, who always knew how to get out of a difficult situation. Like any daughter, she trusted her father to solve life's problems.

'Read it girl!' His hand moved menacingly from her knee towards one of her inner thighs as he stretched them wider. Crying again, she sobbed through the text.

'The new guard is known to me...Karol Androzj; since the days of being a student in Bonn. Three englishmen they trust me and we can formulate the escape. The night before escape, me, I, Karol Androzj cannot sleep. My one eye is focused on six sleeping eyes of the Royal Air Force. I love my Wife. I loved Her. I had to kill Her. I love to fly. I loved to fly. They killed my skill. I am the son of Kosciuszko. I did possess in Warsaw, a private plane, one of the few. The war come and later the Germans come and occupy my town. My father in America, stayed, where he is, as it happened with my aircraft. So, my Wife I kill and the Germans they pay me, they do for it. One jew less. They need me no more and so they massacre us and my ability to fly. Several jews less. Three english men they have eyes, two eyes with which to see and to fly. This new plan it is dangerous. Can I have a guarantee that if they escape with the tools I make them that they will come back, these three Englishmen, to rescue me. So, I will forfeit the three englishmen because I am not sure. The keys I will take, when my German friend gives them to me and the uniform I will take and the passport and out I will walk of this safest prison of the Germans.'

Here there were several blank pages and then *'Again I am thinking of the Warsaw Ghetto and considering the people that conditions as this will breed. Indiscriminately people breed for lust and comfort. Creatures must survive and to do this they quarrel.*

Quarrels provoke the War and the War is the solution to the surpluspopulation…' (all one word.)

'I am sick and this cell stinks. The airmen they wake me up and tell me they will promise that England will compensate for all that I suffer.'
That was all.

'Read on,' commanded the man. He turned the page for her, to save her having to put the book on her lap to turn the pages with her one free hand. It was blank, so was the next. All the pages were blank. On the next to last page she read:

'Later they told me he lived for ninety days. One airman, he lived for ninety days in a cupboard.'

That was all it said.

'Will you let me make the love to you now?'

Roz looked at the airman, uncomprehending. The Pole repeated the question and licked his lips and tough moustache. 'Please make love to me, will you now?'

He gently took the bandages from her left wrist and her ankles. She had not understood the manuscript. It all had been written at a later date, belying the present tense he employed. It had not been written in the prison. What puzzled her most, although it had clearly been written in retrospect, all the pages were stained and marked with age, in dull post-war ink, except for the last page which looked clean, almost fresh. The last entry was also written in ballpoint pen. Two sentences only, written in ballpoint. There were surely no ballpoints so soon after the war. It had been written that day. Why?

'Please let me make the love to you my dear. I need you.'

'No.'

'Then just call me by my name. I need it that you call me by my name. Please make love to me Roz.'

'No...' she hesitated. How could she give this monster a name? An English name. Or did he mean his Polish name Karol? ... 'No...George...' she stammered.

Surprisingly he helped her to her feet and allowed her to straighten her dressing gown. He put the key back in the door but before he turned it, he said, 'If you of this speak to a person, one person, anyone, you know I will harm you. You know I can harm you; people harmed me.' And then this wicked and war-damaged man just opened the door.

She went back to her own room in the hotel, and in the bathroom she was sick.

She was trembling and shaking. Roz lay on the bed and tried to sort it all out.

She remembered the baby inside her, the polyp that had moved. She was fifteen weeks pregnant. It moved again.

Roz was sure it would survive.

Now, with a new wave of feeling, she was sure she wanted it to survive. The natural instinct of motherhood had survived.

(iii)

An hour later Roz woke up shaking to answer the 'phone ringing in her bedroom at the Rif Hotel. She trembled and answered it hesitantly, but this time it *was* Gerry.

It was surprising even after such a shock how normal Roz's voice sounded. Nevertheless, she must have looked unearthly as she walked into Gerry's room a few minutes later. Suddenly there was no need for courage or pretence. Here was Gerry, her lover; the father of her child; here at the precise moment when Roz needed him.

He was standing up as she entered the room and she walked straight into his arms.

'Roz?' The short man was surprised. He frowned slightly and a quizzical slightly amused light flashed through his grey eyes. 'What's the matter?'

She began to cry and the man sensed that the matter was serious. He allowed the young girl to remain in his arms and when the sobs subsided he looked into her eyes, red and sore from the tears.

'It's moved, Gerry,' she sobbed. He's moved again.'

Gerry looked at the size fourteen dress and he understood. His face went white. 'You should've told me, Roz,' was all he said and the tears ran faster down her face. Her mascara smarted. Her body heaved. The whole awfulness of that afternoon rose up from her stomach into her throat, beating inside her like blows from a mallet. After a few minutes the pain of the tears, magnified by the silent sobbing, reduced the trembling and Gerry, holding her very firmly, led her to the couch and laid her down. He knelt beside her.

'Gerry, I am pregnant.'

'There Roz, you should never cry like that again. You could lose the baby. You should've told me before. How many weeks is it? How could it happen? I took precautions.' He never questioned paternity. It was as though Roz could not reply. Gerry took her hand and together they were silent for many minutes.

'You're wonderful' Gerry spoke quietly, his heavy Yorkshire tone almost indiscernible. 'I thought I was infertile. My own child!' and he gently put his hand on her stomach. Immediately the fear and memory of her treatment earlier returned. She became rigid. Gerry looked alarmed.

'Roz, darling, of course, you don't think like that. I'm being selfish. Of course, you will want me to arrange an abortion.'

With the mention of the word abortion, Roz felt she was going to be sick. George Kenyon standing over her, stretching, stretching her legs apart. The memory rose up before her and she passed out.

When she came round, Gerry was anxiously soothing her face with a damp flannel which smelt faintly of aftershave in a paternal way. 'Oh Roz, my own clever darling. You must tell me what you want. You must tell me what to do.' He patted her with his thick hand, further conveying a fatherly rather than a lover's concern. It didn't reassure her and she knew she was going to be sick. She stood up and hurriedly made for the bathroom. Gerry followed her and gently wiped her brow and when it was all over led her back to the bed.

There she fell asleep. She slept for half an hour. When she woke Gerry was beside her, his arm gently round her. 'I want your child Gerry. I want him so badly.' She seemed more relaxed. 'George Kenyon...'

she said, 'Gerry I don't know whether he was trying to rape me or abort me.' She told him the story, the whole story, slowly. The sweat ran from her. She told the tale so slowly that Gerry had to work hard not to interrupt the flow, and reflected on how little he knew of this new person in his life.

Roz, on the other hand, knew that the feelings she had for Gerry were an overwhelming love, with the same intensity that she loved her father; but the thought that she had known him for such a short time made him also a stranger was not present. Nor was uppermost that the emotion she felt was not the same as her feelings for Derek. When she had finished she felt the child move again.

'I should have taken you home from Roger's bar. I just could not be sure. A long time ago, I knew a Polish airman in Germany. I just couldn't be sure that it was that same man in the bar. It was a long time ago.'

'Were you in Germany, Gerry? You never mentioned it.'

'Yes! For too long I was in Germany.'

Something was fitting into place.

'Were you a prisoner of war?' Since he didn't answer Roz squeezed his hand. 'Poor old you,' the silly words were full of sympathy and understanding, but still Roz did not understand the full significance of the relationship between George Kenyon and Gerald Duncan. She had reacted like a child, and she hated herself for it.

Gerry reached for a bowl of pink pistachio nuts and put them on the white candlewick bedspread and for a while they sat apart, with their feet on the floor, splitting open the nuts, enjoying their sweet and salty flavour.

'I was a prisoner Roz, in a prison near Munich and when your Polish pilot escaped from this prison the Germans didn't suspect the guard. I think this guard knew they wouldn't. Instead, they took the survivors of a British bomber crew who would have escaped with the Pole if he had followed instructions; the Germans took these survivors into a large walled courtyard and they added more English prisoners to make the number up to thirteen. We were a group; I remember their names today. Thirteen captured airmen: Mike, Victor, Maurice, Albert, Dixie Dean, Bob, Dick, Chalky White, Harold, Frank, Leslie, John Sykes and Dunc. Strange I only remember John Sykes, Dixie Dean and Chalky White had surnames. They then faced us against a wall where bullet holes featured in the damp plaster. Stale blood stained the wall and fresh blood was still running in trickles down to pools on the stone floor. We, thirteen men, were ordered to hold hands above our heads and after they had ached for fifteen minutes in this position the German soldiers yelled that we were to put them to our side. Then the Gestapo fired and twelve men sank to the floor and hit the wet surface of blood so that it splashed the one prisoner still standing. The only German to speak English ordered this one man still standing to feel the pulse of his dead companions and to report if they were actually dead. I was this survivor and since then I've felt guilt. Guilt that I survived. Then the Gestapo took me and locked me alone in a cupboard, six feet wide and five feet high, with one small ventilator in the door. They fed me and left me. The doctors say it was probably for about ninety days, three and a half months…I wouldn't know.

'You know Roz, I have never spoken of this to anyone since I left the rehabilitation hospital, until today, when for some reason I told the story to Ben and that madman called George in Roger's Bar. You know I honestly didn't recognise the Pole for Karol Androzoj Kosciuszko. He was very thin, then, he literally did have one eye. George Kenyon looks better now.

'The Germans had deliberately not killed me. I was the Captain of the bomber and they hadn't learnt all they needed from the crew. Do you know I remember so little about that cupboard? They must have exercised me I suppose. Otherwise, I would be a cripple, wouldn't I? I couldn't have survived without exercise, could I? I can't remember.

'One month after VE Day I was released by the allies. They sent me home and gave me a warm comfortable bed until I began to forget about the cupboard and the secrets I had never told the Germans…at least I don't think I did.

'Telling you this now, I only believe it happened to some other fellow. It might be a story I've read. In time, this happens and in time, I hope today's awful experience for you, my darling will mean as little.'

Roz thought she would never forget it.

'When I came out of the hospital I wasn't harmed physically. I was a strong man and I soon remembered that I had a pretty wife called Holly and I owed her a honeymoon, although it was November and more than eighteen months since our wedding. You see we had been married in 1944 and after thirty-six hours leave I went back to the Air Force. I hadn't seen my very young wife since our wedding night. She was younger than you when I married her.'

For Roz, suddenly there was comprehension. The whole tragedy of this newly married wartime couple; destined never to beget children and now here inside her was Gerry's child. Of course, he could never marry her. He couldn't.

'And in St. Ives on our much belated honeymoon, where the sea crashed against the quay, where the beaches were of golden sand,' the small plump man who was now middle-aged continued, 'the farmer's wife spoilt us and fattened us up on fresh farm butter and Cornish cream, delicacies city folk wouldn't taste for many more years and I almost forgot the Polish airman with one eye. Except I couldn't make love to my wife. You see I always blamed him, not for my own discomfort, but more for the death of my twelve colleagues. And if they couldn't love, why should I? And that's how it was Roz. To you, Karol Andrzoj was making a confession. I was mistaken to tell my story in Roger's bar this afternoon. Some force jogged only half my memory. Strange isn't it that I shouldn't recognise the man that I hated and against whom I've borne such a grudge all these years. I've been trying so hard to forget that I'd almost succeeded. This afternoon I thought it was Roger's exuberant character that drew the story from me. Now I know it was the strange forces of telepathy that caused it for I was thinking of Germany before I even walked into the bar and saw Karol. And still I didn't place him; I knew I'd met him but not where. I wonder if I ever would if you hadn't come to me now with your terrible story?'

Roz could not tell Gerry at this point that she had prayed to Gerry to save her, and just at that point, he had actually walked into the bar. It seemed much too coincidental.

199

'And I'm sorry for the Pole,' Gerry continued. 'In a way... He may never be given the gift to forget his terrible past. What he did to you this afternoon was a dreadful thing, but Roz, if you are not harmed by this incident...if my baby is born to you, alive and well, find it in your heart to forgive and forget this awful man. The war did dreadful things to men, made monsters of civilised beings, walking corpses of princely souls; none of us who experienced it first hand, came away totally unscathed. It had to alter our lives. You can't live through an experience like that without being affected. And I think I'll be happier if our sad story is never told again. I think you are also the only person who knows both sides of the story. I think the solicitors in London must have told Karol that I'd survived and how I survived. I know he actually dared to present himself in London to the addresses we gave him and ask for naturalisation. He did that in November of 1945. I didn't think there was any point in impeding his request. After all his only crime was cowardice, he thought we would let him down if he let us get away first and there was a genuine risk that he would be caught. Seeing me today has shaken his memory and he probably did only add that last sentence in his diary today.

'You know he was pretty drunk in Roger's. I expect by tomorrow he'll have forgotten the whole incident. Unless you remind him.'

'Gerry, I love you. Really. I want your child. I'm excited to bear it. Gerry, ...'

'Roz. you have the child of another coward. You must remember that. I should never have made love to you. Holly's been a good wife, although she might've disappointed me in some ways. Until I met you I was faithful to her. It's not as though we were careless. I knew there might be some slight risk, but honestly, I thought I was impotent. Holly's told me that I've been impotent for years, but what she really means is I'm a lousy lover. Oh, Roz, I'm sorry. Give me time to think.'

'Of course. I've been thinking of nothing else for three months. I was never going to tell you.'

'But you have, and I'm glad. You made me into the thing I've most wanted to be. A father.' He kissed her with the same intensity and in the same natural way as he had done the last time in Manchester before they had said goodbye.

'But I'm also sad, because now I love you as I've never loved anyone before, and because I can do nothing about that love I'm hurting you.'

The 'phone rang and Gerry answered it. Roz brushed the pink nutshells from the bedspread and tried not to listen as Gerry clearly made arrangements for an early morning take-off. He hung the 'phone back on the wall bracket and lifted Roz by her armpits from her seated position. When she was standing he felt her waist and kissed her neck.

The 'phone call had neatly solved one of the problems.

'I'm leaving, early in the morning. But I'm taking George Kenyon with me. My first office, Leslie, has gone sick it seems. Kenyon can stand in and we'll leave Leslie in your tender care until he is better. For one thing, I don't like the thought of Ben, inexperienced as he is as a Captain having such an unreliable type as Kenyon to back him up. We also have a third pilot on our aircraft, in training but spot on reliable. I'm leaving you Roz, but I love you. This must be good-bye.'

'Goodbye for now?' said Roz as a question.

'Yes,' he said automatically.

Roz's eyes were wide and beautiful, her small face had the delicate features often associated with Asian women, but that was its appeal. Her eyes were very green when she was sad and she wanted to screw them up and catch the tears. She was used to the total support of her adoring father and she could not quite accustom herself to the fact that Gerry had to leave her at this critical point in her life. She hoped she was not going to cry again. She should not feel so let down. There was every emotion expressed across her face and the agony of parting was reflected in her pupils and the worried gaze, which circled her eyes in very fine lines; like the lines of age in the stump of an old oak tree. She was too young to frown.

'I understand Gerry.'

'Yes Roz, I know you do. And what happens next must be what we both want. Always remember that I love you so much.

'I'm off to Tenerife (correctly he said Tenereefee) at five this morning, and then back to Malta and onwards east until we come back, via Jersey of all places, to Yeadon. Christmas excepted I've worked over 120 hours this month and it's the winter season, the quiet season! Gone are the days when I never worked in the winter, just whiled away my time in Cyprus. I think someone will have to complain to BALPA. The next thing we know and every other Englishman will be flying abroad for his hols. Ten years ago, there wasn't such a thing as a tourist, by 1970 they'll have destroyed the very thing they wanted to see. Mark my words, it can only get worse!'

'Poor Gerry. And you know we've had five miserable days in this stinking town. All over Christmas and now New Year. Heaven knows what this will do to Ben!' He doesn't drink any the less you know for being in command!

'That's a good thing about leaving Leslie Black with you. Leslie doesn't drink, so he may be able to help sober Ben up – if you can keep Ben on sixteen hours Roz before take-off you'll have done well.'

'Your guess is as good as mine how much Ben will drink, and he's proposed to me four times this trip already!'

'And that, young Roz, is something you must promise me never to do. Under the circumstances, it would never work. Promise you won't attempt to manufacture a father for the baby?'

She managed a smile. 'Promise! Don't work too hard'' She left him then. She left Gerry. Turning the copper doorknob, she was concentrating on the heavy weight presented by the varnished mahogany door. When she closed it, she felt she had enclosed the core of her life.

It was then that she saw Ben Smith, sitting on the fire extinguisher, outside Captain Duncan's hotel room. It was as though she had closed the door on one problem. This was the great watershed, the way forward was downhill, decelerating for the time being at least, but certainly with new dilemmas about to present themselves.

It was eight o'clock. Ben by now was showing signs of being drunk.

Now then young Roz, you got a light? I've waited long time for this light. It spoils a cigarette to keep it hanging around, waiting for a light like this. That'z the first point.' he paused. The unlit cigarette hung from his mouth. The red Pyrene fire extinguisher shuddered against the man's weight and the new Captain's eyes flickered, solid blue from beneath black bushy brows and lashes and he spoke again. 'Zecond point, this, you should never go into a man's room, 'specially a senior Captain's. And third, thiz is important you shouldn't get caught coming out. Now how about coming to tell Uncle Ben all about it? And Roz chanced to see a rare dimple form in the man's chin as he seized her arm and unlocked his door, helped her in and locked it again behind them. She did not dare to protest. Same old scene, but this time with amiable Ben. She was not frightened. She was more afraid of the attention a scene of refusal on the landing would attract. Her relationship with Ben had always been one of easy trust and friendship.

'Now then love, pour us a drink. Now, don't you go and get the most respectable and therefore the most respected Captain in the Company a bad name, will you?' She did not know whether he was referring to himself or to Gerry.

Since she didn't immediately pour Ben a drink he poured himself a whisky from half a bottle of Grant's Standfast and handed another to her without asking her if she wanted it. He lit the cigarette finally, but left his drink on the table. Suddenly he became sober. Roz sat on the bed head and Ben joined her. He began to talk.

'You know the company came onto me after that night in Cheshire. You remember in Bowdon when I disgraced myself by getting into your bed. Apparently, I must've made some sort of racket for the hotel reported us. I said it was my fault entirely and not yours, but the devil of it is that I can't remember a damn thing about any of it.

204

'Don't worry Ben. I've forgiven you.' How the actions of that night had changed the course of her life, she thought laconically.

'But I hope it wasn't too personal.'

'But of course!' she joked and had never felt less like joking. Gerry was going away, they had said goodbye, but when would she see him again. He had made no long-term plans.

'The point is that this square old management warned me that if I'm caught again I'll get the sack. I haven't told you before tonight, because frankly, well you how I feel about you anyway, well you know I've been wearing kid gloves since the affair, ... I mean, oh hell, Roz, you know how I feel. I'm embarrassed. Sorry. That's the word...sorry.' He ran his fingers through his thick black hair.

Sorry - thought Roz. The child would grow; it would go on growing. Soon it would show and everyone would notice. Ben took another puff of his cigarette and reached over for his glass for a swig of whisky. Roz knew of course that within a matter of weeks she would have to give up her job and the prospect of creeping home and announcing that she had got herself pregnant directly after her father's little homily did not appeal.

Ben began to tell silly jokes. They were not quite 'nice'.

Roz found she was not listening. Something would turn up. If she did nothing someone was bound to help.

Ben was now sitting untidily on the bed with creases in his 18-ounce trousers. He might have slept in his suit. He also needed someone to love him. Tears formed in Roz's eyes. She must spend them another time. How uncomplicated life would be if it were Ben she loved and not Gerry.

'I must go and change for dinner Ben, sweetie.' She rose from her perch at the bed end. 'Thanks for the drink. See you! Sober up now and we'll have dinner together.'

Surely, she should be confined to a sick room screaming 'rape', with reporters and doctors around and police chasing George Kenyon through the Kashbar. Oddly she still felt elated. A victory in life with adrenaline still rushing through her blood. She had found Gerry as her ally.

Ben unexpectedly pulled himself from his crumpled position and kissed her. She allowed him to do so, but when she stiffened in the middle of his big bear like embrace he let her go and did not comment. Roz walked out of Captain Smith's room without saying anything more. In the corridor, just as she closed the door she met a rather sad looking English girl, employed as a receptionist. Because she was not guilty she could make her exit confidently. In spite of this internal reassurance, it was the third pilot's room she had left in three hours. Behind the receptionist walked George Kenyon, the Polish pilot.

He was following the girl with his soft unhurried step, his thin mid-European features accentuated by the harsh light in the corridor. He didn't say anything to Roz, so neither did she to him.

She went back to her own room, and tried to piece together this most traumatic afternoon.

Over the past eight weeks, since her worst suspicions were confirmed, life had lost its charm and her world had become fraught with dilemma. That afternoon the missing pieces had slotted into the central jigsaw but leaving the edges unfinished, a never-ending, always expanding puzzle like a bad dream.

But now she had decided not to pray or hope for an abortion or miscarriage, that afternoon she had decided to deliver Gerry's child.

It was after nine o'clock when Roz went downstairs for dinner. Ben was alone, drinking soft juices in the hotel lounge waiting for someone to talk to and he had changed his suit. She was very sun-tanned, although her dress was a little tight it gave away nothing and the enormous blue and grey checks of the cloth matched and complimented the contemporary bathing pool, which could be seen through the huge glass wall of the bar; the very pool in which Roz had been dreaming of indulging earlier in Roger's bar; only six hours ago, it might have been a life time.

Ben gave her an admiring glance. Nobody had yet mentioned that she had put on weight and she knew for nearly four months pregnant she was still very small.

'I'm sorry dear because you look your best tonight, but as the ship's funds are running low I wonder if you would mind if we two just popped out to a little seafood bar I know in town, instead of dinner. I was expecting Gerry and George, but since they haven't shown up I think we'll make do with our own company. Just need to mind the pennies for New Year. You know Roz, whenever I night-stop with you there're always other men competing for you. Wonder where George is? A bit squiffy in Roger's if you ask me, glad we're not flying on tomorrow. Wouldn't be surprised if we don't see him tonight. He was well away when we left Roger's this afternoon.'

Did Roz tell him now that she knew George would have received orders that he was flying on with Captain Duncan, or did she let Ben find out in his own good time? In his own good time, she decided.

They walked along the seafront, turning left out of the hotel towards the Kashbar. Roz was certain that Ben's choice of eating-house would be rough and native. The more money saved for beer meant the less spent on food and when Ben led her into a side street before they came to the actual native quarter she was glad. The restaurant was a large hall with a tiled black and white floor, wooden scrubbed tables and a bar which looked like a fishmonger's counter. For no reason, the hall was decorated with dancing African characters, reflecting an era when no-one thought to comment on such a choice.

They sat at the bar and Roz ordered a coke. She was beginning to tire of alcohol. What a way to spend Christmas. She wondered if there was any snow in England.

She drank one drink and refused any others.

Ben said in his Northern accent, 'What's up lass, you a bit peaky?'

The sawdust on the floor was beginning to spoil Roz's shoes but it covered up the pieces of mullet, which she was repeatedly dropping to the floor. She ate the large pieces of outsize tomato and cucumber, which had been served on the side plate.

'What's the matter, Miss?' Roz jumped. Gerry was the only person who had used the term 'miss' before. It was one of his ways in flight. It was generally a title which Roz could not abide, although when Gerry enunciated it, it made her feel dominated, which he intended and that was different.

'Nothing Ben,' she replied momentarily hating him. 'I've a slight headache that's all.'

'You would tell me if I did anything wrong that night near Manchester, wouldn't you?'

'Oh, Jesus!' thought Roz, nearly speaking aloud. That's what it is. He thinks he's made it. Oh! What a mess! He really would be watching her tummy soon. Perhaps he had already noticed.

They both smiled. Inanely. An old trick came happily to Roz's mind.

Anything, she thought to change the subject.

It was one she had learnt soon after Coca-Cola became fashionable in Britain. She hoped it was one of which Ben was unaware.

'I'll have a coke. Just a coke. Have you a penny, Ben, preferably an old one?'

Ben watched as Roz dropped the penny he gave her into the glass of coke. 'I'll give you a bright new penny back,' and she waited as the acid fizzed and she fished out a shining bright Britannia from the glass. 'Of course, if I left it in longer it would come cleaner than that...might even disappear altogether, they tell me teeth, baby teeth dissolve right away!'

Ben smiled, but seemed unimpressed, or perhaps he knew that Coca-Cola were going to eliminate the mystery ingredient.

'But think what it does to your innards!' she persisted.

'Oh, the alcohol puts that to rights.' Ben smiled cheerfully.   They inspected the date on the coin. 1936 and an uncrowned Edward.

Then their efforts at invigorating small talk failed completely. They paid the bill, called for a

Chrysler taxi, although the Rif was not much further than two hundred yards from the restaurant.

'Care for a night-cap?' asked Ben on arrival, hope registered by his raised shaggy eyebrows.

'Rather not, thanks all the same.'

Roz unlocked her own door and closed it behind her. To be honest she had only gone out for dinner because she was too scared to stay in. She was surprised that Gerry had not considered that. She was confused and she was exhausted; the day and circumstances had won. It had been too full of coincidence for credibility. She had hoped to tell no one she was pregnant. But how could she have hidden it? When there was proof for the entire world to see. Which cave could she have crawled into to hide? Julie hadn't suspected yet, but she was surely about to do so.

Julie lived with her, saw her en route to the bathroom, brought her tea in bed after late flights and borrowed her dresses, soon she must guess. Roz considered stuffing her bra with padding and purchasing larger dresses to confuse everyone into thinking she had just become grossly overweight. After all, in pregnancy it was only because your tummy was so comparatively fatter that people sensed the condition at all. Children never notice, do they? The obvious thing, she thought was to hope she wouldn't carry too much water and hope the baby stayed as proportionally small as he was now. He was? She was? Well, at least since the events of the afternoon he had ceased to be an 'it.'

Lying sleeplessly in the air-conditioned room in Tangier, Roz recalled the long journey by public transport to the General Hospital in Leeds, where she had had the pregnancy confirmed.

In her cane-shopping basket, she had carefully put the milk bottle containing her precious sample. There had been the problem of sealing it and she had settled for greaseproof paper secured with string. Thence the expectant urine changed onto three buses carefully and arrived well shaken at the Path. Lab, but intact. Without a murmur, they had accepted the offering.

'Couldn't find something larger for it, I suppose?' they had enquired. 'Remember we only need half an ounce next time!' There was to be no next time.

Three weeks later, four days before they left for a trip to Cairo with Bill Turner, the doctor let her have the result.

'Rather too late for an abortion, love,' he had said. 'Don't try it, and I mean that. Damn bad luck. If you could've come to me at once and said it was rape I might've arranged it for you. Funny the labs. take so long to analyse a simple sample in a matter of life and death ... so sorry! Just a manner of speaking, didn't mean to upset you. Ha! Ha! Forget it!'

Forget it? How? She must admit the doctor had abandoned his sense of humour and become quite helpful, pledging his support and giving the details of the adoptive procedure. Nonetheless, it was Gerry's child and her own that they were all so readily and coolly planning for adoption.

Odd though. The thing she and Gerry had planned so determinedly against was the thing he most wanted. And perversely so did she. She would sleep now.

The 'phone rang as the first waves of sleep drifted over her. It shook her.

'Roz love, I've bought you a pretty necklace, from the Arab woman outside the hotel. May I come and give it to you?'

'At twelve o'clock at night? I'd rather you didn't Ben.'

'Just a little grog together,' her captain pleaded. 'I'm sorry; it is Christmas after all Roz. It's alright for these married men; they've children and Christmas trees. I've just my bottle. Geoff's so grown up now he doesn't notice whether I'm home or not. Just so long as his Gran cooks his Christmas dinner he's alright with his T.V. I know I've been miserably drunk this trip. I'm sorry Roz. Really.'

Poor lonely Ben. He could be the solution to her problems but one she realised she could not entertain.

'Goodnight Ben, I'm sorry. The answer's no.' she yawned as if to convince him, trying to make her action fully audible over the receiver. 'I'm going to sleep now. I was asleep when you woke me.'

Very shortly there was a tap on the thick door. She did not answer.

Presently the knock was repeated. Perhaps it was Gerry. She opened the door.

It was not Gerry.

'Oh! Hallo. What can I do for you?' She said rudely.

Twisting another half bottle of Scotch in his fingers Ben announced his intention like the small boy who was uncertain whether to doff his cap before or after he crossed the threshold.

'Thought you might've changed your mind?' Hope again in the blue eyes.

At this precise moment, the lift door slammed and round the corner came George Kenyon.

212

'It is a pity we can't have a party,' she said acidly. 'But the answer is no, even if it does mean that certain people are spending the small hours on the landings of the Rif Hotel, knocking on the doors of young ladies.' And she shut the door on the pair of them.

Too late, she had learnt what all the hostesses eventually learn.

SEVEN: INEVITABLY...

24 June 1972

(i)

It was possibly the first warm sunny day of that dreadful summer.

In the quiet of the walled garden, Rosalind was shielded by her parasol and she removed her bikini. With some envy, she thought of the present-day teenagers who would think nothing of her permissiveness, her guilt-ridden indulgence. She had been daring to wear a bikini on that first visit to Greece, she remembered. Now, even in solitude, this was the first time she had dared to sunbathe in the nude. She began to revel in the feeling of the hot sun on her naked skin. Her paler than pale breasts, never before exposed to the sun, drew the warmth from her sensitive skin pulling it into a feverish climax, and she touched her nipples. She lay quite still and forbade herself to turn over as the hot sun burnt her white skin in waves between the gusts of wind.

Rosalind reduced herself to a deep humiliation which she could only hope to release with physical expression; the administration of abreaction in the remembrance of puppy love. Her husband never manifested an interest in the subtler ways of loving. Rosalind needed more modest surroundings and she went inside where slowly in a cool bath she reminded herself of Gerry, of his gentle way of loving, the feeling he gave her of belonging. After all these years he was

214

still so important. Reluctantly and shamefully she allowed herself the excesses of memory and she lay down again in the sun, to yield to the calm. But it took two hours to return to normality and she forced herself to walk around feeling a curious mixture of punishment, salacity and satisfaction from the doubtful rewards of her thoughts and efforts.

It was June.

The month was always painful.

It was the month of their nuptials. The month of the Andrew's birthday. The sign of Gemini and more particularly the sign of Cancer.

Cast a horoscope for Andrew and admit to her own omen.

Today was also a birthday for Rosalind.

How strange that her past life was still clear in parts but remained as a memory like a book once read. Gerry had said she would forget. She had not forgotten. Where was he now?

January 1961

(ii)

Captain Smith and Roz Peters arrived back in Yeadon two days after the New Year. For all their revellery at the Velazquez Hotel, dining in the magnificent dining room overlooking Tangier, where they had carefully booked a table, the evening had not been an outstanding success. Captain Smith had saved a great deal of night-stop allowance for the festivity and blown the entire amount on booze. Roz didn't know what else she had expected, and Ben, of course, had pressed amorous attentions upon Roz, but Roz was fast learning how to manage these occasions. The presence of the first officer left behind by Gerry and other aircrew who joined them, diffused the situation, although it did not cure all of Roz's nerves.

The New Year meant little to the Moslems and despite the international flavour of the New Year's dinner, the Arabian atmosphere and the encouragement of some European and American residents in the cosmopolitan city Roz longed for the solidarity of an English New Year's Eve ball or the foolish pageantry of the Scottish Hogmanay, even the doubtful escapades performed in Trafalgar Square.

They arrived back in Yeadon to find Yorkshire cold and snow threatened.

She shivered in the crew room and having checked her in-flight bar with customs and catering with Gil, Roz had gone straight home to her flat. Here she arrived as the snow began to fall and found Julie in her

216

deep blue and gold trimmed uniform, clearly about to depart.

'Happy New Year, love. I'm just off to Palma. Glad I caught you though before I rush off.'

Roz had made up her mind to confide in Julie when she arrived home, now here she was in her usual mad jig of a rush.

Since George Kenyon's refined torture Roz had started with morning sickness, something she had escaped in the early stages. It wasn't technically morning sickness, more a feeling of fright every time she thought about the Pole, or indeed of Gerry, or of the baby. It hit her stomach and bowel in a way which reduced her to pure terror. The baby was really becoming quite lively. She had felt his little limbs kick every day since the New Year.

Thankfully she had only twenty passengers on the return flight from Tangier.

They had refuelled at Bordeaux and been offered a good lunch at the airport restaurant. She was surprised that she was hungry but the fresh blue trout made the most appetising meal she had had since leaving England. She had also been surprised how well the baby had travelled through the winter weather they had experienced coming in from the Bay of Biscay. Perhaps after all she would be able to keep flying for longer than she had first imagined. If she stayed small and well, perhaps she could fly until the last month, if she could let her skirt out. It was always difficult to persuade the company to refit you with another uniform even if you did get fat; Roz thought of Daisy Yorke who had grown fatter every day until really her jacket would not fasten across her bust and her skirt was permanently stretched and creased across her tummy, and that was pure greed.

If Daisy could get away with it, so could she.

She suddenly thought of the reasonably voluminous tropical overalls they were to be issued with that summer, in light blue cotton, they were going to cover a multitude of sins. Perhaps she would be able to wear just that and a rain cape. She could just tell Julie that she was running to fat that week, make a joke of all the beer on night-stops and the lunchboxes and then she could ask the Chief Stewardess for a larger size than her original uniform.

It was true there was nothing like the French cakes or the Italian puddings left by slimming passengers for tempting greedy hostesses in the galley; everyone knew that.

Roz looked at Julie, her chief stewardess and her confidence faded. There was something about an outgoing hostess of course, which set her apart from one who had just completed a rough flight with poorly passengers and upset coffee cups, even so, Julie really was immaculate.

There followed another of the waves of fear and vacuous pain that she had been less skilled at handling recently.

Roz knew she was going to have to persuade more than nature to act in her interests, but she did not think it was a fallacy that one's hair and complexion in pregnancy improved, hers was already showing a certain radiance and even in a fairly windy and cool Tangier she had managed to catch a little sun, nonetheless more was needed and the feeling that her womb would drop out of her lower body in excruciating pain continued to panic her.

What's the matter Roz? You've looked like a ghost since you walked in. You weren't air-sick, were you?' The thought obviously amused Julie, who laughed shaking her brown hair, which she kept short, as was the rule for every girl employed by Ferryair. To Roz, this felt cruel, another heavy blow in the lowest part of the stomach.

'No, I wasn't sick. Just that fuzzy nasty head feeling, you know what I mean. One is better standing up, but Ben Smith had us all strapped in our seats, including me. It wasn't too awful but I must say I wish we could use the Whistlers for longer trips, the Viscounts do seem to get above the weather.'

'Depends; not if it is very rough, but we're whistling down to Palma tonight, so we should be alright.'

'Are you stopping over?' Roz asked the question hopefully.

'Nope, not technically anyway. Due back at three this morning. In this weather though, anything is possible. Look how it is snowing, now! In these conditions, I always wish we were Zurich or Geneva based. The Swiss bad weather facilities are so superior. If we do get back on schedule I'll have a bit of a lie-in, if you don't mind. Crikey. One needs Eskimo suits to face this sort of thing. As Julie opened the door to the Arctic conditions the snow and hail raced in from the great white void outside. Roz was glad she was not taking off in such weather.

As she shut the door the sickness got the better of her. An awful thought told her that this was her problem, her problem alone. With the best will in the world, Gerry would not be able to help.

219

The child must be born. She wondered if birth was as painful as the stories said. She wondered if the love she felt for Gerry would help the pain. The love she felt for the baby. The baby had to be adopted. Why? There could be no real love for the baby.

It was impossible for her to make a home for the baby. There could be no more love for Gerry. It was quite impossible.

She had yet to consider whether she could even expect help from Gerry.

She really did feel alone.

The Harpic that Julie had put down the loo made her retch again.

She felt better. She stood up, flushed the toilet and went into the bathroom to wash her face. Although it was only four o'clock in the afternoon she left a note on the kitchen table that she didn't want to be disturbed until breakfast. She hoped Julie would understand when she came in from Majorca at three in the morning. Notwithstanding that Julie had said she wanted to sleep in, normally Roz would have got up and made her a cup of tea. It was kind of a tradition among the female crews who roomed together that when one was on a night flight, others welcomed them home!

In bed, she rolled over onto her swollen stomach and felt the slight bulge that was her baby growing and growing.

She woke as a car door slammed. It was five o'clock and very dark and cold. In Morocco, the town would be waking, markets opening up. It would be warmer.

Here Julie must be coming in from Palma. Roz put on her dressing gown, for despite her note to Julie she now felt rested, and she went into the kitchen.

It was colder in the kitchen.

Julie was making a cup of coffee. Her skirt was creased, her light blue blouse coming adrift from the waistband. She was obviously tired and not the immaculate hostess who had departed a few hours earlier.

An aircraft brown paper 'sick bag' lay on the table. Julie picked it up and turned it upside down. Thirty bob; one pound note and four half-crowns dropped out.

'That's it. Palma! Empty out and a full load of pax back. Every bloody one of the idiots had bought 200 cigarettes at the airport. I sold five loose packets and one packet of two hundred to a silly geezer who thought he'd be able to fool customs because it was the middle of the night. Best of luck to him, I say! Even the crew were non-smokers.

'Palma is a certain full trip usually, and if we're lucky and sell a full complement of ciggys on the way out and then again on the way back, and whisky, gin and brandy, we net seventy or eighty pounds. Ten percent on that is worth having.

'Yep,' said Roz unenthusiastically. Julie gave her friend a long hard look.

'For goodness sake Roz Peters! You've looked like sin for week. What is getting you down? One of the crew been at you? I thought you liked this life.'

'Nothing's up.' Roz lied, wishing Julie would make the coffee quickly. She lit the electric fire. 'That's why our electricity bill is always so high. We should claim expenses for having to live through the night. Everything you do except using the telephone is twice as costly at night; lights, taxis, more heat...'

'But at least we don't spend much on food and entertainment by flying at night. Somehow a snack will always do instead of a meal.' Julie sat down on the big armchair. Roz sat on the floor in front of the fire.

'Yes, but don't you see that is what is making us fat. I shall have to start slimming soon.' Roz said it lamely and wished she had not spoken. Now Julie would be sure to guess. She went on hurriedly, warming her hands against the bars of the electric fire, 'My father is thinking of putting central heating in at home.'

Julie ignored the remark.

'Did you have a good trip?' Roz tried again. 'Ours was lousy. That awful freelance George Kenyon, he's dreadful.' And she wished she hadn't said that either. 'He is so opinionated and Tangier was awful. It just wasn't warm enough, and yet it wasn't cold enough to remind you that it was Christmas.'

'Roz, really you do worry me. You used to have such good trips. It's not Ben Smith, is it, he's not made you pregnant, has he?' Julie stared at the redhead.

Roz went white and twisted her hands together.

Julie noticed.

'No,' said Roz truthfully. It was not Ben that had made her pregnant.

'Are you sure? You've put on a lot of weight. You're right, you should slim.'

Roz knew Julie realised that she was lying. 'And you're off your food. You put on weight and you eat like a bird.' The daughter of the chairman and managing director of the company did not want to be caught sharing a flat with a pregnant stewardess.

'Oh 'Hell's Bells, Jules. I suppose I don't feel well. I'm always sick. Why, oh, why?'

'Well, I'll tell you why, Roz Peters. You are pregnant. I've lived with girls for three years now and I've always known when they are on heat. Damn it love, with our antiquated loo those little tubes don't flush down the first time, you haven't used a Tampax for months!'

Roz was crying. 'I don't think I am, really Julie.'

'Roz. Sweetie. I know you took a sample to the hospital. I saw it. I know you are going to the Doctor, he rang while you were away, I promise I won't tell a soul. I only said I was worried about you, to cover up for you. To pave the way for you to tell me all about it. You see sweetie, you really do look pale. I'm going to help you.'

'You can't help Julie. There is a sickness and a pain in my stomach always. What's going to happen? I thought when you had babies you felt well. I feel wretched. Everything aches and I'm always tired.

EIGHT: THURSDAY'S CHILD HAS FAR TO GO

July 1972

(i)

Rosalind walked alone from the car park into Harrogate's Great Yorkshire Showground. Yorkshire people were proud of this permanent agricultural monument. It lay adjacent to the town where the sharp boundary between building and farmland was accentuated by the clean modern lines of the I.C.I. factory, a business solid in its foundations. It was inconceivable that things would ever be different. This was the secure early seventies.

Her husband had said they would meet in the Member's Enclosure.

'Where people come to see and to be seen,' he said scathingly. 'Hardly any of them interested in actual cattle, let alone sheep and pigs.'

'Then how do you explain all the horsey people one sees, or the doggie faced owners at the Hound Show'. His wife had laughed.

'Oh, jumping and hounds! That's a different matter entirely. A different matter entirely to the cattle and machinery. You wander round the real exhibits this year and see the genuine people of Yorkshire. None of your gin and tonic drinkers there'.

'And what if you aren't a member of that exclusive club?' Rosalind said, thinking that she and her husband were some of the people she knew who still did drink a fair amount of gin. It no longer seemed to be the smart drink it was ten years ago, particularly among the younger set.

But she knew what her husband meant. No sooner would she walk into the Member's Enclosure bar than she would see Daddy with his friends, glasses in hand, all with smart hats, lady friends wearing theirs, Daddy's resting on top of his shooting stick.

With them, it would be a cast of friends all wearing similar uniform of privilege. Then unlike the majority of these 'really best people' who would go in the direction of the distinctive luncheon tent, they would adjourn to Daddy's stand, easily one of the most impressive of the show, where they would be entertained to a champagne buffet infinitely superior to the one reserved for Members. Indeed, all this was so predictable that the day ran completely true to form without a hitch of an alteration or a change to expectations.

Rosalind's expectations were however stereotyped and her spouse could not help thinking that as middle age made her facial features thicker, fatter, enlarging that delicate almost Asian bone structure so his wife was growing more as he remembered her mother Helene. She had died several years before they were married, but he still remembered the ever-correct social climbing woman who would have been his mother in law. A woman he had known from afar; everyone in the district had known who the Peters family were. Now Rosalind's more neutral Trans-Atlantic accent was

225

turning more northern, higher pitched and more 'refined'. It was not a change that he could say particularly pleased him. In any other dictionary, it could be defined as a snob. In recent years, she had always seemed on her guard as though she was hiding some secret from him.

That night, as planned, they dined alone at Pool Court, one of the better restaurants of that time in Yorkshire. As a couple, they looked well. He sampled a delicious pate and she had an avocado appetiser, which they followed with exotic curried apple soup. Finally, they enjoyed a wonderful experience with salmon and after a bottle of Montrachet, they both mellowed considerably.

Driving home, Rosalind snuggled closer to her husband than he usually permitted and for once he drove a little slower. Suddenly she said, 'Are you glad we married each other, darling'?

'What a question. Of course, I'm glad, you little goose!' He tried to rationalise his automatic answer with his thoughts earlier in the day.

That was the editor in him. He hadn't always been an editor, or even a journalist but from his youth, it had been recognised he had a way with words. She often wondered what his thoughts really were. Only with Lucinda, her cousin, her father's adopted daughter, did he seem to unwind, but Roz didn't mind, she loved Lucinda too.

'You didn't know much about me when we got engaged did you?'

'Enough, I would think. Indeed, I knew plenty about your family and I would've thought that would suffice. Why do you ask? Have you something on your conscience?'

How typical!

'No', she answered and lapsed into silence, whilst her husband increased his speed.

That night they made love, silently, in case they woke the children.

Afterwards, feeling soft and satisfied she pulled the sheet around her and immediately fell asleep. It was a warm night. The first warm night of the year and it was mid-July.

He had woken her ten minutes later.

'Don't you need your nightie on? Your back will play up if you're cold'.

Reluctantly she struggled with its length and pulled it over her head. It made the act of sex seem deliberate, almost ugly. She thought of Gerry. Making love had been making love with Gerry, but immediately she knew that was ridiculous, she had hardly known Gerry. With her husband, it was pleasurable and satisfying, very satisfying. He made her feel good, but there might be others in the world who could make her feel as good. There was no one who could make her feel love as Gerry had made her feel love.

She thought of her visit to the doctor, a friend. She had gone yesterday and he had said the coil was perhaps making her anaemic and causing the discomfort of which she had complained. He had prescribed the pill. As he examined her he remarked on her suntan; there were no bikini marks.

Rosalind had been fitted with a coil since her marriage. The children were adopted; the twins. The adoption society knew nothing of Roz's fear.

Her panic fear of conception and pregnancy.

227

22 June 1961

There was sweat on her brow, under her arms, between her thighs, between her breasts. A mist was forming over her eyes as she tried to relax with the pain that gripped her groin in waves. It hurt. More than she had ever imagined. Perhaps she should have taken Julie's advice. Perhaps she should have attended the clinic. There they apparently had some new idea of breathing exercises to help you in childbirth.

A nurse was holding Roz's hand. Temporarily, though it was surprisingly kind of her. The two other women, the midwife and another nurse were rushing about the rooms.

Every so often one of them popped in.

'Keep going,' she said cheerfully and left. The kind nurse also left.

'Keep going.' she said as she went. Roz had been 'going' for six hours. Six hours of pain every five minutes. She remembered the words of the Polish pilot in Tangier. 'The pleasure of childbirth is a pain denied to man.' Well, they could have it. It wasn't at all romantic. There was no way that suffering was made less, simply because you had loved the man; most particularly when the man hadn't been seen for weeks,

It was hot outside.

It was hot inside.

Months ago, weeks ago, days ago, every time she had thought of childbirth she had wondered whether the pain would remind her of the night she had loved

228

Gerry. The feeling of submission now culminating, in giving birth. Well now she had her answer, it didn't.

Another pain caught her pelvis. Her stomach tightened. She tried to relax but it didn't help. She screamed.

It was senseless. A nurse came in.

'Don't scream' she said, just like that. 'It frightens the others who haven't started.' She went out. A birth factory.

Here women in agony came and went. Came for the pain and left with the little bundle that would mould their lives.

Roz had seen one departing as she came in. Happy with her little bundle but still pale of face; her man at her side positively beaming. It was simply amazing what he had created.

The loving husband in his new role of father, arm round his wife, gazing down at their creation which he felt he had such a part in; a curt but happy nod to the nurses, slightly too embarrassed to express thanks but with his chest puffed up like a cock. The wife in her expected role of mother, prepared, but not confident perhaps, holding the baby as though she might drop it, more as one would hold a new puppy, but also happy, full of thanks and gratitude to the hospital, the pain already forgotten. 'Grateful thanks to staff'. Who? Who, Roz would like to ask them was doing all the work?

Another pain.

The nurse had gone out. Roz gathered up her pillow and dragged it over her face, she bit it. Perhaps they'd give her a leather strap to bite on soon.

'Gerry' she thought, 'if only…' Two women came in. They were dressed in white. They opened her legs and they looked at the naked pelvis. They brought

229

further rubber sheets and they yanked Roz on to them. They brought a bowl of hot water.

Roz didn't think she could bear the pain anymore.

'You can start pushing now' they told her. "Labour means exactly what it says," said a book Roz had once read. "Hard work, that's why it is called labour: every mother thinks this hard work is amply compensated when she has the baby in her arms."

Well here was a young mother who was going to disprove your theory, Author. What punishment worse than this could be drawn up for fornication and adultery? Her baby, whose baby? Gerry's child, their child of love. And who will love it now?

Another appalling pain.

The nurse pushed the gas onto Roz's face. Its thick rubber mouthpiece made Roz want to retch. Below her abdomen, hands were prying, feeling, disturbing.

'Push,' said one.

'Is she keeping the baby?' said another.

'No! Silly girl. They don't learn, do they?'

I want to keep my baby - Roz wanted to cry, I want my baby.

Tears formed in front of her eyes. They all looked like the Pole.

She inhaled more gas.

They were torturing her.

She screamed.

Again, they clamped the rubber back over her mouth.

She would scream as much as she wanted. She did not care how much she upset the other bitches in the ward, waiting to take her place in the labour room. They at least will be able to forget about it as soon as they took the little brats home and could wrap themselves back into their dear hubby's arms.

The pain was worse. She couldn't believe it, but it was.

She inhaled more gas. The figures looked busy, concerned. A doctor came in. 'Did she sign the form?' he asked. Of course, she signed the form, Roz was cross. They had all encouraged it; 'for the child's good,' they had all said.

'Give it a proper start. Adoption is better than illegitimacy,' the Matron had said at the home for unmarried mothers. 'Better not to see the child at all. Sign the form.'

Even if the child would know all about his wonderful father, even if Roz could love him, would his adoptive parents love him more; Roz had wondered.

But she wouldn't be able to tell the child about his wonderful father. Not unless she told the world about this father. At the moment, the world was still guessing as to the paternal parentage. And still the figures around Roz's bed were busy. And the pains came quickly and so hard that there was scarcely any respite.

'It's hard work for her,' said the doctor. 'I think she will tear badly. Better whip her up to the theatre, Sister.' He moved to walk out of the room. 'Better they never see the child too. Better they don't feel the birth, they don't become too emotional that way!' He said it softly but Roz heard him. The gas had made her drowsy, but she wanted her baby now.

He was hers. She wanted to hear him cry. He might be a girl. She didn't need an anaesthetic. She was getting used to the pain.

'Stop pushing now love. The Doctor says you're to go up to theatre. You can stop pushing now, I said.'

They brought in a trolley. They were lifting her, rolling her onto the stretcher. Roz wanted to give birth by herself.

Suddenly the pain no longer seemed like pain.

Clearly, she could see Gerry. His soft gentle manners; his gentle wry smile, amused; his grey-blue eyes; his aristocratic nose. And then they were pushing her helpless along the long corridor into the dark lift. She didn't want the anaesthetic. They said you talked in your sleep.

She might give them the name of the father. Everyone was asking her the name of the father.

She wouldn't tell them.

At that moment, the baby took over. No more pain, just an overwhelming satisfying desire to push and expel the little body from her womb.

'I think he's coming,' she said quietly.

And the three-gowned figures looked at her as the lift moved up.

They wheeled her out. She saw the theatre.

'Pethidine' said someone.

'No,' said someone nearer. 'Take off the blanket.'

They lifted her knees and looked at her exposed vulva.

'The head,' they said wisely.

'Don't push, just wait for the doctor.'

Roz pushed and felt the thrill and motion as the baby's head was expelled between her legs.

'Quick,' said another nurse.

The doctor arrived. 'What a place to have a baby!' He laughed. 'On a trolley! One more push and we'll have her.'

'Is it a she?' Roz asked.

'You push and I'll tell you. She's got bright red hair anyway.' He laughed again.

The final contraction and Roz's baby slipped from her. Immediately she was tired.

'A boy,' said the doctor. 'A baby boy with red hair like yourself. And no stitches after all!' He patted her thigh. 'Well done, now when you go home young lady, you have a nice rest and forget all about it, you soon will,' and he walked away.

Why did well-meaning people keep telling Roz that she would forget her experiences? This was one event she would never forget, nor did she wish to do so.

Two young nurses picked up the baby and hurried away as Roz felt the after-birth slip from her like an anti-climax. A third nurse cleaned her up and moved her onto another trolley.

The form she had signed had said she would not ask to see the baby.

This is what it was like to have a stillbirth.

The doctor had been kind to suggest she might have an anaesthetic.

A small red-haired baby boy, a tiny baby.

A porter was hovering around, uncertain where to wheel the trolley from its position obstructing the corridor outside the theatre. A staff nurse came up. 'Take her back to Ward II.'

(iii)

In the ward, they helped her onto her bed. Roz smiled weakly at the two girls in adjacent beds. There was an empty cot near the foot of the bed.

'How's the baby?' asked one.

'Where is it?' asked the other.

The nurse drew the curtains round Roz's bed, screening her from the rest of the ward and Roz fell asleep.

She awoke as the curtains were parted. One of the nurses from the theatre, not one from the delivery room gave Roz a small cotton bundle.

Roz cradled the soft infant. She let the shawl fall until the child's arms were free from the cotton and he clung to his mother. His little hand below her shoulder gently tapped and rubbed his mother with incredible love.

Roz's baby!

'Are you breast-feeding?' asked the nurse.

'I don't know.'

'But you must know. Didn't they ask you before the birth?'

'No, they didn't mention it,' said Roz truthfully thinking of the form saying she wouldn't see the baby, let alone feed it.

'Well, do you want to do so?'

'Yes.'

'Come on then, start immediately, never wait, it helps to bring the milk in.' She undid Roz's nightie. It was one that Roz had deliberately bought last week to look like the other nursing mothers with fastenings down the front to quickly expose her breasts. As she had thought before the birth, if the child was taken away from her she could always pretend to have had a stillbirth.

In effect, if they were going to deprive her of her child that is what it amounted to, a piece of living flesh, stolen and torn from her womb. With the cutting of the cord, Roz had assumed that the child would cease to be hers and yet here she was with the nurse thrusting the child's mouth onto her nipple, squeezing her breast and massaging it as well, and the tiny little mouth nuzzled the papilla like a baby bird.

The tiny boy seemed to have some trouble adjusting to the traumatic way of feeding and several times he spat the nipple out and each time the nurse thrust him rudely back.

'I did three months in maternity,' she said. 'It's better than theatre. You'll just have the colostrum for the first two or three days. Very good for your baby.'

The baby didn't appear to agree, he was happier being fed the easier way with a cord from his tummy directly linked to his food supply. Roz rather resented the young nurse's urgent fight with her son and she gently held her nipple forward and put his little mouth against the nipple to discourage the nurse from pressing her baby onto her again. This time the baby sucked and Roz felt the tingle of pleasure as she held him closely in the crook of her arm.

Roz needed her baby. She wanted to keep him.

But she had signed the form. The form of consent to adoption, the initial procedure was in a long rigmarole of forms and consents and legal niceties.

235

The curtains were drawn back. The Sister in all her blue glory regarded the maternal scene in amazement.

'Nurse! This young mother has signed *the* form.' She was about to drag the baby from Roz. 'Nurse you're not on this ward. You are in the theatre. Who gave you permission to be here?'

'Sister MacKintosh asked me to take this young lady's baby down and make them both comfortable. She gave birth before they could get her to theatre, on the trolley. She never said anything about the form.'

'Well, Sister MacKintosh should not interfere with my ward. You've caused untold heartbreak for *Miss* Peters. *Untold anguish.* Go back to the theatre. Let me have the baby.' Rather than using the normal calm tones of a professional this Sister was speaking in a most dramatic fashion.

'Please, Sister,' Roz's voice was hardly audible and very timid. 'I know what I'm saying. I would like to keep my baby. I've changed my mind.'

'This is the silliest mistake I've ever heard of; of course, you've changed your mind. And in three weeks time, you will have changed your mind again. Now you are experiencing breast-feeding. In three weeks time, you will be washing nappies and not getting one decent night's sleep. Of course, you've changed your mind! Mercifully in this hospital, we don't get many cases like yours, but we always advise the mothers in the same way. Come on give me your baby before you do any more harm.'

Roz began to cry.

The Sister softened. 'Well for tonight you can keep him, in the cot. But if you still persist in taking the course of unhappiness we'll need to get in touch with the Matron of your Home, your doctor and perhaps a solicitor. You've signed *the* form, *Miss* Peters.' She drew back the curtains. The girls in the neighbouring beds were trying to keep straight faces.

'Bottle-feeding for the infant from now on though. Do you understand?' Sister continued on her tour of inspection of her ward.

A bell rang. The doors of the ward flew open and in poured all the Dads.

Roz crept under the sheets to hide her grief. As her sobs subsided, (however unhappy, it is difficult to cry silently in public,) the general happy sound from the ward penetrated her loose bedcovering. She pushed her hair out of the sheets, still covering most of her face and lay rigid and still, thinking and listening to the general babble.

Lying on the hard bed surrounded by West Riding maternity Roz realised that her problems were not over as she hoped that they would be before the birth. If she were to keep her son they really had not yet begun.

The irony was that if she had confided in Julie before she went to the doctor she would have discovered that not only was Julie's mother, Mrs. Rhodes, deeply committed with the home for unmarried mothers, but she might have been able to help with regards an abortion. Perhaps with the right advice at the beginning that was the course she would have taken. That might have been the better solution.

Instead, because she left her confession to Julie so late, Julie became embarrassed, deciding for herself that abortion for her friend was out of the question, and surprisingly reluctant to confide in her mother, until the baby was very nearly due. In this way, Roz had missed out on benefiting from all Mrs. Rhodes' experience and judgment. Roz suspected that Julie did not even tell her mother that they were friends. The position was also greatly complicated by the fact that Roz knew that her father and Julie's father, Lionel Rhodes, the airline's chairman, were business colleagues. But she thought this was a fact of which Julie was not aware.

Roz lifted herself up, wiped her swollen eyes and looked at the small sleeping child, now lying in the crib alongside her bed.

His red hair was lighter than hers. Who would adopt a child with a shock of ginger hair, although she expected it would darken? Even in his gentle little face she could see Gerry's masculine profile, a look of determination. The eyelids covered the round little eyes, relaxed and sleeping, the strong nose and Roz remembered that she had not registered the colour of his eyes before he shut them in sleep. Then she recalled that most babies have blue eyes at birth.

How she wished that she could proudly show him to his father. But even if they let her keep her son, she could not give him what he deserved.

What should she call him? Obviously not Gerald. Not James, her father's name. Her father! Roz felt a sinking feeling in her stomach. How could she tell her father?

A nurse came in. She drew the curtains again round the bed and produced a feeding bottle. 'Sister has said you aren't to breast-feed, we'll give you some'ut to take the milk away, but you can give Baby 'is bottle if you like,' she announced in the broad vowels of Yorkshire.

Take the milk away? What did she mean? Pills or were they going to electrically milk her like a cow? She had heard tales of women who had too much milk being milked to give to babies who were exceptionally tiny at birth. 'I don't want to be a wet nurse, thank you very much,' she said, sure in her mind that they would take advantage of an unmarried mother with no husband to speak up for her. The nurse looked surprised.

'What do you mean, a wet nurse? Giving my milk away when you won't allow me to give it to my son.'

'Oh, you silly girl! Someone 'as been telling you fairy stories. I mean we shall give you some pills to take your milk away, so that your breasts don't 'urt, so you don't get mastitis or some'ut.' She picked up the baby and handed him to his mother, loosening his shawl to expose the harsh starched hospital nightie he was wearing. 'I'll show you how to change his nappy later. 'He's only got two ounces, see how much milk 'e'll take. Do you know how to give a bottle?'

'Not really,' Roz grinned weakly.

'You young mothers, you're all the same!' But kindly she put the baby into the crook of Roz's arm, covered him with his shawl and shook the bottle with her right hand until a drop fell onto the back of her left hand.

'First, you test the temperature. If it is just warm to your 'and, it is OK for Baby. Then you 'old it like this, to stop the air giving Baby wind.' She put the bottle in Roz's hand, cradling it underneath and she put the teat in Roz's son's mouth.

'Now don't worry, if 'e doesn't get the 'ang of it straight away. It always takes a bit of time. Hold the bottle so that 'e has to tug a little with the mouth. That way 'e'll learn to start sucking quicker.' And her baby did suck, eagerly and contentedly. The nurse stood by and when the fluid level was reduced gently pulled the teat from the baby.

239

'Now you wind Baby like this.' She picked the child up and putting him over her shoulder rubbed him between the shoulder blades. 'When 'e 'as burped give him the rest of 'is milk. Then I'll change 'is nappy.'

This little mite had no father…Roz corrected her thoughts; he was a little boy whose father did not know he had a son.

Roz thought of the letter which she had written to Gerry.

She had left it, this one attempt to communicate with him, in his crew room pigeon-hole, the day she had resigned, giving two weeks' notice and had worried for days lest someone else had picked the letter up, opened it and read it.

Yet she dare not send it to his home for fear of his wife, Holly, discovering Gerry's indiscretion.

She had written with no attempt of endearment at the beginning:

"It is hard to write, despite the very real understanding you gave the problem, but I know that I shall have to take full responsibility myself. For I will be able to look after myself and I have received lots of help from friends.

"I cannot write in this letter what I am trying to say. But perhaps you can read between the lines. The important thing is I have promised myself that I shall be discreet, that this is our secret. That I will never tell anyone, ever. In a year's time, I shall have forgotten the whole incident. That is what you really want, isn't it?

"God bless, goodbye."

She had not even signed it, but wrote the words, *"please destroy this."*

Feeding a baby gave too much time to be reflective and Roz's conscience was aroused and she went white. She had protected the man she loved but what damage was she about to do to this baby boy?

Would the child's father care for his newly born son, would he ever know about him, did he care about Roz's feelings? These were questions Roz never addressed. They were simply too painful.

The last months of the pregnancy had been spent in a state of absolute calm, and although dejection and depression were the main themes of the mood, she had floated through the months with a turgescent patience.

It was as though the same protective skin and cushion of water, which surrounded the unborn child, protected the mother also. And throughout she remained devoted to Gerry's memory.

It was Roz's swollen pride, her calm, that had irritated Julie, who when defeated in her quest for the paternity of Roz's bastard had lost interest in the adulteress and gone her own way.

For Roz, the important fact remained, that the course of her life having been adjusted by a turn of fate, she could at least protect the memory of that one night of pure love and not defile the esoteric experience, which without Ben having been so drunk would never have happened. To her friend's disgust, she remained silent and kept her secret and Gerry's confidence. It was a romantic notion, wholly misplaced by one so young.

Gerry had eventually replied to her letter. Five hundred pounds!

"Don't send this cheque back," he had written. "I am not paying you off. In a way you

241

will understand, you will know you have found manhood for me and for other reasons too, I will love you."

This was the single endearment in the typed missive, which also like Roz's letter was unsigned. Had Roz been less naïve she might have spotted a lack of trust perhaps even suspected a one-sided relationship.

The letter went on: "You realise that I cannot marry you. Would we be happy? You with a querulous old man, me with a young wife I would always feel I had strangled in her prime. Would you have married me but for this accident? Of course not. And as I write the words the conviction of their truth leaves me. Yes, you might well have wished to marry me, so let me not surmise anymore.

I am married to a strange and motherly woman, but a woman of mixed emotions, because she believes I am impotent. I could never leave her, for I am to her both her child and her lover. I cannot leave her for something which was not of her doing, her fault. This would be crueller to her than I am being to you now. Your letter was touching. In no sense could it be called a love letter and yet your love for me reached out and held me. I did read between the lines. Be strong my young redhead, in these next months. Remember I am alive and my thoughts are with yours. Do not write to me again, not to the crew room! It interferes with my flying! Afterwards we may meet. The money is for you; to make you as comfortable as you can be during your confinement. I do not want you to

```
keep the child; this would be worse than
I marry you.
        Go fly my little bird."
```

The letter had arrived the second day after Julie had been
rostered out to Cairo for a week on the Viscount. A copy
of the roster was always posted up in the crew room.
Gerry had appreciated that Roz would need to be alone
when she received such a large sum of money, or this is
how she read the situation.

Poor Roz was looking with as much spirit as she
could muster for some thread of trust and love to cling
on to. It said much for her courage that she read nothing
but love into the words.

The baby had finished his bottled milk. Roz
looked around the ward, but there was no sign of the
nurse. She held the child to her, against her breast, no
longer naked, but covered by the thin material of her
nightdress. She shivered. The letter Roz had received, as
a document to prove her son had a father, was worthless.

It was absolutely worthless. How could she
show a questioning teenager a letter that was unsigned,
typed, which could have been written by anyone and
say, 'this was written by your most wonderful father. I
cannot disclose his name because I made myself promise
I would not disgrace his name.'

Eventually, Roz would destroy the letter by
burning it.

You could obviously only keep illegitimate
children where the question of paternity did not enter
into it. And yet keep her son Roz knew she must. She
looked at him now asleep in her arms. He looked so
peaceful. Presently the nurse came back and took the
child from the mother and placed him in his crib again,

which was removed back to the foot of the bed. The mother was ordered to sleep herself.

Roz hadn't written to Gerry again, nor had she seen him. Three days after she had received his letter Julie had flown in from Egypt.

'I've bad news Roz.' It was February and a blast of cold air entered the room as Julie came in, obviously dying to tell Roz the bad news.

'Ben Smith's been fired!' Julie looked expectantly at Roz.

Roz had stared back.

Julie's statement was charged with accusation, yet there was no question of Roz denying it for Julie had not actually accused Roz of anything. Julie assumed from now on that Ben was the father of Roz's bastard.

'Why was Ben fired?' Roz had asked some time later.

'Nobody seems to know. Thought you might.'

'What will he do?'

'You tell me! You always said he was good with words. Perhaps he'll become a writer.'

'That's not very practical. Everyone knows you need to be trained to become a journalist.'

'You seem very protective of him?'

Roz shrugged, it seemed pointless to continue the discussion. Let her think what she liked. Roz had felt she was moving in one direction and the rest of the world in the other, but she didn't care. The comradeship she had once shared with Julie had gone.

Roz was a stranger, a curious animal, living within someone else's house and just occasionally when Julie was feeling generous or sorry for Roz, she treated her like a pet, metaphorically stroking her, patting her, until Roz got in her way again, and then she lashed her

244

with words and sarcasm and Roz had crept back to the solitude of the bedroom or increasingly the bathroom where she had lain in a hot bath trying to hide the bulge with her face cloth, hoping it would go away.

In a way Roz did not blame Julie, she thought she would have reacted the same way, had it been Julie who needed the love and help. She was disgusted with herself, and as with a pet that behaved disgustingly, a human keeper will often fluctuate between emotions of forgiveness and caring to those of impatience, just because the animal has not come up to expectations. That was it, Roz felt substandard, a second-rate citizen, an animal who had succumbed to instinctive desires, not a member of an order of higher intelligence. It was mortifying.

She was tortured by guilt, guilt because Ben had lost his job.

Had Ben been fired because of her principles, because she had protected Gerry, but unwittingly and unfairly exposed Ben?

Back and forth Roz's tortured mind had rolled; and Ben had been such a cuddly type; she had to admit she had a very soft spot for him.

Obviously, Ben was suspect. But would they fire him because a stewardess with whom he had flown was pregnant? Did the Company know she was pregnant?

Finally, Roz gave up thought; it was easier that way. Ben had been reprimanded for visiting her room in the hotel in Cheshire. The hotelkeeper had reported the noise Ben had made. He was habitually drunk on long stopovers. He had been warned. Whatever the reason, she decided, it was a fate that Ben Smith deserved.

It was, she had happily exonerated her conscience, disgraceful that aircrew became so drunk and then flew the public the following day with an almighty hangover.

Roz recalled the fateful Manchester/Paris flight, when she had had to administer oxygen to Ben, before the passengers, one of whom had been her own father, had been allowed on board. Oxygen was an instant cure for a hangover.

It was his due, and anyway, Roz felt it was all justified, for if Ben had not been so drunk that previous night she would never have needed to enlist Gerry's help and all this might never have occurred.

There was no point in worrying about Ben.

But there were times when Roz had woken in the middle of the long restless night, not quite so convinced. Should she try to see Ben? She knew he lived in a small terraced cottage near Guiseley. He like Gerry had been considering buying one of the new bungalows being built nearby. Both he and Gerry had discussed it on the very first flight she had made with them to Hamburg. Now Ben was out of work would he be able to afford it for himself and his son.

(iv)

The Sister opened the curtains and came into Roz's cubicle. She was tall and unusually young for her rank, but her face was lined and her hair drawn back across the brow under her cap.

'Now Miss Peters, far be it for me to dissuade you from keeping your baby if you really want to, but have you considered the full implication of all this?'

Roz remained silent, but in truth, she had not had a chance to reply before the Sister said, 'I understand you're to be resident at the Roselea Home for the next week after your discharge from the hospital, the day after tomorrow. In fact, I understand that you were admitted on the 48-hour confinement because your doctor was frightened of complications if you had the baby at Roselea. I much prefer it when you unmarried mothers don't come into hospital though. Hospitals are too upsetting for your sort.'

'Yes, Sister.'

'Well, at least the complications didn't arise. Well, not of that nature anyway. Now Miss Peters, about the baby! How can you be sure you want to keep this baby?'

'I am.' Roz mumbled. But already the fire was dying in her conviction. 'I'm sure.'

'Well then, I have to ask you some questions and I'll take down notes here to show both the Doctor and Matron. This happens frequently when babies are born fatherless in hospital. You needn't think of yourself as unique, but most mothers see the sensible solution in the end. As I said before it is too upsetting for you young girls to see the other fathers and happily married families here. But in nearly every case the young woman goes back to Roselea and there realises the full implication of her rash decision and again reverses it. It just makes a lot of paperwork for us here at the hospital.' As Roz still didn't reply she went on, 'well now Miss Peters, do your parents know about the baby?'

'My mother's dead.'

'How often this happens! No maternal influence to guide you. What about your father? Surely, he would give some support? Fathers nearly always do understand you know, contrary to the popular television image, they rarely throw their daughters out on the street. And if you now intend to keep your baby surely you must consider telling your father. Have you no sisters?'

Roz's eyes flashed when she thought of Lucinda but she didn't answer.

Would Lucinda understand? The perfect Lucinda how could she understand? Life had gone too smoothly for Lucinda. No, that wasn't strictly true, was it? Lucinda had been orphaned and adopted by Roz's parents. And she wasn't a sister.

'I've a cousin,' said Roz suddenly. 'She's my adopted sister, but she's married.'

'Does that make any difference? Well now, are we going to tell your father or cousin, or are you?'

'I will.' Heaven forbid! Roz admitted to herself that it was the one issue she had avoided thinking about. Somehow if the child were to be adopted it didn't seem important to tell her family, rather it seemed essential that she didn't.

'Have you any means of supporting it?' Roz wished the old bully wouldn't keep referring to her son as 'It.'

'Yes.'

'How?'

'Perhaps my father. Perhaps the baby's father.'

'But it says here that you don't know who the baby's father is!'

Now the woman was inferring that she was promiscuous. 'I don't, not really, it is just that I mean....' Oh Hell! thought Roz, why does she ask all these questions? She was so tired. Too much gas.

'*Miss* Peters,' laying great emphasis on Roz's single state. 'Who is the father?'

Still young, the mother whose twenty-first birthday was imminent hoped she sounded petulant. She gave a little smile to fuel the flames.

'Well now, if *you* don't know, how can he support the child? You might have to support the child yourself – on national assistance!'

Roz recognised the note of triumph in the Sister's voice. Silly Bitch!

'I've a little money in the Post Office.'

'How much?'

'Must I answer that?'

'If you want us to help you, we must know these facts. You'll have to tell Matron too.'

'About five hundred quid.' Roz didn't add that she had also an expected trust fund of sixty thousand pounds to inherit on her twenty-first birthday. It seemed pointless, even though this was a vast sum.

'And where will you live?'

'I don't know.'

Miss Peters, it occurs to me that you haven't really given this much thought. Your baby will need a good solid background. You, yourself are obviously sufficiently well-educated to realise that if you haven't any money at least you must provide it with a good home. You must understand that you receive only so much National Assistance and as soon as the child is old enough to go into a day nursery you will probably have to go out to work. What is your employment?'

'I'm an air-hostess.' A look of understanding passed over the Sister's face.

At this time in the sixties the word stewardess, simply to avoid such looks, was gradually replacing the word hostess.

'But you won't be able to carry on with that will you dear? I mean I understand you young things are often away for days at a time. What about the baby then?'

'I'm also a trained secretary. I'm not an air-hostess anymore.' The antagonism between the two women was increasing.

'Well Miss Peters, I feel you should abide by your original decision and have the child adopted. You're not yet twenty-one years old you know. You've a lifetime ahead of you. Few men ask a girl with a child to marry them. You should consider the child. It's not just that your son may not have the joy of a father, but also, he may never have the companionship and love of siblings. In adoption, it is the family life that we are able to offer the child that is so important. However, I'll go away now and make my report to the doctor and Roselea. You look tired, now have a little sleep. Think about what I've said.'

She didn't give Roz a chance to reply.

Roz woke about two hours later. A nurse was standing over her.

'Here's Baby, mother,' she cooed. 'Is it a little girl or a boy?'

'A boy.'

'Oo!' The nurse's squeak was high pitched, immature and excitable. Roz shuddered. 'Daddy will be pleased,' continued the woman, in reality not much older than Roz. Roz was beginning to realise why the doctor had been loath to bring her into hospital for delivery.

'See! He's hungry,' the irritating nurse went on. 'You're not feeding him, are you?' She appeared to know the answer to her question without Roz's reply and produced a bottle of Cow and Gate. 'When you've finished you can have a bath.'

Roz felt very sore and swollen and it promised well, the thought of a warm bath pleased her. She remembered before the birth the difficulty she had experienced in getting in and getting out of a bath and she thought with pleasure of a normal figure again. She could only persuade her son to take half his feed, he gave a tiny burp and Roz handed him back to the nurse to change his nappy, anxious to indulge in the deep waters of a warm bath as soon as possible. The nurse laid the child in his crib. Immediately he began to yell.

'Leave him,' ordered the nurse. 'He'll soon learn not to try it on. Put on your dressing gown and bring your washing things.'

Roz followed her to the bathroom, unhappy to leave the tiny babe, his cries straining the muscles of her heart as much as his. It really hurt. What a shock it must be to face the great cold world after the cocoon of a mother's womb. She wondered what babies felt before they were born and when they started to think. Could they experience the actual birth or did they not begin to live until the first cry? Roz supposed they felt pain but really the crux of their world was discomfort. If their experience involved discomfort, warmth or cold, hunger or wind, they registered disapproval, but this was only

251

once they learnt to cry, what if they were distressed in the womb?

What a simple existence it would be when emotion played no part and she tried to recall when she had first felt emotion and realised that it had begun very early, long before she could remember. The discomfort of leaving mother's warm cradling arms was really the first emotion experienced and that was why her child was crying. The first hurt, almost anger, certainly not discomfort, for he was warm, dry and fed.

Roz was given a chair to sit on while the nurse filled the bath. There was a large scrubbing brush on a handle and a big plastic container standing on the rim of the bath against the green waterproofed and painted walls. The steam condensed against the walls making them appear slimy.

There was also a weighing scale in the room and Roz meant to weigh herself when she got out of the bath. Already she felt lighter but her tummy did not look much less extended. Roz supposed it took time.

The nurse threw in a large handful of powder from the container.

'Salt,' she explained. 'Sister said you had a small tear, not enough for a stitch. It helps to heal the wound. Get in and stay in for five minutes, no more. The bell is here; ring if you feel faint and when you're ready to get out. We'll have to help you out, the first time.'

The nurse left and Roz took off her blue dressing gown and stepped in. She lowered herself gently into the water, which as her body cut the surface whipped her sore and swollen parts as the salt did its work. She tried to stand to get out, but she was too weak. Helplessly she lay in the salty water feeling the unexpected agony as acutely as she did with the birth pains. She was too weak and tired to wash herself. The shock of the water felt to have enlarged the whole overworked part of her body.

'Gerry darling,' Roz whispered. 'Please come and help me now.' She began to cry, salt water running down her cheeks to the salted bathwater. She wiped her tears and smiled a little ruefully and rang the bell.

'You've had a quick bath!'

'It stings.'

'It is good for you. It's only a little,' said the nurse.

'Good for me! It nearly killed me. After all I've gone through too!'

'You must be more sensitive than most, pain tolerances are different,' said the woman seriously. She didn't give Roz time to weigh herself, and anyway, Roz couldn't stand without assistance. Back in the ward, she collapsed thankfully into her remade bed. The baby, she had ceased to worry about under the duress of her bath, was asleep anyway.

The large girl in the next bed leant over. 'Them baths give you a bit of a shock at first, don't they? Never mind lass, yer'll get used to them after a day or so.'

'Most unpleasant,' said Roz, reluctant to be drawn in the conversation.

'Ticularly for you, I'd say, not having an 'usband and all. No shoulder to cry on always makes it feel worse, don't it?'

'I'm very sleepy. Do you mind? You don't need to worry about me. I've got used to the situation now.' Probably the girl meant well, Roz thought, just unable to express herself. She settled down to sleep, but she seemed to be woken almost at once with supper, later to have her temperature recorded and finally after she really thought she might rest, to feed the baby.

At last, they moved the babies to the Nursery and Roz believed she would sleep at last, but they woke her again at midnight to feed again and thereafter she did not sleep for the crying she could hear coming from the nursery. She wondered if it was her own nameless son. When she was considering adoption, she had hoped they would call him 'Peter', now with his only identification, 'Baby Peters 6lbs. 1oz. June 22, 1961' written on a tag around his ankle she realised his surname would necessitate thinking again, if she were to keep him.

Could she really keep her baby?

For the remainder of the night, she turned the problem over and over in her mind. In the frightening gloom, she thought of explaining it all to her father, who had not seen her since before Christmas. She thought of arriving back at Julie's flat with the baby, Julie expecting it to be adopted, a reward for her patient but rather obviously performed duty in shielding Roz from the world whilst her tummy issued forth its enormous secret.

With the act of birth the curtain should have been lowered and the play over. Now if she were to arrive home with the child it would have scarcely begun.

During the months of pregnancy, she hadn't been proud of her condition and this had exaggerated her swollen stomach creating a heavy, ugly and loathsome walk. She had noticed other expectant mothers, compared their lightness of step to her own, but now with the baby safely delivered she did feel different. Her shame had also been converted to pride.

Julie's attitude had not increased her confidence. For instance, Roz found Julie never confided in her about her own personal life. She did not even know if Julie had any current boyfriends; she was out a lot and she appeared to entertain her friends away from the flat. It was good in a way that there was little rapport. She felt certain that Julie would not have talked about her condition to her parents. This was important so the news did not travel to her father.

Almost instinctively, saving it for a rainy day, Roz spent none of the money that Gerry had sent. She put it in a deposit account in the Post Office and did not tell Julie. She still received an allowance of ten pounds a month from her father, who in his last letter had promised to cut it out if she didn't go home within the next two weeks.

Well, she would do so, in ten days. She could rest at home...but with the baby?

This allowance had just covered the ten pounds needed for the flat each month and Roz had existed on the generosity of Julie to a greater extent than perhaps she realised. She knew Julie grumbled behind her back, but let her. She had found that she didn't qualify for a maternity allowance unless she had paid her full unemployment insurance stamp up to eleven weeks before the baby was born, but the grant of sixteen quid was substantial, together with nearly three pounds a week for the last eleven weeks of her confinement, and a free pint of milk daily.

Julie had resisted handing in the tokens from Roz's milk token book at first, but finally had capitulated feeling more shame than Roz from the milkman's enquiring look.

'You air-hostesses!' He had said. 'It's true then, what they say about flying fast then? Fast in the air, fast on the ground!' He was only joking and fortunately, Julie laughed, but Roz had blushed.

In comparison with her problems, the dole money had seemed an insult to Roz and she had failed to queue for it. This, she knew had made Julie angry. True, Roz had little else to do with her days, but Julie didn't feel as self-conscious as she did and because of the law, Julie could not collect it for her.

Roz might have met Ben if she had collected it regularly.

In later weeks, she had become very worried about Ben. Once she had set off to walk over from the flat to Guiseley, but it was a long way, and halfway there she had lost courage and returned to the flat. If Ben had not been drunk he would not have got into such a mess. All that would come of helping Ben out of his predicament would be to point an accusing finger in Gerry's direction.

Some days she never left the flat. She jealously drank her one-pint of milk and often a pint of water. She had a passion for tomatoes, cornflakes and for marmite sandwiches. Otherwise, she scarcely disturbed the budget at all. She forced herself to eat one egg twice a week and a piece of meat once a week. She eagerly accepted fish, but Julie never seemed to buy much and she was usually too embarrassed to go shopping for herself.

She had found an old gold ring, which could be reversed to hide the small ruby stone on the underside of her third left-hand finger. Wearing this she occasionally took the bus and went for long solitary walks towards Otley Chevin. She would walk up to the edge of the escarpment and look over Wharfedale toward Almscliff Crag. The space that she saw lightened her load and promised that beyond there was a better life than this. Although she didn't actually put on much weight her tummy was distended and felt heavy. Her coat was nowhere near voluminous enough and she was glad when the warmer months came the borrowed maternity clothes came into season. She was either too hot or too cold and always restless throughout the pregnancy.

If the weather was poor she stayed at home with the cheap magazines on which she preferred to spend her money rather than food. She bought nothing for the baby she was not going to keep.

Sometimes if Julie was out she played the gramophone, but Julie complained that Roz was using unnecessary electricity if she found out, and that it was bad enough that she was spending extra on heating and lighting now that she wasn't working. Once Roz helped herself to a martini whilst Julie was out, but when Julie found out on her return, Roz thought Julie was going to hit the roof so she never did it again.

She didn't really crave for alcohol. It was physical touch and someone to hug or kiss her that she wished for most. When Julie was at home she spoke very little and when she was out she cried from time to time.

Once, about eight weeks before the birth, Julie had taken Roz to meet her mother in a discreet café near Leeds.

She had made it quite obvious that Roz worked for at the airport hinting that it was in the Operations Office and she made it equally obvious that Roz was no real friend of Julie's and certainly no hint that they had ever shared a flat. And in a way Roz understood, she felt she might have introduced Julie to her own mother in the same way under the circumstances. Mrs. Rhodes had been sympathetic and said she would get in touch with

Roz's doctor and arrange for the adoption. Roz hadn't told her who the father was when she had asked.

With morning, Roz's despair had lifted a little, at six o'clock the maternity ward broke into a hustle of activity. It wasn't long after another bath before Roz was subjected to another torture common to maternity hospitals in the sixties, when she was persuaded to open her bowels against her better instincts.

'Must keep them moved,' was obviously the motto but the pain from the swollen orifice and haemorrhoids, which had constantly troubled her for the last four months, was almost unbearable. At least, Roz reflected grimly, her efforts kept her from dwelling too much on other problems, but she was tired from the lack of sleep that she had a job to keep her eyes open when they brought the baby for her to feed.

The other mothers on the ward looked so happy. Could the discomfort of childbirth be minimised to such an extent by the presence of a husband?

Then they brought Baby back for his bath and life took on meaning again.

Everything was brought to hand, the soap for his hair, under his arms and his body, a clean towel, large enough to wrap him completely and talcum powder, pins and clean napkins. Roz sat on the chair and held her son while the nurse tested the water. She gently put him into the warm water, holding him with her arms underneath. He was happy and content and the nurse told Roz how lucky she was, as most babies hated water at first and screaming they became almost impossible to hold. Gently and lovingly Roz was able to dry the tiny creature, dust him with powder and put his nappy on.

She cuddled him for a while. Tomorrow she thought she would be able to take him back to the home and there she would have to decide whether to keep this small living thing they had created in one short hour of love.

Keep the baby she was sure she must, but how could she?

The girl in the next bed received her third bowl of flowers; the girl in the other bed had at least six arrangements and many more cards arranged around her possessions. Roz had nothing.

A little later a second post arrived.

She was surprised to receive two letters. One was a card 'congratulating' her from Julie and it was difficult to decide whether it had been chosen carelessly or deliberately. Out of wedlock, Roz did not care to consider the physical act of birth as an achievement.

The other envelope contained another card; perhaps more suitably worded; 'Grin & Chin Up! Old Spud!' and the picture rose larger than life from the cardboard; an old large potato together with a chinless face imposed on it. Inside was written:

'At least you're not boiled alive, mashed, chipped or peeled!' It was signed 'Reg'.

Every Thursday, throughout her indisposition Roz had utilised the same park bench. At first, he had passed, saying merely "good afternoon," but after two or three weeks he had sat at the other end of the bench.

'Cold, isn't it, today?' he had said in March. 'A deceptive month, isn't it?'

'Very,' she had replied. Reg was only young, certainly younger than Gerry, about twenty-six, Roz had guessed. Gradually he had told her that he was married, with two children and his wife now expecting twins. He was a schoolteacher; they were both Welsh and short of money. On Thursdays, he took a stroll in his free period, trying to find inspiration for a T.V. script.

Was Roz married? His Welsh voice was friendly; it was not an impertinent question. Neither was the following query; but she was expecting a baby?

He was very sympathetic. He told her of the double shock of his wife's conception, twins due in April, completely unexpected. They were Socialists, with a capital S. He bemoaned their financial circumstances, continually hooked on hire purchase and extended credit but a strong belief that a new government would relieve all his problems. He passionately believed this.

He was not really Roz's type of person.

His main concern was with the overpopulation of the world. He maintained that no one should have more than two children or there would be no resources for future generations. He was convinced that by 1970 that you would need a licence to produce children. Abortion would be legal and encouraged he had said.

He was horrified that he and his wife had committed such a sin and were to be a six persons family.

One afternoon expounding on the decisions, with which he and his wife had been faced when they found they were expecting the twins, he went deep into the case for abortion.

'It's a very simple operation you know. Absolutely no need for all the ballyhoo and rigmarole surrounding it, there isn't.' His soft Welsh tongue would emphasise, 'you young things you know, you really ought to be made to take this contraceptive pill, you should.' But he was often laughing and not criticising Roz personally.

Reg had really helped to bring Roz's misfortune back into perspective. In due time the twins were born and for a few weeks, Roz did not see him. Then in early May he was back again, giving her advice, describing the twins' advent into the world in detail.

Roz speculated if Reg would help her now her own son was born. He might be in favour of her keeping the child. He would know how to help her. She knew where he lived; she knew he would help, although she had never met his wife.

There was a nagging doubt that Reg's wife might not be so willing to help her. After all Roz's son had no named father. There was always the question why Reg had not invited Roz to meet his wife already.

Perhaps Lucinda would help? Perhaps she really would…but how? She who had caused much trouble in Roz's life already.

But by the time the Doctor made his evening rounds, Roz was beginning to feel much happier than she had been for weeks, someone was bound to help. Perhaps she felt better because at last she was more rested. She was even considering such mundane chores as washing her hair, being able to bend over the basin again, instead of having to wash it uncomfortably in the bath, which in keeping with the times had no shower in the bath. Primarily she was looking forward to wearing her own clothes again.

'Well young lady,' said the doctor, so loudly that Roz blushed.

'Hear you want to keep this handsome son of yours. Don't propose to say anything. I've seen the report the Sister has made and I think the best thing is to

261

get you and your youngest back to Roselea. To this end I have asked for an ambulance to be here in half an hour. You're a strong lass and your son is equally robust and you'll get good care at Roselea.'

NINE: "AND DID YOU EVER SEE AN OYSTER WALK UPSTAIRS...?"

August 1972

(i)

William Weighton was still struggling with the problem of replacing all the three journalists he had fired in May. He didn't often speak of his work, to his wife Rosalind, but as she watched him down his second gin William told her that in Tom Morton's place he had engaged a new journalist called Benjamin Smith.

Unlikely to be the Ben Smith she had once known at Ferryair, who was never known as Benjamin. Even so, the thought did not stop her heart missing a beat, however far-fetched it was. The Ben she had known was a pilot, not a writer.

As Rosalind tried to sleep she could not quite dismiss from her mind the consideration that the last time she had seen the Ben Smith she had known that he had been a council maintenance man. Such an occupation, was not her fault or of her doing.

She felt guilty that in nine years since her last visit to Yeadon, she had thought often of Gerry Duncan, but rarely of Ben. She would have liked to meet Gerry just once more.

The next morning, she was still attempting to piece the scanty fears together. Unfortunately, like a difficult jigsaw, they didn't fit any better by light of day.

She had simply decided to stop worrying, it would be a completely impossible coincidence that the

263

heavy drinking Ben Smith she knew could have turned into William's new journalist when the 'phone rang.

It was William. 'The Chairman has asked your father if we can use the house you have for rent on Savile Park for this new man Smith? Can you ring the caretaker and ask him to make everything habitable?'

She swallowed hard, foolishly, she told herself, a mere coincidence.

William Weighton continued. 'I've just met him and his wife, both very decent people. You'll do your best with the house, won't you darling? They don't know a soul in Halifax. It will be good if we can try to be a little neighbourly. Oh, by the way, they've five, *five*, children!'

So that ruled it out, thought Rosalind with some relief. It would be more than an extraordinary circumstance if it were the same Ben, even though Guiseley was probably only fifteen miles from Halifax.

For one thing, the Ben Smith she knew was not married.

Even if he had married since they last met, it was unlikely that he would have had five children at his age.

Five children! When she had known Ben, there had been Geoffrey. And another thing, Ben had simply not been newspaper material, but she thought again of the definitely untidy, alcoholic, but equally loveable person she had known.

Strangely enough, she could not quite remember his physical features. Stranger, nor could she remember those of Gerry, not absolutely clearly. Yet if she met him in the street, she would recognise him, she was sure.

If it was the same Ben, and possibly it could be, he could have news of Gerry. Indeed, with Guiseley being so close to them, even though it was a place she rarely gave a second thought to nowadays, it would be more of a coincidence if it was the same Ben Smith.

She decided to drive over to Savile Park. It was raining. She put on her raincoat. It was pure silk, but proofed; an extravagant present from William last time he was in Knightsbridge. He was always a generous man.

The 'phone rang again.

'We've just found out the ages of the Smith children,' said William's secretary. 'William says you'll have to put the adult boy in the attic rooms, and tell the caretaker to arrange the other rooms to allow for an eleven years old boy and three younger children.

I don't know their sexes. Perhaps the eleven years old should go in the attic with his elder brother?'

Rosalind knew now that it could not possibly be the same Ben Smith, even allowing for Geoffrey as the adult child, even making allowances for Ben marrying again, eleven years ago she knew Ben and there was no baby at that time.

She was disappointed.

(ii)

The middle of August was warm. The garden had reached a zenith.

Rosalind gathered flowers, and in the peaceful garden, her thoughts turned to the bizarre conversation she had had with William the evening previously. She had expressed an opinion to William that women having more than one child might not be brave, but merely incredible animals trying to achieve satisfaction through the act of birth. William had clearly not understood, not following her reasoning at all. He was male and knew nothing of her own childbearing experience. The twins were adopted.

Now she was preoccupied by the strange thought that there was a fine line between pain and pleasure.

Satisfaction, she had told him, was just the right word. After the passing of time, even a few days, the memory of pain in childbirth would diminish, the memory would be of the pleasure of the birth.

One would therefore happily allow oneself to be seduced into the same situation again, knowing that, when one has endured nine months of discomfort and the hours of climax of the actual birth, the satisfaction from this act was paramount, and more, the total submission of woman would dwarf the importance of the child that was emerging from the swollen womb. Gradually however in the minutes following the birth, the baby would assert himself and the confidence of the woman would lessen as the memory of nature's greatest climax was overwhelmed by maternal instinct.

That, believed Rosalind, was the theory but only Rosalind could not put it into practice. Her women friends had several babies; some women chose to have large families. Rosalind could not forget the pain, even yet, and as the twins were adopted she could not own up to her experience of childbirth. William, therefore, knew nothing of the pain of childbirth.

Perhaps, she thought, it remained the greatest subconscious gift a woman could give to a man she loved. Only to Rosalind it had not quite felt that when William had asked for love.

She thought of the good grace with which William, who didn't know she took the pill after years of being fitted with a coil, had allowed her to accept the twins. All these years and he knew nothing of the child and the pain; the mental anguish arising from just thinking of him, a ginger-haired boy who must be eleven years old, was intolerable.

Anyone who had suffered such mental anguish would verify that physical pain was preferable. Her only son.

But Rosalind's twins were adopted because William thought she was barren.

William knew nothing of her contraceptive devices. Nor for that matter did the Adoption Society.

23 June 1961

(iii)

Half an hour after the doctor spoke to her and still in her old blue dressing gown Roz was travelling to the other side of Leeds in a small ambulance, the baby asleep on her knees and a young nurse at her side.

'You've upset the applecart, 'aven't you? I gather there was someone 'specting to adopt your baby. Adoption society have been ringing 'ospital all t'day to see if you'd made up yer mind. I expect you'll change it though. I'd a friend who kept 'er babbee once. It's in care now though.' The nurse droned on in the flat pessimistic tones of the West Riding. She was a pretty girl and the heavy somewhat masculine voice was a shock. 'She couldn't manage. Poor little blighter, it could 'ave had a proper 'ome, if she'd 'ad 'im adopted at birth. You know 'ow it is, people don't like adopting them two-year-olds or t'older ones. Last I 'eard 'e was in a h'orphanage,' she finished triumphantly haitches all over the place.

The nurse looked happy to talk all evening. Roz was glad when they reached Roselea Home. A beautiful Georgian mansion, but its glory faded now. Since the war, few families had been able to afford the upkeep on such suburban masterpieces and as more and more people moved out into Wharfedale and the villages around Harrogate, so the neighbourhood took on a new role, part student accommodation, part offices and part institutions such as this one. Only thirty years previously the house would have echoed to children's voices, nannies with charges in prams, domestic staff and a chauffeur polishing the family's Daimler.

It was eight o'clock and she was surprised to see Julie's mother, Mrs. Rhodes with the Matron when she entered the hall.

'I've put her into the single room Nurse,' Matron said to the uniformed junior standing nearby. 'If you would show Miss Peters up to her room, Mrs. Rhodes and I will be able to talk to her in a minute or two.

True to Matron's word, Roz became subjected to a barrage of questions immediately she was unpacked.

'Are prospective adoptive babies in such short supply that you must haggle for mine?' Roz was finally driven to ask bitterly.

'Miss Peters,' the matron answered in the calm tone of a woman only just keeping her temper. 'That isn't the point. It is true that we always have more adoptive parents than babies, thank goodness, at least white ones, indeed you can thank your lucky stars that you didn't foolishly conceive a coloured child.'

'And if you don't mind me saying so, that's also hardly the point,' Roz counteracted, her hazel green eyes flashing angrily and the knuckles of her hands went white. 'Black people don't frighten me.'

'Oh dear,' continued Mrs. Rhodes, sympathetically stepping in for Matron, but still sounding patronising. 'We're trying to help you; when you came to see me with my daughter, I might add, you were adamant that you didn't want to keep the child. Now I'm in charge of mothers who wish their babies to be adopted, if we had thought you so indecisive or that you wished to keep the child, my colleague would've

269

looked after you and perhaps been of more assistance to you. Now then dear, you must tell me what has made you change your mind.'

What a world of words, thought Roz. Everyone was influencing each other with a lot of words, all of them potential psychiatrists.

'Is it only that you were mistakenly allowed to see the child and, worse, allowed to look after him in the hospital? My dear, if that is the only reason you most certainly will discover in time that you've made the wrong decision. You will almost undoubtedly revert to your original decision in time and grow to resent the child.'

'I wanted my baby during childbirth. That's when I decided.' Roz was uncooperative and deliberately not objective. Not many months the other side of adolescence it was not surprising she was confused. Did she want the child? Was she really only trying to bring attention to herself in what must be the most traumatic experience of her life? Was she excusing her guilt by making a fuss, so that for the rest of her life she could tell herself that in all conscience she had tried to keep the child?

'Well my dear, we shall be in tomorrow to see that your decision is final. We'd found a wonderful home for your child. I couldn't have found him nicer adoptive parents, and able to provide for him amply too!' Roz was surprised that Mrs. Rhodes had given in so readily. A tiny flicker of doubt crossed her mind, was she really causing this scene for effect?' She thought Mrs. Rhodes looked very dignified, like her mother would have looked; in her smart navy and white check suit and a navy hat. She wished her mother were alive.

Lucinda would be smart when she was matronly. As for herself....

'It is a mistake to let these mothers have their babies in hospital,' snapped the Matron, herself a neatly dressed woman. 'The result is always the same upset for the mother and child. It always takes the same course. By tomorrow, Mrs. Rhodes, she will realise that we're right. You'll see!'

'I hope so, Matron. I do hope so.' Thus, they left Roz to have the last word. They left Roz and curiously she slept. Nobody brought the baby near her.

She did not wake until the following morning.

At ten o'clock the next morning Roz had a visitor. It was Julie.

Roz was embarrassed and Julie's larger than life smile and the expression of 'doing one's duty' was similar to the one her mother had worn the evening before.

'I hear it was a little boy,' Julie said uneasily and unnecessarily since she had already sent Roz a card congratulating her on the birth of a son.

'Yes, they haven't let me see him since I arrived back here. I've asked for him several times this morning.'

'I know. Mother rang me last night. They think you've changed your mind too late and that you're still emotionally influenced by the experience of childbirth. I tend to agree. What would we do with a baby?'

'We?'

'Well you'll have to live somewhere, I meant the expression figuratively and you must remember Roz that he won't be a baby forever. You could perhaps stay on at the flat for a couple of months, but Mummy's bound to find out that you're living with me and she won't approve.' Julie sounded very superior. 'And I'm sure she has absolutely no idea that your father knows my father.' That simple statement completely stopped Roz's thoughts in their tracks, but she must not weaken. It was important to stay on course.

'She'll have to visit you every so often to make sure that you're looking after the babe alright,' Julie ploughed on, 'at least someone will from the Society. And then he grows older and all your life is going to be devoted to looking after this illegitimate son.'

'I know, all of it...but he is my son, and I loved his father and I want to keep him. How can you tell me that I can find more satisfaction than this? You don't know that I'll have any more children; this may be my last chance. I may never get married. No one may ask me. I could die old and lonely when all the time somewhere in the world there would be a son, my son who could have kept me company.'

'But that's selfish. Sweetie, it just isn't reason enough. You haven't thought of the difficulties of bringing up a child on your own, particularly a boy. Have you really considered whether it is fair to deny the child full parentage and a home when he has been offered one? My mother broke all the Association's rules yesterday when she told you she had found a good home for him, but she has; and a much better one than you could ever offer ... middle-class people, with money, a childless couple and do remember adoptive parents are taking on their task voluntarily. Even if a fellow offered to marry you tomorrow, even if you were sure he would make you a good husband, he would also be taking on your mistake as well as you, and it takes a saint to do that successfully. Roz, instead of looking for a husband for yourself, you would subconsciously always be looking for a father for your son, a substitute father, not someone either to act as the father of a dead man's son, but someone to take on the lover and child of another man. You will be seeking a miracle and you may not find it.'

'Julie, you've been sent by your mother to talk me out of this, so I forgive you, but honestly, you're wasted in your job, you're the one who should be working for the Adoption Society. What a saleswoman, but I'm sorry ducky, it just doesn't wash.'

'If that's the way you feel, I can't do anymore. There's a letter from your father. I've brought it with me. Even he doesn't know, does he? You've been quite clever to conceal it. Next weekend you could go back to Halifax, and visit him as though nothing has happened. You could go into your local pub on Saturday and meet the most handsome fellow you could imagine. You could begin to live again!'

'Thanks, Julie, I know you mean well. But please leave this to me. I do want my baby. I'm going to call him Andrew. Simply because it is such a nice name. I'll find my own accommodation. I don't say I wouldn't be grateful for the use of the flat for a few days until I can do this, but I am completely self-sufficient. I've quite a bit of money put away. Today is my birthday. I'm twenty-one! This day next year I'm due to inherit a trust fund which would mean I needn't work, if I live simply and invest it.'

Roz hadn't meant to tell anyone that. She looked at the slim trim girl with short neat brown hair who sat on the edge of her bed. Once she had trusted Julie, now she wasn't sure. Somehow it felt to be cheating to allow all these busybodies the satisfaction of knowing she was financially secure. 'Don't tell anyone about the money, please Julie. Everyone is concerned for the child, but don't you think if you're really honest with yourself that one real parent is better than none?' Roz was tired; she lay back on the pillows and smiled sadly.

'Most adoptions are very satisfactory, more so often than real parentage, because the parents want the children so badly in the first place and there are people who make quite sure that they do. My mother says that if everyone had to suffer such difficulties before getting a child, like these poor adoptive parents do, there would be better marriages and less cruelty to kids. Less broken homes and more tolerance and because you only had a child if you could prove you desperately wanted one, there would be less violence, teddy boys and things.'

'I don't entirely follow you; children often bring a stability to a marriage that wasn't there before. Are you going to adopt children just to prove to the world that you really want them? It isn't just because you have love-sex with your lover or husband that they were conceived!' Rosalind thought she had scored a point. 'Another thought occurs to me Julie, in all this, say the adoptive parents for my baby Andrew are killed, perhaps in an air crash or a car crash and I'm still living, perfectly well, normal and able to look after this child that I wasn't encouraged to keep. But I don't know he is now an orphan? You can't generalise. Anything might happen in life. No-one can foresee the future and surely this is a decision that I've to take on my own?' Since Julie took this in silently Roz went on, 'Please Julie, thank you for coming but my mind is made up. Have a word with Matron for me and ask if I could have Andrew in here, do you think you could?'

274

'I don't think so, love. I've only come as a friend.'

Some friendship, thought Roz bitterly, confirming her thought as Julie added 'but I'll tell Mummy that your heart's set on keeping the child. I expect I'll have to see if I can find you a room or a flat somewhere. I suppose you could stay with me for a week or so.'

'Bless you, Julie. I knew you'd help.' But neither girl sounded very sincere and Julie left giving Roz a light kiss.

'I don't approve mind you, and Happy Birthday...I'm sorry that I forgot it.'

'I'd have liked Andrew to be born on this day you know.'

Julie closed the door behind her and Roz opened her father's letter.

Out fell a cheque for fifty pounds.

"Darling Pan" the letter read with her father reverting subconsciously to the childhood name he had always called her. *"I am so anxious about you. Now it is your birthday and it seems incredible that you haven't arranged to come home for this weekend. Your letters have been so vague since Christmas. You mention little of your work and you never send postcards from these places you visit. Only one since January, postmarked Yeadon, and "Sorry I forgot to post this when I was in Rome."* (Roz remembered asking Julie to buy the card when she was in Italy for this very purpose, it had been careless not post it from abroad; but too complicated.)

"Darling if you are in trouble you must come home. I am the person to help you. Lucinda has also become so

*troubled that yesterday she rang the airline. They told
her that you've resigned! Your letters have specifically
mentioned flying, albeit vaguely since that time.*

*"Who are you flying for and why did you not mention
you had changed airlines? I believe you need me. I
shan't be cross and to this end, I am coming for you on
Saturday to bring you home for a few days. You must be
entitled to a few days holiday whoever you're working
for, whatever you are doing! Can you, please, arrange
the time to do this?*

"Happy Birthday darling. All my love from Daddy."

"P.S. Lucinda and Derek have had their baby - a girl."

The shock was enormous. For as long as Roz could
remember her father had ridden over her affairs. From
the time, she was a child to the present day she had never
know him show concern unless her life was interfering
with the smooth running of his existence.

Almost more traumatic was the news of the birth
of Lucinda's baby. Clearly, it would be perfect. Tiny,
engaging and pretty, unless of course, it had the ill luck
to inherit her mother's teeth. But without the teeth she
could not have the attractive lisp.

These thoughts were pure cattiness and getting
her nowhere.

Roz felt strangely exhausted. Suddenly the fight
had gone out of her, left her empty. She had had a baby.
So, what? Lucinda and Derek had managed to upstage
her, even on that.

She knew she would stand no chance of keeping
the child if her father discovered his existence before she
could establish him well and permanently into her
pattern of life. She had hoped to persuade the Home to
keep the child for two days whilst she went to Halifax to

see her father, at the weekend. How, she thought acrimoniously, when she was really fighting a losing battle anyway? Was there no one who could help her keep her child, it was obvious that she could not gain the support of her father or of the Home. Even with Reg, she was counting on the support of his wife, a stranger, and adding more difficulties to the unease of their own fraught life.

Roz rang the bell at her bedside. It was the news that Andrew had a cousin which had affected her decision most.

The nurse came in her own time. Roz supposed she might have had a haemorrhage in the fifteen minutes that elapsed.

'Yes?'

'Tell Matron,' she said steadily tossing her auburn hair defiantly, 'tell Matron that she can have my child. I'm not keeping him. Now go away and leave me in peace for two days. Only bring me my food. I don't want to see anyone. I also would like some notepaper and an envelope.'

But Roz's instructions were not to be. In much less time than it took the nurse to answer her bell initially, the Matron burst into her room.

'Now then, my girl. It is all very well behaving like some temperamental schoolgirl, but you're a responsible adult now. I'm glad you've made the right decision, but you won't make it an excuse to talk and dictate to my nurse as you did.' Her anger seemed real and her cheeks were flushed. 'You'll put on your dressing gown and you'll go through into the dayroom where the other ladies are. Your things will be transferred to the main bedroom. We need this single room for more unfortunate cases than yours.

'Your baby will be looked after; you'll have no need to see him. Fortunately, you've already signed the form and it hasn't been revoked. I shall ring the prospective adopters and tell them they can have the baby in two weeks' time.

'Normally we don't allow them to go to the parents until they're at least a month old, but we've been very fortunate in securing parents for your baby boy who are very well thought of in their district.

'Now I must tell you this because it is the law, I have to. But I hope sincerely you won't change your mind. In three months, you'll be asked to sign a form releasing your responsibility for the child forever. After you've signed this form you've no redress and the child legally belongs to its adopting parents only. Since in the past, you've shown a marked tendency to change your mind I now beg of you not to let your son go to his new parents if you intend to change your mind again. I cannot emphasis too strongly the appalling distress for these new parents if their baby is whipped away after they've cared for him for the first vital months of his life.

'Nurse will move your things and show you to the day room. None of the young ladies there have decided to keep their babies. Have you any questions?'

'Can my baby be named by me?'

'No, I'm afraid not.'

'Not even if you suggested to the parents that I would like him to be called Andrew.'

'Well I'll mention it to Mrs. Rhodes, but it's not allowed.'

The Matron left without waiting for Roz to reply. It had been a feature of the whole incident that people had very little desire to hear Roz's own point of view. Only Julie had ever really allowed her to voice her opinion. Even she, Roz felt had done it for effect rather than the importance to the well-being of the child or Roz's future life.

Roz felt it was all very negative. She was completely exhausted with the whole business. She felt emotionally drained, which she told herself sharply, was the sudden cessation of breast-feeding. In that directive, they were right on the maternity ward; she should not have started it.

She would write to her father and tell him not to send the car, but that she would travel home making her own way by bus on Friday. In the meantime, she would rest and take advantage of the accommodation she was paying for so dearly at Roselea.

No fiat of impudent orders from either the Matron or the nurses would now disturb her convalescence.

She had no wish to communicate with the other girls. They were as emotionally involved in their own problems as she was in hers. She realised that she would quickly recover strength if there were no baby to keep her awake at nights. She found she was able to control her emotions surprisingly quickly and suddenly she was alive again for the first time in eight months. A child who was no longer a responsibility must cease to exist. Her father would never know about Andrew, and she would never see the child again.

As for her non-attendance at Bankfield Hall, her father's home, couldn't it just be a very dishy boyfriend, who had sadly ditched her just this week?

It was a risk, but Roz knew she'd take it.

It happened all the time with young girls, infatuation, and suddenly, nothing. Now that she had capitulated over the adoption of her son she even suspected that Julie and Mrs. Rhodes would help her out of any difficulty, assuming the worst that her father or Lucinda had been in direct touch with Lionel Rhodes; and it wasn't likely that Lionel Rhodes himself would know she had resigned, simply too important to be concerned with the minutiae of the lives of his staff. It would be the operations manager they would be put through to. With Mrs. Rhodes on her side 'for doing the sensible thing,' she could at least infer that Lionel Rhodes had been mistaken about her resignation. The obvious solutions are often the ones that work best.

Certainly, a boyfriend should be a good enough reason for her father to believe she had not felt like a visit home. It sounded an excellent answer to her problem and she spent the next twenty minutes before the nurse came to move her, thinking up a wonderful and likely relationship with a young East Riding farmer whom she would call Simon. Indeed, Simon could be cast in the role of baby's father should she be bullied about that one still! Why had she never dreamt this scenario up before?

It was so plausible that she almost believed it.

And Mrs. Rhodes, well, she probably still thought Roz worked as a secretary at the airport, in Operations. The woman had far too many other matters on her mind to worry about Rosalind's personal life. Again, Roz congratulated herself on her imagination!

(iv)

Roz's visit home went well. She arrived, as planned, eight days after the birth of Andrew. Her father accepted her apology and the story she weaved about the fictitious 'Simon' and Roz did not feel it was necessary to go into details - he didn't expect it. It was sufficient that the episode had prevented her from visiting home and her father showed some concern, such as would befit a daughter who had suffered from a broken romance. The atmosphere was easy and friendly.

'Just so long as you're not in trouble, Rosalind; that is all I was worrying about!' And he opened a bottle of champagne, which she enjoyed.

After this James Peters said very little. Roz thought he might not have been easily convinced, but fortunately, her figure had quickly returned to normal, and the incident had done nothing more than show a slight thickening around the waist and somewhat heavier breasts than normal. All easily translated into compensatory eating after her tragic affair with Simon.

As Roz left Bankfield Hall at the end of her visit her father pressed two five-pound notes into her hand.

'Come home sooner this time, pet. I miss you, you know. I'll always find you a job nearer home if you would consider it.'

Roz said she would consider it and thanked him politely for a lovely weekend. The only flaw in the visit had been her own visit to see Lucinda and Derek and their new baby, Felicity. Even the name of the child upset her and on seeing the baby, Roz had broken into uncontrollable sobs, but everyone concerned had put it down to Roz's special relationship with Derek and Lucinda.

Roz loved her cousin Lucinda, as much as she loved anyone. Both Derek and Lucinda made an enormous effort to be kind to her and Lucinda persuaded Derek to take Roz to a party while she looked after Felicity. There was a rock and roll band and Derek even made an attempt to teach Roz to twist, a dance which was taking over from the jive.

Although she did attempt to go back to Yeadon Airport, she never made it further than the flat, where Julie, the Chief Stewardess showed her the memorandum, which had been issued when Ben lost his job. It was highly irregular of Julie to do this, but she seemed determined that Roz should see it. It merely suggested that Ben was drinking more than was safe in his type of employment, although it did not say so in many words and took several sentences to reach the point. It did not mention anything about Ben entertaining hostesses in his room.

Nevertheless, Roz still felt slightly responsible and after two weeks she set out to see Ben, at home, in Guiseley.

Sensitive, intelligent Ben had lost his job. Destroyed himself through drink, was it her fault?

Of course, she knew Ben had been crazy about her, a lot of other people in the company also knew this.

She walked down into the village of Yeadon and took a bus to the small grey town of Guiseley. It was near enough to walk, but she wasn't inclined to do so. She had often done her shopping in Guiseley and walked back to Yeadon for the exercise and she knew her way around easily. The new houses looked finished. Beyond them, she could see the small row of cottages where she thought Ben still lived. It was not unattractive, being a terrace with a good deal of sculptured stonework in the Victorian mode, with neat little gardens to the front, but in the sixties, many of these houses were uncared for and yet to be restored. They were not yet in fashion again. Not for Ben, now, the new bungalows he had desired so much a few months ago. She crossed the road and walked up the long flight of steps, which would lead her to Ben's cottage.

She was tired after her walk and the exertion of the steps. She paused to draw breath and wondered how long it would be before she could consider herself physically fit again. The new houses were about five hundred yards up the road. Ben's small house was nearly opposite her on the left.

She turned towards the cottage. A man was walking down the footpath pushing a pram. She wished there was no evidence of babies in the world. But it seemed, that at that moment, everywhere she turned, there was a baby, reminding her; overwhelming her with maternal instinct.

The pram was about twenty-five yards from her. The man pushing it was an older man, possibly a young grandfather. She was so used to not wearing glasses that she had left hers at home. The Company rule had been not to employ stewardesses who wore glasses, so Roz did not wear hers, and few people wore contact lenses at this time.

But she could see the man now. She stopped quite still and looked at the pram and then at the man and back at the pram.

The pram was empty.

'You look surprised', said the man. 'Our baby arrived only yesterday and I've just collected this pram from friends which they're lending to us. But then, men don't often push empty prams about do they?'

Roz felt rooted to the ground, the mere sight of a baby or a pram was quite sufficient in her present state to throw her off her balance, but this was more than she could take.

'My wife was a little taken aback too,' continued the man, noticing Roz's white face. 'We only had our adoption application passed a month ago and we didn't expect a baby so soon.'

'That's marvellous!' Despite the emotion trembling in Roz's voice, she might be talking to a complete stranger. 'Is it a girl or a boy?' she asked.

'A boy.' Gerry spoke quietly and his steel grey eyes glanced involuntarily towards Roz's flatter stomach. 'And your news?'

'Also, a boy. He's going to be adopted next week.'

'And here have I just adopted another man's child, when your son and my son will be adopted in the same week!' The man and the young woman stood facing each other; their expressions were worthy of a Grand Opera and the slight breeze on that hot July day helped the sun to burn their skin. It was difficult to talk and the man who seemed, not months, as he should, but years older than when she had last seen him. Short, heavy set he was to Roz a little less than she remembered, yet…

She had not seen him since Tangier. He went on staring at the auburn-haired girl, who in turn had matured. 'All these years, Holly and I've waited to have a child, for years we've been on the adoption lists but somehow the right child never came up and *now* how can I adopt a child while you have my child, my own child? How can I do it?' And Gerry looked angrily at the girl. 'How could you Roz, why did it happen this way?' There was malice, temper and a twist to his usually firm voice which made Roz alarmed and distressed.

Had this man known why they had fired his friend? Had he allowed Ben to take the blame for his own deed? Did she feel different now, different from how she had felt before the birth?

The man lent heavily on the handle of the empty pram.

'A month ago, my wife met Elsie Rhodes, Lionel's wife, they've been friends since schooldays. After all these years she persuaded us to adopt a child which she said would come from good stock. Holly agreed if the child were a boy. What are you doing here anyway?' He asked still angry, his tone still brutal, but Roz did not answer his question.

She shook her head. 'Did you say Mrs. Rhodes, do you mean Julie Rhodes' mother?'

'Yes,' he replied curtly. She hadn't been listening. 'Julie is Lionel and Elsie's daughter.'

'Then the baby you've got, probably came from the home where I had mine. If mine wasn't so young, if you'd just waited another week, or so, you might have got mine,' and Roz laughed and the shock of her harsh laugh made her cry. 'Do you hear what I said Gerry Duncan, you might have adopted *my* baby, your own son?' And there wasn't a soul on that quiet July day in the residential suburb of Guiseley who could hear the cry of anguish as it echoed across the wide valley. Except, that is, the rather stout middle-aged man with an empty pram, and he allowed the girl's almost silent hysteria to subside before he spoke.

He put the brake on the pram, moving closer to the girl, but appearing reluctant to touch her. 'On what day was your baby born?'

'On the 22nd June. I called him Andrew. He looked like you.' And Roz turned and ran; she ran down the hillside to the long steps, which led to the mill, which Gerry's grandfather had built and Gerry had to abandon his precious baby-carriage and run fast to catch the fleeing girl. When he caught her, he slapped her across the face and the blow marked her fair skin, so recently caught by the sun and wind.

'And if it should please you, young lady, we, Holly and I also call our son Andrew. We call him Andrew because the Matron from the home where he was born said the child's mother had particularly requested it. He was also born on June 22nd, and we were especially given him because he had red hair like Holly's.'

He looked ashen, but he was more worried about the girl whom he thought might faint. 'You see,' he said lamely, 'these things happen. By chance.'

'I never want to see him, he's yours now Gerry. Thank God! Your own son! He has a birthmark on his left heel. You look for that, it looks like a pear. Then you'll know for certain that you have your own son. And of course, you will never tell Holly he is your real son, your natural son, will you?'

'No, I'll never tell Holly. But each time I see your son I shall think of you.' But Gerry still did not touch Roz. Rather he turned to walk back to his pram again, but almost as an afterthought he asked quietly. 'Are you alright? Can you find your way home? What have all these months been like for you?'

'Pure hell. But now I've never been so happy. It has all been worth it. I've never been so happy in my life. Goodbye Gerry! I think I've given you what you want, exactly. Now I'm leaving Yeadon and Guiseley. I'm going to pick up my stuff from Julie's flat and leave you all to it. I've just decided and I'm going back to Halifax. I think that is what fate intended. I need never worry about my son again.'

She waved to the man. She had loved him once. The man that had been a lover. At the bottom of the steps she remembered Ben, but she continued back along the road towards the bus for Leeds. There seemed no need to track down Ben now.

Once there had been Derek. She had forgotten him. She would forget Ben. Would she forget Gerry?

TEN: HOROSCOPE

6 September 1972

(i)

A cloud quite unexpectedly hid the sun where minutes ago the three women had had the impression of sitting under a glorious Indian summer sky of blue.

'Do you feel cold, either of you?' Rosalind asked her best friend, Penny Sky, and a new acquaintance, the wife of Benjamin Smith, recently employed by her husband William. The three women were sitting on the patio watching the children play in the walled garden, having been entertained to lunch by Rosalind. It was Rosalind's attempt to introduce the newcomer to her own friends, but as she had predicted it had been an uphill task.

'Yes, actually I do feel chill,' said Penny Sky. 'I'll fetch my jacket,' and she left, almost with an audible sigh of relief. She found the conversation of Mrs. Smith inane. Rosalind was always full of good deeds, but Penny could have done without this. It was a waste of her time and she scarcely concealed it.

'Do you want to go inside? Would you rather?' Rosalind asked Mrs. Smith. She stared at the woman. She could not help it. She was much older than the Ben she remembered, it was impossible that she could be the wife of the pilot she had known. That was it, she thought, she should simply ask the woman if her husband was a pilot? No, he was a journalist, she knew

288

that! Silly question! Watch what you say Rosalind, she chided herself.

'I think the sun will come out again soon, don't you? I'll have to be getting home anyway, very soon. Carolyn will be wanting her tea.'

'Sure? You won't stay for tea?' asked Rosalind sincerity not strong in her voice. Go on; ask her if her husband flies planes. But instead, she heard herself say, 'Penny is staying - and I always give the twins tea at half-past four so you're welcome.'

Rosalind Weighton watched the three younger Smith children, her own six years old twins and the older children of tiny dark-haired Penny Sky. There were tricycles, sand and children spread all over the grass. The tent had collapsed and the noise was terrific. It was lucky the house on the hill had no near neighbours.

'Thank you no, we must get home,' and now it was Rosalind's turn to breathe a sigh of relief. She had been hoping for this in order to have a word with her good friend, Penny Sky Rhyl-Jones, on her own.

Rosalind had yet to meet Benjamin Smith, employed by her husband in the summer, and it was the first time she had entertained his family.

If she was truthful she went to considerable lengths to avoid meeting him, continually justifying to herself the impossibility of it being the same man. 'It would be such a coincidence, such a common name,' she would repeat to herself. Much continued to pain her, give her nightmares and re-ignite old stresses. It was as though she was ashamed of her younger days, indeed as well she might be.

She wished Penny Sky would hurry up, what could she be doing inside for so long. She had relied on Penny Sky's support on this occasion.

She gathered it was the Smith woman's second marriage.

'You were very courageous to start another young family, Ivy,' said Rosalind frantically trying to lift the conversation above the weather, the baby Carolyn's immediate needs and the price of infant feed. There was much she wanted to talk to Penny about, and here she was making useless small talk to this middle-aged frumpish bore, whose presence just stirred up other traumatic memories. Ivy: what kind of a name was that? So old-fashioned. Happily, the children would be back at school next week and she might get away without arranging any more such planned entertainments until the Christmas holidays.

'I don't think I'd much choice. Benjamin's a Catholic. He is now very devout and sincere. When Carolyn was born this year, it nearly killed me, but it was nothing to the discomfort I suffered when I was carrying Julian and the pain when he was born.' She laughed uneasily. She was also embarrassed.

Such awful small talk. If the woman didn't leave soon she was bound to say something really stupid. 'By the way,' Ivy Smith continued in a tone which announced that she had been primed to ask, 'Tell me, how is Mr. Peters, your father? Your husband says he hasn't been well.'

'Daddy! Oh, he's a lot better. The doctors are quite pleased. Mild heart attack, they said, but he must go slowly. When were you and your husband married?' Now, why had she asked that, Rosalind wondered? She must take it easy, it would not do to sound too curious.

'1964. July 14th, I was thirty-eight the same day,' Ivy stammered, because it was a lie. She was not legally married to Ben Smith. Ivy was her given first name, but it was only recently that she had started to use it, her pet childhood name too painfully reminding her of her first husband and the tragic end to that marriage.

'How extremely odd, another family plagued with birthdays under the sign of Cancer,' and Rosalind blushed, because aside from Andrew and nobody was talking about Andrew, it was only she who had a Cancerian birthday. 'You were married the year after I married William.'

As Penny Sky Rhyl-Jones returned the older woman said pleasantly, 'you're both so lucky to have youth on your side. You can imagine what these tiny ones do to me at my age!'

Rosalind shivered, but managed to wink at Penny without the visitor seeing. The woman was a fussy old hen; Rosalind at thirty-two did not want to think she would be too old to cope with babies when she was in her mid-forties. She changed the subject defensively. 'I just wish that William had not gone to Munich.'

Then, at that moment, she began again to think about Andrew. Must she think about him; all day, every day, even when she consciously tried to forget him?

Her eleven-year-old bastard son. Why think of him at all. It was all in the past now. Her life was full enough without thinking about him.

'It's terrible, isn't it?' Penny Sky was referring to the Olympic Games, to which Rosalind had felt, before yesterday, that her husband was making a very privileged visit. 'My papers didn't say the hostages were dead. I'd an awful shock when I heard the news on the radio this morning. What a so-called exhibition of peace!'

'It's the Germans I feel sorry for...they go to enormous lengths to make this particular Olympic Games more than a symbol of peace, almost an apology for the Games held in Berlin in 1936 and two small forces bring their own war into another camp and the whole hatred is stirred up again.'

Rosalind spoke, with feeling. 'What's worse is that everyone again feels it is a Jewish sacrifice. Last night on the news I was thrilled to hear that the West German police had been successful in killing only one of the terrorists and that the hostages were still alive, and this morning we hear that this is anything but the truth.'

'My first husband was very pro-Jewish. He was a prisoner of war. The Germans treated him very roughly.' Mrs. Smith spoke proudly, but Rosalind shivered and the other two women noticed.

The 'phone rang. It was William.

'Here I am. Back home.' His voice did not mask his relief. 'I'm at Manchester Airport. Awful trouble getting a flight from Munich. You should have been here'; criticism implied that she wasn't.' She hadn't expected him to run away and she had a curious feeling that she was mentally accusing him of being a coward. She said goodbye and put down the receiver. She thought he should have stayed until he had seen what he hoped to see in Germany. After all, he was a newspaper-man.

She returned to the garden. Ivy Smith was collecting together all the paraphernalia of a small children's outing.

(ii)

It had been raining in the small town of Guiseley. A man protected by a thick yellow mackintosh was working on some road works. He appeared to be fixing one of the modern concrete streetlights which the council had recently installed above the houses which were by now spreading out dormitory style along country roads. A portable radio was turned on and Roz could hear the Beatles song 'Love Me Do!' as she approached.

The older houses were still full of cottage character, small, square and even, with grey Yorkshire slate roofs. The newer houses were almost international, conformist and uninteresting and had none of the charm of the old industrial architecture that Rosalind remembered from two years previously. Two years ago, when things had been very different and now there was a whole new scenario. Fate had clearly picked her up, given her life a good shake, and put it down again.

Part of Guiseley's uniqueness was due to its geographical position, twixt and between as the estate agents' jargon went, the industrial suburbs of Leeds and Bradford and the beautiful countryside of the Yorkshire Dales which began in Airedale, and to which valley side Guiseley could just be said to cling. It was also very close to the new and growing airport but not greatly affected by it. With the general clean up throughout the West Riding, the town was beginning to collect some status with commuters.

Like all towns at this time, mid-twentieth century, it was still the heart supplying the pulse and character of the place. It was in the centre that the man was working.

On warm days, the town smelt of fresh bread and of industry and on wet days it smelt of the moors.

The man working on the electric lights was Ben Smith.

On this June Saturday, he was unaware that Roz Peters was standing in the doorway of a dress shop and she would not have liked him to see her. Ben Smith was not her quarry. In any case, it was two years since he had seen her and much had passed in that time.

She was not looking at the flowered skirts in the window with their hemlines now daringly raised above the knee; she was merely sheltering from the rain, whilst she thought things out. Soon she covered her red curls with her headscarf and moved on down the street.

Earlier in the week, men obviously had been resurfacing the road. In parts, they had laid open the tarmac and the earth underneath was dusty. Over the dusty area was the largest sheet of polythene Roz had ever seen. This modern equipment had been secured to the ground against the strong winds of the north with many large broken stones and the overall effect was absurd.

It had taken some courage to bring her to this part of the town.

From the dress shop, Roz had an advantage lookout. Gerry would not know he was being observed. The dormer bungalow, where Gerry Duncan must still live, with his wife, was an example of suburban perfection, even in the soft rain of the morning.

What had thrown Rosalind was the discovery of Ben Smith working on the lamppost.

So instead of just being able to watch Gerry's front door, she also had to be sure that Ben did not see her. Being a Saturday she had worked out that there was a more than a high chance that if she waited long enough someone might come out of the house and that could well be Gerry. Married men seemed to do errands on a Saturday.

Indeed, her discomfort did not last long, for, as though spellbound, she watched the front door of Gerry's smart new home open, Gerry himself appeared, closed the front door and walked down to the village.

Gerry reached the shops without once looking in Roz's direction.

He pushed open the door of a 'Do-it-yourself Shop' and walked in.

Roz felt ill. There was still no need to speak to Gerry but she badly wanted to give him the news.

She could turn and run for her own car in the safety of the car park before he came out of the shop. She could just as easily go home to Halifax.

Gerry had not seen her.

Walking straight into a puddle she splashed her stocking as she crossed the road. She had never met his wife, but she did know quite a lot about her.

Gerry had spoken often about Holly.

Roz walked to stand outside the joiner's shop and waited.

'Hallo,' he said as he came out of the shop. It was as though she had met him by appointment. There was no hint of the usual quizzical smile, but a strange flicker of pleasure at the corner of his mouth, and Roz's nerves vanished.

'I'm getting married.'

Having spoken she felt the statement might be premature.

It was two years since she had spoken to Gerry.

'You don't know him,' she further volunteered.

Gerry studied the green eyes. 'Is he rich?' He asked in true Yorkshire fashion.

'Fairly. He's clever. He's making money. He's a newspaper editor in partnership with the owner of the paper.'

'Well mannered? A gentleman?'

'Naturally.'

'Then you don't need my permission, do you?'

He took her hand and he pressed it very hard until she felt her veins rise as strings to her fingers, until she felt his rough palm, her body tingled. Ten minutes before Gerry Duncan had been the man she had once loved. Now he was the man she still did love. This was a crazy position in which to put herself.

'That old joiner nearly lost himself a job just now with that fancy new "DO-IT-YOURSELF" sign. I had forgotten he was a sign-writer. I was about to drive into Leeds to have a nameplate inscribed for our house. I only remembered that he did that sort of work as I was crossing the road. And damn it...I've gone and told him 'White Gates' when Holly insisted it should read only one "White Gate". She thinks it sounds better. I ask you? Well, she'll have to put up with it. I'm not going back into the shop, to put it right, with you here. You might run away!'

Roz opened her mouth. Only a splutter was emitted. 'I might.'

'Oh, come on with you lass! Don't tell me you're nervous.' He smiled.

They walked slowly down the street without asking each other where they were going.

'My dear Roz, you tell me that you are getting married. I tell you that Holly is expecting me to be out all day, to go up to Leeds for lunch. Tell me who says fate is not on our side? I missed you so much. Thought about you so often.'

They both noticed Ben Smith still adjusting the lighting, with his back to them, and despite his protective clothing obviously getting wetter all the time.

It was fairly clear he hadn't seen them.

'Do you think they pay him well?' she asked.

'He deserves to be!' Gerry shrugged. 'Poor devil! Had everything going for him when he was promoted; made up to Captain sooner than most men, and the silly bugger still couldn't control his drinking.' The swear word jarred and Roz realised it was probably the first time she had heard Gerry swear; he really used to disapprove of his crews using strong language.

She realised also how she had become conditioned to the milder manners of William and her home environment. Gerry went on, 'Ben should have been a writer. He was too creative to hold down a demanding job like flying. Remember all the time he devoted to scribbling notes in his diary whilst on trips. Some of his observations and travel jottings were brilliant. And he doesn't devote enough time to his son, young Geoffrey. The lad's our village postman now. But he doesn't relish the job.'

In the two years since she had seen him, Gerry had aged. He was still fair-haired, but many grey hairs were also prominent, and he was a lot balder than she remembered him being. A little stouter too, although he was always heavily built. He was not the image she had carried in her mind. She was disappointed and supposed that she had been accustomed to William, who was not only more distinguished but was more her own age. In fact, she felt more than a little shame that the attraction for Gerry had been there in the first place, and worse that she could still recognise the same attraction.

Gerry was still discussing Geoffrey Smith. 'He's fifteen. He had to leave school this year. I gather he's not bright but he's cheerful enough. I feel rather responsible for the child. I think perhaps I should have done something for him, but you know how it is, Ben and I drifted apart after he left the company. I gather that Ben frequents Alcoholics Anonymous now. I wonder if we let him down? What do you think?'

Roz thought she ought to make some effort to answer. She wished she had not brought the subject up. Did Gerry know that Ben probably wondered if he was the father of her child? Did Ben even know that Roz had had a child? All Ben probably knew for certain was that he had been fired for entertaining and probably making love to some girl in his hotel bedroom or her hotel bedroom, and the whole thing had been dressed up under the umbrella of drinking too much. He'd been unlucky. He'd been caught by the system. He'd been drunk and he probably felt he'd been fired justly. But just how much did Gerry know about Ben's redundancy? Had he also been wrestling with his conscience? Gerry was the chief Pilot for the Company.

And Roz, who knew the true facts, had no desire to try to put matters right, and this amazed her. Why didn't she care, she who cared so much about justice?

It was past.

She was getting married.

That she might see Ben again in very different circumstances was highly unlikely and of course, the thought didn't occur to her.

'Have you got a car?' he asked. 'Shall we go for a drive?'

They sped north under a sombre sky without saying any more about Ben. Their conversation brief and skirted round all the real issues they wanted to discuss; both were embarrassed and uncomfortable.

The car parted the surface film from the wet road and almost floated over the town boundary. Here the drystone walls began to give way to some hedges, which behind ditches divided the flat fields, but once down Pool Bank the countryside took on a definite look of the Dales. Here and there an occasional yellow field of oil-seed rape glared poisonously amongst the soft English fields in the valleys, fields full of cows. The contrast was almost arrogant and it seemed as though the cows deliberately shunned the elegant yellow flowers that had drifted across the walls into the pastures. A tramp on Roz's left suddenly decided to cross the road nearly leaving his manoeuvre too late and she had to brake to avoid him. The tramp seemed oblivious to danger.

'His animal existence is very basic isn't it Gerry? Look at his dreadful clothes!' Gerry laughed and her remark sounded almost feudal, but he glanced again at the dark tramp through the side-driving mirror.

'He looks as though he's wearing three coats, each garment minus the left sleeve. He must be hot.' One thin arm was naked and its hand clutched a white enamel billycan.

'I do hope someone will give him a right sleeved coat before winter.' Roz spoke wondering if she would be the person to supply the old coat if the tramp knocked at the door of her house. She thought of the lovely Pennine house where she and William would live after the wedding that month, and then again about the tramp.

'Do they get fed?'

'Yes,' reassured Gerry. 'I expect they keep a cunning mental note of places where they were well received last year. They're rather like the birds you know, migrating with the seasons, also there is a keen intelligence system, a grapevine, which operates and the word soon spreads when someone is willing to fill their cups. They leave a sign language on each gatepost indicating hospitality, fierce dogs or otherwise.' Gerry spoke like a man of her father's generation, which he nearly was.

They stopped at a cottage café, near Fountains Abbey, and there they lunched on ham and salad, tea and bread and butter, watching the full flight of some wild geese through the small window with leaded lights, watching each other.

They spoke rarely and all the while the woman proprietor stayed discreetly in the kitchen. They were the only customers in the tiny cottage restaurant. Their silence might be associated with their suspicions that they looked foolish, he forty, she twenty years younger, he going bald, she fresh and pretty, he with his thick north country tongue, a discord to her light tones. It was an uneasiness, which had not existed when they'd worked together.

They finished their meal and Gerry left the little oak table disturbing the fold of its plain cotton cloth with his jacket and after lightly knocking on the oak door he went into the kitchen.

He paid the woman fifteen shillings from his Moroccan leather wallet, and hesitatingly proffered the change.

She was a large woman and wore neither adornments, nor rings on her fingers. She looked neat, her hair drawn tightly over her head and fixed heavily down in two plaits on the top. The parting, which ran down the back of the head to the nape of her neck, was centred and quite straight. She disapproved of the couple. She gave the two half-crowns back to Gerry with a sneer.

'My brother wouldn't thank you for them. It is our pleasure.' In the tone of her one sentence, she gave them her life history.

'Well thank you, anyway. We've enjoyed the meal.' Roz was glad the woman wasn't a wife. She would have pitied the poor man such a dour spouse. Self-righteousness shouldn't be rewarded with a husband. Roz was too young, too inexperienced to think other than the air of righteousness must be caused by spinsterhood. At that moment, her own body was warm and loved by many people.

They walked outside. The rain had stopped leaving the grass wet and the air damp. They wandered from the cafe towards the wooded hollow in the valley where the beautiful abbey lay, once in all its glory now, in splendid ruins, and he asked, 'when is the wedding?'

'Saturday,' she said glibly and wondered did he really care?

She was glad she was young. She felt to possess a glorious power. She had been young enough to ride over the damage that Gerry had done to her. Now by seeking him out, so cruelly, just before her inevitable marriage, she felt to be punishing him, for his treatment of her. Anyway, the attraction she felt for Gerry was nothing to the pride she would feel in marriage to William Weighton on Saturday.

She merely needed to know how her son Andrew was faring.

They walked down the road, with the lovely Fountains Hall on their left, its beautiful Jacobean windows dwarfing the scale of the large house so that in comparison to other mansions it seemed a mere dolls house.

Marriage was a safeguard against age. That is why she had accepted William's proposal. She did not want to recognise age, but she did worry about change. They say time doesn't exist; it is merely an invention of the mind to explain change. Change was frightening; it was most frightening to experience these contrary emotions on re-meeting Gerry. Suddenly she held out her hand for Gerry to take.

He took it in his warm strong hand, and she wondered if it was because the ruins had come into sight and overwhelmed her by their majesty and their simple beauty, or whether it was because of their walk in silence.

He said, 'It's the boy's birthday on Saturday. Did you remember that when you chose the date for your marriage?'

Neither of them had mentioned Andrew before this,

All this time and it was if the two years old did not exist.

Her red-haired curls were tossed in defiance. 'Of course, sir!' She was mocking him.

Gerry squeezed the girl's hand. She was more arrogant and self-assured than he remembered her. 'I suppose it is a day when we shall always remember each other.' He used the words ruefully and despite the dimples in his cheeks there were no smiles. Perhaps he was reminded of another anniversary, perhaps he was reminded that the reason his wife Holly had been anxious to accept that particular adopted son was that the boy's birthday was also the date of their own wedding anniversary. Such things were important to Holly. In many ways, his dominant wife was very immature.

What was this girl thinking now, he wondered?

He spoke. He had hoped to keep what he was about to say a secret. It had been difficult, and that was why he had not mentioned Andrew before. If only Roz would realise how he was in inner turmoil and why her meeting was not in his plan.

'Your son has poor eyesight. He's nearly blind. There is however one specialist who might be able to help him. We hope.'

Roz thought of the boy, young and helpless and suddenly all her confidence was sapped from her. She was immediately angry with Gerry for spoiling her pleasantly organised thoughts. She could not speak, she was angry. Why tell her something that was going to spoil things, at this special and well-organised time in her life.

Suddenly the dark clouds rolled forward and the imposing ruins, which previously held much hope for Roz, under the backdrop of a light blue sky, took on a dark and cold aspect. The stones were full of secrets, not all of them nice.

It started to rain again and without waiting for the shower to get heavier Gerry put his arm firmly round the girl's waist and they ran for the car.

The monastery must wait for another day. In the sombre light, the valley had become narrow and sinister, the wide green well-kept grassy space which had welcomed them, suddenly bid them go and the huge trees which dotted the green space shook with awful warnings.

By the time they had reached Roz's car, and she had located the key for the locked door, Roz's dress was drenched. It was not surprising, in their enclosed world, that they had not realised that they had walked so far along towards the Studley Royal water gardens, and it had taken them twenty minutes to hurry back to shelter.

Once in the car Gerry felt the cool green striped dress and told her it was wet through. She took it off and spread it carefully over the back seat to dry. The huge trees in the car park cast a shadow, investing a serious air to their position.

The leather seat was seductive and curiously unpleasant and she shivered more from its effect than the cold. The little car had been a present from William, when they had become engaged.

Gerry studied her hazel eyes; today they were green eyes. 'You've the green eyes of a goddess', he told her. 'Green, just like Cyprus. And Cyprus is the home of Aphrodite, and one day it will be my home. At the moment, I've other responsibilities. But Cyprus has been my goddess. Just as you're now my goddesses. Cyprus, Roz, Aphrodite?' he murmured.

It didn't make much sense to Roz although she knew of his love for the island, and it was slightly touching. She had little way of knowing its full significance.

He moved the palms of his strong hands over her firm body and removed her brassiere and suspender belt.

He left her stockings on. When his hands reached her waist, he turned them over and kneaded his knuckles into her flesh. Roz began to cry, but they were gentle tears, tears of remembrance for all the wasted love, tears of resignation. Sadly, he went on stroking and caressing her body and she put up no resistance.

He allowed himself only to stretch her senses, pulling her nerves from the veins, stimulating the skin and kissing the soft body.

It was his deliberate treatment of a would-be bride.

At no time did he betray himself. He didn't undress.

Gerry, she thought, still loved her deeply, and she saw the one tear as it escaped from the corner of his eye. She knew nothing of his inner turmoil.

Nevertheless, throughout the seduction, if that is what it was, she could think of William, still with a certain amount of satisfaction; indeed, she made herself think of William. She was excited by the marriage, a marriage of dreams. This event was a slightly uneasy experience, pleasurable, in some way, but for the disgust that arose in her at her actions.

It crossed her mind that having done it once, the effect could be achieved again, whenever she was bored by William; that is what people did nowadays, nobody remained faithful any more, that was frightfully old fashioned. Whenever William was out of the country on business, as he was in New York this week, she could perhaps see Gerry, or someone else even.

The hardest part of the day had been actually deciding to drive to Guiseley, only just off the road to Harrogate, which she often used, although she had never actually been back to Guiseley since she left it nearly two years ago. Once in Guiseley, the rest had been quite easy...a matter of luck that she had actually bumped into Gerry, as she did, but not surprising, considering that it was such a small place.

Suddenly her thoughts were silenced by Gerry's actions, which took on more urgency. Her mind stopped thinking, she only felt. The feeling had nothing to do with love or excitement, with right or wrong, it was just there, she could not stop it. The feelings were solely concerned with going forward, with increasing the sensation of going forward until the whole experience came to a natural conclusion. And all the time Gerry remained in the driver's seat, fully clothed, and the rain drummed down on the metal roof of the car. Until this moment, no other man, not even William had touched her in this way, not since she and Gerry had last touched.

When it was over, Roz smiled, but was silent until Gerry said her dress would be dry. He slipped it over her head and she searched for a comb in her bag, while he started the engine of her car.

'Do you remember that old Mercedes you once had?'

He looked surprised. 'Yes, a hangover from the days of the Berlin Airlift. Not a lot of girls notice a chap's car.'

'Oh, you'd be surprised. A wise girl judges a man's pocket on the car he runs.'

'Really, then if you run this, what does William run?'

'He likes Rovers, drives them for preference...he says they have more to them than Daddy's Bentley.'

'You live and learn!' scoffed Gerry with more than a hint of his old sarcasm. 'What's he like, this William?

'Like you!' said Roz, surprised at the sudden comparison. 'Rather like you. Fair hair, sexy eyes, perhaps less hair even than you, although he's younger.'

It was a funny thing, but in having to marry William, that is she had to marry William if she wanted to get married, because clearly, she could not have married Gerry, but life and love, particularly love had ceased to have the same meaning that they did two years ago.

Was she being unfaithful to Gerry in marrying William, was that the reason that it did not seem to matter if she was unfaithful to William?

How could she possibly be unfaithful to William? It was Gerry that she was 'wedded' to in the purest sense. At no time did she think to ask Gerry how he felt, nor would she have thought it appropriate to do so, she just assumed that was how it was.

Once back in Guiseley Gerry told her, 'I'll be there on Saturday, you know. To watch you wed!' And he opened the door of the car and got out immediately.

'Despite your son's birthday?' she said, suddenly desperate that he shouldn't leave like this.

'Despite my own wedding anniversary. We'll have been married nineteen years on Saturday, Holly and I.'

'I didn't know,' she murmured. 'You told me nothing more about Andrew.'

'You don't want to know,' he said firmly. 'You've signed away your rights to Andrew, remember.' It was cruel, but for the best. 'But I'll tell you something, he's a lovely child, he'll be alright...and he has been

307

such a great joy to me, the best gift anyone, particularly you could have given me.' If she noticed the past tense she did not remark upon it.

He didn't need to say, 'I love you,' after that, it would have been superfluous. She reached into her handbag and drew out an invitation card and a pen, and on it, she scribbled the Captain's name and gave it to him. Did the availability of this card prove she had been intending to meet him?

She changed into the driving seat, closed the door of her white Lancia herself and gave a little wave before moving off.

She was crying, but she told herself sternly that the tears were for Andrew. For Gerry's own two years old reflection. A child going blind. His second birthday on Saturday, and in a few days' time, she would also have a birthday.

They would be on honeymoon.

Cast a horoscope for Cancer, she thought dryly.

ELEVEN: THEY BUILD CHIMNEYS HIGHER THAN SPIRES

October 1972

(i)

The first days in October were unseasonably warm, like summer. The sun was shining when the 'phone rang in the little Scottish bothy. Rosalind answered it as a cloud diluted the brilliant warmth. From the little window of the cottage, she could see the mountains of the Cairngorms, framed by a blue sky. The heather was tinting them purple and a cacophony of colour shouted from the draped trees.

William's voice crackled over the line from Yorkshire.

'Rosalind. I've news, and I'm afraid it's bad.'

She knew immediately what this would be.

'It's about your father. Darling, he's had another heart attack.'

'Is he dead?'

'He's very ill.'

'I'll come home tonight.'

'No, darling. I'm coming up for you. I'll fly to Inverness. There's no way you should drive when you're upset. I'll be with you about midnight. We'll come home tomorrow. There's not much we can do, he's unconscious.'

The sun went down over the mountains and the heat left the Spey Valley.

It had been a gorgeous day. The family had known for some time of the fragility of James Peters' heart. Every day had become precious without much being said. It had created an unbelievable tension within the family and yet it had brought Rosalind closer to William.

Rosalind wondered how she would explain the death of their beloved grandfather to her twins, at the point in their life when they were most attached to him. In her mind, she knew he would be unlikely to make a full recovery.

She had walked that afternoon with her daughters through the Queens Forest and not given a thought to her ailing father. Now she had returned to this telephoned news. In the forest, the sun had warmed the resinous scent of the pines and the shade from the tree's long branches was welcome.

She had relaxed. Later she had taken the young children on to the beach at Loch Morlich and they had watched the boats and Alice had built a curious sand castle on the rough grit beach which Sara had immediately laid waste and thus declared war, which had threatened to spoil a good day.

Now she had this news to give them.

At midnight William arrived in a taxi.

In the morning, they put the kids into Rosalind's car. They didn't understand why they should forfeit such a splendid holiday just because Grandpa was ill. Rosalind packed the luggage as best she could and William paid for the forthcoming week's rent to a very disgruntled Scotsman. The man as puerile as the children seemed incapable of understanding that someone could not use pre-booked accommodation due to circumstances beyond their control and he had no intention of reducing the income, which was outstanding because of these circumstances.

Rosalind told him that no doubt with all the Americans around that he would have no difficulty in re-letting the cottage and thereby earning double on its rent.

He seemed reluctant to believe this and spat hard on the ground as they climbed into the car.

It did nothing to relieve the tension which Rosalind felt.

The Toledo was bursting at the seams, even with luggage on the roof. Gone was the day when the Weighton's could run a superior or luxury family car and also afford a racy little sports car for their jaunts together; William's car was now very much a family version. They took the long road to Edinburgh. There was a mist on the hills as they climbed up from Newtonmore. It was very depressing. The railway ran beside the road, climbing also, its straight functional lines gracefully pushing the rails up through the mist like a trail from a jet plane. They looked cruel and flagrant a man-made imposition on the barren inhospitable land and suddenly they broke through the cloud and the grey whisky town of Dalwhinnie presented a happy face with children playing between the houses in the sun whilst the mist swirled below them.

By the time they reached Pitlochry, which also basked in glorious sunshine the pattern of the day had been established. William and Rosalind said little and Rosalind kept herself busy trying to keep the twins occupied. The car was cramped and now after being cold in the mountains, everyone was too hot.

The delicate Scottish glens, wearing their magnificent autumnal mantle were ignored on this southern journey. They were originally planning to take four slow days to come home, motoring slowly down to Loch Ness and back to England.

Now her father was dying.

Rosalind did not know whether she would see him again. Would she ever speak with him again? What had she left unsaid? So many things she should have told him, but would she tell him now, if she had the opportunity? More importantly, if he died, he would take with him so many answers to so many problems, so much advice, so much unsaid.

The car dropped out of the Highlands into Perthshire as fast as a swooping eagle and from the stark-naked beauty of the mountains, the golden lights of the trees and the patterns and shadows they made on the earth beneath became almost indescribably vivid.

Rosalind, of course, had never told her father about Andrew.

She had never told anyone, save those who knew at the time of the birth. Most of the journey she thought about Andrew.

It wasn't unusual; she spent many hours thinking about him. An immense sense of guilt flooded through her.

Outside the grey-black town of Edinburgh, they stopped for lunch.

Throughout, most of the family ate in silence and Rosalind ate very little although William cautioned her when she ordered a third whisky and soda.

The children behaved atrociously, spilling drinks and fighting over the last bap roll, which Sara actually threw to Rosalind in an attempt to prevent her sister eating it. Rosalind lost her temper.

They arrived in Huddersfield at seven o'clock, all dizzy and fatigued from the constant movement.

Nevertheless, they went straight to the Nuffield Nursing Home. The children remained in the car, tired and bad-tempered.

The nurses told William quietly that Mr. Peters had died at five-thirty that evening. Rosalind felt nothing, no tears, no emotion, just an empty space; a void, empty cavern where they said there was a heart. William put his arms round his wife but she did not respond to his sympathy.

She did not even feel emotion. She smiled sadly and thanked the nurses turned and walked back to the car, where Alice was in tears and fighting with Sara over the contents of their mother's handbag.

Sitting in the front seat Rosalind said to the children, 'Mummy is sad because Grandpa died this afternoon.'

William added, 'So be extra good children, for Mummy, will you please?'

'Does that mean we won't see him again?' asked Alice.

'Yes, darling,' said her Daddy quietly and the tears began, at last, to flow down from Rosalind's vacant eyes. A realistic childish statement bringing home the harsh facts.

'Never mind,' said Sara, 'we've still got Granny and Grandpa Weighton and Great-granny Weighton, two grannies left and one grandpa.'

In bed, the Librium which William had made Rosalind take seemed to have an adverse effect. He suspected she had drunk some of the whisky that she had bought in Aviemore and packed in her suitcase, straight from the bottle, but he wisely said nothing.

'Aren't you asleep darling?' William fumbled his way into bed two hours after his wife. 'Don't worry.

It can't help. Don't for Heaven's sake start planning the funeral now. We'll do that tomorrow.'

Rosalind wished that were the total of her worries, a funeral, at least that would be over in a week. Her father would never now know these things, always Rosalind had prayed that he would never find out that he had a grandson and now he was dead, her prayer answered and she wished her father was still alive. Rosalind felt she had almost wished him dead.

'I know how easy it is for me to speak but honestly darling, your father went peacefully, there was no pain, it really was for the best.' She remained silent, but her husband persevered.

'What is it darling? You've been upset for months, before your father was ill even. Why are you always edgy? I give you everything you want. Everything I can?' Trust William to choose this night for justifying his chauvinistic instincts.

'Not tonight, I can't enter into that sort of discussion tonight.'

'You're a strange girl. You've no spark, not like you had when we were first married. You haven't had all summer.'

'William,' said Rosalind desperately. 'Would you have any spark in you if your father had just died?'

'No, but I wish he'd had a grandson, a real grandson.'

'Oh no,' Rosalind froze. William was trying to cuddle her, tonight of all nights. 'Don't William, not now, not tonight, please don't.'

'Sorry. Just thought it might help. I do love you!'

'I love you!' At that moment, she didn't. Had she ever loved William? Needed him perhaps. But love.

After Derek, after Gerry. And there was another secret. How could William follow that? She wished she were back in Scotland, without William.

22 June 1963

(ii)

Curiously Gerry woke late. Usually, the child woke them both, but today, because he was working, Holly must have taken the boy down to breakfast quietly. He smiled gratefully and almost contentedly. His wife was good to him in such little ways. The smile faded as his memory was jogged by recalling the day, the date. It was their wedding anniversary. He wondered why it was always presumed that men would forget this occasion. He was never allowed to do so. For nineteen years on this date, he had reminded Holly that he had loved her, once, and he supposed in a way he did so still. He loved the child more.

Nineteen years ago, when England was still at war with Germany, it had been a June wedding. The churches were booked many weeks in advance; it seemed all the soldiers wished to be married. Lovely desirable auburn-haired Holly and he recalled the longing to be married as soon as possible, to possess the creature, which would then belong to him. The leave had lasted a mere thirty-six hours, but it had given Holly the white wedding she wanted with all the important friends and relatives.

It was obviously a short wedding night.

Holly had been sweetness and light. She had kissed Gerald's cheeks, his forehead, she had stroked his hair but she had shaken him with her insistence that this was not to be their honeymoon. That would wait, and in that she was adamant. She remained a virgin.

Gerry had supposed that her wish for a short engagement, the glorious if hastily prepared wedding feast and the following night were to be for his benefit. Like all his comrades he expected to be presented with an heir as soon as possible; a tangible image as reward for his soldiering.

The somersaulting plane had fallen into the grounds of a German castle. It must have done so, for only that could explain how he had come to be in that German castle seventeen days after the June wedding.

He preferred to remember nothing about the succeeding months, the escape, which failed, or the terror of the terrible thin Pole. The Pole had one eye, which in retrospect Gerry would place in the centre of the Pole's forehead. At first, the Polish Officer had appeared intelligent and the men had trusted him, believing him like the Cyclops and capable of shepherding a flock to freedom.

To help Gerry forget these things and the painful six months in hospital after the end of the war, with the blinding headaches, he had always made a point of liking Poles and Germans, and particularly Jews.

Nine months after the end of the war Gerry returned to civilian life but still Holly practised her own resistance and when at last the war-weary hero's patience wore out he virtually raped his own very young wife.

Except he found that he could not.

Try as he may, on many occasions, anything along these lines, tender, organised or forceful it was not possible.

The couple fell to blaming each other, not to each other, but silently and resentfully. Had they sought the sort of help that became fashionable in later decades they might have realised that the fault was not within them but brought about by outside forces which could have been talked through and the problems addressed. Holly continued to think of Gerry as impotent and occasionally say so, and Gerry thought of her as barren but never said as much.

The surprise in his life had been his adopted son. He was two years old today. He really loved Andrew. This love was causing him a problem. None excepting himself and the child's mother knew he was the child's father.

And the girl Roz, the child's mother, had chosen this anniversary for her wedding.

He took the pills the doctor had prescribed for the pain.

The child was eating a boiled egg as Gerald walked into the kitchen.

'Humpty Dumpy Dadda,' said the yellow apparition in the high chair.

'And all the king's horses and all the king's men couldn't put Humpty Dumpty together again, Happy Birthday Nicky-Licky'' Nicholas was the child's second name and one which Gerry often used when he found the name Andrew brought back too many memories of the child's real mother. Gerald kissed his wife and his carrot red-haired son. 'I bet you never knew the original author of that nursery rhyme? Lewis Carroll; it isn't really a traditional rhyme,' Gerry told his wife,

But Gerald's wife looked up from the birthday cards she was opening for the toddler and only said. 'I wish you wouldn't 'ie' us all the time Gerald. I don't like Holly Berry, and Nicky Licky is horrid. Next thing you know the kids around here will put an 'er' instead of an 'ie' and that will be awful.'

'Nicky-Licky' said the baby,

'They will anyway dear.'

Gerald gave her the parcel he had been holding behind his back. 'To celebrate not just the boy's birthday but also our wedding anniversary.'

Holly unwrapped it to display an exquisite Dresden figure. She smiled and said thank you. She said, 'it's a wicked zodiac is Cancer.' The fact that it was Dresden was a deliberate attempt by her husband to show that he did not hold a grudge against the world, and she knew it. She took a letter from the bottom of the pile of opened cards.

'I didn't want to spoil this day, but I think you should see this. It's from the specialist. He says he thinks they should operate on the lad's eyes this month. He sounds fairly hopeful, but they will only do one eye this year. He'll be three before they tackle the second one and only if the first operation is successful. I can't bear the thought of his remembering the first operation when they come to do the second. Why can't they do them both at once?'

Gerald didn't answer. He didn't know what to say. He loved Andrew much too much. He couldn't stand the strain. He could take pain, he had demonstrated that much. But he couldn't subject Andrew to pain. There was always the risk that one operation would not be successful, and then where would they be. A one-eyed son? The one-eyed cyclops?

'We're going to see Mr. Robinson next week. Perhaps he'll tell us.' Holly's words sounded unconvincing. 'Where are you going today? Is it a long flight?'

'Fairly short flight', he lied. And he wondered why he had lied.

Since he was working, he could not possibly go to Halifax for Roz's wedding, there simply wasn't time, and he had never intended to go anyway. It was much more important to be at home for his son's birthday tea, and if he flew to Cyprus, there was no way he could be home for tea.

The rain, which had drenched Ascot that week, had stopped and for once it was a hot June day. Gerry's hand reached from the steering wheel to open the window on the left-hand side and picking up his brief-case from the left-hand passenger's seat he dropped it into the rear. He took a shining ivory card from his wallet memorised the inscription and replaced the card in the wallet and both to his inside pocket in his uniform jacket.

He switched on the ignition of the car and resigned himself to working on a Saturday. The radio broadcast was interrupted by a gale warning for shipping and Gerry played, as he often did, the game of deducing the flying weather from the situation over the North Sea.

He reversed the car from the garage. Whatever the weather man might be saying about a hot day it was one of those windy days when the world felt to be going around whilst the racing clouds remained stationary in the sky.

The printed silver words had said:

"Mr. James Peters requests the pleasure of your company
at the marriage of his daughter Pandora Rosalind
to Mr. William Keith Weighton
at St. Jude's Church, Halifax,
on Saturday, June 22nd, 1963, at 2.30 o'clock
and afterwards at Bankfield Hall."

It was Saturday and really not very much different to any other Saturday, except of course that he must work whilst others got married. It requested his pleasure but he must work. The Company had failed to tell him that he was rostered out for Paris until yesterday.

The announcer was giving out a report on the road traffic situation.

It was really not very far from Yeadon to Halifax. Possibly he could be re-rostered; possibly they would find a standby for his schedule. He could always ask in the Kremlin...; the radio announcer was finishing, 'have a good weekend everyone and remember to drive carefully.' This year was to see the start of Radio playing Big Brother for road safety.

He didn't know why he didn't want Roz to marry, but he didn't. He was jealous. He'd no right to be jealous, but he was and it mattered.

No matter that he had never made one move to contact Roz since she had conceived his child.

No matter that he had kept his feelings to himself since he first set eyes on Roz.

No matter that the auburn-haired Roz had given him everything he had hoped for from the red-haired Holly.

If Roz had not found him in Guiseley on two occasions, the first the day they adopted Andrew, and then a week ago, then he would not have had any knowledge the son Holly thought was adopted was his natural son, but worse was that Roz had become inaccessible by marrying another.

In his pocket was passenger ticket to Nicosia, one of three. He had suggested to Holly that they went to Cyprus for their anniversary but she did not want to take

Andrew abroad. The sunlight might affect his eyes she said. So, the surprise and impulse purchase yesterday remained in his pocket.

He fingered the ticket gently.

He loved Cyprus.

He loved Andrew more.

He couldn't go on living with Holly without telling her the truth.

Poor Andrew.

He hated that Pole. He hated all Germans.

It was an impossible situation.

He loved Cyprus.

The pain in his head was worse than ever.

How could he justify not telling his son that he was his natural father?

The pain had been worse since the day that Rosalind told him he was Andrew's father.

On no day had it been so bad as this day. If he went back to the doctor he would lose his licence, to fly.

He loved to fly.

It was Saturday and it was June. There were very many weddings in June. In the churches, all over England, the notes of Mendelssohn would echo through the hollow pipes.

There were many people who drove in June.

All over the roads in England the ambulances would hurry with their bells ringing.

(iv)

A leaf fluttered through the open window and gently rested on the wicker chair. A dark cloud passed over the sun and the room darkened.

There was going to be a storm.

Rosalind picked up the leaf and pressed it in her hands. It matched the colour of her parchment dress, her bridal gown. The leaf crumbled and fell gracelessly to the floor. The leaf was pale, brown and dead but it was only the early month of summer. It was June. Rosalind looked at her watch, a small gold present from her groom. It was ten past two o'clock.

She looked out of the window at the black thunderclouds and she wondered how much she really loved William. If she indeed actually loved him? He really was rather like Gerry, both to look at and to talk to. William was younger but still considerably older than she was.

William wasn't married.

Yet.

She put on the gramophone. She chose Mahler's Fifth Symphony and wondered where her father was. The house seemed empty. A bride should not be left alone on her wedding day. Not for those few crucial minutes before the long walk up the aisle began.

Five minutes ago, the huge white car, strung with white ribbons, flowers and a horseshoe had carried her six bridesmaids away. Tiny Felicity, her cousin's toddler had really been too young to be a bridesmaid, but no one could resist the temptation of dressing up the two-year-old in all that finery. She had been crying as the wedding car left the house.

Now five minutes of silence had followed in the huge house.

Her own world of superlatives.

Not hers, those of her father and the new world she was entering, that of her husband-to-be, of her cousin, or her friends, where only the best will do.

Was she ashamed of her good fortune?

Was it good fortune indeed?

She thought of her son, she could picture him vividly. He, whose second birthday it was. Today, her wedding day,

Everyone had gone to church. She had chosen the wedding date, as she had manipulated many events in her life.

And she was nearly crying. Dry hot tears that were the pain of thought.

Andrew. And Gerry.

Now from the drawing-room window, she could see her father talking to Hugh Rhyl-Jones, William's usher. A friend since University days and now a psychiatrist. He would drive the huge veteran Rolls Royce that would take him, Hugh Rhyl-Jones, Pandora Rosalind and James Peters to St. Jude's Church.

More superlatives.

The men turned and walked into the house.

Her father came into the room, followed by Hugh. Rosalind scarcely knew him. He was William's friend. He had recently moved to the Lake District to take up a post at a hospital there.

'My darling,' said Rosalind's father, 'you're beautiful, a radiant bride, indeed, eh, Hugh?'

He opened a bottle of champagne and poured three glasses.

'To the bride.'

Rosalind was weary. The excitement earlier in the morning, hairdressers, dressmakers to fit her into her own gown, six bridesmaids, all to fit into their own gowns of pale parchment, a little darker than her own. She had insisted that they all look perfect and she had spent several minutes arranging the fold of their garments.

And all the time, if Felicity hadn't been crying she had been running in and out of rooms, picking up things she shouldn't have and Lucinda seemed nowhere about to calm the child. So, Rosalind was tired, but she couldn't sit in her wedding dress, and she had pursed her lips, pushed forward and slightly upward the strong chin and she smiled and drank her own health. It was the point of no return. Thirty-three months of chastity was presumably to be rewarded that night by a groom who supposed he had a virgin bride.

Chastity, that is, save for Gerry's gentle loving just days before.

Her father took her glass. In five weeks' time, she would see the house again, as a guest, never more as a resident. In the meantime, she would show William the glories that were Greece.

Hugh opened the double doors for her; throwing them open as a butler would with much ceremony to accommodate the folds and tresses of her bridal gown. Her father rearranged her veil, over her green eyes, over her auburn hair.

Rosalind felt to be in purdah.

They walked slowly to the resplendent Rolls, both men helping her into the vehicle. Donning their top hats, they stepped in and drove through the village.

Here they paused whilst Hugh popped out and opened her door to display the bride to an elderly lady sitting by arrangement in the doorway of her cottage. She blew a kiss. Rosalind felt cold but she smiled warmly and graciously as was expected of her. As a child in wartime Roz had bought sweets from this very old lady. As a child, Roz had shared all her secrets with this lady. The car drove on.

Heads turned. People stared and suddenly the stage fright left her.

She was a princess for a day.

At least she was not a Catholic and at least she could repair her mistakes; also, she could teach herself to make the marriage work, it was a voluntary institution after all.

They arrived at the Church. A mist of confusion blocked out all but the important faces. In the porch, the five girls and the baby girl were waiting.

Now began Roz's debut into her new world.

The world of her birth-right; but was it a world of conformity which she would willingly accept? Rosalind recalled her father's joy, when a year ago she had announced her engagement to William.

Briefly, she thought of the humility and tenderness she had experienced whilst living amongst Gerry's world. Even in the style and life of humbler folk, there was a gentleness and sincerity that she could not characterise in her own circle of aspiring aristocrats, perhaps time would bring a greater liberalism within all the classes, without exploiting those who must follow behind those who succeed. Now she was marrying her own kind.

Yet even at this late stage, fate threw in a strange card.

She'd never met Gerry's wife Holly, but it was only this week when going through the wedding guests for the second time that she had learnt that Ainley Armroyd, a rather steady friend of William's, and about to be married himself, had an elder sister married to a pilot operating out of Yeadon. The coincidence was too strange to dismiss. Yet had Ainley not rung her, seeking an invitation for his fiancée Fiona, she might never have known for certain. He attempted to introduce his fiancée as from the same school as his sister, thereby he thought, justifying his request for an invitation.

As Rosalind had listened sympathetically to Ainley's request on the 'phone she had been reduced to a jelly almost literally when Ainley had concluded; 'You know, eh, my sister, Holly? Married to a chap at Ferryair, operating out of Yeadon. He and I don't get on, so she never comes this way now.'

'No,' Rosalind told him, she had never met his sister Holly.

To meet Gerry's wife would be more than she could bear. It just did not bear thinking about; the woman who was looking after her son.

'Pity,' said Ainley, without feeling. 'Because she'll not come this way, not now, not if I can help it, that is whilst she's still married to that chap. No, she'll not come here.' And having been assured that it would be all right to bring Fiona, his fiancée, ('from the same school as Holly') he had rung off. She didn't mention the call to William. How could she?

Again...there was Andrew. Two years old and there with Holly.

Suddenly she knew there would be no more natural children.

She could not allow that.

In marrying William, she had been simply ensuring her future, as all those around her seemed to be doing, Lucinda and Derek, Ainley and now Fiona. That William was a nice, well-bred, polite, good-looking man had seemed of prime importance, if he was to father her children.

But no, he was not going to do that - how could she mother other children when she had deserted Andrew, her own?

Again, a sense of depression seemed to cause a great vacuum in her stomach, she wished that time would begin to go anticlockwise.

Her tummy contracted again as the elegant bridesmaids came down from the steps to greet her and the first of the dark clouds arrived from the East, bringing the first drops of rain.

Roz looked at the church clock.

It was twenty to three.

She was ten minutes late.

Precisely half an hour ago she had looked at her new watch.

The dark clouds that had appeared to threaten her wedding day had indeed arrived at her marriage.

As Rosalind began to walk up the aisle to meet her groom she was thinking of Gerry, who had been invited; and of Gerry's son, who had not. Of course, if circumstances had been different, perhaps both Captain and Mrs. Duncan would have been invited. It was unbelievable that Gerry's wife had been brought up in the same village as she had. Funny she had had no recollection of there being a girl in the village called Holly, but how could she have. Holly would have been married and presumably moved to Guiseley when Rosalind was only a child. They might even have been married in this very church. Rosalind shivered, and those who watched her slow and triumphant progress up the long aisle, who saw her shake, thought it was all down to nerves.

She could hear the torrential rain drumming with its unrelenting rhythm on the paved courtyard through the open porch. How lucky she had been not to get wet. She thought of her attendants with whom she had been so pleased in their pale parchment dresses, carrying the lilac coloured posies in small baskets with lilac ribbons around the bust and collar and the large lilac picture hats and of her own bridal gown with its intricate folds and delicate material.

That it might rain in June had never occurred to her. Rain somehow signified bad fortune, but it was June and it was her glorious day.

One single tear dropped down Roz's painted cheek.

This indeed was her last chance.

She took her father's arm, I love you. I love YOU, but William I give you my troth.

A calm wave unknotted her stomach and the music of Bach filled her veins.

Alone to her nuptials and Rosalind wished she was a virgin.

Not once that day did she think of Derek, although somewhere in the vast crowd his eyes watched her as did those of Lucinda, his wife; Rosalind's cousin.

A lot of water flows under a bridge after a flood.

TWELVE: MID SUMMER

24 June 1963

(i)

The newly married couple spent the first two nights of their honeymoon in London and then took a night flight out to Corfu on the eve of Rosalind's birthday.

The Yorkshire Post carried a story of a horrendous car crash on Pool Bank, but in spite of his interest as a newspaperman, the Weightons did not see the newspaper.

A wrecked car had been found but there was no sign of the driver.

The report said that the car belonged to a pilot with the local airline Ferryair.

A witness who came across the accident said that there were obvious signs of a crash on the bend and a car had come to rest against a tree, perched perilously over the bank; a dazed man had been seen sitting on a fence about two hundred yards before the accident but the driver of the other car had not initially connected the two until after he had driven to Pool village to report it and to get help.

When the help arrived with the ambulance and the police, the car had already toppled over the edge of the bank and was on its roof well below the road.

There was still no sign of the occupant.

Although William did hear that Ainley Armroyd had lost his brother-in-law, on his return to his office from Greece, he did not think to mention it to Roz.

After all, Ainley was not a close friend of hers.

There was a bit of gossip locally because Captain Duncan still had not been found but it was not likely to be repeated in the circles in which Rosalind moved.

(ii)

Time was not the healer Rosalind had been told it was.

At the beginning of June, nearly six months ago now, she had spent two days getting her father's property on Savile Park ready for the Smith family to rent. Her father's secretary, Ann, had come down with Rosalind and together they had swept out the bare rooms and opened the windows to air the house.

The removal van had arrived and Ann had explained how Mrs. Smith had just had a baby and they were to arrange the furniture and carpets as best they could, Although the floors were parquet throughout the ground floor, the upstairs was left with the original threadbare Indian carpets. They decided to leave the curtains for Mrs. Smith to arrange. The nursery was probably the most successful room, all women probably respond to the thought of a tiny baby. Rosalind had gone home and waited but no more was said about the Smiths and finally last September she had taken up the challenge on her own, and through Ann, she had arranged for Mrs. Smith to visit her for tea, with the children. And still, she was no nearer discovering if the name of Ben Smith was just a coincidence.

Then one November evening William had come home for dinner and announced that Benjamin and Ivy Smith would like them to go round for coffee that evening to say thank you for their assistance.

This was the chance she had been waiting for. This was the chance to see if this was, in fact, the Ben Smith she had known ten years ago?

It was a cold evening and Rosalind had put on a pale green worsted trouser suit.

Benjamin Smith had opened the door when they rang the bell, Rosalind would not have recognised him, had she not been half expecting to see him. He didn't recognise her.

'How do you do?' William had asked, although he had seen Benjamin earlier that day in the editorial department. 'My wife, Rosalind, this is Mr. Smith,' very formally he added, 'Benjamin Smith.' He had stepped back to allow his wife to shake hands with the tidy gentleman, now boasting a dark moustache, neatly trimmed and a thick pair of rimless square glasses hiding the bushy eyebrows and accentuating the blue eyes.

'Hallo Ben!' she had spoken quietly, but she couldn't quite control the surprise. It had amused her to see Ben's second glance, the slow look of recognition and the interminable time it took him to put a name to her face.

'I say,' William had spluttered in his best public-school accent, 'Do you two know each other or something?'

Rosalind Weighton had laughed. Ben was still stammering, trying to put a name to her face, 'Why, it's Roz Peters, of course it is, Oh, goodness, I just don't believe it!'

They studied each other; she had looked at the round friendly face of the neat poised reporter and wondered what had happened to the untidy lovable airline pilot, more often drunk than sober, that she had known ten years ago. He remembered a young girl; very pretty, petite and overpowering with her glorious copper coloured hair. The woman, Rosalind, was more mature, her long hair still curling, still auburn. Her figure still

334

lithe and she was wearing a very pale green trouser suit. He remembered how she had always been fond of green.

They had stood silently, staring and William had felt very uncomfortable.

A young man walked down the stairs and she had exclaimed, 'Why this must be Geoffrey!' He was twenty-four years of age and was followed down the stairs by a younger boy.

This Rosalind had assumed was the eleven years old she had been told about. Still she puzzled how Ben could have a son of that age when eleven years ago she knew he wasn't married. Good looking and, like Ben and Geoffrey, the boy wore thick glasses.

'This is my stepson,' Ben had said. Stepson would mean that it was his second wife's child by a previous marriage, Rosalind was less puzzled.

Ben had spoken to the child. 'How was school, son?' The boy nodded. 'He really has settled down well in this town, we were lucky it was such a long half term when we arrived, gave us time to settle him in before starting school.' The boy had dark auburn hair.

William had said. 'Well now, you're a big family aren't you Ben? Three younger ones as well, I hear? However, now you seem to know my wife so well do tell me where you met each other.' If William's breeding made him in any way superior to his employees his tone on this occasion confirmed it.

The host had ushered the Weightons into his sitting room and slowly he closed the door. His sons had vanished in the direction of the kitchen. Ben, who had displayed a degree of self-control, stood squarely and facing his new boss's wife said, 'Roz, I am surprised at you! Surely you have told your husband everything there is to know about the incorrigible Benjamin Smith you

335

once knew in Ferryair? Greece, Cairo, Tangier, you name it; we've been there! And together,' he added wickedly.

William had turned to look at his wife, as though in some new light.

She had laughed a little too lightly. 'Oh, Ben, shsh, ssh! So that diary you used to keep served you in good stead; you really are a journalist' and then the question she had waited so long to ask followed before she could stop herself. 'By the way, do you ever come across Gerry Duncan these days?'

She knew she had spoken out of turn. Too quickly, Ben had looked horrified. Perhaps after all these years Ben was the only person who had suspected anything between her and Gerry, but she had not been ready for the shock that followed.

Ben had turned to check the door was closed. 'Has no one told you Roz?' She had waited while Ben paused. 'He's gone. He left his wife; he simply disappeared. On June 22nd, 1963. His wedding anniversary.'

'June 22nd... and in 1963 our wedding day...1963', had said William, catching nothing of the tension.

But Ben had hardly noticed the interruption.

'Nine years ago! He simply disappeared, feigned a car crash, at first everyone thought he was dead. The papers reported his death, his car was found damaged and abandoned but there was nobody, and for years we thought he had suffered from amnesia, but now we know that wasn't the case.'

The door had opened and a tall handsome auburn-haired woman had walked in. 'This is Ivy,' said Ben....

'This is William's wife, Rosalind,' he continued. 'But then, you've met! You had an afternoon together in the summer? And I can't believe it but Roz worked with me at Ferryair! You know I've spoken about Roz Peters. This is her!'

'Oh,' said the woman, 'I'll get the drinks,' and she turned and went out of the room. Her hair colouring was exactly that of her oldest son.'

'I'm glad I was there to look after her, it was an awful shock…'

Roz looked blank.

Ben could not see that a piece of the jigsaw was missing but William knew. 'Ivy is Ainley Armroyd's sister, she was married to a pilot at Ferryair – the guy who went missing, I thought you knew…' said William.

'You might remember her as Holly,' said Ben, 'in the trauma that followed Gerry's disappearance, the fact that we can never legally marry, my partner, or wife as she prefers to be thought of, has reverted to her given Christian name, Ivy. Although she was born here, lived around here as a child called Holly, it has been easier for her to blend in under the alias of Ivy Smith.'

Gerry's wife, ex-wife, now Roz knew that was who she was, was exactly as Gerry had described her. As she returned into the room Ben had laughed nervously...'As I was trying to explain, Roz was a good friend of mine in Ferryair.'

'I never mixed with Gerald's flying friends,' said Ivy, 'but I do remember the name, although it is Benjamin here, who has spoken most about you.'

And Rosalind had believed the danger passed and the colour returned to her face.

Then Ivy made things worse, far worse, 'Ben used to talk about you a lot when we first met. He would ask everyone, why you had left Yeadon, and nobody had the answer. Isn't it strange that we should re-meet you like this?'

'I'm glad you met Ben.' Rosalind hoped she sounded normal. 'I used to feel so sorry for him and his son. It's good for them both to have a family life. Do you realise that Geoffrey is only six years younger than me?' Rosalind blushed again, was this information that she should have so readily available? She really must not sound familiar with Ben's history.

Mrs. Smith looked surprised. She spoke to Rosalind interrupting her thoughts. 'Did you know Ben well?' Rosalind should have seen that question coming her way, the conversation had been leading up to it.

Ben's stepson had re-entered the room during the introductions. The boy had stood unobtrusively behind his adoptive mother and Rosalind did not notice him at first. Andrew had auburn hair, even deeper and richer than Roz's and he had walked into the room like his father. His walk was an imitation of Gerry's and Rosalind had confused it with Ben's when she had first met the boy in the hall.

'Andrew's eleven.' Ivy had spoken to relieve the silence, but there was a bitterness in her voice, 'his birthday was the day his adoptive father went missing;' the anniversary recalled a distasteful event, and was clearly not to be celebrated.

Rosalind had then fainted.

When she came round, William looked perplexed but helped her up and seated her in a large armchair. Mrs. Smith had seemed completely unperturbed, if not a little puzzled why her guest should faint.

In the silence that followed Ivy Smith tried again.

'I hear you know my dear brother Ainley,' she had said to William.

Early December 1972

(iii)

It was a lovely winter's day, mild and sunny as well. William was in Dublin for a few days and Rosalind resented this trip only a month after her father's death.

She grieved, more than she had imagined she would mourn. In most ways William didn't understand and she felt he had given her very little sympathy. In many ways, she did not blame him. So much in her life was now hard to cope with and there were days when she felt she was losing her sanity completely.

She had coped with the arrival of the Smith family and the great secret that it threatened to expose. She had been polite and welcoming to Gerry's wife and had not enquired as much as she would like, so she really knew very little more than she had learnt that evening a week ago.

She perhaps should not have been surprised because some months after she had married, en route to Harrogate to do some shopping, she had turned off on the spur of the moment to Guiseley and seen a 'For Sale' sign on the gatepost at White Gates. Alarmed that this would mean she would never see Gerry again, she had retreated to a 'phone booth to look up his telephone number. The only entry she found was for an I. Smith at White Gates. This had confused her thoroughly, and also depressed her and she went back a month later to find the sign now had 'Sold' written across it.

Still not privy to the gossip and mystery surrounding Ainley Armroyd's brother-in-law, she had no one to discuss the problem with.

Now with the arrival of the Smiths in Halifax old wounds had been opened.

Some people were obviously more insular than others. Rosalind felt she had been driven to that insularity by fate; like Sean MacStiofain slowly starving himself to death in a hospital outside Dublin. Starving himself, excruciatingly torturing himself in the name of the Irish Republic and thus feeding the cause.

Rosalind was worried about William in Dublin. It was an unsettled place to be at this time. The riots of the north seemed to be fanned by the flames of the hunger strike towards the southern Irish capital.

Rosalind was also worried on her own account.

In the last few days, Rosalind had learned to live with her secret and at first it seemed easier to keep it than involve the entire Smith and Weighton family in emotion and shock. But now she felt the need to talk to Ben.

Most of all, Rosalind worried that one day she would find the selfish need to tell her handsome son the truth.

Surely the child had the ultimate right to know the truth? To recognise his bond and blood relationship with the Peters/Weighton family. He had never known his father was his real father and too young to appreciate his influence in those early formative years.

Not only did Andrew Nicholas Shaw Duncan have a mother, but also the man who had adopted him originally was his real father, yet how could Rosalind tell him this? Particularly as his real father had deserted him. Had his father gone, just because the pressure to own up to the child was so great? Gone before the child remembered him?

How could Rosalind tell this to William, any of this to William, or even to Ben? In particular, to Holly. She still thought of her as Holly, not Ivy Smith? How could she tell anyone? It was simply a fact of life that none of them would ever know the truth.

Broadminded though he pretended to be William always seemed to be horrified by the casual reminiscences unearthed by Benjamin Smith of his wife's flying days, a reaction, which Roz felt, was forced. Indeed, Benjamin himself, now with a neat moustache and rimless spectacles was scarcely recognisable as the old reprobate and Rosalind wondered whether Ben presented a threatening image towards her husband.

Worse she knew at intervals, even in public, Rosalind would have to continue to meet the Smiths. It would be torture. Some of these occasions would demand that Rosalind should spend some time engaged in conversation with Ivy Smith, like the occasion when Rosalind had invited her to lunch, in September and they had sat in the garden. But then she had no idea of the difficult jigsaw her actions had created.

Gerry's ex-wife in her wisdom had discussed the problems of having a family with an adopted child, and a stepson, brought up among natural children of the marriage, only at the time Rosalind had not known that Ivy Smith was Gerry's ex-wife.

Ivy had remarked quite seriously, that it was good that Andrew should wear such thick glasses, like his stepfather and his stepbrother Geoffrey. She had also compared her own red hair and Andrew's auburn hair. She thought these physical likenesses were important for

342

Andrew, they made him less conspicuous as the only adopted child in such a large family. She appeared not to worry that the boy might go blind, one day.

She had told Rosalind that at the time of her first husband's disappearance it had been arranged for Andrew to undergo surgery to restore his sight, but after Gerald's disappearance she had never got around to arranging it.

Rosalind had asked with some concern, whether it was too late for the operation, but Ivy had quickly dismissed the subject, without committing herself and had gone on to say how delighted she was with Julian's progress at his primary school, Julian was obviously going to be clever and Rosalind dared not interfere anymore.

The silent tears had increased and so had the Librium doses and more worryingly the intake of alcohol; that was a lethal combination.

Certainly, since Ben had come on the scene, there had been a certain marital change, not least seemed to be William's frequent visits to Rosalind's cousin, Lucinda. But Rosalind was extraordinarily fond of her cousin and told herself she didn't consider her to be a rival. Her worries were mostly imagined. So, she told herself.

All the time Rosalind was nursing her guilty secret. She was frightened of her own emotions. She was terrified.

She quickly realised that Andrew was an independent child, lonely perhaps, apparently always exploring the town by himself, or playing football with friends. He was never still. He was Gerry's child, and he did not fit into the Smith household. He was the rightful heir to the Peters fortune. He was a grandson, the only grandson and one which James Peters had never known he had. Indeed, he was the only natural grandchild.

She felt she must speak to Ben alone.

(iv)

It was strange how Rosalind, thought Ben, as he replaced the receiver on its rest, was like Noah's wife. There was the safety of the big waterproofed ark, supplied and stocked by William, but she always wanted to get off.

Rosalind Weighton had just rung Ben and asked him to take her for lunch at the Bridge Inn.

Of course, it would be nice to have lunch with Rosalind, but despite the fact that she had assured him that her husband would not mind, Ben felt he had grown to know his editor very well in the last few months and Ben felt William would mind very much. He knew that William was in Dublin.

But he felt excited, like a small boy again, and he scattered a few papers around his desk to make him look busy when Roz arrived.

This was a different mood entirely to the one he experienced with Ivy. Ivy ordered him to be the dominant partner. It was a complex emotion and it worked in so much that it had improved his outward confidence, but it was not his natural mood. He had always been able to be himself with Roz Peters.

Thinking of Roz reminded him of his first wife, the young girl called Eileen, who now seemed many lives away - as though their time spent together had been something he had read about in a book.

Eileen, wife and playmate in a game of marriage; they had laughed and loved and played so that Ben never took the pain seriously when his young wife cried. But Geoffrey had rudely forced himself into the

345

world and the doctor dallied in arriving and nobody believed that Eileen was dead.

He had resented his son Geoffrey, because of it. There was no question about it; he really had neglected his first son dreadfully. Perhaps that is why he tried so hard with young Andrew. A good job he did, because the same could not be said for Ivy's attention.

To remember Eileen, to hear her cries of pain, to compare her with Roz made a strange comparison but a considerably stranger one should it be with Ivy. Ivy was a strange lady. A woman who had confessed to Ben, that he was the first real lover that she had had, indeed that she had always resisted making love to her first husband when she was married. Now she was nothing short of randy, and at her age! And so much older than Ben! Then there was the curious moment that she had changed her name: admittedly it was her given name, but one not even her family used. Ainley and Holly Armroyd had been as much part of the Halifax scene as had Pandora Rosalind Peters nearly two decades later. But Ben knew nothing of Roz's past or her family history, he was a comer-in to the town and, with his new partner and their large family, they simply blended in.

At that precise moment Roz arrived in the reporters' office.

'Hallo Ben! Extremely good of you to take me out for lunch. Here's the file I've brought in from William. You should have had it days ago.'

Ben staggered to his feet. He pushed his hands through his thick dark hair and she noticed none were grey. She was wearing the same green trouser suit she had worn that first evening that they had re-met.

'Hallo old girl! This really is a treat. Not often an old man gets the chance to take such a pretty girl out to lunch!' His confidence was surprising him; it was supreme. He had not thought that he could control the situation when Roz had rung. A momentary thought for Ivy only confirmed something he had always suspected; his true wife was Eileen and all other women in his life were merely friends, to a greater or lesser degree.

He eyed Roz up and down.

'Come on, hurry, let's move,' he pushed the papers aside demeaning any importance he might have hoped they would create. 'Offices are an anathema for a tearaway like me. I'm a wild bird at heart, aeroplanes are my métier...'

Ben's car was in the carpark. He opened the door for her and she stepped elegantly into the Cortina. He quickly brushed her forehead with his lips and she looked up in alarm.

'For goodness sake, people might see us!'

'You sound like my wife' Ben arched his eyebrows. 'Anyway, who cares if someone does see us?'

'I do. What would William say - if he knew?'

'He would recognise a gentlemanly courtesy when he saw one. You're looking lovely and this is my way of telling you so.' He closed the car door and walked round the mustard coloured vehicle to the driving seat. They took the Ripponden road from town.

'Was it my child that you had?' There was no point in beating about the bush.

'No, Ben, it was not your child.' She flushed. 'I tried to find you one day to tell you, before I left Yeadon.' Roz remembered meeting Gerry pushing the empty pram. She remembered after that how the original errand to see Ben seemed unimportant, and how she had turned and gone back without attempting to visit him.

'Ben nobody knows about that baby, not even William. *You must promise* not to tell anyone.'

She lied of course. There was no point in telling him that Gerry had known.

'Of course, not Roz! I presume the child was adopted.'

'I couldn't keep him, so yes, he was adopted;' she replied, hesitation in her voice evident.

Ben noticed how pale she was.

'When I heard you were pregnant, I thought I was responsible.'

'I thought nobody knew, except Julie Rhodes.'

'Oh Roz, do you really think Julie kept quiet about it. It was the talk of the airport bar, of course. Everyone wanted to know who the father might be, and all the time I thought it was me...'

'Ben...now listen to me. You never made love to me. Never. You were drunk. I merely kissed you and kicked you out of my room, after you had made enough noise to wake all Manchester.'

'I don't believe you. All these years I've been reliving that night in my dreams, believing that I fathered your child and now you're telling me that I haven't even had the pleasure of making love to you.'

'That's right.'

Ben took his eyes off the road to look quickly at the woman. They were approaching a roundabout. The girl had gone quite white and was pressing her hands together, biting her lips nervously. The car swerved a little as Ben found the roundabout closer than he thought and he took a minor road towards Lancashire.

'This isn't the way to the Bridge Inn,' Roz said quietly.

'I know that.' Ben's reply was curt.

348

She trembled but kept silent. Strange that she should have thought that no one knew she had had an illegitimate child. Of course, it was obvious now, the whole of the company would have known. That is why Gerry kept completely out of her way. In a way that made her feel a bit better, for she had often felt deep down that he had let her down, she had tried to rationalise her thoughts but she had been hurt at the time. And the pain lingered. If she was honest it still deeply affected her.

They drove in silence for a couple of minutes. She was nervous. She trusted Ben, but where was he driving?

She could think of nothing to say. However indifferent her feelings had been recently for William, she had no intention of being unfaithful to him. Over the years their marriage had been built up, created and she had no intention of putting it on a downward path at this stage. She had learnt her lesson and she was certain of that emotion at least.

When Ben turned into the narrow lane where the overhanging trees were barren and stark in the pale winter sunlight she was visibly shaking. He carefully parked out of the mud and switched the engine off.

'We can't talk in pubs, and I can't talk and concentrate on driving. We've never had the opportunity to put all the things we should have done into perspective.' He put his hand firmly on Roz's knee. The woman let out a piercing nervous scream and Ben's huge blue eyes distorted in terror.

'What on earth is the matter with you? I'm not going to rape you, for goodness sake.' The girl was sobbing, the tension of years of living a lie, flowing down her pale cheeks.

'But you want to.'

'Of course not. Admittedly I desire you, but only if you want it too and certainly not here. I'm far too old for the back seats of cars. Roz, I've never stopped worrying about you since you left Ferryair. Whether or not your child was mine, our lives are too closely involved for me not to recognise that something is worrying you, has been worrying you since you fainted in our sitting room.'

'Don't ask me! I can't tell you!' The woman was hysterical. Ben put his arm round the shaking woman hesitantly and she surprisingly stopped trembling.

'After you had left that evening a couple of weeks ago,' Ben said, 'I stood quite still in the hall. Ivy took the coffee cups into the kitchen and banged them about a bit because I didn't follow her.' He smiled a little devilishly. 'I listened to her clearing the kitchen; she's a creature of habit and has to lay the table for breakfast however late it is, however tired she is. When she had finished messing about she came into the sitting room to persuade me up to our Catholic bed. I went as bidden to avoid a scene. But I lay there and thought about you. I've always been in love with you Roz, since I first met you. When you left Yeadon, I resigned myself to the life that fate has mapped out and I never expected to see you again. After I lost my job with Ferryair, Geoff stopped doing so well at school, and I was worried about his future. Eventually, I realised the demon drink was destroying me. I started attending AA meetings. I found some work with the council. In the evenings I began to write, I went to the Tech. We struggled along until Geoff got a job at the post office and then things began to improve a little. I began to feel I could do a little better with the writing and I went into Bradford, where there is a small newspaper who took me on as a sub.'

Roz smiled a rueful smile. She realised alcoholism took a terrible toll.

'Anyway,' Ben chattered on, 'at this time Gerry Duncan had disappeared, and as I knew Holly, as she was called then, I tried to help her through the trauma. Partnership seemed a good investment, if a shock to my bachelor state. She is a fairly wealthy woman and financially independent, and at the time of Gerry's disappearance it was impossible to get a divorce because he had gone missing. So, we just lived together. But she took my name Smith because she said it made her anonymous. Just as choosing her birth name Ivy did. Everyone knew of the disappearance of Gerald Duncan.

'Haven't you ever heard anything from him?'

'Oh yes, Ainley, Ivy's brother tracked Gerry down in Cyprus, two years ago. It wasn't difficult. They had a house there for holidays, before they adopted Andrew. He'd sold it and bought another. Ainley couldn't pin him down, either on financial arrangements or with a divorce. Gerry didn't seem to care. Ainley had hardly ever met him, he'd even refused to have him in the family home, when he and his sister were married; something to do with obeying his father's wishes there was a big age difference between Ainley and his sister. But he said Gerald wasn't the same person that his sister had married. Living some sort of hippy-like existence.'

'How odd!'

'Yes, quite out of character apparently, but the point is Ivy isn't my legal wife. It's not something we broadcast however. She is actually older than I am and she was nearly forty when we unexpectedly had our first child Julian. She had told me she was infertile; she was

351

totally convinced she was barren. Conception came as a tremendous shock to us both and it followed at her age that it was a difficult birth, and I was quite worried I would lose her, as well as Eileen, my first wife, in childbirth.'

'Poor Ivy,' remarked Rosalind quietly. 'I don't think men quite understand the trauma that women must experience with birth. You know you're the first person that I've been able to mention that to. After all, with adopted twins I'm not supposed to have any experience of childbirth.'

'I understand. But really, quite apart from childbirth being both risky and painful at Ivy's age, I honestly think she enjoyed it. It fulfilled a need within her. In fact, once she found she could conceive she became quite obsessive about it. Both Rosalind and Carolyn were procreated by making love in the full knowledge that in my Catholic household a baby would eventually follow. I simply can't come to terms with contraception.

'It was like a love game. She would deliberately tease me and ask me for babies, not for love, and even now I must stroke and press her tummy after love-making, deliberately reminding her of the purpose of our mutual satisfaction. She will then stretch her whole body and whisper, 'I hope we've made another baby.''

Rosalind shuddered but Ben only noticed the negative reaction and not the disgust and repulsion she felt on hearing these intimate bedroom secrets.

Still, he doggedly continued his saga, 'Anyway, the two girls followed on after Julian with less than a year between them and with each birth Ivy suffered terribly, but it didn't seem to put her off asking for more.'

'Shut up Ben! It's your life. I just don't want to know.'

'But don't you see, I've got to tell you. I'm not a devout Catholic but I take my manhood seriously enough. After Carolyn's birth, we were shaken to be told no more children.'

'Pull yourself together. You aren't Catholic...certainly not a practising one, you never were and never will be. I know that. Part of Ivy's obsession has rubbed off on you; you're as obsessed with making kids as she is about having them. You should both see a shrink. Really you should.'

'No, you don't understand. It's you that doesn't understand. Listen Roz; when I make love to Ivy I know that if we make a baby, I put her life at risk. Lovemaking is rationed therefore to the first night of her monthly cycle, the only time I know is safe. Psychiatrists can't cure that!'

'Why are you telling me this? It's your private life.'

'I have to tell you, because it is you that I love, Roz. Always has been.'

'Rubbish Ben Smith! Too much has happened and things are different now. Whatever you may think, whatever you may sense I'm totally committed to William and my twins. I admit I might have been indifferent when I married him, but I've grown to love William now, and that is how it is. It is the way it has to be.'

'You don't really seem to understand what I'm saying, trying to say. What I am trying to tell you is that I immediately become impotent as soon as I suspect my woman is using contraceptives. Ivy has to use contraceptives. I pretend she doesn't, but it doesn't work and we don't make love anymore. I do really need to make babies not love.'

Rosalind thought he looked such an ordinary lovable person; he didn't have any of these hang-ups when she had first met him.

'I could do with a drink.' He said suddenly.

'Shall we go and eat?' she asked. 'After all, that was the prime object of the exercise and what I intended when I invited you. For old times' sake!'

'Do you want to?' Ben sounded reluctant. There was a hint of embarrassment in his voice. He had embarrassed Roz. He had talked too much and yet he had to emphasise he was teetotal. It could not be like old times.

'Of course, I want to. So, would you if you'd been living on fish fingers with the children at six whilst your husband stood up to the inclemency of Irish hooligans. For the first time in a fortnight I'm quite peckish.'

'Alright.' Ben sounded peeved, like a spoilt child. 'It was just the first chance I've had to talk to you and I'd hoped to hear your side of the story. And when he smiled softly his old dimple came back into his chin.

'There's nothing to tell. I had a baby; he was a boy. It was stupid of me. The baby wasn't yours. At least you don't go on record as the father of a bastard and I'd be obliged if you didn't mention the fact again to me or to anyone else.' She was cross.

'I've been on edge since you moved to this town, for fear you let it out. That was why I fainted in your house. I'm sorry, if I embarrassed you or Holly Duncan.' In her anger, the name with which she always associated Gerry's wife, the adoptive mother of her son, slipped out.

'Did you know Holly in the days when we were aircrew?'

Roz went bright pink. 'No,' she said. 'I never met her.'

At the inn, he ordered a double tonic for himself and a Campari for Roz.

'Holly doesn't drink, either.' Ben said and looked uncomfortable, well aware that they had slipped back into the language of their first meeting. 'Her family called her Holly, because of the Christmas carol, the Holly and the Ivy.'

'Really,' said Roz. 'I never would have guessed!'

At lunch though, he suddenly ordered a bottle of wine. Roz tried to discourage him, but decided she was not his keeper.

After lunch, it was obvious that Ben could neither go back to the newspaper nor home to Ivy.

Rosalind drove the mustard coloured Cortina slowly back to the Weighton's moorland home and parked it inside the empty garage. William had taken the Rover to the airport. She shut the garage doors.

'Come on, you silly chump, we'll have to make you cups of coffee. Strong black coffee. Then I'll have to collect the children from school. Funny how your capacity decreases as you get older, I feel a teeny-weeny bit tipsy myself! Do you remember the old days? Pink gins, a dozen Vodka and limes, do you know I thought nothing of it and I was a mere twenty years old. Never had a hangover either. Really you might say I've had a very narrow escape from alcoholism.'

'I didn't escape.' Said Ben and smirked. 'But' he went on, 'I like to think an alcoholic has to feel guilty. The stuff was cheap in Ferryair so we never felt guilty and consequently, we didn't get so tight. Now you've given me a taste for it again! I expect I shall be in for it when I get home tonight. Ivy doesn't drink. Period. She thinks because she rescued me from the doldrums that I shouldn't either. She'll smell it a mile off. "Where have you been?" or "Must you come home smelling like a public-house?" or "If you come any closer to me you'll intoxicate me from your breath." Charming! I ask you! Why do women change when they have a family? Is it the mother-hen instinct? Protecting their little brood all the time from the bad habits of the randy cock? Cock a doodle doo! My dame has lost her shoe. My master's lost his fiddling stick and doesn't know what to do! What's a fiddling stick Roz?'

'Come off it Ben, sober up for goodness sake.'

'What Ivy always conveniently forgets is that I rescued her from the doldrums too. God! She was low when Gerry hopped it! You haven't changed Roz. Lucky old William. Does the bastard appreciate you?'

'But I've changed Ben. I'm a shadow of my former self. William keeps reminding me how I've changed and you know I blame him. He always wanted me to be the right person to do the right thing and I'm always conscious of trying to please him. I'm always trying to make him proud but I think I fail miserably. And sometimes I think this is a form of guilt. Guilt for my past; it's always with me; this thought for my first child. My son!'

'Don't you ever wonder what your child is doing? Where he is?'

'I'm constantly reminded of him. If only you knew how! Hell!' She looked straight at Ben. How nice it would be to tell someone, anyone, about her son, about Andrew. Why not tell Ben, after all, he should know.

356

How surprised he would be to know that it was Andrew, Ivy's adopted son, who was Roz's bastard.

'I daren't go home just yet.' Ben wriggled in his inebriated state and looked as though he intended to settle in the comfortable dralon covered chair, which enhanced the Weighton's elegant sitting room.

'Why don't you ring a friend, and get her to pick your kids up?'

'I'll ring Penny-Sky...hang on...' Afterwards, she said, 'you know I can now see Ivy's point of view. That shows how much I've changed. A few years ago, we used to hear tales of pilot's wives kicking up a fuss when hostesses had parties in their flats or when the same aircrew was constantly rostered together for night-stops. I used to think, stupid bitches, why do they get into such a great flap? After all, they're not making love to us, only having a good time... a little booze never did anyone any harm! But you know when it happens, when you get married, you feel vulnerable, so dependent, you have to exercise your rights. And years ago, in my innocence, I really did believe we did no harm.'

'And maybe you have just conveniently forgotten that half the girls did actually go to bed with the fellas, and you know it! You're just excusing your own conscience.'

'No, I know I made that one slip. But it was only once, a mistake, and most of the time we didn't chase the married pilots. We had more sense!'

'Who was it? Who was the father?' Ben coaxed.

'Now, after all this time why should I tell you? I've never told anyone. No one. Only the father knew.' Curiously she used the past tense here. 'No-one else knows, do you understand that? No-one.' She tossed her red hair back, but it didn't have the bounce of her fine hair of her youth.

'Steady on old girl. I only asked!' And she knew that Ben, simple Ben, who for years had suffered unnecessarily under the burden of thinking he had fathered an illegitimate child was too naïve to suspect his friend Gerry, provided she played it really cool and never gave any hint of such.

'Anyway, it's the wives fault. If they can't provide enough love and amusement in their own homes to keep their man on the straight and narrow they deserve what they get. They are probably always nagging them, you see in those days youth was on our side and innocence too.'

'That wasn't quite what you said a minute ago. You were just saying how difficult it was to provide the love and amusement, because immediately you got married all you girls were consumed by a great big insecurity problem.'

'You're confusing me. In the old days, I liked to believe everyone was good. I didn't realise that man was naturally a polygamous creature and every woman conversely a monogamist and that her nagging is only a form of love gone out of control. I know William will always come home, barring accidents, so I'm full of guilt for the poor wives who suffer because their husbands are continually subjected to temptation. Temptations brought about by the Eves in their prime, who like air-stewardesses find it amusing to flirt and seduce the Adams of this world with their forbidden fruit.

'But at least today,' she continued, 'your wife has been spared the worry of wondering all day where you are, whether you're alright, whether you're drunk, because as you say it is a long time since you did go off the rails. And she thinks you're in the office. My job now is to sober you up enough to send you home to your wife, full of peppermints and black coffee so that she will think you've had a good day at the paper.' And she thought of William and how she knew he had been seeking the comfort of Lucinda. Was it just an innocent get-together or something more serious?

'Well Roz, there is something else which sobers a man up very quickly!'

'What's that?' Rosalind was caught off guard, thinking of her own problems and failed to notice the twinkle in Ben's blue eyes.

'A good shag.'

She stared at him and lifted her hand and moved towards him.

She slapped him hard across the cheek. 'And that probably works faster than any other method,' the girl snapped in rage.

But Ben had seen red. He rose angrily and catching hold of her, he picked her up, walked to the white panelled door, turned the brass handle and with the strength of a giant carried her through the house until he found a bedroom. A strong man, her kicks and flaying arms seemed to have little effect. Pinning her down on the bed, while the slim beautiful young mother screamed, he took her shoes, tights and pants from her.

At this point, Ben knew he had won.

For years he had resisted taking this girl. Now the resistance left her hazel eyes and the man released his hold.

For years Roz had lived with the knowledge that she was lost to touch.

William, always the gentleman, rarely made his wife feel desired.

Once would not hurt. She was on the pill. The pill had revolutionised their world in a way that ten years ago she would not have dreamt possible. In western society, increasingly it was used not only for contraception, but to regularise the woman's monthly cycle, and thereby releasing the woman from the chronic period pain that for all time had kept woman less than equal to man.

As they climaxed together Rosalind had a thought, she had forgotten her pill last night, and not remembered it that morning.

THIRTEEN: CONUNDRUM

12 December 1972

(i)

Tuesday was an awkward day for the twins to break up from school. William had taken the morning off to watch the performance of the nativity and carols. The twins had been cast as shepherds, wearing striped blankets folded and sewn down both sides with a slit in the front for praying hands and carrying gifts.

Alice had complained that the headdress was heavy and that it had given her a headache and she had been tetchy all day since. Sara had shown much more confidence and led the children off the stage. There were a lot of proud dads present and tearful mums.

Rosalind herself felt out of sorts and now, at teatime, she was glad the day was over. 'Can you get yourselves ready for bed?' she asked the twins as she washed out the teapot, stuffing teabags down the waste-disposal where they shouldn't go.

The Weightons were hoping to go up to Aviemore in the New Year to finish off the Scottish holiday which had been so unfortunately interrupted when James Peters died.

Alice was running the bath water. Sara was running up and down the landing chattering excitedly. Alice came down into the kitchen with no clothes on. 'I wanted you to see these spots,' said the child importantly.

There were three large red pimples and in one a slight blister, all on the child's chest. It did not need much thought to diagnose chicken pox. Gone were the hopes of skiing and the New Year in Scotland. Rosalind rang William, although it was only an hour before he would normally leave the office for home.

Her period, which had always been regular since she went on the pill, should have come. It hadn't. But she couldn't possibly be pregnant. She could not possibly be pregnant.

William had made love to her once since he came home from Eire. He had been so tired.

Rosalind told William on the 'phone about the twins' spots. She was fed up. He was also and said he'd be home in half an hour and that there had been no need to ring. She didn't mention the curse. She could not possibly be pregnant. There was no way she could go through the process of birth now. All these years she had guarded against it.

She was thirty-two years old, would be thirty-three if it was born, and she would have to explain to all the specialists that this wasn't her first baby, that there wasn't really any cause for alarm about that. No cause for alarm? And now with all the worries brought on by seeing Andrew, almost every week, when she picked him up from the squash club for Ivy Smith, and by arrangement gave him his tea. No, she could not be actually pregnant.

(ii)

The weather had been colder but the fog which had plagued the country had lifted and there was an enlightened look to the sky. Nevertheless, Rosalind could not feel that spring was on the way. This year there would surely be no spring.

The tension had been unbearable over Christmas and every time the carol *The Holly and the Ivy* was played on the radio or television Roz had difficulty avoiding the blushes which naturally went with her red hair; yet it was almost as though Christmas was deliberately arranged in the mid-winter for by the time it was over and the festivities abated, the clearing up accomplished there was generally a hint of spring in the air. Not this year though.

On Christmas Eve, Rosalind had looked at herself in the mirror and just above her right eyebrow was the tell-tale pimple.

At first, she had laughed. The children hadn't been ill and Rosalind felt extraordinarily well. Her mother had always said women could not carry a child with illness in the first month and the sign of the pox was surely going to be a blessing in disguise and relieve her other worries.

Did chicken pox really scar your skin forever or was that the scare put about to prevent children picking the scabs?

Oh, bother! What a mess! She resigned herself to fate and stood petrified watching the one red pimple grow, redder, larger, slowly perhaps as a flower bud, and all the time it vied with her other vexations for attention.

Rosalind did not feel poorly, perhaps the chicken pox was not as serious as everyone tried to make out. William did not even know she was pregnant yet.

Maybe she wasn't pregnant.

After all, she was only a fortnight overdue. Certainly, she had chicken pox.

Having clarified everything, she had called for William.

'Happy Christmas darlings! Mummy's got chicken pox too!' And Rosalind had yelled with hysterical laughter. 'Come and look, everyone, your Mummy's got spots!'

But even as she had shouted a fierce flush had engulfed her face and body.

She knew she had a temperature and a splitting headache. She went to bed.

It was Christmas Eve.

Still, the children hadn't been very ill. Perhaps, Rosalind thought, she would also get it very lightly.

On Christmas Day, however, Rosalind was barely with the world and on Boxing Day, the Weighton grandparents who insisted on coming to help William cook the family dinner, walked into their daughter-in-law's bedroom with a glass of champagne for the near delirious patient.

Her temperature had soared; her body perspired. She was on the rack. Her skin was inflamed with irritation and itching and the headache was nearly making her unconscious. The champagne was a bad idea.

She'd fallen into a semi-conscious doze and in her head, she heard herself say, 'Oh Gerry, darling, I'm dying...look after the boy for me...look after Andrew.'

And the dream had increased and she dreamt of the seafront at Rhodes and the olive tree that grew through the roof of the restaurant where they had once eaten, where the dusk was indistinguishable from the night or the day and in Greece one was conscious of neither light nor dark. Then after they had made their tummies pregnant with taramasalata and stuffed vine leaves they were drowning in a sea of red hibiscus flowers. She felt herself going under and she woke to find she felt a little better and the fever had left her. William was standing near her.

'You were talking in your sleep.'

'One thing is for certain. You wouldn't need to employ the Mafia to find out my secrets. And to think I only laughed when the Queen had chicken pox! I can't remember what I said when your parents were here. I was delirious. I don't remember what I dreamt.' She was nearly asleep again with the effort of talking and with the fever that had left her exhausted.

Nearly a month later her face was still badly scabbed and scarred; though with great control she had tried to refrain from picking the spots.

There was still no period. This meant she had missed yet another month. Tomorrow she knew she would have to go to the doctor.

It was not surprising that the Monte Carlo rally had been squeezed out of the press. It had been a week of climaxes. Shares had toppled rapidly on the British market; Sean MacStiofain was to be returned to prison from the hospital where he had lost the courage to starve himself to death. A volcano had made a whole township homeless in Iceland. Lyndon Johnson had died on the eve of the Vietnam peace agreement and Rosalind's whole body cried for the Texan family he had loved. She felt particularly emotional. She had cried for the children smothered by napalm and the women still to be raped and the men to be tortured and slaughtered within the now private war of the Far East and she cried for the child which was now confirmed as hers within her, the child of which William still did not know.

She was crying visibly when the new announcer on television mentioned that Alexandros Onassis had also died; in hospital after a serious operation whilst in a coma, following his Athens air crash.

'Why are you crying?' William had asked.

'For Jackie Kennedy. Jacqueline Onassis, I mean...'

'Why for her?'

'Would you like to lose a stepson and then a very old friend and colleague of your first husband, all in twenty-four hours?'

'Oh, I shouldn't worry your pretty little head about that sort of thing. I don't think there was much love lost between the Johnsons and the Kennedys. They were just political associates. It will be interesting to see what history makes of the American politicians of the sixties.'

But Rosalind went on crying.

'I met Lucinda in town today. She told me their dog was run over. Killed outright.'

'Oh, come on Rosalind, dry the eyes. What is the matter lately? I mean, I know all illnesses like chicken pox at your age can take it out of you, but really look darling, here comes the good news! Darling, I've

366

had a vasectomy! I had it done quietly in November when you thought I was in Dublin.'

Rosalind stopped crying and gasped.

'It was a sore experience but I didn't want to tell you at the time. I wanted to give you a surprise when the tests gave the all clear. A sort of surprise Christmas present, but you were too ill at Christmas to tell you about it. I've known for years about your contraceptive arrangements. One can't have a friend for a doctor, like Hugh, without him confiding in the other partner when he thinks things are getting on top of another friend. And he thought your fear of giving birth, and all the elaborate arrangements you were engaging in to conceal the fact from me, to adopt the twins and so on, were getting out of hand. So how about that for some really good news?'

Hugh Rhyl-Jones was a psychiatrist, the brother-in-law of Rosalind's friend Penny Sky, the Weightons thought they had no need of such a doctor, but Rosalind had often confided in him. Often going to great lengths to seek him out without William knowing. Nowadays Hugh lived in the Lake District. He was a particularly kind man.

'But William,' she said, 'that sort of decision has to be a joint decision. You should have asked me first! I might have wanted children…in the end.'

'No, no. You don't want more children. You're scared stiff of the birth process. I mean you don't want to be on the pill at your age!'

'But you still should have discussed it with me.'

'True, too true. How right you are! Legally too, as it happens you should have signed a form saying you approved et cetera. However, I'm afraid I took the liberty of confiding all our problems to Hugh. It pays to have a psychiatrist as good as Hugh as a friend you

367

know. He agreed with me, that under the circumstances: get the deed done first and then get you sign afterwards. He didn't want you upset, any further.

She had to tell William, now. Now or never.

'You see, I'm pregnant. I must have been pregnant before you had the operation. And I daren't go through with it. You're right, I'm scared.'

She moaned. 'I'm terrified, Bill.'

'How many months gone?'

'Three', she said wildly, trying to hedge her bets. 'Maybe two, I don't know.'

'But darling, it can't be. I didn't make love to you for a month before I had the op. I couldn't bring myself to do it, having once committed myself mentally to the operation, I couldn't make love for the last time, in case it really was the last time it felt good. You see I was terrified too, about having the thing and the sperm count has been nil for two months now. And now you tell me you're pregnant. I'm telling you! You can't be! Not with my child!'

'I am pregnant. It must be your child.'

She lied.

And William who trusted his wife didn't think to disbelieve her.

He resolved to go back for another sperm count.

Later that night Rosalind finally fell asleep. She dreamt.

There was a carcase hanging from every tree, and the sun which shone through the cold bones echoed a close imitation of the shapes, casting a shadow of delicate lacework over a barren earth.

A fire was raging and the wind screeched and the massive hands of God were trying to tie the bodies to the scorched trees so that now they were suspended nearer to His Heaven, but nearer to the foul earth.

The world had died.

FOURTEEN: AFTERBIRTH

(i)

On September 2nd, 1973 both Ivy Smith and Rosalind Weighton gave birth to baby girls.

The Smith baby weighed eight pounds and was twenty-two inches long.

The Weighton girl weighed five pounds and thirteen ounces and was twenty inches long. Mrs. Smith was delivered of her child in the Intensive Care Unit of a Leeds hospital. Mrs. Weighton delivered her child in the Nuffield Nursing Home. There they all asked her if the baby was premature? She was such a little mite, they all said. But Dr. Hugh Rhyl-Jones said if anything the baby was five weeks overdue. One of those strange quirks of nature, he had said with a soft Welsh emphasis on his words.

A priest immediately christened the Smith girl Eileen Joy, and she was red-haired.

The Weighton daughter, who was named Geraldine, had her name changed before the day was out to Zoë Jane. She had very dark brown hair and solid blue eyes.

(ii)

On September 2nd, 1975, little Eileen Joy Smith asked her young friend, Zoë to her second birthday party. Apart from their completely different hair colourings, the two little girls could be taken for twins.

It was Eileen's elder brother Andrew, who although adopted by his parents bore some resemblance to his baby sister, because of their similar hair colour and he remarked on this likeness. But he also said he looked even more like Zoë than his baby sister, Eileen did to him.

It was all rather curious.

(iii)

William loved his new daughter. He was amazed at the depth of his love. It also improved his relationship with Rosalind.

Rosalind continued to live the lie that her life had been for many years now. It was merely a bigger lie and curiously not as stressful. She did realise that for as long as she lived in this bubble of secrecy and deceit she was as incarcerated as any prisoner in any jail. Her jailer was fear. Fear that she would expose her own shortcomings; two short moments of foolhardy behaviour that she was condemned to regret all her life. Yet to own up to William might release her from her torment or there again it might make matters worse.

At night, she tried to lie still but dreams turned to nightmares. She woke up screaming one night. 'Hush, there,' said William, 'it's alright.'

'But it's not,' she sobbed. 'I was dreaming. The taxmen were interrogating Daddy's body. They wouldn't listen to me. I was Daddy's ghost. I was in his body, in his coffin. The sun was shining through the trees echoing the shapes of dried bones; casting a shadow of a delicate network over the earth.

'It was horrible. I was on some sort of 'phone, like a walky-talky, pressing a call button and laughing hysterically every time I got through to the taxmen. I scared them to death because they knew Daddy was dead and I must be a ghost!'

'Quite right,' said William, 'hounding your honest father like that. There never was a more upright kindly businessman.' But Rosalind just sobbed more.

Although she did see Ivy Smith from time to time, it was mainly on a casual basis as young women with young children meet from time to time. The families did not socialise more than helping each other out with the chores thrown up by rearing children. There was no question of reciprocal dinner parties and Rosalind never made any effort to see or ask after Ben.

She did hear that he had thrown himself into Alcoholics Anonymous (after his spectacular lapse when he was with Rosalind) becoming a leading light within that institution and attending meetings almost obsessively. And she did discuss this with William, stressing the support an alcoholic and his family would require.

'It is the most devastating disease. The Government should do much more for these poor stricken people, with more clinics, more support generally. I heard a programme on the radio which said that even if the diseased person, and it is a disease you know, even if that person gave up drink, if they were what did they call dry, they could still be a dry drunk. All their life they may never take another drink, but they could be still in an obsessive mode and quickly turn their obsession with alcohol into another equally damaging obsession, gambling, over-eating, even sex. I think that is the case with Ben.'

She regretted that she had opened her mouth.

'What makes you say that?' asked William sharply.

'Well just look at the number of children that elderly Ivy has had to bear.'

'Had to bear? What do you mean?'

'Well put it this way. I wouldn't have so many children at her age. Ben said the births were really difficult.'

'Ben? When did you speak to him about his intimate family details?'

Rosalind blushed. 'On the first night I met him, at his house, you remember.'

'No, I don't remember. Perhaps it was something Ivy has told you at the tea-parties you indulge in. Goodness knows what gossip women find to talk about.'

He had let her off the hook.

As long as one did not dwell on the past, or what if, or what might be, she found life could continue quite normally, and she really appreciated William's attention. The three girls were lovely, the older twins adoring their pretty little sister, and from Rosalind's point of view she could keep herself informed of Andrew's well-being. It was wonderful to see him from time to time, to have news of his successes even if she worried a good deal about his eyesight.

In a nutshell, the Weighton family was moderately happy, moderately well off.

As Hugh said to Roz, the day he met her in a Manchester street after the birth of Zoë, when he confirmed that it was he who had inferred that the child was born five weeks overdue, thus taking the heat out of the timescale with regard to William's vasectomy, 'the secret of life is to avoid the highs and the lows'.

She would be eternally grateful to Hugh, the groomsman at her wedding who had made sure she got to the church on time.

The End.

AUTHOR'S NOTES

Change between eras are often imperceptible:

This is a book of the sixties and seventies when not all was politically correct. As such I have left a few instances of the colloquial language of the time, although I have drawn attention to the fact that by present-day standards this is not acceptable. If this breaks the flow of the novel I apologise. Calling a person black or coloured (or worse) in the 1960s was normal and no one would have challenged such a remark, but now it can be marked as racist or politically incorrect. Other derogatory terms would also be commonplace and I have avoided using these.

Before the onset of climate change in the early 21st century the early signs of spring including bird-song belonged to March and not to the winter months.

Aircrew, along with most of the nation tired of the stress of war and rationing were much more relaxed and casual. Many of the pilots were hard-drinking skilled airmen straight out of the wartime RAF or Berlin Airlift and although there was an 8 hour no drinking ban in place it was not always adhered to before a flight. Because of the cost of fuel, some aircraft and crew ferrying people from place to place on what was called an 'air-cruise' would stay with the passengers, enjoying several days in foreign parts. Cockpit, not flight deck, air hostess not cabin crew/flight attendants were the usual words.

Money values have inflated so much in the last half-century that it is difficult to imagine that £500 in 1960 is worth about £8000 four decades later;
£60,000 in 1960 probably the equivalent of about £800,000 - £900,000 in the early twenty-first century

Librium was the catchall drug of the seventies, like the Prozac of the noughties.

Much of this book concerns the strict codes of conduct of a society coming out of the huge trauma left by two World Wars and consequent austerity. Particularly frowned upon was illegitimacy and those that strayed from sex within marriage found they were caught by the confines of an unmentionable taboo. Likewise, the path to adoption was fraught with complications and secrecy.

Greece has never been a stable country, politically. Occupied for millennia from the times of the Romans through Byzantine times and the Ottomans to the time of the Greek War of Independence 1821-1827, it succumbed to the German/Italian invasion of WW2, a civil war immediately after and a Junta in the early seventies. Constantine Karamanlis twice Prime Minister of Greece and twice President was a remarkable man who did much to bring Greece up to date and into the modern world. He was to retire into exile in Paris only to be recalled after the colonels fell from grace in the seventies.

Athens grew in sophistication from chronic austerity only slowly around the 1960s, and much of what could be seen and appreciated lasted until just before the Olympic Games in 2004, although the city itself and its population expanded rapidly in the second half of the 20th century. Greece prospered with new hotels, restaurants, tourist shops but much of the character of the city remained distinctly Greek. For example, the prestigious restaurant Floca, so famous in the 1960s, after 2000 took on a new lease of life in line with expansion of many businesses in the early millennium, with chocolate shops in other upcoming towns such as Nafplio in the Peloponnese and with service station cafes Flocafe vying with Goody's, (also Greek) on the new motorways that tore through the bedrock of Greece. Such is progress and progress should have been the Greek inheritance but for the catastrophic economic collapse wrought on Greece by the global crisis of 2008. Yet many of Europe's top businesses were founded in Greece in the pre-war period.

The scenes in Greece in this book are set firmly in the period of joy when Greece finds democracy once again the early 1960s.

If you enjoyed this book I would be very grateful if you could take a little time to write a review.

For your interest, this is what some other reviewers have said about the series JIGSAW ....

BEFORE - GREEK LETTERS QUARTET VOLUME 1

...As I have visited many of the places in the Peloponnese written about in this book, I found reading this sensitively written story especially nostalgic. It tells the reader about the hard times suffered by the Greeks circa 1827 and of the young idealistic Grecophile, Samuel, who, in search of adventure and fortune, finds out a lot about himself and the nature of the Greeks he befriends along the way. I especially enjoyed the lovely descriptions of the Greek landscape and I am looking forward to reading the following books... **C.C. 5* review on amazon.co.uk**

...This is one of those rare books that tells a terrific story set in a world about which I, as the reader, knew absolutely nothing, but which engages from the first page. It set me off finding out more about this period of history, and the creation of modern Greece. The story told here is both epic and deeply personal; set against a crossroads of East and West, it shows the hinge of historical events which have ultimately resulted in so much of the world we know today. The characters are well-rounded, with believable flaws and convincingly realistic ambitions, and the writing propels the reader seamlessly into the wider tale with some magnificent descriptions of the natural grandeur of the region, as well as some sensitive character-driven scenes which complement the action. It is a complex story, demanding some concentration, but rewards a careful read, and is certainly not lacking in 'racier' descriptions of sex and violence. The book put me in mind of a number of other works - strangely, perhaps, the feel is often similar to the sweeping fantasy works of writers such as George Martin or Robert Jordan - and there is the attention to period detail one would expect of a populist historian - but in its theme and treatment, it is original and exciting, and the quality of the writing makes this book a great read completely in its own right. Recommended! **A.W. 5* review on amazon.co.uk**

...If you are interested in Greece and its history this is the book for you. Told as a story, it describes the struggle that Greece had to become independent in the Greek War of Independence. A wonderful read to take on your summer holiday to Greece! **O.P.W. 5* review on amazon.co.uk**

AND AFTER – GREEK LETTERS QUARTET VOLUME 2

... set in Victorian England and Greece, this is a continuation of the life and times of wealthy investor, philhellene, and amateur conductor Samuel Carr. Samuel is well intentioned, but he has secrets. He leaves Greece and his son by his first wife and doesn't return for 15 years because his second marriage is potentially compromising. Throughout the novel, a former servant, Soula, blackmails Samuel and tries in other ways to undermine him. By the end of his life, Samuel learns the truth about his first wife and his second marriage. The death of Samuel doesn't end this multi-generational saga. At the end of this volume, readers are already engaged in the fates of Samuel's extended family in Greece and England in the twentieth century. Like the first volume in this series, accurate historical details bring to life a distant time and provide the setting for a complicated, compelling plot. **Williamsburg V.A. 5 * review from amazon.com**

THE EYES HAVE IT - GREEK LETTERS QUARTET VOLUME 3

This historical novel continues the Carr family saga ...the two main characters are Helene and Phil. The first part of the story focuses on Helene, born in 1906 in Edwardian England. The author does an expert job of recreating the texture of life before, during, and after the Great War. This evocative part of the book recounts a time made popular in several TV mini-series. About midway through the novel, the scene shifts to Helene's encounter and love affair with her cousin Phil in Greece. Although Helene is the main character in this novel, Phil's story is also an important part of the book. It's clear that the author has in-depth knowledge of, and love for, Greek history, geography, and culture. Stembridge's carefully researched novel is bolstered with notes and a bibliography, and it should be of interest to both general readers and history enthusiasts. The book ends in 1943, for this reader, too soon. I wanted a more complete resolution to Helene's and Phil's stories. Perhaps that will come in the next volume of GREEK LETTERS. **Williamsburg V.A. 5 * review from amazon.com**

BRIGHT DAFFODIL YELLOW - COMING OF AGE SERIES

...Bright Daffodil Yellow opens with aging former airline pilot Gerald Duncan posing as a Greek Cypriot innkeeper named Stephanos in the delightful romantic harbor town of Kyrenia of the early 1970s. Colonial Cyprus has long gone and the Turkish forces have not yet arrived while Gerald is lusting after a young English girl named Maeve. From the very start the reader knows Duncan is in trouble, pursued by relatives of former loves and indeed a marriage. As the Turks invade, Duncan flees the Island and in the turmoil, adopts another identity in England. One feels like laughing at this hopeless creature as he earnestly seeks the freedom of obscurity only to survive an Underground railway disaster and be thrust into the exposing spotlight of national television. Duncan's great ambition is to be a loving parent for the two sons he fathered by two different women -- and stay free. It's a wonderful but fascinating and taunting story, well written and seemingly reminiscent of Lawrence Durrell who also lived on Cyprus in another age, frequented Kyrenia (Bitter Lemons) and wrote of the loves and agonies of men and women in The Alexandria Quartet. The author's knowledge of Cyprus and the English Lake District is highly evident, plus she has the ability to portray characters with deep meaningful words. This along with the peculiar, unpredictable and pathetic exploits of a freedom seeker keeps one turning the pages to discover this Romeo's fate. Incidentally, his encounter with a Harley Street plastic surgeon is classic. A truly delightful saga. **R.E. Upstate New York. 5* review on amazon.com**

...Set in the 1970s, with an intricately woven plot, Suzi Stembridge's sparkling novel ... soon shifts to Wales and the Lake District of the UK. It's the story of the many identities of Gerald Duncan, a former British pilot, prisoner of war, and lover whose life intersects with multiple women. Will he manage to accept responsibility for his life, his loves, and his sons? Or will he be successful in finding freedom? From a deadly train crash to a dangerous walk in the Lake District, the story will captivate readers. Duncan's nemesis, Ainley, a richly drawn, despicable character, pursues Duncan relentlessly, tying together a host of memorable characters. **Williamsburg V.A. 5 * review from amazon.com**

MUCH MORE THAN HURT - GREEK LETTERS QUARTET VOLUME 4

The concluding book of a most intriguing and ingenious set of stories of a very complex family over several generation. This book is a fascinating read in its own right, but most people who read this one will be more than tempted to peruse the others in the series, all of which are written by an author with a very vivid imagination, great knowledge of the subjects, and exceptional talent. **little h. 5* review on Amazon.co.uk**

....the reader is reintroduced to the wonderful characters that populated her earlier novels. Each of the novels in the series stands alone although they work best if read together. Her characters are all on journeys to understand themselves and their complicated heritage. This novel, like the others in the series, takes place in Greece and Northern England....carefully researched and provides insight into the human condition and the social history of the nineteenth and twentieth centuries... Stembridge very cleverly gives a synopsis of books one and two of the series by writing about the same events from a different characters' points of view. In the conclusion she references the other novels in the series. With these ingenious and effective means she ties together the four novels in the series. If you love generational novels with memorable characters and exotic locales, you will enjoy this series. **Williamsburg V.A. 5 * review from amazon.com**

Printed in Great Britain
by Amazon